James Lee Burke is the author of many novels, and the critically acclaimed, bestselling Detective Dave Robicheaux series. He won the Edgar Award for both *Cimarron Rose* and *Black Cherry Blues* and *Sunset Limited* was awarded the CWA Dagger. *Two for Texas* was adapted for television, and *Heaven's Prisoners* and *In the Electric Mist* for film. Burke has been a Breadloaf Fellow and Guggenheim Fellow, has been awarded the Grand Master Award by the Mystery Writers of America and has been nominated for a Pulitzer award. He lives with his wife, Pearl, in Missoula, Montana.

www.jamesleeburke.com

James Lee Burke

LAY DOWN MY
SWORD AND SHIELD

ORION

An Orion paperback

First published in Great Britain in 2003
by Orion Fiction,
an imprint of the Orion Publishing Group Ltd,
Carmelite House, 50 Victoria Embankment
London EC4Y 0DZ

An Hachette UK company

1 3 5 7 9 10 8 6 4 2

Reissued 2005, 2011, 2021

First published in the USA in 1971 by
The Countryman Press, Inc., Woodstock

A CIP catalogue record for this book
is available from the British Library.

ISBN 978 1 3987 0639 2

Printed and bound in Great Britain by Clays Ltd,
Elcograf S.p.A.

www.orionbooks.co.uk

This book is for my father,
James L. Burke Sr.,
who taught me most of the good things
I know about

LAY DOWN MY
SWORD AND SHIELD

chapter one

Almost ninety years ago during the Sutton-Taylor feud, John Wesley Hardin drilled a half dozen .44 pistol balls into one of the wood columns on my front porch. My grandfather, Old Hack, lived in the house then, and he used to describe how Wes Hardin had ridden drunk all night from San Antonio when he had heard that Hack had promised to lock him in jail if he ever came back into DeWitt County again. The sun had just risen, and it was raining slightly when Hardin rode into the yard, his black suit streaked with mud, horse sweat, and whiskey; he had a shotgun tied across his saddle horn with a strip of leather and his navy Colt was already cocked in his hand.

'You, Hack! Get out here. And don't bring none of your Lincoln riggers with you or I'll kill them, too.'

(My grandfather was sheriff and justice of the peace, and the Reconstruction government had forced him to take on two Negro federal soldiers as deputies. Of the forty-two men that Hardin eventually killed, many were Negroes, whom he hated as much as he did carpetbaggers and law officers.)

Hardin began shooting at the front porch, cocking and firing while the horse reared and pitched sideways with each explosion in its ears. Wes's face was red with whiskey, his eyes were dilated, and when the horse whirled in a circle he whipped the pistol down between its ears. He emptied the rest of the chambers, the fire and black powder smoke roaring from the barrel, and all six shots hit the wood column in a neat vertical line.

Hack had been up early that morning with one of his mares that was in foal, and when he saw Wes Hardin through the barn window he took the Winchester from the leather saddle scabbard nailed against the wall and waited for Wes to empty his pistol. Then he stepped out into the lot, his cotton nightshirt tucked inside his trousers, blood and membrane on his hands and forearms, and pumped a shell into the chamber. Wes jerked around backwards in the saddle when he heard the action work behind him.

'You goddamn sonofabitch,' Hack said. 'Start to untie that shotgun and I'll put a new asshole in the middle of your face.'

Hardin laid his pistol against his thigh, and turned his horse in a half circle.

'You come up behind me, do you?' he said. 'Get your pistol and let me reload and I'll pay them nigger deputies for burying you.'

'I told you not to come back to DeWitt. Now you shot up my house and probably run off half my Mexicans. I'm going to put you in jail and wrap chains all over you, then I'm taking you into my court for attempted assault on a law officer. Move off that horse.'

Wes looked steadily at Hack, his killer's eyes intent and frozen as though he were staring into a flame. Then he brought his boots out of the stirrups, slashed his spurs into the horse's sides, and bent low over the neck with his fingers in the mane as the horse charged towards the front gate. But Hack leaped forward at the same time and swung the Winchester barrel down with both hands on Hardin's head and knocked him sideways out of the saddle into the mud. There was a three-inch split in his scalp at the base of the hairline, and when he tried to raise himself to his feet, Hack kicked him squarely in the face twice with his boot heel. Then he put him in the back of a vegetable wagon, locked his wrists in manacles, tied trace chains around his body and nailed the end links to the floorboards.

And that's how John Wesley Hardin went to jail in DeWitt County, Texas. He never came back to fight Hack again, and no other law officer ever got the better of him, except John Selman, who drove a pistol ball through his eye in an El Paso saloon in 1895.

As I stood there on my front porch that hot, breathless July day, leaning against the column with the six bullet holes, now worn and smooth, I could see Hack's whitewashed marker under the pin oaks in the Holland family cemetery. The trees were still in the heat, the leaves filmed with dust, and the shade was dappled on the headstones. Four generations of my family were buried there: Son Holland, a Tennessee mountain man from the Cumberlands who came to Texas in 1835 and fought at the battle of San Jacinto for Texas' independence, was a friend of Sam Houston, later received twelve hundred acres from the Texas Republic, and died of old age while impressing horses for the Confederacy; Hack's two older brothers, who rode with the Texas cavalry under General Hood at the battle of Atlanta; Great Uncle Tip, who made the first drive up the Chisholm Trail and married an Indian squaw; Sidney, a Baptist preacher and alcoholic, who always carried two revolvers and a derringer and killed six men; Winfro, murdered in a brothel during the Sutton-Taylor feud, his body dragged on a rope back and forth in front of the house by drunken cowboys; Jefferson, who had two years' business college in Austin and decided to compete with the King and XIT ranches in the cattle market and lost six hundred acres of Holland land as a result; and Sam, my father – Hackberry's son – a genteel man with a rheumatic heart, a one-time southern historian at the University of Texas and later a United States congressman during the New Deal, and finally a suicide.

Out beyond the cemetery the low, green hills sloped down towards the river, which was now low and brown, and the crests were covered with blackjack, live oak, and mesquite. The cotton in the fields was in bloom, the rows evenly spaced and stretched out straight as a rifle shot, and the tomatoes had come out big and red in the early summer showers. The sun flashed brilliantly on the windmill blades, now idle in the still air, and in the distance the clapboard and shingle homes of the Mexican farm workers looked like flattened matchboxes in the heat. My three natural-gas wells pumped monotonously up and down, the pipes on the well heads dripping moisture from the intense cold inside, and occasionally I could smell the slightly nauseating odor of crude gas. The wells were located in the middle of the cotton acreage, the derricks long since torn down, and the cotton rows were cut back from the well heads in surgically perfect squares, which always suggested to me a pastoral reverence towards the Texas oil industry.

The front lane was spread with white gravel, the adjoining fields planted with Bermuda grass, and white wood fences ran both the length of the lane and the main road where my property ended. The lawn was mowed and clipped, watered each day by a Negro man whom my wife hired to take care of the rose gardens, and there were magnolia and orange trees on each side of the porch. The main portion of the house had been built by Hackberry in 1876, although the logs of Son Holland's original cabin were in our kitchen walls, and it had changed little since. My wife had added a latticework verandah on the second story, with large ferns in earthen pots, and a screened-in side porch where we used to eat iced-tea dinners on summer evenings. After we began to take our meals separately, the porch was used as a cocktail bar for her lawn parties, complete with a professional bartender in a white jacket who shaved ice into mint julep glasses for the Daughters of the Confederacy, the Junior League, and the Texas Democratic Women's Club.

But regardless of the Sunday afternoon lawn parties, the political women with their hard eyes and cool drinks, the white boxes filled with roses, the air-conditioning units in the windows, it was still Old Hack's place, and sometimes at night when I was alone in the library the house seemed to creak with his angry presence.

I suppose that's why I always felt that I was a guest in the house rather than its owner. Even though I was named for Hack, I never had the gunfighter blood that ran in the Holland family. I was a Navy hospital corpsman during the Korean War and spent three months in Seoul passing out penicillin tablets for clap

5

until I was finally sent up to the firing line, and I was there only six days before I was shot through both calves and captured by the Chinese. So my one attempt at Hack's gunfighter ethic was aborted, and I spent thirty-two months in three P.O.W. camps. However, I'll tell you more later about my war record, my wound and purple heart, and my testimony at a turncoat's court-martial, since they all became part of my credentials as a Democratic candidate for Congress.

I lit a cigar and walked down the glaring white lane to where my car was parked in the shade of an oak tree. I had showered and changed clothes a half hour before, but already my shirt and coat were damp, and the sun broke against my dark glasses like a hot green scorch. I sat back in the leather seat of the Cadillac and turned on the ignition and the air conditioner, and for just a moment, as the stale warm air blew through the vents, I could smell the concentrated odor of the gas wells, that scent of four thousand dollars a month guaranteed income from Texaco, Inc. I dropped the car into low, pushed slowly down on the accelerator, and I felt all three hundred fifty horses throb up smoothly through the bottom of my boot. The gravel pinged under the fenders, and I rumbled over the cattle guard onto the main road, then pushed the accelerator to the floor and listened to the tires whine over the soft tar surfacing. My white fences whipped by the windows, clicking like broken sticks against the corner of my eye, and I steered with three fingers ninety miles an hour around the chuck holes and depressions, biting gently down on my cigar and watching the shadows on the fields race with me towards San Antonio and Houston. Several times

6

when drunk I had driven one hundred and twenty miles an hour at night over the same road, hillbilly and gospel music from Del Rio thundering out of the radio, and the next morning I would sweat through those whiskey hangovers and see yellow flashes of light in my mind, the Cadillac rolling over in the field, the white fence gaping among the shattered boards, and I would be inside, bleeding blackly between the steering wheel and the crushed roof.

But sober I drove with magic in my hands, an air-cooled omnipotence encircling me as the road sucked under the long frame of my automobile.

As I neared Yoakum I unscrewed the cap of my whiskey flask and took a drink. The white ranch houses and the barns, the cattle and horses in the fields, the acres of cotton, and the solitary oak trees rolled by me. The sun reflected in a white flash off the hood of the car, and ahead the road seemed to swim in the heat. A thin breeze had started to blow, and dust devils spun along the dry edge of the corn fields. On the top of a slope the blades of a windmill turned into the breeze and began spinning rapidly; then the water sluiced out in a long white spray into the trough. At the edge of town I passed the rows of Negro and Mexican shacks, all alike even though some of them were built decades apart, all weathered gray, the porches collapsing, tarpaper nailed in uneven shapes on the roofs, the dirt yards littered with broken toys, tangled wire, dirty children, plastic Clorox bottles, and garbage set out to rot in boxes. In the back, old cars with rusted engines and spider-webbed windows sat among the weeds, faded overalls and denim shirts hung on the washlines, and the scrub

7

brush that grew in the gravel along the railroad bed was streaked black by passing locomotives.

I sipped again from the flask and put it in the glove compartment. It was Saturday, and Yoakum was crowded with ranchers and farmers, women in cotton-print dresses, Mexican and Negro field workers, pickup trucks and battered cars, and young boys on the corner in lacquered straw hats and starched blue jeans that were as stiff as cardboard. On Main Street the old high sidewalks had iron tethering rings set in them, and the wood colonnade, built in 1900, extended over the walk from the brick storefronts. Old men in white shirts with clip-on bow ties sat in the shade, spitting tobacco juice on the concrete and looking out at the traffic with their narrow, sunburned faces. At the end of the street was the stucco and log jail where my grandfather had locked up Wes Hardin. It was set back in a lot filled with weeds, and the roof and one of the walls had caved in. The broken timbers and powdered stone lay in a heap on the floor, and kids had smashed beer bottles against the bars and had left used contraceptives in the corners. But on one wall you could still read the worn inscription that an inmate had scratched there with a nail in 1880: *J. W. Hardin says he will kill Hack Holland for nigger meat.*

I had always wondered if Hack ever worried about Hardin breaking out of prison, or about Hardin's relatives catching him in the back with a shotgun. But evidently he was never afraid of anything, because when Hardin was released from prison after fourteen years Hack sent him a telegram that read: "*Your cousins say you still want to gun me. If this is true I will send you a train ticket to San Antonio and we can meet briefly at the depot.'*

Through law school at Baylor I used one of Hack's .44 Colts as a paperweight. The bluing had worn off the metal, and the mahogany grips were cracked, but the spring and hammer still worked and the heavy cylinder would rotate properly in place when I cocked it. After I started law practice with my brother in Austin, I hung the pistol on my office wall next to a 1925 picture of Hack as an old man, with my father in a white straw hat. I had my law degree and Phi Beta Kappa certificate framed in glass on the wall, also; but the gun, Hack's creased face and long white bobbed hair dominated the office.

It was almost two o'clock and over one hundred degrees when I reached San Antonio. The skyline was rigid in the heat, and on the hills above the city I could see the white stucco homes and red-tiled roofs of the rich with their terraced gardens and mimosa trees. I turned into the Mexican district and drove through blocks of secondhand clothing stores, Baptist missions, finance companies, and pawnshops. Slender pachucos in pegged slacks and maroon shirts buttoned at the cuff, with oiled hair combed back in ducktails, leaned idly against the front of pool halls and wino bars.

I pulled into the Mission Motel, a dirty white building constructed to look like the Alamo. There were arches and small bell towers along an outer wall that faced the street. Cracked earthen jars, containing dead plants, stood in an imitation courtyard in front of the office. The bricks in the courtyard had settled from the rains and Johnson grass grew between the cracks. I took a room that I'd had before, a plaster-of-

Paris box with a double bed (an electric, coin-operated vibrating machine built in), a threadworn carpet, walls painted canvas yellow, and a bucket of ice and two thick restaurant glasses placed on the dresser. I cut the seal on a bottle of Jack Daniels and poured a glass half full over ice. I sat on the edge of the bed, lit a cigar, and drank the whiskey slowly for five minutes. The red curtains were pulled across the window, but I could still see the hot circle of the sun in the sky. I finished the glass and had another. Then I felt it begin to take me. I had always liked to drink, and I'd found that during the drinking process the best feeling came right before you knew you were drunk, that lucid moment of control and perception when all the doors in your mind spring open and the mysteries suddenly reduce to a simple equation.

I dialed an unlisted number given to me three years ago by R. C. Richardson, a Dallas oilman whom I'd kept out of prison after he defrauded the government of fifty thousand dollars on a farm subsidy. He had written out a ten-thousand-dollar check on my office desk, his huge stomach hanging over his cowboy belt, and handed me his business card with the number penciled on the back.

'I don't know if lawyers like Mexican chili, but you won't find none better than this,' he said.

He was crude, but he was right in that it was one of the best call-girl services in Texas – expensive, select, and professional for that ethic. I always felt that the money and organization must have come from the Mafia in Galveston, because none of the girls or the woman who answered the phone seemed to be afraid that the client might be a cop.

The woman on the phone sounded like a voice from

an answering service. There was no inflection, accent, or tonal quality that you could identify with a region or with anyone whom you had ever met. I used to imagine what she might have looked like. She must have answered calls from hundreds of men in motel rooms and empty houses, their voices nervous, slightly drunk, hoarse with embarrassment and passion, cautious in fear of rejection. I wondered if those countless confessions of need and inadequacy had given her a devil's insight into the respectable world, or if she was merely a mindless drone. I couldn't identify her with the image of a fat, bleached madam with glass rings on her fingers, who would be altogether too human for the voice over the phone. Finally, I had come to think of her as a hard, asexual spinster, thin and colorless, who must have developed a quiet and cynical sense of power in her ability to manipulate the sex lives of others without any involvement on her part.

As always she was discreet and subtly indirect in asking me what type of girl I wanted and for what services. And as always I made a point of leaving my motel registration name – R. C. Richardson.

I hung up the phone and poured another whiskey over ice. Thirty minutes later the girl arrived in a taxi. She was Mexican, tall, well dressed in expensive clothes, and she had a delicate quality to her carriage. Her black hair was combed over her shoulders, and her white complexion would have been perfect except for two small pits in one cheek. She had high breasts and a good ass, and her legs were well formed against her tight skirt. She smiled at me and I saw that one of her back teeth was missing.

'You want a whiskey and water?' I said.

'It's too hot now. I'm not supposed to drink in the afternoon, anyway,' she said. She sat in a chair, took a cigarette from her purse, and lit it.

'Have one just the same.' I poured a shot into a second glass.

'It won't make me do anything extra for you, Mr Richardson.'

'People in Dallas call me R.C. You can use my name in the Petroleum Club and it's better than a Diners card.'

'I don't think you'll get your money's worth if you drink much more,' she said.

'Watch. I'm a real gunfighter when I get loaded.'

I stood up and took off my shirt and tie. The whiskey had started to hum in my head.

'You should pay me before we start,' she said. She smoked and looked straight ahead.

My white linen coat hung on the back of a chair. I took my billfold from the inside pocket and counted out seventy-five dollars on the dresser top.

'Does any of your organization come out of Galveston?' I said.

'We don't learn about those things.'

'You must meet some of the juice behind it. An occasional Italian hood wearing sunglasses and a sharkskin suit.'

'Your date is for two hours, Mr Richardson.'

'Take a drink. What about that voice on the phone? Has she ever been laid herself?'

The girl set her cigarette on the dresser edge, slipped her shoes off, and rolled her hose down. I drank a long swallow from my glass.

'Maybe she's Lucky Luciano's grandmother smoking a reefer into the receiver,' I said.

'You must not get a chance to talk much.'

She stood up, put her arms around my neck, and pressed her stomach hard against me. I could smell the perfume in her hair. She moved the flat of her hand down my back and bit my lip lightly with her eyes closed.

'Don't you think we should start?' she said.

I kissed her mouth and could taste the whiskey on my own breath.

'Why don't you have a drink?' I said. 'I don't like a woman to wither under me because of Jack Daniels.'

'You're married, aren't you?' She smiled and worked her fingers under my belt.

'I just don't enjoy women who look like they're in pain when you bend over them. It's part of my R. C. Richardson genteel ethic.'

'You must be a strange man to live with.'

'Give me a try sometime.'

She pushed her stomach into me again, then dropped her arms and finished undressing. She had a wonderful body, the kind you rarely see in whores, with high breasts and brown nipples, long legs tanned on the edge of some gangster's swimming pool, a flat stomach kept in form by twenty-five situps a night, the buttocks pale right below the bathing-suit line, and a small pachuco cross with three rays tattooed inside one thigh.

I took off my trousers and shorts and laid them across the top of the chair. I picked up my cigar from the ash tray and looked into the full-length mirror on the closet door. At age thirty-five I had gained fifteen pounds since I played varsity baseball as a sophomore at Baylor. I had a little fat above the thigh bones, the veins in my legs were purple under the skin, and my hair had receded a little at the part; but otherwise I was as trim as I had been when I shut out almost every team in the Southwestern Conference. There was no fat in my chest or stomach, and there was still a ridge of muscle in the back part of my upper left arm from two years of throwing a Carl Hubbell screwball. My shoulders had grown slightly stooped, but I still stood over six feet barefooted, and the bit of grey in my sand-colored hair made me look more like a mature courtroom lawyer than an aging man. Then there was my war wound, two holes in each calf, white and scarred over, placed in an even, diagonal line as though they had been driven there by an archer's arrow.

We made love on the bed for an hour, stopping only for me to pour another glass. My head was swimming with whiskey, my heart was beating, and my skin felt hot to my own touch. The floor was unlevel when I walked to the bottle on the dresser, and my breathing became heavier and more hoarse in my throat. We went through all the positions which she knew and all the experiments I could think of, re-creating the fantasies of adolescent masturbation. She was a good whore. She affected passion without being deliberately obvious, and she tensed her body and widened her legs at the right moment. After the third time when I didn't think I could go again she bent over my stomach and kissed me and used her hands until I was ready to enter her. She was soft inside, and she hadn't been at her trade enough years yet to enlarge too much. She raised herself on her elbows so that her breasts hung close to my face, and constricted the muscles in her stomach and twisted one thigh sideways each time we moved until I began to feel it

14

swell inside me, then build in force like a large stone rolling downhill over the lip of a canyon, and burst away outside of me with the empty tranquility of an opium dream.

Then I fell into an exhausted whiskey stupor. The dust in the air looked like weevil worms turning in the shaft of sunlight that struck against the Jack Daniels bottle. The girl got up off the bed and began dressing, and a few moments later I heard the door click shut after her. I was sweating heavily, even in the air conditioning, and I leaned my head over the edge of the bed to make the room stop spinning. There were flashes of color behind my closed eyes, and obscene echoes of the things I had said to the girl when the stone began to roll downhill. My throat and mouth were dry from the whiskey and heavy breathing, the veins in my head started to dilate with hangover, and I wanted to get into the shower and sit on the floor under the cold water until I washed all the heat out of my body; but instead I fell deeper into a delirium and then the dream began.

I had many dreams left over from Korea. Sometimes I would dig a grave in frozen ground while Sergeant Tien Kwong stood over me with his burp-gun, occasionally jabbing the short barrel into my neck, his eyes flat with hatred. At other times the sergeant and I would return to the colonel's interrogation room, where I sat in a straight-backed chair and looked at nothing and said nothing until the sergeant brought my head down on his knee and broke my nose. Or sometimes I was alone, naked in the center of the compound, where we were allowed to wash under the water spigot and scrub the lice out of the seams of our clothing once a week. And each time I went there and turned the rusted iron valve I saw the words embossed on the surface – *Manufactured in Akron, Ohio.*

But this afternoon I was back in 'the Shooting Gallery,' a very special place for me, because it was there that my six days on the firing line ended. That afternoon had been quiet, and we had moved into a dry irrigation ditch that bordered a two-mile plain of rice farms with bare, artillery-scarred foothills on the far side. In the twilight I could see the shattered trees and torn craters from the 105's, and one hill, from which the North Koreans had started an attack, had been burned black with napalm strikes. We had heard that the First Marine Division had made contact with some Chinese at the Choshin, but our area was thought to be secure. They had two miles of open space to cross before they could reach us, and we had strung wire and mines outside our perimeter, although it was considered unnecessary because the North Koreans didn't have enough troops in the hills to pull a straight-on offensive. At seven-thirty the searchlights went on and illuminated the rice fields and devastated slopes; then the nightly bugles and megaphone lectures against American capitalism started. The reverberating cacophony and the unnatural white light on the hills and corrugated rice fields seemed like an experiment in insanity held on the moon's surface. Sometimes the North Koreans would fail to pick up the phonograph needle and the record would scratch out static for several minutes, echoing down off the hills like someone raking his fingernails across a blackboard. Then the searchlights would change angle and sweep across the sky, reflecting momentarily on the clouds, and settle on another distant hilltop pocked with brown holes.

I sat with my back against the ditch and tried to sleep. My blanket was draped around me like iron in the cold, and my feet ached inside my boots. I had gotten wet that afternoon crossing a rice paddy, and grains of ice had started to form inside my clothes. Even with my stocking cap pulled low under my helmet, my ears felt as though they had been beaten with boards. In the distance I heard one of our tanks clanking down a road; then a .30 caliber machine gun began firing far off on our right flank. 'What's that fucking asshole doing?' a corporal next to me said. He was a tall hillbilly boy from north Alabama. His blanket was pulled up over his helmet, and he had cut away his glove around the first finger of his right hand. I had a small bottle of codeine in my pack, and I started to take it out for a drink. It didn't taste as good as whiskey, but it warmed you inside like canned heat. The machine gun fell silent a moment, then began firing again with longer bursts, followed by a B.A.R. and the irregular popping of small-arms fire. 'What the hell is going on?' the corporal said. He raised up on his knees with his M-1 in his hands. Suddenly, flares began bursting in the sky, burning in white halos above the corrugated fields. The corporal's face was as pale as candlewax in the light, his lips tight and bloodless.

The first mortar rounds struck outside our wire and exploded the mines we had strung earlier. Yellow and orange flames erupted out of the earth and flicked around the strands of concertina wire. I could feel the suck of hot air from the vacuum, my ears roared with the thunder of freight trains crashing into one

17

another, and the wall of the ditch slammed into my head like a sledge. The rim of my helmet had cut a neat slit across my nose, and I could taste the blood draining in a wet streak over my mouth. Somewhere down the line, among the shower of rocks and frozen earth, the tremors reverberating through the ground, the locomotive engines blowing apart, I heard a Marine shout, a prolonged voice rising out of a furnace, 'DOOOOOOOOOOOC!' I started to crawl along the floor of the ditch on my hands and knees, then the Chinese corrected their angle of fire and marched the barrage right down the center of our line.

Somehow I had believed that if I ever bought one it would come as a result of some choice I had made; that I would be killed after some positive act of my own – no matter how unconscious or reckless – but there would still be a type of control in my death. However, now I knew that I was going to die in the middle of a fire-storm. I had no more chance of resisting my death than if God crashed His fist down on top of me. The shells burst in jagged intervals along the ditch, blowing men and weapons in every direction. The corporal was suddenly frozen in an explosion of light and dirt behind him. His mouth and eyes were wide, his helmet pitted and torn with shrapnel. He seemed to pirouette in slow motion, the weight of his tall body resting inside one boot, then he fell backwards across me. The blood ran from his stocking cap like pieces of string over his face. He opened and closed his mouth with a wet, sucking sound, the saliva thick on his tongue. He coughed once, quietly and deep in his throat; then his eyes fixed on a phosphorescent flare burning above us.

Moments later the fire-storm ended, almost too

quickly, because it seemed that nothing that intense and murderous could ever end, that it would perpetuate itself indefinitely with its own cataclysmic force. I pushed the corporal off me, my ears ringing in the silence (or what seemed like silence, since automatic weapons had begun firing again on both sides of us). The corporal's helmet rolled off his head, and I saw a long incision, like a scalpel cut, across the crown of his skull. The dead were strewn in unnatural positions along the ditch, some of them half-buried in mounds of dirt from the caved-in walls, their bodies twisted and broken as though they had been dropped from airplanes. The faces of the wounded were white with shock and concussion. Down the line a man was screaming.

'Are you hit, Doc?' It was the first lieutenant. He carried his carbine in one hand. His left arm hung limply by his side.

'I'm all right.' Our voices sounded far away from me.

'Get ready to move the wounded out of here. The right flank is getting their ass knocked off. We're supposed to get artillery in five minutes and pull.'

'You're bleeding pretty heavy, Lieutenant.'

'Get every man moving you can. We're going to have gooks coming up our ass.'

However, the artillery cover never came, and we were overrun fifteen minutes later. Our automatic weapons men killed Chinese by the hundreds as they advanced across the rice fields. We packed snow on the barrels of the .30 caliber machine guns to keep them from melting, and the bottom of the ditch was littered with spent shell casings and empty ammunition boxes. The dead lay in quilted rows as far as I could see. They moved forward and died, then another wave took their place. The bugles began blowing again, potato mashers exploded in our wire, and every time a weapon locked empty or a Marine was hit they moved closer to the ditch. Our only tank was burning behind us, the lieutenant was shot through the mouth, and all of our N.C.O.s were dead. We fired our last rounds, fixed bayonets in a silly Alamo gesture, and then the Chinese swarmed over us.

They ran along the edge of the ditch, firing point-blank into us with their burpguns. They shot the dead and the living alike, in the hysterical relief that comes with the victory of living through an attack. Their weapons weren't designed for accuracy, but they could dump almost a full clip into a man who was closer than twenty feet. For the first time in my life I ran from an enemy. I dropped the handles of a stretcher with a wounded Marine on it and ran across the bodies, the ammunition boxes, the bent bazookas, the knocked-out machine guns, the lieutenant spitting blood and parts of teeth on his coat, and suddenly I saw a young Chinese boy, not over seventeen, his thin, yellow face pinched with cold, standing above me in tennis shoes and quilted clothes. I guess (as I remember it) that I threw my arms out in front of me to prevent that spray of flame and bullets from entering my face and chest, but the gesture was unnecessary because he was a poor marksman and he never got above my knees. I felt a pain like a shaft of ice through both legs, and I toppled over as though a bad comic had just kicked me deftly across the shins.

My Korean recall, born out of Jack Daniels and sexual exhaustion, ended here. I awoke at six-thirty, sweating, my head thick with afternoon whiskey. For a half hour I sat on the shower tile under the cold water, chewing an unlit cigar. The white indentions in my calves felt like rubber under my thumb.

chapter two

The Shamrock-Hilton Hotel in Houston was crowded
that night with Democrats from all over Texas. They
came in party loyalty almost seven hundred strong –
the daughters of forgotten wars, the state committee
from Austin, the A.F.L.-C.I.O. fat boys, the oil-depletion wheelers, manicured newspaper publishers, slick
public relations men, millionaire women dressed in
Neiman-Marcus clothes with Piney Woods accents,
young lawyers on their way up in state politics (each of
them with a clear eye, hard grip, and a square,
cologned jaw like Fearless Fosdick), the ten-percen-
ters, the new rich who bought their children's way
into Randolph-Macon, the ranchers with a bright eye
on the agriculture subsidy, a few semi-acceptable
Mafia characters from Galveston, several ex-hacks,
doormen, flunkies, and baggage carriers from Lyndon's entourage, three Hollywood movie stars who
had been born in Texas, an astronaut, one crippled
commander of the Veterans of the Spanish-American
War who sat in a wheelchair, an alcoholic baseball
player who used to pitch for the Houston Buffaloes
before he went up to the Cardinals, some highly paid
prostitutes, an Air Force general who has probably
won a footnote in military history for his dedication

in the fire-bombing of Dresden, and United States Senator Allen B. Dowling.

I had driven from San Antonio in two and one half hours, highballing wide-open like a blue shot through small towns and farm communities, while drunken cowboys drinking beer in front of saloons stared at me in disbelief. I pulled into the white circular drive of the Shamrock and waited in the line of cars for the band of uniformed Negro porters to take over my luggage, my Cadillac, and even my attempt to open a door by myself. They moved about with the quick, electric motion of rubberbands snapping, their teeth white, their faces black and cordial, obsequious and yet confidently efficient. I imagined that they could have cut all our throats with pleasure. They reminded me of Negro troops in Korea when they were dealing with Mr Skins, a white officer. They could go about a job in a way that deserved group citations, and at the same time insult an officer and laugh in his face without doing anything for which they could be reprimanded unless the officer wanted to appear a public fool.

I idled the car up to the glass doors at the entrance; one Negro pulled open the car door for me, another got behind the wheel, and a third took my suitcase from the trunk. I handed out one-dollar tips to each of them (with the stupid feeling of an artificial situation that you have when you pay a shoeshine boy), and followed the third porter into the hotel. And I wondered, looking at his gray, uniformed back, the muscles stiff and flat under the cloth, *Would you really like to tick a razor across my jugular, you uprooted descendant of Ham, divested of your heritage, dropped clumsily and illiterate into a south Texas cotton patch, where you could labor and exhaust yourself and kind through the next several generations on tenant shares? Yes, I guess you could, with a neat, sharp corner of the blade that you would draw gingerly along the vein.*

But I still had a fair edge on from the Jack Daniels, the Mexican girl, and the dream, and I imagine that is why I suddenly had such strange insights into that black mind walking before me.

I gave my name at the desk and was told that my wife had taken a suite of rooms on the tenth floor. She and my brother Bailey had come to Houston yesterday when the convention started, and I was supposed to join them today at noon for lunch on the terrace with several of the oil-depletion boys who had all types of money to sink into a young congressman's career. However, I didn't have to speak before the convention until ten that night, and I didn't think that I could take a full day of laughing conversation, racial jokes, polite gin by the swimming pool, and powdered, middle-aged oil wives who whispered banal remarks like slivers of glass in my ear. I had met all of them before in Dallas, Austin, Fort Worth, and El Paso, and they were always true to themselves, regardless of the place or occasion. The men wore their same Oshman western suits and low-topped boots, the diamond rings from Zale's that looked out of place on their fat hands, the string ties or open-neck sports shirts that directed attention away from the swift eyes and the broken veins in the cheeks. They spoke of huge finance with indifference, but I knew that their groins tingled with pleasure at the same time. Their women liked me because I was young and good-looking, successful as a lawyer, tanned from

24

playing in fashionable tennis courts, and with an inner steeled effort I could clink the ice in my glass and look pleasant and easy while they told about all the trivial problems in their insipid lives (in this respect I was very self-disciplined, because I always knew when to excuse myself and walk away before the inner rigidity broke apart).

Besides, I really didn't need them to be elected congressional representative from my district. The Holland name and my father's reputation would assure almost any member of my family a political position if he wanted it. Also, people still remembered when I returned from the war as a wounded hospital corpsman, dressed in Marine tropicals with a walking cane, an ex-P.O.W. who had resisted brainwashing for thirty-two months while other American troops were signing confessions, informing on each other, and defecting to the Chinese.

Finally, my Republican opponent was a seedy racist, so fanatical even in his business dealings that his insurance agency failed. At different times he had belonged to the John Birch and Paul Revere societies, the Independent Million, the White Citizens League, and the Dixiecrat Party. He was a mean and obnoxious drunk, a bully towards his wife and children, and I don't know why the Republicans let him run, except for the fact that he could always raise money from fools like himself and they hadn't won an election in DeWitt since Reconstruction, anyway.

Verisa had taken a five-room suite with a cocktail bar, deep rugs, oil paintings on the walls, potted rubber plants, and a porch that overlooked the swimming pool far below. The porter set my suitcase down and closed the door behind me. I could see the anger in Verisa's eyes. She sat on the couch in a white evening gown, her legs crossed tightly, with the tip of one high-heeled shoe pointed into the coffee table. Her auburn hair was brushed to a metallic shine, and her skin looked as bloodless and smooth as marble. If I had been closer to her I could have smelled the touch of perfume behind her ears, the powdered breasts, the hinted scent of her sex, a light taste of gin on her breath. She looked at me briefly, then turned her eyes away and lit a cigarette. The toe of the shoe flicked momentarily into a carved design in the side of the table. She was always able to hold her anger in well. She had learned part of that at Randolph-Macon and the rest from living with me. She could reduce flying rage to a hot cigarette ash or a few whispered and rushed words in the corner of a cocktail party, or maybe one burst of heat after we were home; but the pointed flick of the shoe was a fleshy bite into my genitals for seven years of marriage, broken young-girl dreams, her embarrassment when I brought oil-field workers or soldiers from Fort Sam Houston to the country club, my drunken discussions in the middle of the night about my Korean War guilt, and for the stoic and futile resignation she had adopted, out of all her social disappointments, in hopes of becoming the wife of a Texas congressman on his way to the Senate and that opulent world of power which goes far beyond any of the things you can buy or destroy with money.

'Hack, don't you give a goddamn?' she said quietly, still looking straight ahead.

'What did I miss?'

'A day of my making excuses for you, and right now I'm rather sick of it.'

'Lunch by the pool with the Dallas aristocracy can't be that awful.'

'I'm not in a flippant mood, Hack. I don't enjoy apologizing or lying for you, and I don't like sitting three hours by myself with boorish business people.'

'Those are the cultured boys with the money. The fellows who oil all the wheels and make Frankenstein run properly.'

I went to the bar and poured a double shot of whiskey over ice. It clicked pleasantly on the edge of the afternoon drunk, and I felt even more serene in the sexual confidence which I always had towards Verisa after whoring.

'I don't know where you've been, but I suspect it was one of your Okie motel affairs.'

'I had to meet R. C. Richardson in Austin.'

'How much do you pay them? Do they go down on you? That's what they call it in the trade, isn't it?'

'It's something like that.'

'They must be lovely girls. Do they perform any other special things for you?'

'Right now R. C.'s working on a deal to patent hoof and mouth disease. He has federal contracts for Viet Nam that run in millions.'

'Your girl friends probably have had some nice diseases of their own.'

'Let it go, Verisa.'

'Oh, I shouldn't say anything to you? Is that it? I should spend a day of congenial conversation with people who chew on toothpicks, and then meet you pleasantly at the door after you return from screwing a Mexican whore.'

Something inside me flinched at her accuracy. I poured a short drink into the bottom of the glass.

'I bet you've gone to bed with me, not knowing whether they had given you one of their diseases,' she said.

She was really tightening the iron boot now.

'Do you want a highball? I'm going to change clothes.'

'Oh Christ, you've probably done it,' she said, and put her fingers over her mouth.

'I never did that to you.'

'You probably don't even remember. You have to wait two weeks to know, don't you?'

'You're letting it walk away with you.' But she was right. I didn't remember.

'It happened to a girl I knew in college, but she was a dumpy thing who did it in the back seats of cars with Marines and sailors. I didn't believe it ever happened with your husband.'

'Pull off it. You're working towards a real bad conclusion.'

'I wonder that you didn't give me sulfa tablets.'

I fixed her a drink with a squeeze of lemon and set it on the table in front of her.

'I'm sorry that you got strung out today,' I said. 'I thought Bailey would take you to lunch if I didn't make it.'

'Tell me if you really did it to me.'

'Look, it was a shitty day for you. I should have been here to eat lunch with those bastards, or I should have called Bailey and told him to take care of it. But I'm going to change clothes now. We should go downstairs in a few minutes.'

'You must have a very special clock to go by. It starts to work correctly when you feel the corner at your back.'

28

'You ought to drink your highball.'

'Why don't you drink it? It makes you more electric and charming in public,' she said.

'You've gotten it out pretty far in a short time.'

'I might stretch it out so far that you ache.'

'Isn't this just spent effort? If you want to believe that you've won the ballgame in the ninth inning, go ahead. Or maybe you would like me to kiss your ass in apology.'

'You've done that without a need for apologizing. An analyst would have a wonderful time with you.'

'I won't go into embarrassing descriptions, but as I recall you enjoyed every little piece of it.'

'Yes, I remember those sweet experiences. You tried to enact all the things you had learned in a Japanese whorehouse while you slobbered about two boys who died in a Chinese prison camp.'

'You better shut it off in a hurry.'

'What was the boy's name from San Angelo and the Negro sergeant from Georgia?'

'You don't listen when I tell you something, do you?'

'It's just a little bit of recall from things you brought up. Didn't you say they were buried in a latrine? In your words, to lend more American fertilizer to the Korean rice crop.'

'You're fucking in the wrong direction.'

'My, Captain Marvel with his favorite drunk word.'

'This isn't your style. So step back real quick before you find yourself in a bad place.'

'Are you going to hit me? That would make a perfect punctuation mark in my day.'

'Just don't bend it anymore.'

29

'Don't walk away, Hack. If you blow this for us, I'll divorce you and sue for the home. Then I'll repay you in the most fitting way I can think of. I'll cover that historical cemetery of yours with concrete.'

I took the bottle of whiskey and my glass from the bar and slammed the bedroom door behind me. I could feel the anger beating in my head and the veins swelling in my throat. I seldom became angry about anything, but this time she had reached inside me hard and had gotten a good piece between her nails. I drank out of the bottle twice and started to change clothes. My face was flushed with heat in the mirror. I kicked my trousers against the wall and pulled off my shirt, stripping the buttons. I stood in my underwear and had another drink, this time with measured sips. The whiskey began to flatten out inside me, and I felt a single drop of perspiration run down off an eyebrow. Hold it in, sonofabitch, I thought. The Lone Ranger never blows his Kool-Aid. You just give the sheriff a silver bullet and let Tonto pour you a drink. But Verisa had really been off her style this time. She had collected a valise of surgical tools during the day for an entry into all my vital organs. In fact, I didn't know whether to mark this to her debit or credit. As I said, in the past she could always load all of her outrage into a quiet hypodermic needle, thrust subtly into the right place (her best probe, the one she used after I had done something especially painful to that private part of her soul, was to go limp and indifferent under me, her arms spread back on the pillows, during my disabling moment of climax).

I had one more drink, just enough to go over the back of the tongue, then brushed my teeth, took three aspirins and two vitamin pills, and rinsed out my whiskey breath with Listerine. I dressed in an Italian silk shirt, a dark tie, a pressed white suit, and rubbed the polish smooth on my boots with a damp towel. I lit a cigar and breathed out the smoke in the mirror. You're all right, Masked Man, I thought.

I heard Verisa open the front door, then the voices of Bailey and Senator Dowling.

'Hack,' Verisa said, tapping her fingernails lightly on my door. I knew she had already gone into her transformation as the pleasant wife of a congressional candidate. It was amazing how fast it could take place.

I stepped out of the bedroom and shook hands with the Senator.

'How are you, Hack?' he said, his face healthy and cheerful. He was fifty-five years old, but his handshake was still hard and his wrist strong. He was six inches shorter than I, solidly built, his shoulders pulled straight back, and his white hair trimmed close to the scalp. His acetylene-blue eyes were bright and quick, impossible to penetrate, and you knew after he glanced confidently into your face that his lack of height was no disadvantage to him. He had the small, hard chest of a professional soldier, and his tailored suit didn't have a fold or a bulge in it. He wore dentures, and they caused him to lisp slightly with his Texas accent, but otherwise he was solid. Also, Senator Dowling had managed to remain a strong southern figure through five administrations. He had been on many sides over the years, and he always walked out of the ballpark with the winning team (and therein lay his gift, the ability to sense change before anyone else got a whiff of it). He was put into Congress by a one-million-acre southwest Texas corporation ranch in 1940, and in the next two years he paid off his obligations by sponsoring large subsidies for growing nothing on arid land. Then he represented the oil interests, the franchised utility companies, and the Houston and Dallas industries up on antitrust suits. He assured his constituents that he was a segregationist until the Kennedy administration, then he backed one of the first civil rights bills. In the meantime he acquired a three-thousand-acre ranch in the hill country north of Austin, and stock in almost every major corporation in Texas with a defense contract.

'Fine, Senator. How have you been?' I said.

'Good. Relaxing at the ranch. Fishing and playing tennis a little bit before the campaign.'

'Hack, fix the Senator a drink,' Verisa said.

'Thank you. A half jigger and some soda will be fine,' he said.

'You should try the bass in Hack's ponds,' Bailey said. He sat in one of the tall bar chairs with his arm over the back. Good old Bailey, I thought. He could always come through with an inane remark at the right time. He looked like my twin, except five years older and fifteen pounds heavier, with wrinkles in his forehead and neck. Bailey was a practical man who worried about all the wrong things.

'I'd hoped to talk with you earlier today,' the Senator said, and looked straight into my face with those acetylene-blue eyes.

'I had to stop over in Austin with a client. Maybe we can talk after my speech,' I said.

'Verisa says you're having people up for drinks later. I'd rather we have some time between our-selves.'

'Hack, we're invited for breakfast at the River Oaks Country Club in the morning,' Bailey said. 'Maybe the Senator can join us. You all can talk, and then we'll play some doubles.'

'That sounds fine,' the Senator said. 'I could use a couple of sets against an ex-Baylor pitcher.'

The sonofabitch, I thought.

'My opponent hasn't somehow organized his rag-tail legions, has he?'

'Oh no, no. I don't think we need to spend too much time on this gentleman.' He laughed with his healthy smile. 'I wanted to talk with you about several things that will come later in Washington. Your father helped me a great deal when I was first elected to Congress, and I learned then that it's invaluable to have an experienced friend.'

I handed him his highball glass with the half jigger and soda. He had learned to be a cautious person with liquor, and I knew he wouldn't finish the glass I had given him.

'Well, I appreciate it, Senator. But I don't know how good my Baylor arm will be on the court,' I said, biting down inside myself.

'Hack is defensive tonight,' Verisa said.

'He should be,' the Senator said. His eyes took on a deeper blue with his smile.

'I have a weak serve, but I'm hell on defending the net,' I said. 'One flash of the wrist and I drive tennis balls into concrete.'

'We had better go downstairs pretty soon,' Bailey said. His face was flat, but his discomfort showed in the nervous tic of his fingers on his trouser leg.

'I don't expect that our audience will disappear,'

the Senator said. 'They usually have their way of waiting, as a U.S. Senator sometimes does.'

Sorry, you bastard. I'm all out of sackcloth and ashes tonight, I thought. I set my cigar in the ashtray and poured an inch of Jack Daniels into a glass. Bailey's face began to tighten in the silence. Verisa's eyes waited on me, her lips pinched slightly, but I held out. I sipped the whiskey and drew in on the cigar as though the conversation were far removed from me.

'Would you like to drive with us out to the country club in the morning?' Bailey said.

'Thanks. I'll find my way there. From what I understand, Hack drives like he's trying to put A. J. Foyt back in the grease pit,' the Senator said.

'I wouldn't try to beat a Texas boy at his own game, Senator.'

'It depends on what type of game.' His eyes crinkled at me.

'I have a pretty good shutout record in my field.'

'I remember, Hack. I watched you pitch twice. But as I recall you used to have a little trouble with a lefthanded batter.'

'Sometimes you have to bear down a little more.'

He took a thin swallow of his highball, and placed the glass on the bar, his expression assured and pleasant, then looked casually at his watch.

'Bailey's probably right. We should go downstairs. I'll drop up later for a few minutes and say hello to your guests,' he said, and put his hand on the small of my back. 'Then tomorrow we'll see what type of tennis game we can work out.'

I saw the ease come back into Verisa's face, and Bailey stood up stiffly as though he had just been unstrapped from an electric chair. I took my typewritten speech in its leather folder from my suitcase, and we walked down the carpeted corridor towards the elevator like an amiable family of four.

The dining tables in the Shamrock Room were filled. The silver, the crystalware, the white tablecloths, the spangled evening gowns and decanters of wine reflected softly under the lights. The Senator introduced me from the rostrum, and the rows of faces became hushed and polite. Even the fat boys from the oil interests, in their string ties and cowboy boots, looked quietly deferential. I read them my twenty-minute speech of non-language and they applauded thirteen times. Whenever I approached some vague conclusion, pointed at nothing, I could see their eyes grow more intent, their heads nodding slightly, as some private anger with the nation, the universe, or themselves found a consensus in my empty statements, then the hands would begin clapping. They had found a burning spokesman to represent all the outraged goodguys. I was tight enough to be unconscious of my speech's stupidity, and after a while I even felt that I might be saying something meaningful. They rose to their feet when I finished. I shook dozens of hands, smiled with country boy humility at the compliments, and invited half the dining room to Verisa's cocktail party.

The party was a success in every way. Verisa was able to become the radiant wife of a congressional candidate, moving with detached pleasantness between groups of people (the society editors from *The Houston Post* and *The Chronicle* both agreed the next day that Mrs Holland was one of the most lovely hostesses to appear in Texas politics in a long time).

And I was able to make a doubleheader out of the evening: I managed to get drunk twice in one day. The Negro waiters put a fresh whiskey and water in my hand everytime I flicked my eyes in their direction, and within two hours Mr Hyde had begun to prowl obscenely through the hallways of my mind. The room was so crowded by midnight that the air conditioning couldn't clear the smoke, and the noise brought complaints from the floors above and below us. People whom I had never seen before drank three cases of bourbon and Scotch, ate four hundred dollars' worth of catered food, burned cigar holes in the carpet, charged thirty-minute long-distance calls to my room, and threw glasses and bottles off the terrace into the swimming pool. Someone wheeled in the commander from the Veterans of the Spanish–American War, who sat stupefied in one corner, staring out at the bedlam from his atrophied, withered face, until a sentimental W.W. II veteran decided to take him on a careening ride through the corridor. The alcoholic baseball pitcher and I argued about how to throw a crippling beanball, one of the society editors threw up in the bathroom and had to be put in bed by Verisa, and the firebomber of Dresden unzipped the back of a woman's evening dress.

I insulted the astronaut and his wife, who left after a polite five-minute interval, then two of the Negro bartenders quit when an oil broker made a racial remark to them. I took over the bar and poured all the remaining bourbon, gin, and Scotch into a punch bowl, and insisted that everyone in the room have a drink. This resulted in four more people passed out, a clogged toilet, and a group plan to open up the dining room for steak and eggs. Someone brought in a hillbilly singer from a nightclub, who propositioned Verisa, and the Air Force general drank six glasses from the punch bowl and urinated off the balcony. By four A.M. the room was totally destroyed. All the furniture was either burned or broken, the floor was littered with cigar and cigarette butts, the French doors were smashed, the potted plants overturned, and the electric plug in the drink mixer had short-circuited and melted into the wall socket. (Later, I received an eight-hundred-dollar repair bill from the Shamrock-Hilton, and I kindly forwarded it to the Texas Democratic Committee in Austin.)

At five A.M. the last of the guests supported each other out the door, while Verisa accepted their incoherent compliments and told them to visit us at the ranch (she was still radiant, even through her fatigue). I lay down on the bed next to the society editor, and as the false dawn glowed on the horizon and touched the room with its grey light, she rolled her head towards me, her mouth wide with snoring, her face oval and white, and I thought *Good night, good night, sweet Desdemona*, and I fell once more into Mr Hyde's world.

The clay tennis courts at the country club were green and freshly chalked under a hot, blue sky. I sat at a marble-topped table with Bailey under the shade trees, sipping a glass of tomato juice and vodka, while Verisa and the Senator whocked the ball back and forth across the net. Behind the courts the sun shattered off the swimming pool, and children in dripping swimsuits lined up on the diving board. In the distance the smooth green contours of the golf course arched away through the oak trees, and the sandtraps looked like ground white crystal in the light. My hangover was bad. I was sweating unnaturally, shaking inside like a tuning fork vibrating to the wrong chord, and I felt a hard pressure band across one side of my head. My tennis shorts and polo shirt were already wet, although I hadn't been on the court yet, and the vodka wouldn't take hold. Bailey kept talking about our law practice in Austin, my failure to come into the office regularly, and my rudeness to the Senator. His words were like pieces of broken china in my head. He spoke from some abstraction inside himself, looking into my eyes occasionally, his face earnest with the dumb innocence of a nondrinker talking to a man with a bleeding hangover. I lit a cigar, tried to concentrate on the tennis game, and had another vodka and tomato juice.

'It's insane to do these things to yourself,' he said. 'You're hungover three days out of seven, you go into court with your fingers shaking, and in the meantime other people are picking up after you.'

'Are you picking up after me, Bailey?'

'What do you think I did yesterday? And last night you insulted a half dozen people within fifteen minutes.'

'I thought I only got the astronaut.' I wiped the sweat off my forehead on my sleeve and drained the vodka and tomato juice.

'You want to get blasted again?'

'I might unless the conversation changes.'

'It's goddamn insane. You can be in office in a few months. The youngest congressman from the state. After one or two terms you can do anything you want in Texas.'

'I know those things.'

'Then why don't you act like you have a goddamn mind?'

I held my glass up to the waiter for another drink.

'You count on too much from people,' Bailey said.

'Will you go to hell or shut up for about five minutes?'

'You can get angry, but I'm right in what I say.'

'Bailey, would you get away from me a few minutes?'

'You see what that booze does?'

'Goddamn it, go swimming or chase golf balls if you like. Believe me, I'm up to my eyes with it.'

He stood up, his face slightly hurt and angry, and walked across the clipped grass to the clubhouse. I knew that in a half hour he would be back as though nothing had been said, and then later he would start to bore in again. Bailey was a good boy, but he was simply unteachable.

The Senator moved about the court like a man twenty years younger than his age. I have to admit that he looked good out there. The matted grey hair on his chest and his thick, muscular shoulders glistened with sweat, and he whocked the ball in a white streak across the net. For a short man he had a fine driving serve, and his backhand was always accurate and strong. He had a good eye for court distance, and most of his shots just skimmed the top of the net and hit in a low bounce on the clay. Verisa was a good tennis player, but he took her in two easy sets. The Senator was a competitor, and his gentlemanly affectation ended when he entered the games.

They joined me at the table, and the waiter served us a cold lunch of picked shrimp on cracked ice. For the next hour I listened to the Senator's advice on my campaign, the upcoming year in Congress, and contributions from several oil companies (the checks, which already amounted to over sixty-five thousand dollars, had all been deposited by Bailey in a special account in Austin). Then I was told indirectly, with compassion, to avoid public statements on civil rights, at least while in Texas, and that I shouldn't lean too far towards labor, since as a Democrat I could already count on their vote. I nodded my head and listened as intelligently as possible, but my hangover wouldn't let go and few of his sentences seemed to have any relationship to one another. Actually, more than any instruction in Texas politics, he wanted to exact penance from me because of yesterday, and I was in the perfect condition for it – a mental cripple.

'Next week I plan to visit the wounded Viet Nam veterans in Walter Reed,' he said. 'I think it might be good for you to come along.'

'Why's that?'

'You were wounded yourself in Korea. I think the boys like to know that they have congressmen who understand what they've been through.'

'I'm afraid I've had enough of V.A. hospitals, Senator,' I said.

'We'll be there an hour or so. Then you'll be back home the same night.'

'I better pass.'

'Go on, Hack. Bailey will be at the office,' Verisa said.

'No, I don't –'

'You need a trip. Enjoy it,' Bailey said. He had come back from the clubhouse fresh with resolve.

'I spent two months in the V.A. in '53 and I really –' I was smiling in my best convivial way.

'This type of exposure is important to you, Hack,' the Senator said.

Fuck it, I thought. 'All right, Senator. I'll be glad to.'

We finished lunch and played a set of doubles. Verisa and I stood the Senator and Bailey, and the sweat rolled down my face and chest in rivulets. My timing was bad, my movements uncoordinated, and I drove most of my serves into the bottom of the net. My head was thundering from the heat and exertion. The air seemed so humid that it was like steam on my skin. If Bailey hadn't been such a bad player we would have lost the set six games straight, but Verisa managed to keep us only one game behind. I was even proud of her. In her short white tennis skirt and cap with a green visor she was the loveliest thing on the courts. Her legs and shoulders were freckled with suntan, her auburn hair wet and shining on the back of her neck, and you could get a good look at her fine ass when she bent over with her serve.

We went into the final game five to four, and I wanted to beat the Senator very badly. He played confidently, controlling the backline with an easy sweep of his racket in either direction. His thick eyebrows were heavy with perspiration, and his blue eyes refracted a mean success every time he drove the ball into my shoelaces.

However, I soon learned that the Senator's revenge for yesterday wasn't complete yet. I moved up to the net for the final point, Verisa served, and Bailey returned the ball in an easy, high-arching lob. I whocked it with all the strength in my shoulder straight into the Senator. The game should have been over and the set tied, but the Senator caught my drive with one short, forearm chop of the racket, and smashed the ball murderously into my face. My sunglasses broke on the court, my eyes watered uncontrollably, and I felt the blood running from my nose. Through the tears I could see him walking quickly towards me, his face gathered in concern, but there was victory in his eyes.

Later, Verisa drove us back to the hotel while I held a bloodflecked towel filled with ice cubes to my nose. The bridge was already swollen, and there was a sickening taste in the back of my throat. I tilted my head back on the seat and looked with one eye out the window at the stream of angry traffic along South Main. At the court the Senator had apologized in his most empathic manner, the tennis pro arrived with a first-aid kit and tried to push cotton balls up my nose, a Negro waiter put another vodka and tomato juice on the table and left, and now Bailey sat in the backseat talking about going to the hospital for an X-ray.

'Do you think it's broken?' Verisa said.

'No, he just flattened it a little. A warning,' I said. My words were nasal and smothered under the towel.

'It was an accident,' Bailey said. 'You cut the ball right into him.'

'Why don't you get off the goodguymanship ethic? Leave the Boy Scouts for a while, at least till we get to the hotel,' I said. 'He was out to tear my head off.'

'That's hangover paranoia.'

'Oh, shit,' I said.

'How many U.S. Senators would spend their time trying to help a thirty-five-year-old lawyer's political career?'

'Don't you know a sonofabitch when you see one?'

'You're constructing things to fit some strange frame of reference in your own mind.'

'You're an amateur, Bailey. You better learn, to recognize sophisticated viciousness.'

'You're really thinking foolishly.'

'I don't care if you want to look at the world like Little Orphan Annie. But right now I feel like someone took a shit in my head, my nose is full of blood, and if you say anything more I'm going to call the Senator from the hotel and give him my best delivery.'

'You better take us to Herman Hospital,' Bailey said.

'I've had my nose broken before and I know what it feels like. Just turn it off for a few more blocks.'

'I'll have the hotel doctor come to the room,' Verisa said.

'Forget that, too,' I said. 'I'm driving down to the Valley this afternoon. Just as soon as I can get six aspirins down and a double shot of Jack Daniels.'

'You're going to the Valley!' Verisa said. Her head turned sharply at me.

'I got a letter from a Mexican fellow I was in Korea with. He got involved in some trouble with this farm labor union, and he's in the county jail waiting to go up to prison on a five-year sentence.'

'What am I supposed to do in the meantime?' she said.

'Ride back home with Bailey or take a flight. You don't like to drive with me, anyway.'

'So I'm left with the pleasant experience of explaining the condition of the room to the management. Is that it?' she said. 'I imagine that by this time the cleaning woman has run down the hall in hysterics.'

'Ignore them. We didn't do the damage. They know what to expect when they contract for a convention. Particularly when it's composed of lunatics.'

'It's lovely of you to leave me with these things.'

'All right. I'll talk with the manager on the way out. I'll drip a few drops of blood on his desk, talk with him cordially, and then I'll tell him to go to hell.'

'You do what you want, Hack,' she said. 'Get drunk for a week in the Valley, go across the border and find a sweet two-dollar girl, indulge all your disgusting obsessions.'

She turned the car into the hotel drive, and a doorman stepped out to the edge of the walk under the canopy. I rubbed the dampness of the towel over my face.

'I have to go see this man,' I said. 'He was a good friend to me when I went on the line. I was so goddamned scared I couldn't paste a Band-Aid on a scratch.'

'Just don't talk about it,' she said. 'Drive down the road and forget anything else. That's the way you do things best.'

'Listen a minute. I don't enjoy driving three hundred miles in one-hundred-degree heat with a hangover and a bloody nose. But this man has five years hard time to do because of a scuffle on a picket line. He doesn't have a goddamn cent and he can't get a white lawyer to file an appeal for him. Next week he'll be chopping cotton on the prison farm and there won't be a thing I can do for him.'

'We can call the A.C.L.U. You don't have to go down there today,' Bailey said.

'No, you go on, Hack,' she said. 'It would be too

terrible for you to live through one day of putting things together without beginning another adventure.'

'Okay, piss on it,' I said. 'I'll catch air in a few minutes, and you can go back to the ranch and serve cocktails to the D.A.R. Then next week we can take a trip to Walter Reed and shake hands with the basket cases. A war-time V.A. ward should be included on all bus tours. You can meet the dummies in their wheelchairs and the guys without human faces. It's a balling scene.'

Bailey lit his pipe in the back seat and Verisa's eyes were brilliant with anger as the doorman stepped around the front of the car. I lowered the window and dumped the cracked ice in the towel onto the concrete.

People stared at me in the lobby as I walked towards the elevator with the towel under my nose. I still wore my tennis shorts and canvas shoes, with a sports coat over my bloodstreaked polo shirt. Verisa and Bailey walked on each side of me as impervious as granite. Upstairs, I showered and changed into a pair of cream slacks and a soft, maroon shirt, ordered a bottle of Jack Daniels from the bar, and ate a half dozen aspirin in the bathroom. I could hear Verisa making reservations on an afternoon flight to San Antonio. I looked in the mirror at my swollen nose, a slightly puffed upper lip, and the white discoloration in my face, and I decided to leave the whiskey doubleheaders to Grover Alexander or some other better lefthander than I. A bellboy brought the bottle; I took one drink out of it and closed the suitcase. I started to speak to Verisa, but she put a cigarette in her mouth and looked out through the smashed French doors at the oil wells pumping in the distance.

chapter three

The late sun was red on the hills above the Rio Grande. The river was almost dry in places, dividing around bleached sandbars, and in the twilight the water had turned scarlet. On the other side, in Mexico, there were adobe huts and wooden shacks along the banks, and buzzards circled high in the sky. I turned off the air conditioner, rolled down the windows, and let the warm air blow through the car. In the first quick rush of wind I could smell the sweet ripeness of the whole Valley: the citrus groves, the tomato and watermelon fields, the rows of cotton and corn, the manure, and pastures of bluebonnets. The windmills were spinning, and cattle moved lazily towards the troughs. A single scorch of cloud stretched across the sun, which now seemed to grow in size as it dipped into the hills. The base of the pin oaks and blackjack trees grew darker, then the bottom rim of the sky glowed with flame.

I had mended from my hangover during the long drive, and I felt the numb serenity of a longtime dying man who had just received an unexpected extension of life. Then, in that cool moment of reflection, I wondered why I always drank twice as much when I had to make ritual appearances, or why I had gone to

Houston in the first place, since my talk before a few hundred semiliterate oil men had little to do with my probable election, anyway; or lastly, why I had ever entered politics and the world of Senator Allen B. Dowling.

I could guess at the answers to the first two questions, which weren't of particular consequence, except that I didn't want another hangover and defeat at the tennis court like I'd had this morning; but the answer to the third question worked its way through the soft tissue and dropped like an ugly, sharp-edged black diamond into a bright space in the center of my mind. Inside, under all the cynicism, the irreverence towards the icons and totems, my insults to astronauts and country club women, I wanted a part of the power at the top.

I tried to believe that my motive was to atone for Verisa's spent dreams, or that I wanted to equal my father in his law and congressional career, or at least that I was simply an ironic man who felt he could do as good a job as comic-page segregationists; or maybe at worst I was just a pragmatist with knowledge of the money to be made in the dealings between the federal government and the oil interests. But that black diamond had blood crusted on its edges, and I knew that I had the same weaknesses as Verisa and the Senator; I wanted power itself, the tribal recognition that went with it, and that small key to its complexities carried secretly in my watchpocket.

I accelerated the Cadillac through the low hills towards Pueblo Verde. The evening had started to cool, the sky deepened to dark purple, and the last of the sun's afterglow burned into itself in a gathering fire at one small point on the horizon. I didn't care for

47

these moments of reflection, even though they came with the cool release from hangover, and I had learned long ago that solitude and introspection always bring you to Mr Hyde's cage. Every jailer knows that an inmate would rather take a beating with a garden hose than go to solitary, where the snakes start coming out of hibernation and the voices from years ago thunder through long tunnels. The North Koreans and the Chinese knew the same trick, too. The broken noses and smashed finger tips, or even digging your own grave under Sergeant Tien Kwong's burpgun, weren't nearly as effective as six weeks in a dirt hole with an iron sewer grate over your head. There you could concentrate on your guilt for forgotten sins, your inadequacy as a man, your lack of courage when you dropped a wounded Marine on a stretcher and ran, your resentment towards a dying Australian who was always given the largest portion of rice in the shack; or you could look up through the iron slits in the grate at the Chinese sentry who watched you while you squatted like a dog and defecated into a helmet.

So Socrates and his know-thyself ethic were full of shit, I thought, or he never spent time in solitary before he drank the hemlock or drove down a south Texas road on a clear summer evening with Mr Hyde sitting in the passenger's seat.

The main street in Pueblo Verde was almost empty, the wood frame buildings along the high sidewalks locked and darkened. A few old cars and pickup trucks were parked in front of a beer tavern with an insect-encrusted neon sign buzzing above a broken screen door. In the Sunday night quiet I could hear the hillbilly music from the jukebox and the laughter of a half dozen high school kids smoking cigarettes under the oaks in the courthouse square.

The hotel was a two-story wood building with flaking white paint and a latticed verandah. The letters on the ROOMS FOR GUESTS sign were blistered and faded, and the small lobby, with a plastic television set in one corner and wilted flowers in dime-store vases, smelled like dust and old wallpaper. I signed the register while the desk clerk looked over my shoulder at my Cadillac parked in front, then I could feel his eyes become more intent on the side of my face.

'Will you have somebody wake me at seven in the morning?' I said.

'You're getting on the road early, huh?'

'No, I'll be in town.'

'Oh.' His narrow grey face continued to watch me as I followed the Negro hired man with my bag towards the staircase.

My room overlooked the street and the trees on the courthouse lawn. I sent the Negro to the tavern for six bottles of Jax, pulled off my shirt, and turned on the overhead wooden fan. It was probably too late to visit the jail, and also I was too spent to argue with night-duty cops. I sat in a straw armchair with my feet in the open window and pried the cap off a beer with my pocketknife. The foam boiled over the top and ran down cold on my chest. I tilted the bottle and drank it straight to the bottom. I could still feel the highway rushing under my automobile, the mesquite and blackjack sweeping behind me, and I drank two more beers, tasting each cool swallow slowly. Then a breeze began to blow through the window, a train whistle echoed beyond the dark hills, and I fell asleep in the chair with a half-empty bottle held against my bare stomach.

At first I felt only the swaying motion of the boxcar and the vibration of the wheels clicking across the switches. Then I heard my own voice, loud with urgency, telling me to wake up before it started. But it was too late, or that alter-self inside was inept in turning off the right valve, because I now saw the drawn faces of the other men crowded in the boxcar with me. Outside in the night the snow was driving almost parallel to the ground, there was a slick of ice on the floor of the car, and some of the men had already been stripped of their boots by the Chinese. Their feet were beginning to discolor with the first stages of frostbite, and by morning the skin would be an ugly yellow and purple, the toes swollen into balloons. I watched a Greek urinate on his feet, then dry them carefully and rewrap them with his scarf. The wounds in my calves throbbed with each pitch of the car, and the blood had run down into my socks and frozen. But I had been lucky. The Chinese had machine-gunned all our wounded before we were loaded on the train, and I would have been shot, too, except that I had managed to keep limping forward in the line between two Marines. Before the guard slammed the boxcar door and bolted it, I looked out into the snow at the bodies of the men who had been thrown begging in front of the burpguns. Their mouths and eyes were still wide with disbelief and protest, their hair flecked with snow like old men.

In the next fifteen hours the train stopped three times, and each time we heard a boxcar door slide open, hysterical shouts in English and Chinese, and the firing of burpguns. Whenever the train slowed we became a community of fear as each of us listened, motionless, to the decreasing metallic clack of the wheels. Once, while pulled off on a siding, we heard several guards crunching outside in the snow, then they stopped in front of our boxcar. They talked for a minute, laughed, and one of them slid back the iron bolt on the door. I looked dumbly into the black eyes of the Greek who had urinated on his feet, and the heart-racing fear and desperate question mark in his face seemed to join us together in a quick moment of recognition. Then another train roared by us a few feet away, its whistle screaming in our ears, and our boxcar jolted forward, knocking us backward into one another. We heard the bolt slam into place and the guards running towards the caboose.

By morning the car was rancid with excrement and urine. We had no water, and several men broke ice from the floor with their boots and melted it in a helmet over a dozen cigarette lighters. It tasted like wheat chaff, sweat, and manure. The snow had stopped blowing and the sun shone through the cracks in the walls. The light broke in strips on our bodies, and the stench from the corner began to grow more intense. During the night I had been unable to stand up and urinate through a crack in the car wall, and I had to let it run warmly down my thighs. My own odor sickened me. I wondered if the Jews who had been freighted to extermination camps in eastern Europe ever felt the same self-hating, cynical disgust at their condition, lying in their own excretions, or if they tried to tear the boards out of the walls with their fingernails and catch one SS guard around the throat with probing thumbs. My feeling was that they went to their deaths like tired people lined up before a movie which no one wanted to see, revulsed by themselves and the human condition, their naked bodies already shining with the iridescence of the dead.

I woke into the hot morning with a dark area of warm beer in my lap. Two Negro trusties from the jail, the white letter *P* Cloroxed on the backs of their denim shirts, were watering the courthouse lawn. The wet grass was shiny with light, and the shade of the oaks was like a deep bruise on the sidewalks. At the edge of the square there was an open-air fruit market, with canvas stretched on poles over the bins, and Mexican farmhands were unloading cantaloupes and rattlesnake melons from the bed of a stake truck. The sky was clear blue, and the shadows from a few pink clouds moved over the hills.

I dressed in my linen suit with a blue silk shirt and walked down the main street to a cafe. I had a breakfast steak with two fried eggs on top, then smoked a cigar and drank coffee until the courthouse opened. Even though I could feel the July heat rising, it was still a beautiful day, the orchards at the foot of the hills were bursting with green and gold, I was free from the weekend's whiskey, and I didn't want to visit the jail. Most people think that the life of a criminal lawyer is a romantic venture, but it's usually a sordid affair at best. I had never liked dealing with redneck cops, bailbondsmen, county judges with high school educations, or talking with clients at two A.M. in a drunk tank.

I crossed the street to the courthouse and went to the sheriff's office in the back of the building. By the office door there was a glass memorial case filled with junk from the World Wars and Korea – German helmets, bayonets, a Mauser rifle without a bolt, an American Legion medal, canteens, a .30 caliber machine gun with an exploded barrel, and a Chinese bugle. A deputy in a khaki uniform sat behind an army surplus desk, filling out forms with a short pencil. He was lean all over, tall, and his crewcut, glistening head was pale from wearing a hat in the sun. His fingers were crimped over the pencil as he worked out each sentence in printed and longhand letters. His shirt was damp around the shoulders, and his long arms were burned brown and wrinkled with veins.

'Can I help you?' he said without looking up.

'I'd like to see Arturo Gomez.'

He put the pencil down and turned his face up at me. His green, yellow-flecked eyes were flat, his face expressionless.

'Who are you?'

'My name's Hackberry Holland. I'm a lawyer.'

'You ain't his.'

'He's a friend of mine from the service.'

'Well, visiting hour is at two o'clock.'

'I have to go back to Austin this morning. I'd appreciate it if I could talk with him a few minutes.'

The deputy turned the pencil in a circle on the desk top with his finger. There was a hard knot of muscle in the back of his arm.

'You working with these Mexican union people?'

'No.'

'You just drove down from Austin to see a friend in jail?'

'That's right.'

'It won't help him none. He's going up to the state

farm Wednesday. And I expect there might be a few more with him soon.'

'I wouldn't know about that.' I bent over and tipped my cigar ashes into the spittoon, then waited for the deputy to continue the statement which he had prepared long ago for strangers, slick lawyers, and nigger and Mexican lovers.

'You can take it for what it's worth, Mr Holland, but these Mexicans was stirred up by agitators from the outside. They can make fair wages in the field any time they want to work, but they stay drunk on wine half the time or sit in the welfare office.' His yellow-flecked eyes looked into my face. 'Then those union organizers started telling them they could get twice as much money by shutting down the harvest. Just let the cotton and grapefruit rot and they're all going to be nigger-rich. People around here is pretty fed up with it, and it's lucky that a couple of them California Mexicans haven't been drug behind a car yet.'

'As I said, I'm not representing anyone.'

'It's against the rule, but I'll take you down to see Gomez a minute. I just thought you ought to know we ain't pushing these people into a corner they didn't build for themselves.'

I followed him down a staircase into the basement of the building. The rigid angles in his body, the rolled khaki sleeves, and the flush of anger in his neck reminded me of several drill instructors whom I had met at Parris Island. They all had the same intense dedication to perverse abstractions which had been created for them by someone else.

The basement of the courthouse, the jail, had been constructed with large blocks of limestone, sawed and chiseled and set with mortar in uneven squares. The corridor was lighted by two bulbs screwed into sockets on the ceiling, and the cells looked like caves cut back into the rock with iron doors on them. The stone was damp with humidity, and the air was rank with disinfectant, D.D.T., urine, and tobacco smoke. Each of the iron doors had a row of holes perforated in the top, and a slit and apron for a food tray. At the end of the corridor was a large room, with two wide barred doors that swung open like gates, and overhead on the rock in broken white letters were the words *Negro Male*. I could see the spark of hand-rolled cigarettes in the dark, and smell the odor of stale sweat and synthetic wine. There was a wire-screen cage built against one wall, with a small table and two wooden chairs inside. The deputy unlocked the door and opened it.

'Wait in here and I'll bring him out,' he said. He walked back down the corridor and slipped the bolt on one of the cells. He had to use both hands to pull the door open.

Art stepped out into the light, his pupils contracted to small black dots. His denim jail issue was too big for him and his hair hung down over his ears. He was barefoot, his shirt and trousers were unbuttoned, and his thin frame was stooped as he walked towards the cage, as though the rock ceiling was crushing down on him. He had a cigarette in an empty space where a tooth had been, and there was a cobweb scar on the edge of one eye. He had started to get jailhouse pallor, and the two pachuco tattoos on his hands looked like they had just been cut into the skin with brilliant purple ink. I hadn't seen him in five years, when he was contracting tomato harvests in DeWitt County, but it seemed that everything in him had shrunken inwards, hard and brittle as bone. The deputy closed the cage door on us and locked it.

'You can talk ten minutes,' he said, and walked back down the corridor. The light gleamed on his shaved head.

'What about it, Hack? You want to play Russian roulette with me?' Art said, and smiled with the cigarette in his teeth. His long fingers were spread out on the table top.

'How in the hell did you go up for assault because of a picket-line arrest?'

'What happened and what I got tried for ain't the same thing. The Texas Rangers moved in on our picket line because they said we wasn't fifty feet apart. They knocked a couple of our people down, and when I yelled about it they put the arm on me. I pushed this one fat bastard on his ass, and he got up and beat the shit out of me with a blackjack. Man, they're real bad people when they turn loose. I can still see that guy swinging down on me. His eyes was sticking out of his head. He must have saved it up for a long time.'

'What did your lawyer do in the trial?'

'He was appointed by the court. He lives right here in the county and he wanted me to plead guilty. I told him to go fuck himself, so he chewed on his pipe for three days, cross-examined one witness, and shook hands with me after the judge gave me five years.

'Look, Hack, I know I'm leaning on you for a favor, but I want to beat this shit. Our union's got a chance if we don't get broke up. We got a few people in Austin on our side, and some of the locals are afraid enough of the chicano vote that they might come around if we stay solid. But our treasury's broke and I got nobody but kids to organize the pickets and boycotts while I'm in the pen. And I'll tell you straight I don't want to build no five years. Four cents a day chopping cotton ain't good pay.' He smiled again, and took the cigarette from his lips and put it out on the bottom of the table.

'All right, I'll try to file an appeal. It takes time, but maybe with luck I can spring you on bond.'

He took another cigarette from his shirt pocket, popped a kitchen match on his thumbnail, and lit it. The scar tissue around his eye was yellow in the flame. 'A year ago I was ready to charge the hill with a bayonet in my teeth. Corporal Gomez going over the top like gangbusters with a flamethrower. I was ready to build life in the pen for our union, but three months in lockdown here, man, it leaves a dent. Every night when that bastard sticks a plate of grits and fried baloney through the slit I say hello to his fingernails.'

'You know what you're doing is crazy, don't you?'

'Why? Because we're tired of getting shit on?'

'These people have lived one way for a hundred and fifty years,' I said. 'You can't make them change with a picket sign.'

His face sharpened, and his yellow-stained fingers pressed down on the cigarette.

'Yeah, we been eating their shit for just about that long. But we ain't going that route no more. We got more people than the anglos, and this land belonged to us before their white ass ever got on it.'

'You can't alter historical injustice in the present. You're only putting yourself and your people up against an executioner's wall.'

'You can jive about that college bullshit all you want, but we been picking your cotton for six cents a pound. You ever do stoop labor? Your back feels like a ball of fire by noon, and at night you got to sleep on the floor to iron out your spine. All you anglos are so fucking innocent. You got the answers counted out in your palm like pennies. You march off every Christmas and hand out food baskets to the niggers and greaseballs, and then for the next twelve months you congratulate yourself on your Christianity.'

He drew in on the cigarette and pushed his long black hair out of his face. He looked at the table and breathed the smoke out between his lips. 'Okay, man, I'm sorry. I sit in my cell all day and think, and I don't get to talk with nobody except the hack. So I just made you my dart board.'

'Forget it,' I said.

'But learn something about our union before you start to piss on us.'

'All right.'

'Like maybe we ain't just a bunch of uppity niggers.'

"The deputy's going to be back in a minute.'

'Look, watch out for that motherfucker. The other night one of the blacks started screaming in the tank with the DTs, and he kicked him in the head. I think he's a Bircher, and the guys in here say he's got a bad conduct discharge from the Corps for crippling a guy in the brig.'

'Okay, let's finish before he gets back. Were there any Mexicans on the jury?'

'What world do you live in, man?'

'We can use jury selection in an appeal, even though I'd rather hang them on the charge itself. I'll have to get a transcript of the trial and talk with your lawyer.'

'Don't fool with him. I told you he wouldn't pour water on me if I was burning. He's a little fat guy with a bald head, he owns five hundred acres of blackland, and he thinks I was brainwashed in Korea. When I asked him about an appeal he chewed on his pipe and farted.'

'What's his name?'

'That's Mister Cecil Wayne Posey. His office is right across the street.'

'Why didn't you write me before the trial?'

'I don't like to bruise old friends.'

'Well, you sure picked a shitty time to bring in a relief pitcher.'

'You're a good man, Hack. I trust your arm.'

I heard the stairway door slam and the deputy walking down the stone corridor in his brogans.

'I'll be back tomorrow,' I said. 'You want anything?'

'No, just watch after yourself in town. They're pissed, and that southern accent of yours won't help you none when they find out you're working with our union.'

'I don't think they'll roll a congressional candidate around too hard.'

'I mean it, Hack. They don't give a damn who you are. We stepped on their balls with a golf shoe. There ain't been any Klan activity here since the 1920s, and last week they burned a cross on an island in the middle of the river. You better keep your head down, buddy.'

Art lit another cigarette off the butt while the deputy unlocked the cage.

'Tomorrow,' I said.

'Yeah, stay solid, cousin.'

I looked at the black soles of his bare feet as the deputy led him back to his cell. The deputy clanged the door shut, shot the bolt, and stared at me with a fixed gaze while I tore the cellophane wrapper off a cigar. I bit the end off and spit it on the floor. I could feel his hot eyes reaching me through the wire screen. He rattled his change in one pocket with his hand.

'You want to get out of here this morning, Mr Holland?' he said.

Upstairs by the office door a girl leaned against the wall with a carton of cigarettes in her hand. She wore sandals, bleached bluejeans, and a maroon blouse tied in a knot under her breasts. She had on large, amber sunglasses, hoop earrings, and a thin strand of Indian beads around her neck. Her skin was brown, her body lithe and relaxed, and her curly brown hair was burned on the ends by the sun. Her eyes were indifferent through her glasses as she looked at me and the deputy.

'Would you give these to Art Gomez, please?' she said. Her voice was level, withdrawn, almost without tone.

The deputy took the carton of cigarettes and dropped it in his desk drawer without answering. He sat down in his chair and began to sharpen a pencil with his pocketknife into the wastebasket. I knew that each stroke of that knife was cutting into his own resentment at the restraint his job forced upon him in dealing with a hippie girl and a slick, outside lawyer. He bent over his traffic forms, his knuckles white on the pencil, and began to print out his report as though we were not there.

The girl walked back towards the entrance. There

was a pale line of skin above the back of her bluejeans, and her ass had the natural, easy rhythm that most women try to learn for a lifetime. Everything in her was smooth and loose, and her motion had the type of cool unconcern that bothers you in some vague place in the back of your mind.

'Hello,' I said.

She turned around, framed in the square of yellow light through the entrance, and looked at me. She wore no makeup, and in the black shadow over her face she looked like a nun in church suddenly disturbed from prayer.

'I expect you work with Art's union. My name's Hack Holland. I'm trying to file an appeal for Art before he goes up to prison.'

She remained immobile in the light.

'I'd like to meet some of the people in your union,' I said.

'What for?'

'Because I don't know anybody in this town and I might need a little help.'

'There's nothing we can do for you.'

'Why don't you give me a chance to see?'

'You're wasting your time, man.'

'I'd like to see Art out in the next light-year, and from what I understand so far I can't expect any help from his lawyer, the court, or the clerk of records. So I can either wander around town a few more days and talk with people like the deputy in there or cowboys in the beer joint, or I can meet someone who'll tell me what happened on that picket line.'

'We told what happened.'

'You told it in a local trial court that was

prejudiced. I'm going to take the case to the Court of Criminal Appeals in Austin.'

'What's your thing with Art?'

'We were in Korea together.'

'You can't do any good for him. The A.C.L.U. has had our cases in Austin before.'

'Maybe I'm a better lawyer,' I said.

'Believe it, man, you've got a bum trip in mind.'

'I believe in the banzai ethic. At least I'll leave a dark burn across the sky when I go down.'

'You ought to find a better way to pay back army debts.'

'I was a Navy corpsman, and I paid off all my debts in Band-Aids before I was discharged.'

She turned back into the light to walk outside.

'Do you want a ride?' I said.

'I'll walk.'

'You don't want to miss a good experience with the most arrested driver in Texas. Besides, I need some directions.'

'Stay away from our union headquarters if you want to help Art.'

'I don't expect that we'll all end up in the penitentiary if I drive you home.'

We walked down the courthouse sidewalk under the shade of the oak trees to my automobile. The sun had risen high in the sky, and the tar surfacing on the street was hot and soft under our feet. The heat shimmered off the concrete walk in front of the hotel.

We drove into the Negro and Mexican section back of town. The dirt roads were baked hard as rock, and clouds of dust swept up behind my car. The unpainted wood shacks were pushed into one another at odd angles, the ditches strewn with garbage, and the outhouses were built of discarded boards, R.C. Cola signs, and tarpaper.

'I have to see Art's lawyer after I drop you off, but I'll come back a little later,' I said.

'I thought you didn't expect any help from him.'

'I don't, but maybe I can use inadequate defense as a reason for appeal.'

She took a package of cigarettes from her bluejeans pocket and lit one. I glanced at the smooth curve of her breasts as she pushed the package back in her pocket.

'You're pretty sure I've got a loser, aren't you?' I said.

'I just don't think you know very much about the county you're working in.'

'So you're up against some cotton growers who don't want to pay union scale, and a few part-time Klansmen. And you've met a redneck deputy sheriff who probably rents his brains by the week. That doesn't change the law or trial procedure.'

'Wow. You must walk into court with a copy of *The National Review* between your teeth.'

'I've had eight years of law practice, babe, and I haven't lost many cases.'

'I don't believe you've dealt very much with union farm workers, either.'

'I've spent all my life in Texas. I don't expect to find out anything very new about it in this case.'

'Don't you realize the rules in your court don't apply to us? Art's jury brought in a guilty verdict in fifteen minutes, and later the foreman said it took them that long because they sent out for some cold drinks.'

'All right, I can use things just like that in the appeal.'

'I'm not kidding you, man; lose some of those comic-book attitudes if you want to do anything for him,' she said.

'You really know how to turn on the burner, don't you?'

'I'm just telling you about the bag you're trying to pick up.'

'You're a hard girl.'

'Do I get that free with the ride home?' The sunlight through the window was bright on the burned ends of her hair. She had her arm back on the seat while she smoked, and I could see the whiteness at the top of her breasts.

'You're not from Texas. What are you doing here, anyway?'

'Would you like to flip through the celluloid windows in my wallet?'

'It's just a question.'

'It seems like an expensive trip home.'

'Maybe I should put on my chauffeur's cap, and you can sit in the back seat and I'll close the glass behind me.'

'I was a graduate student in social work at Berkeley. I got tired of writing abstract papers about hungry people so I joined the Third World and came out to your lovely state.'

I hit a chuckhole in the road and felt the car slam down on its springs. The dust was so heavy that it had started to filter through the air-conditioning system. Two Negro children were running along the edge of a ditch, throwing stones at an emaciated dog scabbed over with mange. The road reached a deadend in front of a converted general store with a sign above the door that read: *United Farm Workers Local 476*. The glass display windows were yellow and pocked with BB holes, and filmed with dirt on the inside and outside. Strips of Montgomery Ward brick had been nailed over the rotted boards in the walls, the steps had collapsed, cinder blocks were propped under one side of the building to keep it from sagging, and I could almost hear the flies humming around the outhouse in back. A boy of about nineteen, barefoot and without a shirt, sat on the front porch playing a twelve-string Gibson guitar.

'Don't wrinkle your eyes at it, man,' she said. 'We're lucky we could rent anything in this town.'

'I didn't say a thing.'

'I could hear the tumblers click over in your head. You've got the middle class hygiene thing. Anything except green lawns and red brick sends you running up the street.'

'That's a lot of shit.'

'Okay. Thanks for the ride.'

She closed the door and walked down the dusty path to the building. I watched the motion of her hips and her full thighs as she stepped up on the porch, then I turned the Cadillac in a circle and headed back towards town.

I went to Mister Cecil Wayne Posey's office and was told by his junior partner that I could find him at home. His ranch was all blackland, lined with rows of cotton and corn and orange trees. A dozen Mexicans and Negroes were hoeing in the cotton, and horses stood in the groves of live oak trees on the low hills. The large, one-story house had new white paint and a wide screened-in porch, and poplar trees were planted along the front lane. There were two great red barns in back with lightning rods and weather vanes on the peaks, a windmill pumping water into a trough, and rolls of barbed wire and cords of cedar posts stacked against a tractor shed.

As I walked up the lane I heard a woodpecker rattling against a dead limb in the heat. Mr Posey rose from his round-backed wicker chair on the porch and shook hands. The lower portion of his stomach was swollen all the way across the front of his pants. His skin was soft, pudgy to the touch, and his head was almost completely bald except for a few short grey hairs. His eyes were colorless, and his voice had the bland quality of oatmeal. He reminded me of a miniature, upended white whale. When he sat down the watch in his pocket bulged against the cloth like a hard biscuit.

A Negro maid in a lace-trimmed apron served us iced tea with mint leaves and slices of lemon on a silver service, then I began quietly to press Mr Posey for his reasons in not filing an appeal for Art. Actually, my questions, or even my presence there, would probably be considered a violation of professionalism among attorneys, since I was indirectly implying that he had been negligent in the case; but the flicker of insult never showed in his eyes, and if his tone or the pale expression around his mouth indicated anything, it was simply that I was an idealistic young lawyer who had embarked on a fool's errand. He lowered his face into the tea glass when he drank, and momentarily the moisture gave his lips a streak of color.

'I didn't feel there was basis for appeal, Mr Holland,' he said. 'I originally advised Art to plead

66

guilty in hopes of a reduced charge, but he refused, and I doubt if the Court of Criminal Appeals will consider the case of a man who was convicted on the testimony of four Texas Rangers and two bystanders. He did hit the officer twice before he was restrained, and that's the essential and inalterable fact of the case.'

'Who were these bystanders?'

'Two county workmen who were operating a grading machine on the road when the arrests were made.'

I looked at him incredulously.

'Did you feel these men were objective witnesses?' I said.

'They had no interest in the issue. They merely stated what they saw.'

'I understand that most of the people on the picket line testified, also.'

'Unfortunately, most of them have been in local court before, and I'm afraid that their statements were overly familiar to the jury. One young man admitted to the district attorney that he'd been three hundred yards away from the arrest, but he was sure that Art hadn't struck the officer. It's difficult to contest a conviction on evidence of that sort, Mr Holland.'

His face bent into the iced tea glass again, and a drop of perspiration rolled off his temple down his fat cheek. He shifted his buttocks in the wicker chair and crossed his legs. His massive, soft thighs stretched the crease in his slacks flat.

'Art's been organizing a farm workers' union in this county for the past year. Do you believe any members of the jury had preconceived feelings towards him?'

'None that would affect the indictment against him.

He was tried for assaulting a Texas Ranger, not for his involvement in a Mexican union.'

I borrowed a match from Mr Posey and lit a cigar. I looked at him through the curl of flame and smoke and wondered if he had any conception of his irresponsibility in allowing his client to be sentenced to five years in a case that would be considered laughable by a law school moot court.

He put his empty pipe in the center of his teeth, drew in with a wet rattling sound, and farted softly in the back of the chair. I finished my tea, shook hands and thanked him for his help, and walked down the gravel path to my automobile under the trees. Behind me I heard him snap the metal latch into place on the screen door.

I drove back to town and had lunch and two beers at the cafe, then spent an hour in the clerk of records office while an aged secretary made a Xerox copy of the trial transcript for me. There was no breeze through the windows, my sunglasses filmed with moisture in the humidity, and the electric fans did nothing but blow drafts of hot air across the room. The deputy sheriff came in once to drop a pile of his penciled reports on the clerk's desk, and as he walked past me he stared into my face without speaking.

I spent the rest of the afternoon in the hotel, with my feet propped in the window, reading the transcript and sipping whiskey poured over ice. The flies droned dully in the stillness, and occasionally I would hear the hillbilly music from the beer tavern. Across the square the sun slanted on the rows of watermelons and cantaloupes in the open-air fruit market.

The transcript was an incredible record to read.

The trial might have been constructed out of mismatched parts from an absurd movie script about legal procedure. There had been no challenge of the jurors, each of the Texas Rangers contradicted the others, a Baptist minister testified that many of the union members were Communists, and the two county workmen said they had seen a Mexican attack a Ranger, although they had been eating their lunch in the back of a truck a half mile down the road at the time. The three witnesses for the defense were sliced to pieces by the district attorney. They were led into discrediting statements about their own testimony, forced into stumbling admissions about their involvement in revolution, and referred to sixteen times as outside agitators. And Cecil Wayne Posey never raised an objection. Normally, any two pages torn at random from such a comic scenario would be grounds for appeal, but under Texas law the appeal has to be made in local court within ten days of sentencing, unless good cause is shown for an extension, and since Mr Posey's refusal to continue the case had virtually guaranteed that his client would go to prison, I would have to start the whole process over again in Austin.

It was dusk outside now. I threw the transcript in my suitcase, took a cold bath, and shaved, with a glass of whiskey on top of the lavatory. As a rule I didn't try to correct the inadequacies inherent in any system, but in this case I thought I would send a letter to the Texas Bar Association about Mr Posey. Yes, Mr Posey should receive some official recognition for his work, I thought, as I drew the razor blade down in a clean swath through the shaving cream on my cheek.

I ate a steak for supper and drove back to the union headquarters in the Mexican district. There were thunderclouds and heat lightning in the west, an electric flash all the way across the horizon, and then a distant, dry rumble. The air tasted like brass in my mouth. Parts of the dirt road had been sprinkled with garden hoses to wet down the dust, and the cicadas in the trees were deafening with their late evening noise. Fireflies glowed like points of flame in the gathering dusk, and across the river in old Mexico the adobe huts on the mud flat wavered in the light of outdoor cookfires. High up in the sky, caught in the sun's last afterglow, a buzzard floated motionlessly like a black scratch on a tin surface.

I parked the car in front of the union headquarters and walked up the path to the wooden steps. The boy with the Gibson twelve-string still sat on the porch. He had three steel picks on his fingers and a half gallon bottle of dago red next to him. His bare feet were covered with dust, and there were tattoos on each arm. He chorded the guitar and didn't turn his head towards me.

'She's inside, man,' he said.

'Do I knock or let myself in?'

'Just do it.'

I tapped with my knuckle on the screen and waited. I heard dishes rattling in a pan in the back of the building.

'Hey Rie, that guy's back,' the boy shouted over his shoulder.

A moment later the girl walked through a back hallway towards me. Her arms were wet up to the elbow. She had splashed water on her blouse, and her breasts stood out against the cloth.

'Man, like you really want to meet us, don't you?' she said, pushing open the screen with the back of her wrist.

'I decided against watching television in the hotel lobby this evening.'

'Come in the kitchen. I have to finish the dishes.'

The flowered wallpaper in the main room was yellowed and peeling in rotted strips, coated with mold and glue. United Farm Workers signs, pop art posters of Che Guevara and Lyndon Johnson on a motorcycle, and underground newspapers were thumbtacked over the exposed sections of boarding in the walls. A store-window manikin lay on top of the old grocery counter with an empty wine bottle balanced on her stomach. A mobile made of beer-bottle necks clinked in the breeze from an oscillating fan that rattled against the wire guard each time it completed a turn. The single lightbulb suspended from the ceiling gave the whole room a hard yellow cast that hurt the eyes.

I followed her through the hallway into the kitchen. Her brown hips moved as smoothly as water turning in the current. Two young girls, a college boy, and a Negro man were scraping dishes into a garbage can and rinsing them under an iron pump. Through the back window I could see the last red touch of the sun on a sandbar in the middle of the Rio Grande.

'We had a neighborhood dinner tonight,' the girl from Berkeley said. 'There's some tortillas and beans in the icebox or you can get a dish towel.'

'You have a charge account with the supermarket?'

'We get the day-old stuff from the Mexican produce stands,' she said.

'I think I'll just have a whiskey and water if you'll

give me a glass.' I took my silver flask from my coat pocket.

'Help yourself,' she said.

I offered the flask to the others.

'You got it, brother,' the Negro said.

He picked up a tin cup from the sideboard and held it in front of me. His bald, creased head and round black face shone in the half-light. Four of his front teeth were missing, and the others were yellow with snuff. I poured a shot in his cup and then splashed some water in my glass from the pump. I could taste the rust in it.

'So what would you like to find out about the United Farm Workers?' the girl said.

'Nothing. I read the trial transcript and talked with Mr Posey this afternoon. The conviction won't hold.'

The Negro laughed with the cup held before his lips. The college boy straightened up from the garbage can and looked at me as though I had dropped through a hole in the ceiling.

'You believe that?' the Negro said. He was still smiling

'Yes.'

'I mean, you ain't bullshitting? You're coming on for real?' the college boy said. He wore bluejeans and a faded yellow and white University of Texas T-shirt.

'That's right, pal,' I said.

The Negro laughed again and went back to work scraping plates. The two young girls were also smiling.

'Who you working for, man?' the boy said.

'Judge Roy Bean. I float up and down the Pecos River for him on an inner tube.'

'Don't get strung out,' the girl said.

'What am I, the visiting straight man around here?'

The girl dried her hands on a towel and took a bottle of Jax out of the icebox. 'Come on out front,' she said.

'We wasn't trying to give you no truck. We ain't got bad things here,' the Negro said. He grinned at me with his broken, yellow teeth.

In the front room the girl sat in a straight-backed chair, with one leg pulled up on the seat, her arm propped across her knee, and drank out of the beer bottle. Behind her on the wall was a poster with a rectangular, outspread bird on it and the single word *HUELGA*.

'They're kids, and they don't know if you're putting them on or if you're a private detective working for their parents,' she said. 'The black guy has been in the movement since the Progressive Labor Party days, and he's heard a lot of jiveass lawyers talk about appeals.'

'I guess I just don't like people to work out their problems on my head.'

'I told you this afternoon about coming down here.'

'Maybe I should have worn my iron helmet and flack jacket.'

'They don't have any bad will towards you. They're good people.'

'I'm paranoid and suspicious by nature.'

'That's part of the middle-class syndrome, too. It goes along with the hygiene thing.'

'Goddamn, I picked a hell of a ballgame to relieve in. Between you, Cecil Wayne Posey, and that deputy at the jail I feel like I'm standing ten feet from the plate and lobbing volley balls at King Kong.'

She took the bottle from her lips and laughed, and her almond eyes were suddenly full of light. She touched away the foam from the corner of her mouth with two fingers.

'I should have put on my Groucho Marx clothes this evening,' I said. 'You know, an hour or so of Zeppo and the gang throwing pies while your people go up to the pen.'

I finished my drink, and the minerals and iron rust in the water tasted like a gladiator's final toast in the back of my throat.

'You're out of sight,' she said.

I poured a thin shot over the orange flecks in the bottom of the glass and drank it down. The smoky, charcoal-filtered taste of undiluted Jack Daniels, born out of Tennessee limestone springs and rickyards of hickory, rolled down inside me with the lightness of heated air, then I began to feel the amber caution signal flashing somewhere behind my forehead.

'Yeah, I'm a walking freak show. The next time I'll appear with my whole act. Seals blowing horns, monkeys riding unicycles, jugglers, clowns with exploding bombs in their pants.'

'Wow, you really let it hang out,' she said. Her wet eyes were bright with refractions of light.

'It comes free with the ride home.' I poured the rest of the whiskey into my glass. 'Come on, let's drink.'

'What do you do when you're not defending ex-Korean War buddies?' she said.

'I work for the money boys. Oil corporation suits, swindles against the government, the Billy Sol account. I also run for Congress part time.'

'You're putting me on.'

'Buy a copy of *The Austin American* November 5. I'll be smiling at you on the front page.'

'If you're not jiving, you must be an unbelievable guy.'

'You want to talk about my geek act some more?' I said.

'I mean what do you expect? You drop in here from outer space and come on like H. L. Hunt and W. C. Fields at the same time.'

'I was put together from discarded parts.' I finished my glass, and the amber light Hashed red and began to beat violently.

'Tell me, really, why did you come here tonight?'

'I already told you. Television ruptures the blood vessels in my eyes.'

The Negro, the two girls, and the college boy walked out from the kitchen.

'There's a man who likes to drink,' I said.

'You been reading my mail,' the Negro said.

'How about a case of Jax and a bottle of Jack Daniels?' I took a twenty-dollar bill from my wallet.

'We got a few more people coming over tonight,' he said.

'Get two cases. Take my car.'

'It's just down the road. I'd get busted for grand auto in that Cadillac, anyway.'

He took the twenty-dollar bill and stuck it in the pocket of his denim shirt.

'You ain't going to tip me later, are you?' he said.

'I left my planter's hat in the car.'

He laughed and his round black face and brown eyes glistened with good humor. 'You're all right,' he said, and went out the screen door with the college boy.

'You always do this on a case?' the girl said.

'No. I usually don't drink with the people I know.

75

Most of them belong to the ethic of R. C. Richardson and the Dallas Petroleum Club. They like to throw glasses and urinate off hotel balconies. They also like to feel waitresses under the table. R. C. Richardson is a very unique guy. In the last fifteen years he's taken the state and the federal government for a little less than one million dollars. He wears yellow cowboy boots, striped western pants, a string tie, and he has a one-hundred-pound stomach that completely covers his hand-tooled belt. Three days a week he sits in the Kiwanis and Rotary and Chamber of Commerce luncheons and belches on his boiled weenies and sauerkraut, and then rises like a soldier and says the pledge of allegiance with his hand over his heart. But actually, the guy has class. The others around him are clandestine in their midnight dealings and worm's-eye view of the world. They don't have his sincere feeling for vulgarity.'

'He must be an interesting man to work for,' she said.

'Do you have another beer in the icebox?'

'This is the last one. Take it.'

'I never take a girl's last drink. It shows a lack of gentility.'

'You are from outer space.'

I could feel the blood tingling in my hands and face. My scalp started to sweat from the whiskey.

'What's your name, anyway?' I bit the end off a cigar.

'Rie Velasquez.'

'You're not Mexican.'

'No.'

'So what are you?' I reached over and took the beer bottle out of her hand.

'My father was Spanish. He came from Spain during the Civil War.'

I let the beer and foam roll down my throat over the dry taste of the whiskey and cigar smoke.

'Hence, you joined the Third World Liberation Front. The gasoline and dynamite gang.'

'You ought to change your brand of bourbon.'

'Right or wrong? Didn't they incinerate a few college buildings in the last year?'

'Don't you think that sounds a bit dumb?'

'Bullshit. Ten of those people could have a whole city in flames within twenty-four hours.'

She took a cigarette from the pack in her bluejeans and lit it. She pinched the end between her lips as she drew in on the smoke.

'What type of bag do you think we operate out of, man?' she said. 'Did you see any kerosene rags and coal oil hidden under the porch? You believe we all came down here because of your tourist brochures about the scenic loveliness of the Texas desert?'

'I just don't buy that revolution shit.'

'Why don't you read something about the United Farm Workers? They don't have anything to do with revolution. They're tired of being riggers in somebody's watermelon patch.'

'Yow!' the Negro yelled, as he kicked open the screen door with a case of beer on one shoulder and a block of ice wrapped in newspaper on the other. 'Man, we got it. Spodiodi and brew. We're in tall cotton tonight, brothers.'

The college boy carried the second case of beer, and the boy with the guitar had already cut the seal on the bottle of Jack Daniels. They put the two cases on the old grocery counter, and the Negro chopped up the ice with a butcher knife and spread it over the bottles. He opened the first bottle by putting the cap against the edge of the counter and striking downward quickly with the flat of his hand. The white foam showered up over his head and splattered on the floor. He covered the lip of the bottle with his mouth and drank until it was almost empty. The beer streamed down his chin into the matted black hair on his chest.

'Lord, you can't beat that,' he said.

I took the whiskey and poured three inches into my glass.

'You'll drive nails through your stomach like that. Put a little brew on top of it,' the Negro said. He slapped another cap off on the edge of the counter and handed the bottle to me.

'Use this and avoid the slashed hand shot,' Rie said, and threw an opener to the college boy.

Eight Mexican field hands, all dressed in faded denim clothes, overalls, straw hats, and work shoes, came through the screen door in single file as though they had been lined up at a bus stop. They were pot-bellied and short, thin and stooped, tattooed with pachuco crosses and hung with religious medals, scarred and stitched, some of them missing fingers, sunburned almost black, with trousers bagging in the rear and their Indian hair wet and combed straight back over the head.

They had a pint of Old Stag and a gallon milk bottle filled with blackberry wine. The Negro began passing out the Jax, and an hour later the room roared with mariachi songs and Apache screams.

'Let me try that guitar, buddy,' I said to the boy from the front porch. He sat on the floor with his back against the wall and a glass of wine and whiskey between his legs. His face was bloodless and his eyes couldn't fix on my face. I put the strap of the twelve-string around my neck and tried to pick out 'The Wreck of Old '97,' but my fingers felt as though a needle and thread had been drawn through all my knuckles. Then I tried 'The Wildwood Flower' and 'John Hardy,' and each time I began over again I hit more wrong notes or came up on the wrong fret. I smoked somebody's cigarette out of an ashtray, finished my drink, and then started an easy Jimmie Rodgers run that I had learned to pick when I was sixteen. It was worse than before, and I laid the guitar face down on the counter among the scores of empty beer bottles.

'I bet you blow a good one when you're cool,' Rie said. She was sitting in the chair next to me with a small glass of wine in her hand. Her legs were crossed, and the indention across her stomach and the white line of skin above her bluejeans made something drop inside me.

'Give me an hour and I'll boil them cabbages down,' I said.

'Do it tomorrow morning.'

'I'm going to streak out of here like the fireball mail tomorrow morning. My Cadillac and I are going to melt the asphalt between here and Austin.' Someone put the whiskey bottle in my hand, and I took two large swallows and chased it with beer.

'You must have a real dragon inside,' Rie said.

'No, I deal with Captain Hyde. That bastard and I have been together almost fifteen years. However, when he starts acting like an asshole I unscrew my head and throw it in the Rio Grande a couple of times.'

'No kidding, pull it back in, man,' she said.

'I thought you were a hip girl. You're giving me the concerned eye of a Baptist reformer now.'

'I think you're probably a madman.'

'You ought to see me and John Wesley Hardin drunk in the streets of Yoakum. He rides on the fender of my Cadillac, busting parking meters and stoplights with a revolver in each hand.'

The noise became louder. All the beer, whiskey, and wine were gone, and I gave one of the Mexican field hands another twenty dollars to go to the tavern. The twelve-string guitar was passed from hand to hand, tuned in a half dozen discords, two strings broken, and finally dropped in a corner. Someone suggested a knife-throwing contest, and a bread cutter, two bowies, a rippled-bladed Italian stiletto, my pocket knife, a hand ax, and a meat cleaver were flung into the wall until the boards were split and shattered and knocked through on the ground outside.

The room was beginning to tip and blur in front of my eyes. I was smoking a dead cigar butt that I had frayed under my boot heel a few minutes earlier.

'Spodiodi, man. It's the only thing. You got to put them snakes back in the basket,' the Negro said in my face. His eyes were red, and his breath was sour with wine.

'I don't deal in snakes.'

'Man, they're crawling through your face.'

I knew that I had an answer for him, but the words wouldn't rise out of the echoes and flashes of light in my head.

'Shit, let's go down to the river. This place is hotter than a brick kiln,' I said.

'It's all that corn,' the Negro said.

'Come on, Judge Roy Bean is holding court in his inner tube,' I said, and pulled Rie up from her chair by the hand.

'Hey, man,' she said.

I carried the bottle of whiskey by the neck and pulled her through the hallway into the kitchen. The Negro followed us with a beer in each hand and a half dozen bottles stuck down in his trousers.

We walked down the bare slope towards the mud flat. The moon was full and white as ivory in a breathless sky. A rusted Ford coupe with no glass in the windows sat half-submerged in the river. The current eddied and swirled through the gaping window in back and coursed over the top of the seats and the steering wheel. The moon's reflection rippled across the water's brown surface, and I could see the sharp backs of garfish turning by the sandbars. Behind us the Mexican field hands were still singing. The Negro finished one beer and threw the bottle arching high over the river.

'Yow!' he yelled.

'Goddamn, look at it. There's Mexico,' I said. 'Fifty yards and you can drop right through the bottom of the twentieth century.'

Rie sat down on a rotted log with her bare feet in the water. The moonlight turned the burned tips of her hair to points of silver.

'A whole land full of bandit ghosts and Indian legends,' I said. 'You just step through the hole in the hedge, and there's Pancho Villa splashing across the river with pistols and bandoliers hanging all over him. Zapata cutting down *Federales* with his machete.

Illiterate peasants executing French kings. Cortez destroying an entire culture.'

'There's diphtheria in the well water of those adobe huts, too,' Rie said.

'You're like every goddamn Marxist I ever met. No humor or sense of romance.'

'Quit shouting.'

'Isn't that straight?' I said. 'It's the revolutionary mind. You can't realize that man is more a clown than a Satan. You approach everything with a sullen mind and try to convert buffoons into Machiavelli.'

'Oh for God's sake, man.'

I took a drink out of the bottle. The whiskey splashed over my mouth.

'You goddamn people don't know what human evil is. One of these days you and I are going to have some Chinese tea and talk about the Bean Camp together. I'll also give you a couple of footnotes on Pak's Palace and No Name Valley.'

I felt the ground shift under my feet, and I thought I was going to fall. I put my arm on her shoulder to keep my balance.

'There's mudcat nesting in that car. I know how to get them, too,' the Negro said. He took off his shirt and shoes, and laid the remaining bottles of beer in an even line on the bank. 'You just swim your hand under the water and back that shovelmouth into a corner and catch him real fast inside the gill. Come on, brother. I'm going to teach you how to fish like black people.'

He waded out into the river up to his hips and pulled open the rusted car door with both hands. The moon's reflection off the water made his black body glow.

'He does this when he gets drunk,' Rie said. 'You can do it, too, if you want me to take both of you down to the county hospital tonight.'

'That's just what a yankee would say. Don't you know that colored people catch fish when white people couldn't bring them up with a telephone crank?'

I sat down on the mud flat and pulled off my boots. I felt the water soak through the seat of my trousers.

'He had eight stitches the last time he handfished in that car,' she said.

'I don't believe it. That sounds like more Marxist-yankee bullshit.'

I walked out into the river, and the warm, muddy current swirled around my waist and my feet sunk into the silt. The Negro was bent over the top of the front seat with both his arms submerged to the shoulder. His face was concentrated, his eyes looking into nothing, as though his fingers were touching some vital and delicate part of the universe.

'She's backed up and fanning right next to the trunk. She's got young ones under her,' he said.

'Watch her fins.'

'She'll open up in a minute to get a piece of my finger, then I'll grab a whole handful of meat inside her gill.'

He ducked forward, the surface of the water shook and quivered momentarily, and then he drew one hand back with a ragged cut between the thumb and forefinger. The drops of blood squeezed out through the bruised edges of the skin and ran down his wrist. He closed his eyes in pain and sucked the cut.

'I told you to –' Then I heard the sirens rolling in a

low moan down the dusty street in front of the union building.

'Shit,' Rie said from the river bank. I turned around and saw the revolving blue and yellow lights on top of three police cars, winking and flashing in the dark.

'The Man done arrived,' the Negro said, with his cut hand still held before his mouth.

Sheriff's deputies and city police went through the front door of the building, walked around the sides with flashlights, looked in the outhouse, and then focused two car spotlights on us in the river. The electric white glare made my eyes water.

'You people walk towards me with your hands on top of your head!' a voice shouted from behind the light.

'Them dudes can reach out from a long way, can't they?' the Negro said. He flopped both his arms over his bald head and started wading out of the river. The light broke around his body as though he had been carved out of burnt iron.

For some drunk reason I closed the car door carefully in the current and lifted the handle upward into place.

'On your head, punk!' the voice shouted.

'Fuck you,' I said.

Suddenly, both of the arcs were turned directly into my face, and the Negro disappeared from my vision in one brilliant explosion of light.

'Don't screw with them, Hack. Get out of there,' Rie said from the darkness.

I waded out of the shallows with one hand over my eyes. My face burned with the heat from the lights.

'I give you warning. Get them over your head.'

'I told you to go fuck yourself, too.' I tripped on the

mudbank and fell on my elbows. My forearms and one side of my face were covered with wet sand. Rie tried to pick me up by the back of my shirt.

'They'll kill you, Hack. Get up and walk. It's just a disturbing the peace bust. We'll be out in the morning,' she said.

A sheriff's car, with both spotlights burning, drove down the embankment on the hard ground, bounced over a log, and turned to a stop in front of me. As the beams of light changed angle I saw the Mexican field hands lined up against the building, with their arms outstretched before them and their legs widespread, while two policemen shook them down.

The whip aerial on the car rocked back and forth, and the deputy from the jail opened the driver's door and walked towards me. I stood up and put a wet cigar in my mouth. My clothes were filled with sand and mud, and my hair felt like paint on top of my head. His .357 Magnum and the cartridges in his leather belt glinted in the moonlight. There was a line of perspiration down the front of his shirt, and his package of cigarettes stuck up at an angle under the flap of his pocket, which struck me at the time as an odd thing for a military man. His jawbones were as tight as his crewcut scalp.

'I figured that you was you, Mr Holland, and I didn't want nobody dropping the hammer on you for some wetback crossing the river,' he said.

'What have you got? Disturbing the peace? Disorderly conduct?'

'We got all kinds of things. I expect if we look around here a while we might find some dope.'

'Why don't you let these people alone? There wasn't any complaint from this neighborhood.'

'Get in the car, please, miss,' he said to Rie.

'Look, she was out here. She didn't have anything to do with that drunk party.'

He opened the back door of the automobile and took Rie by the elbow.

'Just keep your peckerwood hands in your pockets a minute,' I said.

'What?'

'You heard me, motherfucker.'

'Mr Holland, you can drive out of here tonight in that Cadillac of yours and I'll forget about that. The next time you want to help out the niggers and the wetbacks you just write out a check to the Community Chest and stay out of this county.'

'I'll be all right. Go to Austin tomorrow and put it in for Art,' she said. She sat in the back seat behind the wire-mesh screen.

'Let her out,' I said.

'You really want to push it, Mr Holland?'

'Yeah, I do. From what I understand you have a b.c.d. from the Marine Corps and you do most of your law enforcement on helpless wings in a drunk tank. So why don't you get off the bad ass act?'

'You're under arrest. I don't expect you're going to get out of our jail very soon, either.'

'You're fucking with the Lone Ranger, too, peckerwood,' I said.

He brought his billy out of his back pocket and caught me right above the temple. A shotgun shell exploded in my head, and I fell against the car door and hit the ground on my hands and knees. He kicked me once in the stomach, and my breath rushed out of me as though someone had opened a large hole in the middle of my chest. The inside of my mouth was coated with sand, my eyes bulged, and I started to vomit, then his boot cut across the back of my head with the easy swing of a football player kicking an extra point.

chapter four

Sometime in the early morning hours I woke up on the stone floor of a cell in the bottom of the courthouse. The cell was almost completely black, except for the dim circles of light through the row of holes in the top of the door. Moisture covered the walls, and the toilet in the corner had overflowed. I pulled myself up on the iron bunk and touched the huge swelling above my temple. It was as tight as a baseball, and the blood had congealed in my hair. My head was filled with distant bugles and claps of thunder, and I felt the cell tilt on its axis and try to pitch me off the bunk into the pool of water by the toilet. Then I vomited between my legs.

I raised my head slowly, my eyes throbbing and the sweat running down my face. I found a dry kitchen match in my shirt pocket and popped it on my thumbnail. I held the flame over my wristwatch and saw the smashed crystal and the hands frozen at five after one. My white pants were still wet and streaked with mud, and my shirt was torn off one shoulder. I stumbled against the door and leaned my face down to the food slit.

'Hey, one of you sons of bitches better –' But my

voice broke with the effort of shouting. I tried again, and my words sounded foolish in the stillness.

'Cool that shit, man,' a Negro voice said from down the corridor.

I lay back on the tick mattress with my arm across my eyes. I could smell the urine and stale wine in the cloth, and I imagined that there were lice laying their strings of white eggs along the seams, but I was too sick to care. I slept in delirious intervals, never sure if I was really asleep or dreaming, and my nightmare monsters sat with spread cheeks on my feet and grinned at me with their obscene faces. They appeared in all shapes and sizes of deformity: hunched backs, slanted eyes, split tongues, and lipless mouths. Major Pak was there with his fanatical scream and the electrician's pliers in his clenched hand, the guards in the Bean Camp who let our wounded freeze to death to save fuel, and then Sergeant Tien Kwong leaned over me and inserted the end of his burpgun into my mouth and said, smiling, 'You suck. We give you boiled egg.'

A deputy slipped the bolt on my cell and pulled open the door. I winced in the light and turned my face towards his silhouette. His stomach hung over his cartridge belt. Behind him a Negro trusty was pushing a food cart stacked with tin plates and a tall stainless-steel container of grits.

'You can go now, Mr Holland, but the sheriff wants to talk with you a few minutes first,' the deputy said.

'Where's the man who brought me in?'

'He's off duty.'

'What's his name?' My head ached when I sat up on the bunk.

'You better talk with the sheriff.'

I got to my feet and stepped out into the corridor. The Negro trusty was ladling spoonfuls of grits and fried baloney into tin plates and setting them on the iron aprons of the cell doors. The uneven stone on the floor hurt my bare feet, and my right eye, which had started to stretch tight from the swelling in my temple, watered in the hard yellow light. The deputy and I went down the corridor and up the stairs to the sheriff's office. The fat in his hips and stomach flopped inside his shirt each time he took a step. His black hair was oiled and pasted down flat across his balding pate, and he used the handrail on the staircase as though he were pulling a massive weight uphill.

The sheriff sat behind his desk with a handrolled cigarette between his lips, and my billfold, pocket-knife, and muddy boots in front of him. He wore steel-rimmed glasses, and his ears peeled out from the sides of his head. His face was full of red knots and bumps, a large brown mole on his chin, and his grey hair was mowed right into the scalp, but his flat blue eyes cut through the rest of it like a welder's torch. He put the cigarette out between his fingers in the wastebasket, and started to roll another one from a package of Virginia Extra in his pocket. The tips of his teeth were rotted with nicotine. He curved the cigarette paper under his forefinger and didn't look at me when he spoke.

'My deputy wanted to charge you with attempted assault on a law officer, but I ain't going to do that,' he said. He spread the tobacco evenly in the paper and licked down the edge. 'I'm just going to ask you to go down the road, and that'll be the end of it.'

'Your man is pretty good with his feet and a billy.'

'I reckon that's what happens when you threaten a law officer, don't it?' He put the cigarette in his mouth and turned towards me in his swivel chair.

'I don't suppose that I could bring a charge against him here, but I have a feeling the F.B.I. might be interested in a civil rights violation.'

'You don't seem to understand what I'm saying, Mr Holland. I got my deputy's report right here, co-signed by a city patrolman, and it says you were drunk, resisting arrest, and swinging at an officer with your fists. Now maybe you think that don't mean anything because you're an Austin lawyer, but that ain't worth piss on a rock around here.'

'You're not dealing with a wetback or a college kid, either.' My head felt as though it were filled with water. Through the window I could see the sun striking across the tree tops.

'I know exactly what I'm dealing with. I been sheriff here seven years and I seen them like you by the truckload. You come in from the outside and walk around like your shit don't stink. I don't know what you're doing with them union people, and I don't really give a goddamn, but you better keep out of my jail. The deputy went easy with you last night, and that's pretty hard for him to do when he runs up against your kind. But the next time I'm going to turn him loose.'

'You might also tell your trained sonofabitch that he won't catch me drunk on my hands and knees again, and in the meantime he ought to contact a public defender because I have a notion that he'll need one soon.'

The sheriff struck a match on the arm of the chair and lit his cigarette. He puffed on it several times and flicked the match towards the spittoon. The knots and bumps on his face had turned a deeper red.

'I'm just about to take you back to lockdown and leave you there till you find some other smart-ass lawyer to get you out.'

'No, you're not, because you've already been through my wallet and you saw a couple of cards in there with names of men who could have a sheriff dropped right off the party ticket.'

'I'll tell you something. Tonight I'm going out on patrol myself, and if I catch you anywhere in the county you're going to get educated downstairs and piss blood before you're through. Pick up your stuff and get out of here.'

'What's the bail on the others?'

'Twenty-five dollars a head, and you can have all the niggers and pepper-bellies and hippies you want. Then I'll get my trusties to hose down the cells.'

I picked up my billfold from his desk and put four one-hundred-dollar bills before him.

'That ought to cover it, and some of your water bill, too,' I said.

He figured on a scratch pad with a broken pencil for a moment, smoking the saliva-stained cigarette between his lips.

'No, we owe you fifty dollars, Mr Holland, and we want to be sure you get everything coming to you.' He opened his desk drawer and counted out the money from a cash box and handed it to me. 'Just sign the receipt and you can collect the whole bunch of them and play sticky finger in that union hall till tonight, then I'll be down there and we can talk it over again if you're still around.'

'I don't believe you'll be that anxious to talk when you and your deputy and I meet again.'

'I'm going to let them people out myself. Don't be here when I get back,' he said. He stood up and dropped his cigarette into the spittoon. His flat blue eyes, staring out of that red, knotted face, looked like whorls of swimming color without pupils. He stuck his shirt inside his trousers with the flat of his hand and walked past me with the khaki stiffness of a man who had once more restored structure to his universe.

I sat down in a chair and put my boots on. They were filled with small rocks and mud, and when I stood up again I felt the dizziness and nausea start. I wiped the sweat off my face with my shirt and I wondered how in God's name I could have ever become involved in a fool's situation like this. I was glad there were no reflecting windows or glass doors or mirrors in the sheriff's office, because I was sure that the present image of Hackberry Holland – ripped silk shirt, mud-streaked trousers, swollen temple and blood-matted hair, and face white with concussion and hangover – wouldn't help me resolve my torn concept of self.

I walked outside into the sunlight to wait for Rie. The sun and shadow sliced in patterns across the lawn, and a warm breeze from the river carried with it the smell of the fields. I sat on the concrete steps and let the heat bake into my skin. My clothes and body reeked of the jail, and the odor became stronger as I started to perspire. Two women passing on the sidewalk looked at me in disgust. 'Good morning. How are you ladies today?' I said, and their eyes snapped straight ahead.

A few minutes later Rie and the others came out the

front door. The faces of the Mexicans were lined and bloated with hangover, and the guitar player and college boy looked like definitions of death. Their faces were perfectly white, as though all the blood had been drawn out through a tube. Rie carried her sandals in her hand, and she looked as lovely and alive as a flower turning into the sun.

'Thanks for going the bail,' she said.

'I'll mark it off on my expense account as part of my expanded education. Right now I need to pick up my car, unless our deputy friend set fire to it last night.'

'Rafael's brother has a truck at the fruit stand. He'll take us back.'

'Yeah, I don't think I could walk too far this morning,' I said.

'Say, man, you really took on that bastard, didn't you?' the college boy said. His face was so wan that his lips moved as though they were set in colorless wax.

'Afraid not,' I said. 'It was a one-sided encounter.'

We started walking across the lawn towards the open-air market. My head ached with each step.

'No, man, it takes balls to go up against a prick like that,' he said.

'Stupidity is probably a better word,' I said.

The shade was cool under the trees, and mocking-birds flew through the branches overhead. Across the street a Mexican was wetting down the rows of watermelons in the bins with a hose. Their fat green shapes were beaded with light in the sun. We crossed the street like the ragged remnant of a guerrilla band, and people in passing automobiles twisted their faces around and stuck their heads out of windows at this strange element in the midst of their tranquil Tuesday morning world.

One of the Mexicans and Rie and I got into the cab of a pickup truck and the others climbed in back, and we headed into the poor district. The driver pulled out a half-pint of Four Roses from under the seat and took a drink with one hand on the steering wheel. His face shook with the taste. Then he took three more swallows like he was forcing down hair tonic, and offered the bottle to me.

'Not today,' I said.

He screwed the cap on and passed the bottle out the window of the cab to one of his friends in back. The bottle went from hand to hand until it was empty, then the Negro banged on the roof when we passed the first clapboard beer tavern on the road. He and the Mexicans piled out and went in the screen door, pulling nickels, dimes, and quarters from their bluejeans. Before the truck started up again I could already hear their laughter from inside.

The driver dropped the rest of us off at the union hall. My Cadillac was powdered with white dust so thick that I couldn't see inside the windows.

'Come in and I'll put something on your head,' Rie said. The truck rattled back down the road towards the tavern.

'Unless I figured that sheriff wrong, he's already been to the hotel and my suitcase is waiting for me on the front step.'

'Your eye is starting to close.'

'I keep a couple of glass spares in my glove compartment.'

She put her arm through mine and moved towards the porch. 'All right, no protest,' I said.

'I thought he'd killed you.'

'I don't believe you're a hard girl after all.'

'Your eyelids turned blue. I even cried to make that asshole take you into emergency receiving, and he shot me the finger.'

'Don't worry. I'm going to make this fellow's life a little more interesting for him in the next few weeks.'

'I didn't think you believed in charging the barricade.'

'I don't. There's always ten others like him who'll crawl out of the woodwork to take his place, but you can't fool with the Lone Ranger and Tonto and walk away from it.'

We went inside, and I sat in a chair while she washed the lump on my head with soap and water. The tips of her fingers were as light as wind on the bruised skin.

'There's pieces of rock and dirt in the cut. I'll have to get them out with the tweezers,' she said. 'You should go to the hospital and get a couple of stitches.'

'Do you have a quart of milk in your icebox?'

She went into the kitchen and came back with a carton of buttermilk and a pair of tweezers in a glass of alcohol. I drank the carton half empty in one long chugging swallow, and for just a moment the thick cream felt like cool air and health and sunshine transfused into my body, then she started picking out the pieces of rock from the cut with the edge of the tweezers. Each alcohol nick made the skin around my eye flex and pucker.

'Goddamn, what are you doing? I don't need a lobotomy.'

'You probably don't need blood poisoning, either.'

Her eyes were concentrated with each metallic scratch against my skin.

'Look, let me have the tweezers and give me a mirror. I used to be a pretty fair hospital corpsman.'

'Don't move your head. I almost have it all out.' She bit her lip and squeezed out a splinter of rock from under the cut with her finger. 'There.'

Then she rubbed a cotton pad soaked with alcohol over the lump.

'Listen, goddamn it, there's other ways to clean a cut. They ought to give first-aid courses in the Third World before you kill somebody with shock.'

'Wait a minute,' she said, and went into the kitchen again and returned with a piece of ice wrapped in a clean dish towel. She held it against my head, her almond eyes still fixed with a child's concern.

'A cold compress can't do any good after the first two hours,' I said.

'What was that Bean Camp stuff about last night?'

'Nothing. I create things in my head when I try to run up Jack Daniels' stock a couple of points.'

'Were you in a prison camp during the war?'

'No.'

The whiskey edge was starting to wear off, and grey worms and spots of light swam before my eyes when I tried to stand up. She pressed her hand down on my shoulder.

'You ought to pull the fish hooks out. You're all flames inside,' she said.

'I feel like I've been dismantled twice in three days, and I'm not up to psychoanalysis right now. It seems that every goddamn time my brain is bleeding someone starts boring into my skull with the brace and bit.'

'Okay, man, I'm sorry.'

'I've got a brother that can make you grind your teeth down to the nerve with that same type of morning-after insight. There's nothing like it to send me right through the goddamn wall.'

'So I won't say anything else,' she said.

I felt myself trembling inside, as though all the wheels and gears were starting to shear off against one another at once. My palms were sweating on my knees, and I realized that my real hangover was just beginning.

'Let me have one of your cigarettes,' I said.

She laid the ice compress down, lit a cigarette, and put it in my mouth. The smoke was raw in my throat, and a drop of sweat rolled off my lip onto the paper.

'Does it always take you like that?' she said.

'No, only when I'm stupid enough to get my head kicked in by a redneck cop.'

I smoked the cigarette and exhaled slowly, while my temple and eye beat with pain, then pushed the sweat back into my hair with one hand.

'Look, you're not a drinker, so you don't know the alcoholic syndrome,' I said. 'I'm not a shithead all the time.'

'Sit down. Your cut is bleeding.'

'I'm going down the road. I'll take a couple of those hot beers with me if you don't mind.'

My legs were weak, and the blood seemed to drain downward in my body with the effort of standing.

'You can't drive anywhere now.'

'Watch.'

'You're pulling a dumb scene.'

I started towards the counter where the remaining bottles of Jax stood, and a yellow wave of nausea went through me. The sour taste of buttermilk and last night's whiskey came up in my throat, and I felt a great throbbing weight on my forehead. My cigarette was wet down to the ash from the sweat running off my face.

'Goddamn, I really got one this time,' I said.

'Come in the back, ' she said, and put her arm around my waist. My shirt stuck wetly against my skin.

We went down the hallway through a side door into a small bedroom. The shade on the window was torn, and strips of broken sunlight struck across the floor. An old crucifix was nailed against one wall above a Catholic religious calendar with two withered palms stuck under the top edges. I drew in on the dead cigarette and gagged in the back of my throat. You've just about made the DTs this time, I thought. Work on it again and you'll really get there.

My body felt as rigid as a snapped twig. She pressed me down on the edge of the bed with her hands and turned on a electric fan. The current of air was like wind blowing over ice against my face.

'Lie down and I'll put a dressing on your cut,' she said.

Something was rolling loose inside me, and my fingers were shaking on my knees.

'Look, you don't need–'

'Lie down, Lone Ranger.' Then she leaned over me with her breasts heavy against her blouse, her brown face and wild curly hair a dark silhouette above me, and she pressed me back into the pillow.

She rubbed ointment on the cut in a circular motion with her fingers and taped a piece of gauze over it. I could feel the heat of the sun in her skin and hair, and her eyes were filled with dark shine. I touched the smoothness of her arm with my hand, then the light began to fade beyond the window shade, the fan blew cool over my chest and face, and somewhere out in the hills a train whistle echoed and beat thinly into a brass sky. I heard her close the door softly as on the edge of a dream.

It was afternoon when I awoke, and the wind was blowing hard against the building. The shade flapped back from the window, rattling against the wood-work, and dustdevils spun in the air outside. The boards in the floor quivered from the gusts of wind under the building, and there were grains of sand on my skin. My head was dizzy when I stood up, my face tingling, and I could taste the hot dryness of the air in my mouth. I tripped over the fan and opened the door to the hallway. The sudden draft tore the religious calendar and withered palms from the wall, and the mobile made from beer bottles clattered and twisted in circles on the ceiling in the main room. I leaned against the doorjamb in the numbness of awaking from afternoon sleep. Through the front screen I could see the clouds of dust blowing along the street into the trees. I heard Rie walk out of the kitchen towards me. She held a tall glass of ice water in her hand, and she had put on a pair of white shorts and a navy denim shirt. There were freckles on the tops of her bare feet.

'How do you feel?' she said.

'I'll let you know in a minute.' I took the glass of ice water from her hand and drank it down to the bottom. I didn't believe that I had ever been so thirsty. The coldness ached inside my empty stomach.

'You have bad dreams,' she said.

'Yeah, I've got a whole wheelbarrow full of them.' I

walked past her into the kitchen and put my head under the iron pump. I worked the handle, and the water poured over my neck and shoulders and inside my shirt. I wiped my face slick with the palm of my hand. Down the slope the Rio Grande was rippled and dented by the wind. The brown current was turning white around the wreck of the submerged car.

'You can stay here. You don't have to go back today,' she said.

'I'd better hit it.'

'Wait until the wind storm passes.'

'They don't pass this time of year. That's a three-day affair out there.' The water dripped off my clothes onto the floor.

'You can't see out of your eye.'

'I sight with one eye over my Cadillac hood just like a pistol barrel,' I said.

'I'll ride to the hotel with you.'

'No, the sheriff will probably be hanging around there somewhere. I think you've had enough innings with a lefthanded pitcher for one day.'

The building shook in the wind, and pieces of newspaper blew by the window. Across the river two Mexican children were leading a flat-sided, mange-scarred cow off the mud bank into a shed. Her swollen, red udder swung under her belly.

'I don't want to see you get busted again,' Rie said.

'You take care, babe.' I put my hands on her shoulders and kissed her on the cheek. For just an instant the nipples of her breasts touched me and I turned to water inside. Her mouth and eyes made my heart race. 'I expect I'll be back here eventually and try to do something for that yankee mind of yours.'

'Be careful with yourself, Hack.'

I walked out into the dust and drove to the hotel. Leaves were shredding from the trees on the court-house lawn and blowing along the sidewalk. An empty tomato basket bounced end over end in the middle of the street, and the wood sign over the hotel slammed back and forth on its iron hooks. The fat deputy who had let me out of the cell that morning sat in the swing on the verandah with his feet propped against the railing. He looked off casually at the yellow sky when I passed him, his huge stomach bursting against his shirt buttons.

'Mr Holland, we'll be needing your room tonight,' the desk clerk said inside. His eyes were focused about three inches to the side of my face, then they would flick temporarily across the bridge of my nose and back again to a spot on the far wall.

'By God, that's right, isn't it?' I said. 'The Cattle-men's Association is holding its world convention here this week.'

My room had been cleaned, the bed made, the empty beer bottles carried out, as though I had never been there, and my suitcase was packed and closed and sitting just inside the door, ready to be picked up in one convenient motion. Someone had even put a Gideon Bible on the dresser top.

I paid my bill at the desk, and the clerk managed to show me nothing but the crown of his head while he marked off the ticket and counted out my change.

'You don't sell cigars in here, do you?' I said.

He fumbled in the middle of his counting, his eyelids blinking nervously, and I thought I had him, but he regained his resolve and kept his eyes nailed to the counter. 'No sir, but you can get them right next door,' he said, and turned away to the cash register.

I started down the steps to my car, then I heard the swing flop back empty on its chains and the boards of the porch bend under the deputy's massive weight. Shit, what a time not to have a cigar, I thought.

'Mr Holland, the sheriff wanted me to give you this road map,' he said, pulling it out of the back pocket of his khaki trousers. The paper was pressed into an arc from the curve of his buttocks. 'He don't want you to get lost nowhere on that highway construction before you get into the next county.'

'I guess that would be easy to do unless I had a map. Say, you don't smoke cigars, do you?' I said. 'Let me get a Camel from you, then.'

His eyes looked at me uncomprehendingly out of his white volleyball face. His greased black hair, combed over the balding pate, had grains of sand in it. He pulled a cigarette out of his shirt pocket with two fingers and handed it to me.

'This is goddamn nice of you and the sheriff, and I appreciate it.' I borrowed his lighter, which had a Confederate flag on the side of it, and lit the cigarette. 'Look, I've got two lifetime World Rodeo Association passes that I never use. They're good for box seats at any livestock show or ass-buster in the state. Here, you take them.'

I pulled the two thick, cardboard passes from my billfold and stuck them in his shirt pocket.

'Well, thank you, Mr Holland,' he said.

I went next door to the tavern, bought a box of cigars and a six-pack of cold Jax, and headed down the road in the blowing clouds of dust, the corn stalks rattling in the wind, the gold of the citrus exposed among the swelling green trees, and each time I made a curve between two hills at ninety miles an hour I felt the old omnipotence vibrate smoothly out of the engine through the steering column into my hands. The fields of cotton, watermelons, and tomatoes flashed by me, and the late sun splintered in shafts of light through the dust clouds and struck on the tops of the hills in soft areas of pale green and shadow. Then the country began to become more level, the twilight took on all the violent purple and yellow colors of an apocalypse, and I felt the wind driving with me eastward down a narrow blacktop highway that stretched endlessly across empty land towards the gathering darkness on the horizon.

chapter five

The poplar trees along my front lane were bent in the wind when I got back to the ranch that night. Under the full moon their shadows beat on the white gravel, and the air was full of swirling rose petals from Verisa's gardens. Someone had forgotten to chain the windmill by the barn, and the blades were spinning in a circle of tinny light while the water overflowed from the trough onto the ground. I could see the dark shapes of ruined tomatoes lying in the rows, and some of the cotton had started to strip. Then I saw Sailor Boy, my Tennessee walking horse that I had bought from Spendthrift Farm for six thousand dollars, knocking against the rails in the lot. His nostrils were dilated, his black head shiny with moonlight and fear, and he was running in a broken gait against each of the rick fence corners, rearing his head and kicking dirt and manure in the air. I climbed into the lot with him, worked him back easy against the rails with both my arms outspread, and got a halter over his head. There was a four-inch cut in one flank, and he had broken a shoe and splintered part of a hoof against the barn wall. I led him into a stall, slipped an oats bag over his ears, pulled the rest of the shoe, and dressed the ragged split in his skin. Then I went into the house, my blood roaring.

Verisa was reading a book under a lamp in the living room. She wore her nightgown, and she had two curlers set in the front of her hair. A cigarette was burned down to its filter in the ashtray. She had the nocturnal, isolated composure of a woman who might have lived by herself all her life.

'Question number one: who in the hell left Sailor Boy out in the lot?' I said.

She turned and looked at me, and her face whitened under the lamp.

'What–' I saw her eyes trying to adjust on the swollen side of my head.

'Who left my goddamn horse out in a wind storm?'

'Hack, what in God's name have you done now?'

'I want to know which idiot or combination of idiots left my horse to tear himself up in the lot.'

'I don't know. Why don't you stay home and take care of him yourself?'

'The perfect non-think answer. If his gait is thrown off I'm going to set fire to somebody's hair.'

'You'd better not be talking about me.'

'Read it like you want. It takes a special type of fool to do something that stupid to a fine horse.'

'You just stop your shouting at me.'

'I'll crack the goddamn ceiling if I want. And as long as we're on it, question number two: who forgot to chain the windmill? Which might strike you as a minor thing to consider between book pages, but right now our water table is almost dry and there are some crops that have a tendency to burn when they're not irrigated.'

'I'm getting sick of this,' she said.

'I'm not asking you to walk around in the manure with a cattle prod in your hand. I'd just like you to stick your head out the door occasionally and make sure the whole goddamn place hasn't blown away.'

'I don't know where your present adventure took you, but you must have damaged some of the brain tissue. I'm going to bed. If you want to shout some more, either close the door or go down the road to your tavern.'

'Don't you know what it means to hurt a horse like that?'

'Good night, Hack.'

She set her book down with a marker between the pages and walked past me in her best remote fashion. Her blue nightgown swirled around her legs in a whisper of silk, then she closed the door behind her. I had a drink out of the decanter on the bar, while my chest rose and fell with my breathing. Outside, the trees scratched against the house, and the door on the barn loft kept slamming like a tack hammer in the wind.

In the morning I went to the office in Austin and began work on Art's appeal. I was supposed to help Bailey that week on two large insurance suits, but after he had recovered from staring at my bandaged head and the swollen corner of my eye under my sunglasses, I told him that he would have to carry it alone for a few days. He was still angry from the weekend, and now his exasperation with his younger brother almost made his eyes cross. He sat with one thigh over the corner of my desk, his hands folded, straining like a stoic to retain his patience, while each word tripped out like an expression from a peptic ulcer.

'This is a two-hundred-thousand-dollar deal, Hack,' he said. 'We waited on it for six months.'

'So I'll pick it up next week.'

'We're going to try to settle next week.'

'They're not going to settle. Forget it. We'll be in court a year.'

'Give that case to the A.C.L.U. They handle them all the time.'

'I just want three goddamn uninterrupted days.'

'Even if you win appeal, you won't get him out of prison on bond.'

'I might if I can get some work done and be let alone for any random period of time.'

'What happened in Pueblo Verde?'

'You won't buy a car accident, will you? All right, a peckerwood cop kicked the hell out of me and I spent a night in a drunk tank. I was also indirectly presented with a map from the sheriff so I could find my way out of the county. In the meantime I managed to get a dozen other people arrested. Lastly, I'm going to write off their bail on my expense account. Now you can worry about the wire services picking up a sweet piece of interesting journalism on a congressional candidate. Does that make your day any better?'

'I don't believe you.'

'I have a receipt for the bail if you would like to look at it.'

His stomach swelled as he drew in on his dead pipe. It made a sound that hurt something in the inner ear. His vexed, almost desperate eyes focused out the window. Then his control began to slip, the anger and impotence rose in his face, and he ranted for fifteen minutes in clichés about responsibilities, major accounts, a judge who said that he never wanted me in his chambers again, my career in politics (and its profitable effects on our law practice), and my pending trip to Walter Reed Hospital with Senator Dowling.

'Oh, that's right,' I said. 'We view the Claymore mine and AK-47 cases this weekend. Why don't you come along, Bailey? You missed the Korean show. These guys are a blast.'

He slammed the door behind him, and I lit a cigar and looked up at the picture of Old Hack and my father on the wall. In the faded photograph, now yellow around the edges, his black eyes still burned from his face, which had begun to grow soft and childlike in his old age. His eyes turned directly into mine as I moved the swivel chair in either direction. They were like shattered obsidian, filled with fire and the quiet intensity of a levered rifle. His bobbed hair was as white as his starched shirt, and his stiff black coat looked as though a pistol ball would flatten out against it. Next to him, my father's gentle face and straw skimmer and summer suit made me think of two strangers who had met in the middle of an empty field and had decided to have their picture taken together.

I worked the next three days on the appeal with an energy and freshness that I hadn't felt in years. In fact, I even felt like a criminal lawyer again rather than an expensive manipulator for the R. C. Richardson account. My bottle of Jack Daniels stayed in the desk drawer, and I came to the office at seven in the morning and stayed until dusk. As I said before, the appeal should have been a foregone conclusion, but I began to wonder if any judge in the Austin court would believe that so many absurdities could have actually taken place in one trial. Moreover, each time I went through the transcript I didn't believe it myself. Thursday afternoon, after I'd had the secretary in my office for five hours of dictation and typing, Bailey's patience cracked apart again and he came suddenly through the door, his face stretched tight with anger. (The air conditioner was broken, and we had the windows over the street open. The hot air was like warm water in the room.)

'All right, you can let two hundred thousand dollars go to hell, but I'm still paying half the overhead around here,' he said.

'Bailey, look at this goddamn thing, then tell me that I ought to let this guy sit it out in the pen while some kid lawyer from the A.C.L.U. plays pocket pool with himself.'

'I don't want to look at it. I have a desk covered with twice my ordinary load of work.'

'Then have a drink of water. You look hot.'

'Goddamn it, Hack, you're putting me over the edge.'

'I just want you to glance at what can happen in a legal court without one voice being raised in protest.'

'What did you expect to find down there? Those union people knew the terms when they came in here.'

'I think I heard a deputy sheriff say about the same thing while he was pouring his mouth full of chewing tobacco.'

And once more Bailey slammed out the door, a furious man who would never understand the real reasons for his anger.

I spent Friday night in an Austin motel, and Saturday morning I met the Senator's private plane at the airport. I stood on the hot concrete by the terminal in my white suit, and watched the plane tilt across the sky and approach the runway, its wings and propellers awash with sunlight. One wing lifted upward momentarily in the wind, then balanced again, and the wheels touched on the asphalt as smoothly as a soft slipper. The heat waves bounced off the fuselage, and the sun turned the front windows into mirrors exploding with light. At the end of the runway the pilot feathered one engine and taxied at an angle towards me, and I saw the Senator open the back door and wave one arm, his face smiling.

I walked to the plane, and the backdraft from the propeller blew the tail of my coat over my shoulders. The Senator was grinning in the roar, and he extended his hand and helped me into the compartment. I pulled the door shut after me, locked the handle down, and the plane began to taxi out on the main runway again. The Senator was dressed in slacks, a Hawaiian sports shirt, and calfskin loafers. There was fresh tan on his face and a few freckles along the hair line of his white, crewcropped head. In the opposite seat, with a drink resting on his crossed knee, was a man whom I didn't know, although I sensed at the time that I probably would never forget him. He wore a charcoal business suit, silk shirt with cuff links, a grey tie, and his face was pale and expressionless behind his sunglasses. The mouth was small and compressed, as though he never spoke except with a type of quiet finality, and his manicured, half-moon fingernails and confident reserve reminded me of a very successful corporation executive, but there was something about the hue of his skin and the trace of talcum powder on his neck that darkened the image.

'Hack, this is John Williams, an old friend from Los Angeles,' the Senator said.

We shook hands, and I felt the coldness in his palm from the highball glass.

'How do you do,' he said. Only the mouth moved when he spoke. The face remained as immobile as plastic. He pushed his smoky, metallic hair back on one temple with his fingertips.

The plane gained speed, the engines roaring faster, then it lifted off the runway, and I felt the weightless, empty feeling of dropping unexpectedly in an elevator as the countryside spread out below us and the blocks of neat houses and rows of trees seemed to shrink away into the earth.

John Williams, I thought. The name. Where?

'What happened to your head?' the Senator said. 'I hope you haven't run into another tennis player with a bad aim.'

'A minor car accident.' You *shithead*, I thought.

'Well, John, this man is going to be the youngest congressman from the state in November.'

Williams nodded and took a sip from his drink. I tried to see his eyes through his sunglasses. John Williams, goddamn, where did I see it?

'John's not from Texas, but he's a good friend to the party.'

'I see,' I said.

'I've had him at the ranch for a few days of shooting. I'm trying to convince him that the only place to build industry today is in the Southwest.'

'A beautiful state,' Williams said. His face was turned to me, but it was impossible to read his meaning or intention.

'Do you mind if I have a drink?' I said.

'I'm sorry, Hack. I usually don't drink this early myself, and I forget that other people don't have my same Baptist instincts.' The Senator opened the cabinet door to the bar and folded out a small table from the wall. He picked up three cubes from the ice bucket with the tongs and dropped them into a tall glass and poured in a shot of bourbon.

'I was glad to see you at the airport,' he said. 'I thought maybe we were too forceful last Sunday in getting you to come along.'

'Oh, I keep my promises, Senator.'

'We'll only be there a short while. A couple of the state news services will meet us at the hospital, and then we'll have dinner and take off again this evening.'

'News services?' I said.

'Yes, the local ones. They usually like to cover this sort of thing for the state television stations.'

'I didn't know about that.'

'I see you're a bit new to politics,' Williams said. There was just a touch of a smile at the corner of his mouth, a faint wrinkle in the plastic skin.

'No, no, Hack's father was a congressman. In fact, a very fine one. It's just that Hack had some private reservations at first about visiting Walter Reed.'

'Why's that, Mr Holland?'

'I suppose it's connected with superstition. You know, bad luck,' I said.

'Really?' The skin wrinkled again at the corner of his mouth, and he clinked the ice in his glass. I felt the pulse begin to swell in my neck.

'Probably a silly thing, but I never found much pleasure in visiting a veterans' ward,' I said.

Williams' face remained opaque as he looked at me, but I saw one finger tighten on his glass.

'Maybe it's something about the smell of a dressing on a burn. I really couldn't tell you,' I said.

He continued to stare at me, and I knew that behind those sunglasses his eyes were burning into mine.

'How about another drink, John?'

'I'm fine.'

'I suppose I shouldn't have brought it up. Actually, Hack was wounded in Korea and spent some time in the V.A. after the war.'

'Is that right, Mr Holland?'

'It wasn't of much consequence. A flesh wound. The John Wayne variety,' I said.

'It was a little more serious than that,' the Senator said.

'I'd like to talk with you about your experiences sometime,' Williams said. His voice was as dry as paper.

'They're not very interesting, but anytime you're passing through DeWitt County on your way between Washington and L.A., we'll sure crack a couple of bottles.'

'You'll see John at my ranch. He visits often,' the Senator said. 'Your glass is empty, Hack.'

I wouldn't have believed it, but the Senator was uncomfortable. His acetylene-blue eyes were bright, and his easy laugh had a fine wire of strain in it. He poured another shot in my glass and pressed the stopper hard in the bottle neck with his thumb. And I began to feel that John Williams was a much more formidable person than I had realized.

'If you continue in politics I'm sure we'll see a lot

more of each other,' Williams said. I could almost taste the bile in his teeth. 'It looks like your career is going to be a very good one.'

'I expect that's one of those things you never know about.'

'I wouldn't say that.'

Again, I couldn't tell if there was a second meaning in what he said, or if he used deliberate vagueness to keep his opposition full of unspoken question marks. But I did know that the Senator was still sitting a bit forward in his seat, and his thigh muscles were tensed under the crease of his trousers. Yes, there's a real lesson in this, I thought. Even the predators sometimes have to lie under the reef while the shadows of much larger fish move through the dark waters overhead. I lit my first cigar of the day and squinted at the Senator and Williams through the smoke, and I wondered what umbilical cord connected them.

I didn't say anything else that would test that delicate pattern of membrane behind the Senator's healthy smile, and Williams sensed that the match was over. He set his drink on the table, folded his hands on his knee, and looked out the window like a withdrawn demiurge at the pools of fire in the clouds.

Three hours later I was on my fourth bourbon and water as we began our approach to Dulles Airport.

The air in Washington was humid and hazy with smog. There had been rioting in the Negro district off Pennsylvania Avenue during the week, and from the plane I had seen plumes of smoke blowing across the blocks of red-brick tenement buildings towards the Capitol and the Lincoln Memorial, that island of green and marble and blue water in the center of a colossal slum. Now, standing on the drive among the potted plants in front of the terminal, I could smell just the hint of burned wood in the air, and my eyes watered in the yellow pall that hung over everything in sight.

The Senator's chauffeured Cadillac limousine picked us up, and on the way to Walter Reed I fixed another drink from the portable bar built into the back of the driver's seat. The Senator didn't like it, but he confined his objection to a steady look at the amount of bourbon in my glass. Williams sat silently on the fold-out seat, his back straight and his face turned indifferently to the window; however, I could feel his sense of superiority in the knowledge that I was starting in heavy on the whiskey. That's all right, motherfucker, I thought. Wes Hardin and I will kick your ass any day in the light-year you want to choose.

Two television newsmen from Houston and Fort Worth were waiting for us by the information desk in the main room of the hospital. They were both young, dressed in narrow-cut suits and knitted neckties and button-down collars, and their hair looked as though it were trimmed every day. They had been leaning against the counter with their cameras hanging loosely in their hands, and when they saw the Senator they snapped into motion and came towards us with their leather soles clicking on the marble floor. Their college-boy faces showed the proper deference and energetic respect, and I thought, *ahhh*, there are two young men who will never live within breathing distance of the Fort Worth stockyards.

Three hospital administrators joined us, and we began our tour of the wards holding the Viet Nam wounded. I had a fair edge on from the whiskey, but now I wished that I had made a bigger dent in the bottle. The beds, with high metal rails on the sides, stretched out in long rows, and the afternoon sun slanted across the bodies of the men under the sheets. I had made a cynical remark to Williams about the smell of a dressing on a burn; but that was only part of it. The astringent odor of the antiseptic used to scrub the floors mixed with the reek of the bedpans, the sweaty and itching flesh inside the plaster casts, the urine that sometimes dried in the mattress pads of the paraplegics, and the salve oozing from bandages that covered rows of hard stitches. There was another odor in the air, too, one that might be called imaginary, but I could smell the distant rain forests and the sores that formed on men's bodies from living in wet uniforms and in boots that hardened like iron around the feet. The stench of terror and dried excrement on the buttocks was there, also, and if you wanted to think hard on it you could fill your lungs and catch the sweet-sour grey smell of death.

The Senator shook hands cheerfully from bed to bed, and each time he found a man from Texas he made several banal remarks while the cameras whirred away. A few of the men were bored or irritated at seeing another politician, but the majority of them grinned with their boyish, old men's faces, propped themselves up on their elbows with cigarettes between their fingers, and listened to the Senator's thanks about the job they were doing. Only one time did he have trouble, and that was with a Negro Marine who'd had an arm amputated at the shoulder. The Negro's eyes were bloodshot, and I saw a bottle of paregoric sticking out from under his pillow.

'Don't thank me for nothing, *man*,' he said. 'When

I get out of here you better hide that pink ass behind a wall.'

The cameras stopped whirring, and the Senator smiled and walked to the next bed as though the Negro and his anger were there only as the result of some chance accident not worth considering seriously. Then the cameras started working again, the two newsmen were back to their coverage, and the Marine pulled out his bottle of paregoric and unscrewed the cap by flipping it around with one thumb. His bloodshot eyes continued to stare into the Senator's back.

At the end of each ward the Senator made a speech, and I wondered how many times he had made it in the same wards during World War II and the Korean War. He had probably changed some of the language to suit the particular cause and geographic conquest involved, but the content must have been the same: The people at home support you boys. We're proud of the American fighting man and the sacrifices he's made to defend democracy against Communist aggression. You've taken up the standard that can only be held by the brave, and we're not going to let anyone dishonor that standard. It's been bought at too dear a price . . .

And on and on.

As I watched him I remembered sitting in a similar ward in 1953 after the last pieces of splintered lead had been removed from my legs, and listening to a state representative make almost the same speech. I didn't remember his name, or even what he looked like, but he and the Senator were much alike, because in the intense emotional moment of their delivery they believed they had fought the same battles as the men lying before them, felt the same aching lung-rushing gasp when they were hit, bled into the same dark soil, and had fallen through the same endless morphine deliriums in a battalion aid station.

But the Senator had one better. After all the hackneyed patriotic justifications for losing part of one's life, he outdid himself:

'I bet you boys aren't burning your draft cards!'

And they replied in unison, one hundred strong: 'NO SIR!'

The Senator went through the doorway with the three hospital administrators, who all the time had been smiling as though they were showing off a nursery of hot-house plants, and one of the newsmen turned his camera on me.

'Get that goddamn thing out of my face,' I said.

He didn't hear me over the electric noise of his machine, or he didn't believe what he'd heard, and he kept the lens pointed at the center of my forehead.

'I mean it, pal. I'll break it against the wall.'

He lowered his camera slowly with his mouth partly open and stared at me. He didn't know what he had done wrong, and all the reasons for his presence there in the hospital were evaporating before him. I don't know what my face looked like then, with the cut on my temple and my slightly swollen eye, but evidently it was enough to make a graduate of the Texas University School of Journalism wince. He dropped his eyes to the camera and began adjusting the lens as though the light had changed in the last ten seconds.

'I had a car accident this week and I don't want any of the guys at the country club thinking my wife hit me in the head with a shoe,' I said. I laughed and touched him on the arm.

He smiled, and I saw that his pasteboard frame of reference was secure again. He walked into the next ward after the Senator, and I thought, I hope that thirty-thousand-dollar house in the Fort Worth suburbs will be worth it all, buddy.

Later, back in the Cadillac, with the sun steaming off the hood, I poured a half glass of straight bourbon and took two deep swallows. The yellow haze outside was worse now, and the air-conditioning vents were dripping with moisture.

'That Negro soldier should be brought to the attention of his commanding officer,' Williams said.

'He was a Marine,' I said.

'Regardless, there's no excuse for a remark like that,' he said.

So you're a propriely man as well, I thought.

'It's nothing,' the Senator said. 'His attitudes will change back to normal with time. I've seen many others like him.'

'I didn't like it,' Williams said.

'Maybe he doesn't care to be part of the science of prosthesis,' I said. 'Provided they can fit something on that stub.'

Williams looked at me steadily with his opaque, pale face. For just a second his finger tips ticked on his thigh. I knew that if I could have looked into his eyes I would have seen flames and grotesque mouths wide with silent screams.

'Do you like that brand of bourbon, Mr Holland? I'd like to send you a case of it,' he said.

'Thanks. I'm a Jack Daniels man myself, and I get it on order straight from Lynchburg.'

'You must have a very good relationship with the whiskey manufacturers, then.'

I smoked a cigar and finished my drink in silence while we moved through the late traffic towards the downtown district. When I noticed that Williams was irritated by the smoke I made a point of leaving the cigar butt only partly extinguished in the ashtray. Originally, the Senator had planned for the three of us to have dinner together, one of those charcoal steak and white linen and pleasant conversation affairs that the Senator was fond of; but now it was understood between us that Williams should be dropped off at the Hilton, where he kept a permanent suite.

He stepped out of the car on the sidewalk and bent over to shake hands with me through the open door. In the hot air there was a tinge of his perspiration mixed with the scent of talcum and cologne. The shadow of the building made his skin look synthetic and dead. His sunglasses tipped forward a moment, and I caught a flash of color like burned iron.

'Another time, Mr Holland.'

'Yes, sir,' I said.

We drove to the airport and I waited for the Senator to begin his subtle dissection. I was even looking forward to it. I felt the whiskey in my head now, and I would have liked an extension of last week's tennis match. But he surprised me completely. His attack came down an entirely different street, and I realized then that he probably disliked Williams even more than I did, although for different reasons.

'You weren't in a car accident last week, Hack. You were put in jail with several members of that Mexican farm union.'

I had to wait a moment on that one.

'The sheriff could have charged you with attempted assault on a law officer.'

'Your office reaches much farther than I thought, Senator.'

'You might also know that I made sure the story wouldn't reach the wire services.'

'As a long-time friend of our family you probably also know that I've had other adventures of this sort.'

'Another one like it could end your career in Texas.'

'I don't think either one of us believes that, Senator.'

'I'm not talking about a drunken escapade. If you involve yourself with a radical movement, you'll find yourself on the ticket as an independent. The party won't support you. I don't think your father would enjoy the idea of your associating yourself with people who are trying to destroy our society, either.'

He was after the vulnerable parts now.

'It always seemed to me that my father's work with the New Deal was considered pretty radical at the time,' I said. 'However, I don't have any connection with the United Farm Workers. I was trying to help a friend from the service.'

The sun was starting to set among the purple clouds on the horizon, and through the car window I could see airplanes approaching Dulles with their landing lights on.

'I think you should turn over your friend's case to someone else.'

'Well, in eight years of practice I haven't lost a criminal case, Senator, and I'm usually a pretty good judge about what clients our firm should handle.'

'I hope you are, Hack, and I hope that we don't have this same kind of discussion again.'

The chauffeur pulled into the terminal drive, and I went into the restaurant and had a dozen steak sandwiches made up while the Senator waited for me at the passenger gate. His plane taxied out of the hangar and rolled along the apron of the runway towards us, and in minutes we were back aboard and roaring towards the end of the field.

We lifted off sharply into the sun, the city sparkling below us in the twilight, and the interior of the plane was filled with a diffused red glow. My glass of bourbon and ice rattled on the table with the engines' vibration.

'Who is he, anyway?' I said.

'John Williams? He owns the controlling stock in two of the government's largest missile suppliers.'

chapter six

I spent the next week working on Art's appeal while the July days grew hotter and my broken air conditioner cranked and rattled in the window. The temperature went to one hundred degrees every afternoon, and the sky stayed cloudless and brilliant with sun. The sidewalks and buildings were alive with heat, and sometimes when the air conditioner gave out altogether I'd open the window and the wind would blow into my face like a torch. In the street below, people walked under the hot shade of the awnings away from the sun's glare, their faces squinted against the light and their clothes wet with perspiration. The humidity made your skin feel as though it were crawling with spiders, and when you stepped off a curb into the sun the air suddenly had the taste of an electric scorch.

In the evening, when the day had started to cool, I would drive out into the surrounding hills with the windows of the car down. (I had taken a hotel room in town so I could come to the office early each morning, and also Verisa was holding two cocktail parties at the house that week, and I wasn't up to another round of drinking, and the disaster that always followed, with empty-headed women.)

In the mauve twilight the oak trees and blackjack took on a deeper green, and deer broke through the underbrush and ran frightened across the blacktop road in front of my car, their eyes like frozen brown glass. The air was sweet with the smell of the hills and woods, and jackrabbits and cottontails sat in the short grass with their ears folded back along their flanks. I remembered as a boy how I used to flush them out of a thicket and then whistle shrilly through my teeth and wait for them to stop and look back at me, their ears turned upward in an exact V. A slight breeze blew through the willows growing along the river bank, and I could see the bass and bream breaking the water among the reeds and lily pads. Fishermen in rowboats with flyrods glided silently by the willows, casting popping bugs into the shadows, then the water would explode and a large-mouth bass would climb into the air, shaking the hook in the side of his mouth, and the sun's last rays would flash off his green-silver sides like tinted gold.

One evening, after a flaming day and a one-hour harangue from Bailey about all my deficiencies, I drove down to the Devil's Backbone, a geological fault where the land folded sharply away and you could see fifty miles of Texas all at once. On the top of the ridge, there was a Mexican beer tavern built entirely of flat stones, and as I looked out over the hills at the baked land, the miniature oak trees in the distance, the darkening light in the valleys, and the broken line of fire on the horizon, I felt the breath go out of me and the ground move under my feet. In the wind I could smell the shallow water holes, the hot odor of the mesquite, the carcass of a lost cow that was being pulled apart by buzzards, the wild poppies and bluebonnets, the snakes and the lizards and the dry sand, the moist deer dung in the thickets of blackjack, and the head-reeling resilience of the land itself. I knew that if I stood there long enough, with the shadows spreading across the hills, I would see the ghosts of Apache and Comanche warriors riding their painted horses in single file, their naked bodies hung with scalps and necklaces of human fingers. Or maybe the others who came later, like Bowie and Crockett and Fannin and Milam, with deerskin clothes and powder horn and musket and the self-destructive fury that led them to war against the entire Mexican army.

The stone tavern was cool inside, and the cigarette-burned floor, the yellow mirror behind the bar, the shuffleboard table, and the jukebox with the changing colored lights inside the plastic casing were right out of the 1940s. Cedar-cutters and Mexican farmhands sat at the wooden tables with frosted schooners of beer in their hands, the bartender set down free plates of tortillas, cheese, and hot peppers, and the long-dead voice of Hank Williams rose from the jukebox. The last cinder of the sun faded outside, bugs beat against the screen door, and a brown moon sat low over the hills. I ordered a plate of tacos and a draft beer and watched two cedar-cutters sliding the metal puck through the powdered wax on the shuffleboard. For some reason the Mexican farmhands kept toasting me with their glasses every time they drank, so I bought a round for three tables, and that was the beginning of a good beer drunk.

The next morning I drove to the state penitentiary with my head still full of beer and jukebox music. The blacktop highway stretched through the rolling hills of red clay and cotton and pine trees, and my tires left long lines in the soft tar surfacing. The smell of the Piney Woods was sharp in the heat, and thin cattle grazed in the fields of burned grass. The rivers were almost dry, the sandbars like strips of bleached bone, and flocks of buzzards turned in slow circles over the woods. The corn had started to burn on the edges, and in two more weeks, with no rain, the stalks would wither and the ears would lie rotting in the rows.

As I approached the city limits I saw all the familiar warning signs for this world and the next posted along the roadside:

DO NOT PICK UP HITCHHIKERS
STATE PENITENTIARY NEARBY

PREPARE TO MEET THY GOD

SAVE AMERICA AND IMPEACH EARL WARREN

JESUS DIED FOR YOU HAVE YOU BEEN SAVED

DON'T WORRY
THEY'RE ONLY NINETY MILES AWAY.

And farther on, in a happier mood,

DON'T FAIL TO SEE THE HOME OF
SAM HOUSTON AND JACK'S SNAKE FARM

I stopped at the main gate of the prison and showed my identification to the guard. He wore a khaki uniform and a lacquered straw hat, and his hands and face were tanned the color of old leather. One jaw was swollen with chewing tobacco, and after he had looked at my Texas Bar Association card he spat a stream of brown juice through the rails of the cattleguard, wiped the stain off the corner of his mouth, and handed me a cardboard visitor's pass with the date punched at the bottom.

'Don't try to drive back out till the gate man goes through your car,' he said.

The main complex of buildings was at the end of a yellow gravel road that wound through acres of cotton and string beans. The inmates, in white uniforms, were chopping in the rows, their hoes rising and flashing in the sun, while the guards sat on horseback above them with rifles or shotguns balanced across their saddles. The sun was straight up in the sky, and I could see the dark areas of sweat in the guards' clothes and the flush of heat in the inmates' faces. Except for the motion of the hoes, or a horse slashing his tail against the green flies on his flanks, they all seemed frozen, removed, in the private ritual that exists between jailer and prisoner. Sometimes a trusty, sharpening tools in the shade of the cedar trees at the edge of the field, would carry a water bucket out to the men in the rows, and they would drink from the dipper with the water spilling over their throats and chests, or a guard would dismount and stand in the shade of his horse while the men sat on the ground and smoked for five minutes; but otherwise the static labor of their work day was unrelieved.

The dust clouds from my car blew back across the fields, and occasionally an inmate would raise his head from his concentration on the end of his hoe and look at me, one of the free people who drove with magic on the way to distant places. And as one of the free people I was the enemy, unable to understand even in part what his microcosm was like. From under his beaded forehead his eyes hated me, and at that moment, looking at my air-conditioned car and the acrid cloud of dust that blew into his face, he could have chopped me up with his hoe simply for the way I took the things of the free world for granted – the women, the cold beer, the lazy Saturday mornings, the endless streets I could walk down without ever stopping.

But I did know his world, maybe even better than he did. I knew the sick feeling of hearing a cage door bolted behind you, the fear of returning to solitary confinement and the nightmares it left you with, the caution you used around the violent and the insane, the shame of masturbation and the temptation towards homosexuality, the terror you had when a cocked gun was aimed in your face, the months and years pointed at no conclusion, the jealousy over a guard's favor, and the constant press of bodies around you and the fact that your most base physical functions were always witnessed by dozens of eyes. I knew how the weapons were made and where they were hidden: a nail sharpened on stone and driven through a small block of wood; a double-edged razor wedged in a toothbrush handle; barbed wire wrapped around the end of a club; spoons and strips of tin that could open up wrists and jugular veins; and all of it remained unseen, taped between the thighs, carried inside a bandage, tied on a string down a plumbing pipe, or even pushed into the excrement in the latrine.

The reception building was surrounded by trees and a green lawn. Three trusties were trimming the hedges, edging the sidewalks, and weeding the flower beds. They looked right through me as I walked past them to the entrance. I didn't know why, but I always felt a sense of guilt when I was around prison inmates, as though I should apologize for something. I knew the sequence of absurdities that often put them there, and I knew, also, that the years of punishment and the debilitating ethic that went with it had almost nothing to do with correction; but if I thought too long on any of that I would have to fold my law degree into a paper airplane and sail it out my office window. I looked directly at the Negro clipping the top of the hedge (he was so black that his white uniform looked like an insult on his skin), and he moved the clippers at a downward angle on the side of the hedge so that his face turned away from me.

In the distance I could see one of the crumbling gray blockhouses left over from the last century, and I wondered if that was the one where John Wesley Hardin spent years chained to the wall of a dark cell. They fed him gruel and water, and whipped him every day with a leather strap to break him, and when he was finally taken out to work in the fields they manacled an iron ball to one ankle, and two guards always stood over him with shotguns. He served his hard time like that, fourteen years in chains with the whip and horse quirt laid across the buttocks.

And I remembered the songs that Leadbelly had sung on the same farm: 'The Midnight Special,' 'There Ain't No More Cane on the Brazos,' and 'Shorty George,' and the lines about the 'black Betty,' a four-inch-wide razor strop, three feet long, nailed to a wooden handle.

I sat in the scrubbed reception room and waited for the guard to bring Art from the fields. The room was divided by a long, low-topped counter, and the inmates sat on one side and the visitors on the other, their heads bent towards one another in a futile attempt at privacy. There was a sign on the far wall that read: DO NOT GIVE ANYTHING TO THE PRISONERS; CIGARETTES CAN BE LEFT WITH THE PERSONNEL. At one end of the counter a huge guard, with rings of fat across his stomach, sat in a wooden chair that strained under his weight. There was a dead cigar in his mouth and a filthy spittoon by his feet. Most of his teeth were gone, and he licked his tongue across the strings of tobacco on his gums. His face was like a pie plate, and the washed-out eyes wouldn't focus in a straight line. Occasionally, he looked at his watch and pointed one thick finger at an inmate to tell him that his visiting time was over, then he would suck on the flattened end of his cigar. I could almost hear the digestive juices boiling in his stomach.

Art came through a back door with a guard behind him. His black hair was dripping sweat, and the cobweb scar in the corner of his eye was white against his tan. His palms were grimed and his forearms filmed with dirt and cotton lint. There were black rings in the creases of his neck, and his clothes were rumpled and stained at the knees. He had lost more weight, and the veins in his hands stood out like knotted pieces of cord.

'How long we got, boss man?' he said, taking a package of Bugler tobacco from his shirt pocket.

'Fifteen minutes,' the guard said.

Art sat down and curled a cigarette paper between his fingers. He didn't speak and his eyes remained downcast until the guard had walked back to the door.

'What do you say, cousin?' he said.

'I think we'll get a new trial.'

'Half the guys in here live on new trials. They don't

talk about nothing else. They write letters like paper is going out of style.'

'The difference is that you're not guilty of anything.'

'You know that don't have nothing to do with serving time.'

'Listen, as soon as the appeal goes through I'm going to have you out on bond.'

'That ain't good-guy jive, is it?'

'I don't bullshit a client, Art.'

'All right, you don't. But I'm hanging by my ass in here. This is a rough joint, man.'

'What's happened?'

He rolled the cigarette and folded down the wet seam with his thumb, watching the guard at the end of the counter.

'A couple of the hacks are laying it on. They know I'm with the union, and they're getting off their rocks while they got me in the field. Three days ago the hack said I was dogging it in the cotton and they gave me the apple-box treatment. They take you down to the hole without supper, and all night you have to stand on an upended apple crate, even though you piss your pants. If you fall off, the hole boss gives you a few knots to get your attention.'

He took a book of paper matches from his shirt, split one longways with his thumbnail, and lit his cigarette. He breathed the smoke out through the empty space in his teeth.

'The field boss already told me I'd have to wear out a hoe handle a week if I wanted to earn good time from him,' he said. 'He stays so close on my ass that horse is shifting and pissing all over me. They're going to make me build the whole five, man, and I'll run before I do another month.'

'Don't do that.'

'I'll run or I'll ice one of those bastards. I'm through with that pacifist shit. When I was standing on that box with the hole boss looking down at me from the cage, it hit me what a dumb sonofabitch I've been for the last five years. The anglos want us to be pacifists, just like they taught us that blessed are the poor crap in church. Man, we never knew how blessed we were. They want us to keep our hands in our pockets while they knock the piss out of us.'

'Forget about that running stuff, you hear?'

'It's not something you plan. You start thinking about all that time and your clock gets wound up, and you're ready to go through the wall with your fingernails.'

Art's voice had risen, and the guard was looking at us with his crooked eyes. The fat tissue of his mouth was pressed in a small circle around his dead cigar.

'I spent a little time in a prison compound, too,' I said.

'Then you know what that patience shit sounds like.'

'Give it another couple of weeks and I'll turn every handle I can to have you on the street.'

'I tell you, buddy, if I make the street they'll never get me back in again. New trial or not, they better bring the whole goddamn army with them.'

'You'll walk out of it clean, and I have a feeling that Cecil Wayne Posey's ass is going to get barbecued, at least if I have anything to do with it. Also, the deputy at the jail is going to have a few interviews with the F.B.I.'

'Say, you cats really pulled a scene, didn't you? I heard them bring you in that night. Something hit the cell floor like a sack of cement, and one of the blacks in the drunk tank told me it was a tall blond guy in ice-cream pants. You didn't believe me when I told you to keep your head down.'

'I'm learning. I haven't made a career of getting my head beat in.'

'So I have, huh? The greaseball who always gets his ass caught in the watermelon fence.'

'I met some of the people you have to deal with. I know it's bad.'

'Man, you didn't see nothing. You never got closer to a migrant camp than the highway.'

'I had a small taste of the local law enforcement.'

'I got two purple hearts in my trunk and you can have both of them.' He put out his cigarette, peeled the paper back carefully along the seam, and poured the unused tobacco in his Bugler pack.

'Do I get to be the dart board again?' I said.

'The next time you're in Pueblo Verde get Rie to give you a tour of the farm worker camps. Stick your head in a few of those stinking outdoor toilets, or talk with the kids sitting in doorways with flies swarming over their faces. Have dinner with a few of the families and see how the food sits on your stomach. Get a good breath of the dead rats under the houses and the garbage rotting in the ditches. Check the scene out, man. It really comes alive for you when you breathe it up both nostrils.'

'It looks like I have to stay white when I talk with you, doesn't it?'

'You're a good friend, Hack, but you're a straight and your mind is white as Clorox.'

He got to me with that one.

'What should I be?' I said. 'You want me to apologize because I was born me instead of you?'

'No, man. You still don't see. It's mind style, something you grew up with. Your people go through life like they're looking down a long tunnel and they never see anything on the edges. You roar down the highway a hundred miles an hour and never remember anything later except a motel billboard because everything on the other side of the fence is somebody else's scene. It don't belong to you. It's painted by some screw who lost his brushes and forgot what he was doing.'

'I don't like to tell you that you're full of shit.'

'Take the tour, buddy.'

'I've been on the tour. I grew up around it.'

'No point, cousin. You're right in the middle of the pipe.'

'Another gringo, right? One of the oppressors. A dickhead with the liberal tattoo.'

The guard heard me, and he took the cigar out of his mouth between his fingers and leaned forward, with his stomach folding over his gunbelt. The chair legs splayed slightly under his buttocks, and his crossed eyes were fixed in the smooth fat of his face.

'Look, Hack, if I make the street we're going on a sweet drunk together. We'll hit every chicano joint in San Antonio. We won't have to pay for nothing, either. We'll slop down the booze and ball with brown-skin chicks till our eyes fall out. Yokohama on a three-day pass. A real wild one.'

'You're cooking with butane now,' I said.

'I ain't kidding you. I'm going to wash this jailhouse stink off me in the Guadalupe and buy my

135

own beer truck. We'll just tool around the roads drinking and slinging bottles at the highway signs. Then when I get back to Pueblo Verde they're going to learn what real shit smells like.'

'You want to go back for some more?'

'The ballgame's just starting. We're going to hit them with a strike in August. I don't know if we can win, but a lot of cotton is going to burn in the rows if we don't.'

'Our defense will work like piss in a punchbowl if you have a half dozen new charges against you.'

'I can't sweat that.'

'You'd goddamn better, unless you want to end up here again with another five to do.'

'The only thing we got on our side is us. The cops, the legislature, the farm bureau, the whole fucking bunch – we got to bust them the only way we can, and that's to shut down the harvest until they recognize our union and start to negotiate.'

'You can't make a strike work in the fields. There's ten people standing in line for the job you walk off of.'

'They're going to win in California. We'll win here, too, as long as they can't scare us or turn us against each other. You see, man, that's what their real bag is all about. We twist the screws because of the shacks they give us and the seventy-dollar rents, and they throw out twenty or thirty families and tell them they got to do it because the union's forcing standards on them they can't meet. But people ain't buying that shit anymore.'

The guard looked at his watch and pointed a fat finger at us, then cleared his mouth of tobacco spittle and spat it into the spittoon.

'I left two cartons of cigarettes for you at the desk,' I said.

'Yeah, thanks, man. Look, you were straight when you said two weeks, weren't you?' His dark eyes were concentrated into mine, and one hand opened and closed on his forearm.

'I can't set it on the day.'

'I know that. I ain't dumb about everything.'

'I'll start on the bond as soon as the appeal goes through.'

'Okay,' he said, and smiled for a moment. 'I just don't want to go on the nutmeg and coffee kick and start flogging my rod in the shower like most of the stir freaks in here. Take care, cousin, and look around for that beer truck.'

I walked back outside into the hard light, and I was perspiring before I reached my automobile. The trusty gardeners were sweeping the cut grass from the sidewalk, their faces turned downward, and a crew of men from the fields were walking in file along the road, four abreast, their hoes over their shoulders in military fashion, with two mounted guards on each side of them. The sun had moved farther into the west, and the shadows from the cedar trees fell to the edge of the cotton field. The sunburned faces and necks of the men ran with sweat, and the guards had their hats slanted over their eyes against the sun.

I drove back down the dusty road and stopped at the gate while two guards looked through my car and in the trunk. As I rumbled over the cattleguard and turned onto the highway I felt a strange release from that confined world behind those high walls. The oaks along the road were greener, the sky a more dazzling blue, the hot wind heavier with the smell of the pine woods, the murderous sun less of an enemy. The billboard signs advertising charcoaled steaks and frosted bottles of beer penetrated the eye with their color, and even the weathered farmhouses and barns with metal patent-medicine signs nailed on their sides looked like an agrarian romanticist's finest dream. There's a line of separation between the world of free people and the confined which you never realize exists until you discover yourself on the opposite side. Once there, behind the barbed wire or mesh screens or concrete walls, all objects and natural phenomena have a different color, shape, angle, and association from anything you had ever known previously. And no one who hasn't been there can understand the light-headed opulent feeling of walking back into the free world.

Fifty miles up the road I stopped at a tavern and steak house built on stilts above the edge of a green river. The board walls were grey and peeling, and the open windows were covered with screens to keep out the clouds of mosquitoes in the shadows of the willow trees along the bank. A screened eating porch shaded by a tall cypress tree extended over the water, and I sat at one of the checker-cloth tables and ordered a steak and a pitcher of beer. The bottom of the river was soap rock, a type of smooth grey sandstone that the Indians had used to bathe with, and in the middle, where the current had eroded deeply into the rock over thousands of years, you could see the dark shapes of huge catfish and carp moving in and out of the light and shadow, then the surface would ripple with the wind and they would break apart and dissolve in the sun's refraction. I cut into the steak and soaked up the hot grease with bread, and washed it down with beer. The pitcher and mug were crusted with ice, and the beer was so cold that it made my throat ache. Cowboys and oilfield roughnecks in hardhats were bent over the bar with dozens of empty bottles before them, and the barmaid, in shorts and a sun halter, was opening more bottles as fast as she could pull them from the beer case. Across the river a group of Negroes were cane fishing with worms in the shallows, their black faces shaded with flop straw hats, and the moss in the cypress tree straightened and fell like silk in the wind.

In two more hours I would be back at the ranch, and then Verisa and I would begin to enact our ritual that usually worked itself towards one of three conclusions. The least unpleasant would be a pointless and boring conversation about the office, a new account, a cocktail party at the Junior League, or one of Bailey's trite suggestions for the campaign. Each of us would listen to the other with feigned interest, the head nodding, the eyes flat and withdrawn. Then, after a careful period, I would change clothes and go into the horse lot, or Verisa would remember at that moment that she had planned to invite people to the ranch from Victoria for the weekend.

More unpleasant was the possibility that the control wouldn't be there – the Mexican girl had burned everything on the stove, the gardener had dug out the wrong plants from the flower bed, the odor from the gas wells had made the house smell like a Texas City refinery – and the conversation would quickly deteriorate into a sullen silence and a door slammed sharply in another part of the house.

The last alternative was the worst: nothing would be said when I came into the house until we were forced by geographical necessity to be in the same room together for sixty seconds, and then our exchange would have the significance and intensity of two people talking at a bus stop. I'd spend my time in the library with the door closed, drinking bourbon and playing my guitar, and finally when I was in a drunken fog, my fingers thick on the guitar neck, with the house humming as loud as my own blood and Old Hack's angry ghost walking the front porch, the seams would start to strip and Mr Hyde's bloody eyes would look into mine, and Verisa would have to lock the bedroom door until the next morning.

However, Verisa wasn't always like the person I've described here. When I met her at a country club dance in San Antonio eight years ago she was Verisa Hortense Goodman, the only daughter of a millionaire stock financier, a hard-shell Baptist who never drank or smoked and kept his hard body trim with fifty pushups a day until he dropped dead from a heart attack. That night on the terrace under the mimosa trees the moon-sheen tangled in her auburn hair and her white skin glowed in the light from the Japanese lanterns. Her face was cool and pale, the small mouth achingly beautiful as she looked up at me. There were always men around her, and when she moved across the terrace, her legs like grace in motion against her tight silver gown, the men would follow her, eager, smiling, their own dowdy women left at the drink table. I took her away from her date that night, and we went on a wild ride with a magnum bottle of champagne through the hill country to an open-air German dance pavilion in San Marcos. I had a Porsch convertible then, and I kept it wide open through the black-green hills, drifting across the turns, while she poured the wine in two crystal glasses for us. Her face was happy with adventure and release, her voice loud above the roar of the engine and the wind, and she told me she was sick of country club men and beaux who hadn't outgrown Kappa Sig, and I knew then that I had her.

The next four months were all green and gold days and turquoise evenings, fried chicken picnics on the Guadalupe River, a burning hour under a willow tree in an afternoon shower, tennis and gin rickeys at the club, horseback riding into the hills and swimming in the black coldness of the Comal under the moon. We spent weekends at the bullfights in Monterey, with breakfasts of eggs fried in hot sauce and chicory coffee and boiled milk, and our mornings were filled with sunshine and mad plans for the rest of the day. We danced in beer gardens, hired a mariachi band at a street party in the San Antonio *barrio*, went to cowboy barbecues, and always kept a bottle of champagne in an ice bucket on the back seat of the Porsch. She never tired, and after another furious night of roaring across the countryside from one wonderful place to the next, she would turn her face up to be kissed, her eyes closed and the white edge of her teeth showing between her lips, and I would feel everything in me drain like water poured out of a cup. I'd leave her at her front door, the mockingbirds singing in the grey stillness of first light, and the road back to the ranch would be as lonely and empty as a stretch of moonscape.

We were married in Mexico City and spent the next three weeks fishing for marlin in the Yucatan. I rented a villa on the beach, and at night the waves crested white in the moonlight and broke against the sand

and the Gulf wind blew cool with the smell of salt and seaweed through the open windows in our bedroom. In the mornings we raced horses in the surf, and I taught her how to pick up a handkerchief from the sand at a full gallop. Her skin darkened with tan, and in bed I could feel the heat in her body go into mine. While we ate lobsters in a pavilion on the beach after the afternoon's fishing, her eyes would become merry, flashing at me privately, and I would already see her undressing before our closet mirror.

But later, as the months went by at the ranch, I began to see other things in Verisa that I had overlooked previously. She was conscious of class, and underneath her rebellion towards country club romance and the pale men with family credentials who had courted her, she was attached to her father and the strict standard he had followed and expected in other men. He was the son of a small grocery-store owner, and after he became wealthy he learned, with some pain, the importance of having family lineage as well as money, and he never failed to remind Verisa that she belonged to a very special class of people who did not associate with those beneath their station. She had learned the lesson well, although she was probably never aware of it. She simply didn't recognize the world of ordinary people, those who lived on salaries, rode Greyhound buses, or carried drinks from behind a bar; they were there, but they moved about in another dimension, one that existed in the center of hot cities, drab neighborhoods, and loud, working-men's taverns.

Also, she didn't like drunkenness. Although she considered herself an agnostic, a good deal of her father's devotion to the Baptist church had been left in her (he attributed his financial success to his early redemption at a Dallas revival and the fact that he practiced the teachings of Christ in his business; once he stared me straight in the face and told me that the Jews in the stock market were afraid to deal with a truly Christian man; he also believed that F.D.R. was a Jew). I never liked her father, and I always made a point of serving highballs, filling the room with cigar smoke, and drinking too much when he was at the house. He was glad to have Verisa married into the Holland family, and privately he asked her to name a child after him; so he was always restrained when I poured double shots of whiskey or asked him if he knew a Baptist minister in Dallas who was a grand dragon in the Ku Klux Klan. At first Verisa was indulgent towards my performances with her father, and occasionally, after he had left the house with his face disjointed in concern, she would say something mild, a quiet reproof, in hopes that I would be tolerant of him.

But I couldn't stand his bigotry, his illiterate confidence in the reasons for his success, and his simplistic and sometimes brutal solutions for the world's problems. Also, I resented the influence he'd had on Verisa's mind, that early period when he had infected her with the stupidity of his class. As she grew older I knew she would become more like him, much more sophisticated and intelligent, but nevertheless marked with the rigid social attitudes of the new rich. Worse, as my dislike for him became more open and his weekly visits turned into embarrassing periods of silence in the living room and then finally stopped altogether, I pushed her closer to him and she began to make comparisons between her father and other men who had been *given* everything. Sometime later, after I had come in drunk from a duck-hunting trip, she commented that heavy drinking was a symptom of the weak who couldn't stand up under competition.

I paid my bill at the steak house and took two cans of Jax with me for the drive home. Evidently, I was confused about Verisa's schedule for the week, because one of her afternoon lawn parties was underway when I arrived. The Negro bartender was shaving ice for mint juleps on the screened porch, and blue-haired ladies in sundresses sat around tables on the lawn under the oak trees. *Goddamn, here we go*, I thought. Two men from the state Democratic committee were there, neither of whom I wanted to see, and somebody had ridden Sailor Boy and had left him thirsty in the lot with the saddle still on. I went around the far side of the house and entered the library through the side door, but an insurance executive from Victoria and his wife were there, staring at my gun case with drinks in their hands. They turned their flushed faces at me, smiling. 'Hello. Good to see you,' I said, and went straight through and into the kitchen. Cappie, an old Negro who lived on the back of my property and sometimes barbecued for us, was chopping green onions and peppers with a cleaver on the drainboard. His grey hair was curled in the thick furrows on the back of his neck.

'Cap, get that goddamn saddle off of Sailor Boy and turn him out.'

'There some young ladies been riding him, Mr Holland.'

'Yeah, I know. Nobody thinks he drinks water, either.'

'Yes, sir.'

I started up the staircase to the bedroom, and then one of the Democratic committee men called from behind me and I was caught in the center of it. I drank mint juleps under the oaks with the blue-haired ladies, listened with interest to their compliments about my wife and ranch, explained politely to a mindless co-ed that Sailor Boy was a show horse and shouldn't be ridden into barbed-wire fences, and laughed good-naturedly with the two committee men at their Kiwanian jokes. People came and left, the sun started to set beyond the line of trees on the horizon, and the bartender moved among the groups with a tray of cool drinks, and at dusk Cappie served plates of barbecued links and chicken and potato salad. My head was drumming with the heat, the whiskey, and the endless conversation. Verisa stood next to me with her hand on my arm, accepting invitations to homes that I would not enter unless I was drugged and chained. Finally, at nine o'clock, when the party moved inside out of sheer exhaustion, I took a bottle of bourbon from the bar and drove down the back road to one of the ponds that I'd had stocked with bass. One of Cappie's cane poles was leaned against a willow tree, and I dug some worms out of the wet dirt by the bank and drank whiskey and bottom-fished in the dark until I saw the last headlights wind down my front lane to the blacktop.

During the next ten days I spoke at a free Democratic barbecue in Austin (it was crowded with university students and working people, most of whom stayed at the beer kegs and didn't know or care who was giving the barbecue), addressed two businessmen's luncheons in San Antonio (the American and Texas flags on each side of me, the plastic plants forever green on the linen-covered tables, the rows of intent faces like expressions caught in a waxworks), talked informally at a private club in Houston ('Well, Mr Holland, regardless of the mistake we made in Viet Nam, don't you think we have an obligation to support the fighting men?' 'Granted that colored people have a grievance, do you believe that the answer lies in destruction of property?' 'Frankly, what *is* your position on the oil depletion allowance?'), and spent one roaring drunk afternoon in a tavern with two dozen oilfield roughnecks and pipeliners who all promised to vote for me, although almost none of them came from the district.

The appeal came through at the close of the second week since I had seen Art. The judge who had reviewed the trial record, a hard old man with forty years on the bench, wrote in his decision that 'the conduct of the local court was repugnant, a throwback to frontier barbarism,' and he ordered Art's release from the state penitentiary on appeals bond pending a new trial. I set down the telephone, took a bottle of Jack Daniels and a glass from my desk drawer, and poured a large drink. On my second swallow, with a fresh cigar in my mouth, Bailey walked through the door and hit the broken air conditioner with his fist.

'Why don't you turn the goddamn thing off so the building can stop vibrating a few minutes?' he said. It had been a bad two weeks for Bailey. The heat bothered him much worse than it did me, and we had lost one of our big accounts, which he blamed on me.

He believed that he was developing an ulcer, and each morning he drank a half bottle of some chalky white medicine that left him nauseated for two hours.

'Just turn the knob, Bailey, or you can hit it some more.'

'I see you're getting launched early this afternoon.'

'No, only one drink. Do you know where I can buy a beer truck?'

'What?' A drop of perspiration rolled down from his hair line like a thick, clear vein.

'I tell you what, buddy. Let's lock up the office in about an hour, and I'll take you on a three-day visit to all the Mexican beer joints in San Antonio.'

'Put up the whiskey.'

'Come on. For one time in forty years of Baptist living, close the office early and tie on a real happy one.'

'Did you look at our calendar for this afternoon between drinks?'

'Yeah, R. C. Richardson is about to get burned again, and he needs us to clean up his shit.'

'You accepted him as a client. I don't like the sonofabitch in the office.'

'You don't understand that old country boy, Bailey. He's not a bad guy, as far as sons of bitches go. Anyway, his ass can burn until Monday. Get a glass and sit down. The only ulcer you have is in the head, and you're going to have a few dozen more there unless you let some cool air into that squeezed mind of yours.'

'If you want to get into the bottle and blow half our practice, do it, but shut off that patronizing crap. I've pretty well reached my level of tolerance in the last two weeks.'

'Look, I won appeal today on Art Gomez and the judge has set bond, and you have to admit that we haven't sprung many of our clients from the state pen. So take a drink and lower your blood rate, and I'll pick up Richardson's case early Monday morning.'

'I can't get it through to you, Hack. You've got cement around your head. The office isn't a tennis club where you play between drinks.'

'All right, goddamn, forget it,' I said, and picked up the telephone and dialed the number of a bondsman we dealt with. I turned my eyes away from Bailey's vexed face and waited in the hot stillness for him to leave the room.

The bondsman was named Bobo Dietz. He was a dark, fat man, who always wore purple shirts and patent-leather shoes and a gold ring on his little finger. He had moved to Austin from New Jersey ten years ago, set up a shabby office next to the county jail, and in the time since then he had bought two pawnshops and three grocery stores in the Negro slum. He considered avarice a natural part of man's chemistry, and you were a sucker if you believed otherwise; but he was always efficient and you could count on him to have bail posted and the client on the street a half hour after you set him in motion.

He assured me over the phone, in his hard Camden accent and bad grammar, that the ten-thousand-dollar bond would be made before five o'clock and Art would be released by tomorrow morning. For some reason Bobo liked me, and as always, when I went bail for a client on my own, he wouldn't charge me for anything except expenses. Many times I wondered if there was some strange scar in my personality that attracted people to me like Bobo Dietz and R. C. Richardson.

I turned off the air conditioner and opened all the office windows. The stale afternoon heat and noise from the street rose off the yellow awnings below me. My shirt stuck to my skin, and the odor of gasoline exhaust and hot tar made my eyes water. In the middle of the intersection a big Negro in an undershirt was driving an air-hammer into the concrete. The broken street surfacing shaled back from the bit, and the compressor pumped like a throbbing headache. I sipped another straight drink in the windowsill, sweating in the humidity and the heat of the whiskey, then I decided to give Bailey and his Baptist mentality another try. I took a second glass from the drawer, poured a small shot in the bottom, and walked into his office.

He was dictating to our secretary, his eyes focused into the wall, and I could see in the nervous flick of his fingers on his knee that he expected an angry exchange, profanity (which he hated in front of women), or a quick thrust into one of his sensitive areas (such as his impoverished bachelorhood, the empty weekends in his four-hundred-dollar-a-month apartment). I leaned against the doorjamb, smoking a cigar, with a glass in each hand. He faltered in his dictation, and his eyes moved erratically over the wall.

'Hack, I'll talk to you later.'

'No, we have to shut it down today. It's Friday afternoon and R. C. Richardson will appreciate us a lot more Monday morning. Mrs McFarland, my brother needs to direct me into the cocktail hour today, so you can leave early if you like.'

The secretary rested her pencil on her pad, her eyes

smiling. Her hair was gray, streaked with iron, and her face was cheerful and bright as she waited for the proper moment either to stop work or resume the dictation.

I set Bailey's drink down before him.

'I'd like to finish if –'

'Sorry, you're unplugged for the day, brother,' I said. 'Go ahead, Mrs McFarland. There's a slop chute down the road where I need a warden.'

Bailey saw that I had the first edge of a high on, and he let the secretary go with an apology. (He was the only Southerner I ever knew who could have been a character in a Margaret Mitchell novel.)

'That's too goddamn much,' he said. 'I've had it with this type of irresponsible college-boy shit around the office. When you're not loaded you're coming off a drunk, or you're spending your time on a union agitator's appeal while our biggest account gets picked up by a couple of New York Jews. You've insulted everybody who's tried to help you in the election, you got yourself put in jail because you were too goddamn drunk to know what universe you were in, and you had the balls to file a civil rights complaint against the man who arrested you.'

'Bailey –'

'Just shut up a minute. Senator Dowling kept that story off the wire services, but since you felt so outraged that you had to file a complaint with the F.B.I. we should have some real fine stuff in the newspapers before November. In the meantime you haven't been in a courtroom in three months, and I'm goddamned tired of carrying your load. If you want out of the partnership, I'll sign my name to a check and you can fill in the amount.'

'I started off to have a drink with you, brother, but since you've brought the conversation down to the blood-letting stage, let's look at a couple of things closely. Number one, the criminal cases we've won in court have been handled by me, and our largest paying accounts, keeping Richardson and his kind out of the pen for stealing millions from the state, have been successful because I know how to bend oil regulation laws around a telephone pole. Number two, you haven't been pumping my candidacy for Congress just because you want to see your brother's sweet ass winking at you from Washington, D.C. I don't like to put it rough to you like that, Bailey, but you don't understand anything unless it comes at you like a freight train between the eyes. You have all these fucking respectable attitudes and you heap them out on everybody else's head and ask them to like you for it. You better learn that you have a real load of shit in that wheelbarrow.'

On that note of vicious rapport I received the call from Bobo Dietz. Bailey's face was white, the veins swollen in his neck, his eyes hot as he raised the whiskey to his mouth and I picked up the receiver.

'I don't know what kind of deal this is, Mr Holland,' Dietz said.

'What are you talking about?'

'That man's dead.'

'Look, Dietz –'

'I called the warden. He said a couple of boons chopped him up with bush axes yesterday afternoon.'

chapter seven

It took me a half hour to get the warden on the phone. He didn't want to talk with me, but after I threatened to see him in his home that night he read me the guard's report about Art's death and added his own explanations about the unavoidable violence between the Negro and Mexican inmates.

Two Negroes had hidden a paper bag full of Benzedrex inhalers in the tractor shed, and they had been drinking bottles of codeine stolen from the pharmacy and chewing the cotton Benzedrine rings from at least two dozen inhalers when Art went inside the shed to get a lug wrench. A few minutes passed; a mounted guard working a gang in the cotton field heard a single cry, and by the time he rode to the shed and threw open the door the Negroes had disemboweled Art, torn the flesh from his back like whale meat, and severed one arm from his body.

There wasn't much more to the report. Art had probably been killed with the second or third blow. The Negroes were so incoherent they couldn't talk, and the guard had no idea why they had attacked Art instead of a half dozen other men who had been in and out of the shed earlier, although the warden added that 'a doped-up nigger isn't a human being no longer.' The Negroes had been put in solitary confinement and refused to talk about killing Art, if they even remembered doing it, and Art's body was to be buried in the prison cemetery unless his family was willing to pay for shipment back to Rio Grande City.

I hung up the receiver and sat numbly in the chair with my eyes closed and my fingers trembling on my forehead. So that was it. Just like that. Two crazed men single out another man, for no reason other than the fact that he walked into their bent, angry minds at the wrong time, and then they tear all the thirty-six years of life and soul from his body in seconds. My right hand was still sweating from the heat of the phone receiver and my ears burned with the casual language of the guard's report and the warden's footnotes. I couldn't shut out the vision of the two Negroes dismembering a man who had nothing to do with their lives, their brains boiling in a furnace of satisfaction, just as sometime in the future several other madmen would seat them in a wooden chair fitted with leather straps and buckles and metal hood and place a cotton gag in their mouths and burst every cell in their bodies with thousands of volts of electricity. Bailey poured a drink in a glass and placed it in my hand. I watched the brown light shimmering in the whiskey. My arm felt too weak and lifeless to raise the glass to my mouth.

'I'm sorry, Hack,' Bailey said.

I stood up and set the glass on the desk. My movements seemed wooden, disconnected from one another, as though I had just awoke in the center of a vacuum. I could feel the beat of my pulse swelling into my eardrums. For just a moment the room looked unfamiliar, the ordered arrangement of chairs and desk and file cabinets foreign to anything that was me. I began putting on my coat.

'Where are you going?' Bailey said.

'I'm going to try to explain how a —'

'Sit down a minute and finish your drink.'

'I said I'm going down to the valley and try to explain how a good man was murdered in a prison where he shouldn't have been in the first place. And then I'll explain how I won appeal on a man twenty-four hours after he was dead.'

'Don't let it take you like this, Hack.'

'How should we take it, Bailey? Maybe if I go to work fast I can arrange to have his body shipped home before he's buried in a prison cemetery with a wood marker. And if I'm too late to prevent that, I can always work on a court order to have the body exhumed. And while we're doing all that we can consider that a lynch court had this in mind for him when he was first charged.'

'Here, drink it, and I'll go with you.'

'You wouldn't like it.'

'I'll rent a plane and we'll fly down tonight.'

I drank from the glass, but the whiskey had no taste. I had started to perspire under my coat, and the shapes and late afternoon shadows in the room were as strange as the distorted lines in a dream. Outside, the air-hammer thudded into the asphalt. I felt the sweat dripping off my hair down the back of my neck. The glass was empty in my hand.

'They wouldn't like you, either,' I said.

'Goddamn it, Hack, you can't drive like this.'

'They don't buy that work-with-the-system shit. And I don't feel like telling them the system is all right, except for those twenty-four-hour differences

154

that you have to take into allowance. And I don't like to tell them that I was having drinks with the D.A.R. ladies and shaking hands with the paraplegics while Art's clock was one day behind the court's. Give me another one.'

He put his arm on my elbow and tried to turn me towards the chair.

'Just get the goddamn bottle, Bailey. Pour yourself a super one while you're at it.'

He went to the desk and came back with the bottle of Jack Daniels. He held the stopper in one hand.

'All right, sit down, and I'll call the airport.'

'Would you listen to me just for one goddamn time?' I said. 'I'm not going down to meet with a Rotarian luncheon, and number two I'm not a fucking lunatic who needs his older brother to strap a control harness on his back.'

I took the bottle out of his hand and drank from the neck. I swallowed until the muscles in my throat closed and the whiskey backed up in my mouth.

'There, goddamn. That glues everything a little tighter,' I said.

'Hack.'

I left him standing in the open door with the bottle in his hand, his lined face covered with pinpoints of moisture.

On the four-lane highway west of town I opened up the Cadillac, lowered the windows, and passed long strings of late afternoon traffic, hitting the shoulders and showering gravel over the asphalt. The red sun burned across the tops of the hills and lighted the dark edges of the post oaks and blackjack, and the shadows of the cedar-post fences along the road broke silently against my fenders like a blinking eye. Although I had driven that same highway hundreds of times, the sunset gave a different cast and color to the land than anything I had seen there before. The windmills were motionless in the static air; the cattle in the fields were covered with scarlet, their heads stationary in the short grass, and the neat white ranch houses seemed as devoid of life and movement as an abandoned film set; the irrigation ditches were dry and cracked with drought, the thickets of mesquite like burned scratches against the hill sides, and the few horses in the pastures looked as though they had been misplaced.

The shadows deepened over the hills, the traffic thinned, and I kept the accelerator to the floor for the next fifty miles. The sign boards, the oil rigs, and the three-dollar Okie motels sped past me in the twilight, but none of it would click together as a stable piece of geography that I had lived around all my life. It was removed, unconnected, and the whiskey from my flask made it even emptier and more disjointed. As a Southerner I had been brought up to believe that through conditioning and experience you could accept with some measure of tranquility any of the flaws in the human situation. But death is one flaw that always lands like a fist in the center of the forehead. No matter how many times you see it, or smell its grey rotting odor, or come close to buying it yourself, each time is always like the first. No amount of earlier experience prepares you for it, and after it happens the world is somehow unfairly diminished and bent out of shape.

It was night and just the horn of the moon shone above the hills when I reached Pueblo Verde. Lights glowed inside farmhouses beyond the dark fields and orchards of citrus trees, and the river was as black as gun metal under the starless sky. Everything was closed on the main street except the hotel and beer tavern, and I turned down the rutted road into the Mexican district, wondering what type of inadequate words I would choose to tell Rie and her friends that Art's death had come about the same way that a stupid fool steps on your foot aboard a crowded bus. I understood why Western Union offices always kept a pamphlet of prepared condolences on their counters. Death is the one occasion when words have as much relevance as a housewife talking across her back fence about a broken washing machine.

My flask was empty. I stopped in the Mexican tavern for a fifth of Jack Daniels and had two drinks from the bottle in the car before I pulled up in front of the union headquarters. Bugs flicked against the screen door and turned in the yellow square of light on the porch. One of the windows had a large, spider-webbed hole in the center, and someone had taped a piece of cardboard over it from the inside. *Okay, doc, let's go,* I thought.

I walked up the dirt path and knocked on the door. The Negro and two Mexicans in cowboy shirts and bluejeans were talking at a table piled with cardboard picket signs and bumper stickers. Only the Negro turned his head towards the door when I knocked; the other two kept talking, their faces calmly intense with whatever they were saying, their hands and fingers gesturing in the air with each sentence.

'Say, hello,' I said.

The Negro looked back at the door again, then pushed back his chair and walked towards me with a beer in his hand, his cannonball head shining in the light. He squinted at the screen with his red-rimmed eyes.

'That's my whiskey brother out there, ain't it?' he said. 'Come on in, home. You ain't got to knock around here.'

He pushed open the door for me and put out his large, callused block of a hand.

'Is Rie here?'

'She's laying down. I'll get her.'

'Maybe I should come back tomorrow.'

'No, she'll want to see you. Get yourself a beer off the counter.'

'Look –'

'No, man. It's all right.'

He went into the back of the building, and a few minutes later Rie walked out of the hall into the light. She was barefoot and wearing bluejeans and a flowered shirt, and her curly, sunburned hair was uncombed. I looked once at her face and realized that she already knew about Art's death.

'How you doing, babe?'

'Hello, Hack.'

'I started to call first.'

The skin around her eyes was pale and there was no color in her mouth. I felt empty standing in front of her.

'Do you want to go for a drive?' I said.

Her eyes blinked a moment without really seeing any of us.

'There's a meeting tonight,' she said.

'That's them church people coming tonight,' the Negro said. 'They don't offer us nothing but prayers. You all go on.'

'I know a place to eat across the river,' I said. 'Come on. I might run into a Carta Blanca sign by myself.'

I had peeled off the cellophane wrapper from a cigar and I couldn't find an ashtray to put it in. It seemed that every word I spoke and every movement I made was somehow inappropriate.

'That's right. Go on out of here,' the Negro said. 'I'm going to run them church people off, anyway. Every time they come here they start sniffing at my wine breath.'

She pushed her hair back with her fingers and slipped on a pair of leather moccasins. She was too strong a girl to have cried much, but her face was wan and drawn and the suntan on it looked as though it didn't belong there.

We walked out into the dark, down the path, and I put my arm around her shoulders. When I touched her and felt the trembling in her back I wanted to pull her into me and press her head against my chest.

'I spent three hours thinking of the wrong words to say,' I said.

'You don't need to, Hack.'

'Yes, I do. A man's death deserves an explanation, but I don't have it. Every time I saw a guy buy it in Korea I tried to see some rational equation in death, but it had no more reason or meaning than those faded billboard signs out on the highway.'

'Art's brother phoned this afternoon and told me how he died. It didn't have anything to do with anybody. There's nothing to say about it.'

So I didn't try to say anything else. I turned the Cadillac around in the dust, and we drove back down the corrugated road between the rows of clapboard shacks and dirt yards to the main street. The slip of moon had turned yellow and risen above the hills in the dark sky. The air was hot, motionless, and the oak trees on the square looked as though they had been etched in metal. The deputy who had given me the road map out of town stood under the neon sign in front of the beer tavern, talking with two men in overalls. His khaki shirt was dark around the neck and armpits with perspiration. He took the toothpick out of his mouth and stared hard as the car passed.

'Have they been bothering you?' I said.

'We had three arrests on the picket last week, and two nights ago somebody burned a cross in the front yard. It's strange to walk out on the porch and see something that ugly in the morning light. They'd nailed strips of tires to the wood, and I could still smell the melted rubber.'

'Well, by God, we can do something about the Klan. The F.B.I. wants to nail them any way they can.'

'The local fed thinks it was high school kids, even though some chicanos in the tavern saw a half dozen men in the back of a pickup with the cross propped against the cab.'

'Rie, we have civil rights statutes that can get those men one to ten in Huntsville.'

'We don't care about them.'

'Listen, those men are dangerous and violent people, and they should be in the penitentiary.'

'We've given the farm companies until Monday to sign, and then we shut it down. We have enough people organized now to do it, too.'

'Do you know what's it going to be like when the cotton starts burning in the rows and the citrus goes soft because it wasn't picked in the first week? Those farmers are going to lose their ass, and those K.K.K. bastards will have chains and baseball bats next time.'

'They won't stop the strike.'

'Goddamn, I don't want to see them pouring kerosene on your house, either.'

'Let's don't talk about it any more, Hack. I'm really tired.'

And then I felt that I had selected almost every bad sentence possible in the three hours of driving from Austin to the Valley. I followed the blacktop south of town and crossed the concrete bridge over the Rio Grande. The low, black water rippled through the trash caught in the pilings, willow trees and scrub brush grew along the sandy banks, and the windows of the adobe huts on the Mexican side glowed with candle light and oil lamps. I stopped at the port of entry, and a tired Mexican immigration official in a rumpled khaki uniform and plastic-brim hat told me not to go farther than fifteen miles into the interior without a tourist's permit. Rie's face had the shine of ivory in the light from the official's small office. If I touched my fingers to her cheek I knew the skin would be as cool and dry as stone. All the pain was way down inside her, and it would stay there without ever burning through her composure. Somewhere she had learned how to be a real soldier, I thought. Either in those insane billy-swinging, head-busting campus riots, or maybe in a Mississippi jail where they put cattle prods to civil rights workers, but somewhere she had earned her membership in a private club.

I drove down the bad tar-surfaced highway between tall rows of cedar and poplar trees. The evening star flickered dimly above the bare hills in the west, and a hot breeze had started to blow across the flatland from the Gulf. Most of the adobe houses by the roadside were in ruins, the mudbricks exposed and crumbling, the roofing timbers hanging inside the doorways like long teeth. I could never drive into old Mexico at night without feeling the presence of Villa and Zapata in those dark hills, or the ghosts of Hood's Texas cavalry who chose exile in a foreign country rather than surrender when the Confederacy fell. Even on my drunken excursions to meet three-dollar Mexican whores, the wild smell of the land and the long stretch of burned hills and all the mystery in them cut through my sexual fantasies. Even now, with Rie beside me, her drawn face painfully beautiful as she held a match unevenly to her cigarette, I still heard the jingle of sabers and the cock of rifles, pointed by the thousands down a hill at some forgotten army.

Ten miles from the port of entry there was a small town of flat, adobe buildings, cobbled streets caked with horse manure, whorehouses, two or three dangerous bars, a rural police station, and a cemetery against the hillside with a stucco wall around it. High up on the hill and formed with whitewashed field-stones were the words PEPSI-COLA. The adobe houses were as brown as the land, but the doors were painted blue, fingernail-polish red, and turquoise to prevent spirits from crossing the threshold. Most of the people in the town were poor Indians, but the whorehouses and the bars were run by either the police or marginal gangsters from Monterey. Oilfield workers sat in the open-front cantinas with fifteen-year-old girls, the jukeboxes blaring with mariachi horns, and farther up the narrow main street two policemen in dirty uniforms stood in the lighted doorway of the town's largest whorehouse. One of them beckoned to me as I passed, then he saw Rie and turned his attention to the car behind me.

The *cervezeria* and cafe was across the small square from the church. The owner had hung lights in the mimosa trees over the outdoor tables, and the shadows flickered in webbed patterns on the flagstones and the white oilcloth table covers. In the middle of the square was a weathered bandbox, with a round, peaked roof, and I could see the altar candles burning in the darkness beyond the open door of the church. We sat under the trees, with the dappled shadows breaking across us, and I ordered dinner and two bottles of Carta Blanca.

'Could I have a tequila?' Rie said.

'The stuff they sell here is like pulque. It's a yellow and you can see the threadworms swimming in it.'

'I'd like one just the same.'

The waiter brought us a quart bottle with a cork in it, two slender shot glasses, and a plate of sliced limes and a salt shaker. I poured into our glasses, and she drank it neat, without touching the limes or the water chaser, her eyes fixed on the darkened square. She winced a little with the bitter taste, and for just a moment there was a flush of color in her cheeks.

'That's not the way to do it,' I said.

'Let me have another one.'

'You can burn holes the size of a dime in your stomach with that stuff.'

'I would like for you to pour me another one.'

'All right. Hold the lime in your left hand and put some salt between your thumb and forefinger, then sip it.'

I watched her tilt the glass to her lips and drink it

down in two swallows. She choked slightly in the back of her throat and sucked on the lime.

'It's better the second time,' she said. Her eyes had already gone flat.

'If you like I'll pour some in the ashtray and touch a match to it, and you'll get some idea of the raw alcohol content.'

'I don't think it's as bad as you say.' She drank out of the Carta Blanca bottle and looked past me into the square.

'I've invested a good deal of time in it,' I said.

'It makes you feel quiet inside, doesn't it?'

'Then it pulls open all kinds of doors you usually keep shut.'

'Why don't you teach me how to drink it, then?'

I gave the waiter my best American tourist look of irritated impatience, and he nodded in return and went to the kitchen window to hurry the cook.

'Give me another one,' she said.

'You're not a drinker, Rie. Don't try to compete with the professionals.'

'Here, I've finished the beer and I don't like it. I want you to show me how to drink tequila.'

'The best way is to fill your glass and pour it in your automobile tank.'

'Hack.'

'No, goddamn it.'

'Maybe we should go. It's hot, anyway, isn't it?'

'I don't like to go out on abortive missions.'

'Yes, you do, even to make one point about your knowledge of drinking.'

'Okay, Rie. You nailed me to the wall with that one.' I filled her shot glass and lit a cigar.

'Do you enjoy being angry?'

'No, but I'll be goddamned if I'll take on my idiot brother's role with somebody else.'

'I believe you enjoy it when the blood starts beating in your head.'

'I'm all out of fire tonight, babe. My white flag is tacked to the masthead.'

She sipped out of her glass and fixed her flat eyes on my face. I drew in on the cigar and waited for it.

'Was there anything we could have done?'

'No.'

'Anything at all so he wouldn't have been in that tool shed?'

'It was all done.'

'I visited him the day he was transferred to prison. I watched them take him down the courthouse sidewalk in handcuffs, then I went back on the picket the same afternoon, just like nothing had changed.'

'I turned every lock I could. We were almost home free. It was one of those dumb things that nobody can do anything about.'

She raised the glass again, and her almond eyes looked electric in the light from the trees.

'But it had to be black men who killed him. Not a sadist or a racist guard. Two spades who probably lived everything he did.'

The waiter placed our dinner before us, holding the plates by the bottom with a folded napkin, and looked quickly at Rie, then at me.

'*Dos mas Carta Blanca*,' I said.

'*Si señor*,' he said, and drew his curiosity back inside himself.

'I don't think I'm hungry now,' she said.

'Eat a little bit.'

'I don't want it. I'm sorry.'

'Be a doll.'

'Let's go, Hack.'

'I'll have the waiter wrap it in waxpaper.'

'Please, let's just go.'

I paid the check inside, and the waiter looked offended because we hadn't eaten, until I explained that my wife was ill and told him to keep the rest of the tequila for himself. We drove back down the cobbled street past the loud bars, and a barefoot Indian child in ragged clothes ran along beside my window with his hand outstretched. The two policemen in front of the whorehouse were helping a drunk American in a business suit from his automobile. He leaned against a stone pillar, his face bloated and white with alcohol under the Carta Blanca sign, and gave each of them a bill from his wallet. I shuddered with the recollection of stepping unsteadily out of taxicabs on similar streets and walking through other garish doorways under the slick eyes of uniformed pimps, and I wondered if my face had looked as terrible as the man's under the neon sign.

I accelerated the Cadillac past the last cantinas and turned back onto the dark highway. The moon broke apart in the branches of the tall cedar trees sweeping by me.

'Why did you say we were almost home free?' she said.

Goddamn you, Hack.

'I thought I could have him out with some more time.' I kept my eyes on the highway and didn't look at her when I spoke. 'It's one of those things you can't tell about. You do everything you can and wait for the court to act.'

I could hear her breathing in the dark.

'It could have gone in the other direction,' I said.

'Oh goddamn, Hack,' she said, and put her face against my chest with her hands clenched around my arm. Her tears wet the front of my shirt, and she held onto me tighter each time she tried to stop crying. I pulled her close into me and rubbed the back of her neck and her curly hair; her forehead felt feverish against my cheek and she trembled inside my arm like a frightened girl. I could smell the sun in her hair and the raw tequila on her breath, and I wanted to pull onto the side of the road and press her inside me.

Her face was as white and smooth as alabaster in the light from the dashboard, and when she had stopped crying and tried to sit up straight I held her close against me and pushed my fingers up through her hair. Her eyes were closed, her breasts stopped rising, and I felt the muscles in her back tense once more and then go loose under my palm. She breathed slowly into my neck, and by the time we reached the border she was asleep.

I rolled across the bridge over the Rio Grande, and an immigration official in a Stetson hat looked once at my Texas Bar Association card and waved me through. The hot night air was sweet with the ripe citrus and watermelon, and there was just a taste of salt in the wind from the Gulf. The moon had risen high above the hills now, and a strip of black storm cloud hung off of one yellow horn. I drove slowly over the ruts and chuckholes through the Mexican and Negro district and parked along the broken fence in front of the union headquarters. The light was still on in the front room, and a man was silhouetted behind the screen door with a bottle in his hand. I eased my arm from behind Rie's neck and rested her head against the seat. Her eyelashes were still damp, her cool face caught the softness of the moon, and when she parted her lips slightly in her sleep I felt the blood sink in my heart. I leaned over and kissed her lightly on the mouth. The screen door slammed, and the Negro walked out on the porch. I went around to the other side of the car and picked Rie up carefully in my arms and carried her up the front path. Her eyes opened momentarily, then shut again, and she turned her face into my neck. The Negro held the door back for me, and I laid her down on the bed in the back room and switched on the electric fan. Her hair moved on the pillow in the breeze, and the alabaster color of her face was even more pale and cold in the half light. I heard the Negro opening two bottles of beer in the front room, and I closed the door behind me and went back through the hallway.

'Sometimes people got to get high and boil it out,' the Negro said. He put a bottle of Jax in my hand.

'I'll get some vitamin B and aspirin out of my car. Give it to her if she wakes up before you go to bed.'

'I been on that spodiodi route a long time, man. You ain't got to tell me how to fight it.'

'I guess we went to the same school.'

'There you go,' he said. 'Look, I'm glad you taken her out tonight. Some dudes come by and wanted to give us some shit. For a minute I thought they was really going to get it on.'

'What happened?'

'A couple of carloads of young studs come down the street throwing firecrackers at the houses. Then they parked out front, drinking wine and rolling them cherry bombs up on the porch. I figured they'd get tired of it after a while, but three of them come up to the door and said they wanted to skin out a nigger. Yeah, they said they ain't hung a nigger up on a skinning hook in a long time. They was blowing wine in my face, and I could smell lynch all over them, just like piss on fire. One of them started to pull open the door, and then a dude in the car blew the horn and hollered out, 'Don't waste it on a jig. Let's find them hippy freaks.' Two of them cut, but this stud with the door in his hand wanted a pair of black balls. If the chicanos hadn't started coming out of their houses, the shit would have gone right through the fan, and I'd be up for icing a white kid. Because I tell you, whiskey brother, I give up on the days of letting white people shove a two-by-four up my ass until the splinters are coming out of my mouth.'

I drank from the beer and looked at the Negro's face. For the first time since I had met him I saw the hard glass quality in his eyes, the flicker of humiliation in them, the thin raised scar, now as colorless as plastic, on his lower lip. His gleaming head was covered with drops of perspiration, and the lumps of cartilage behind his ears pulsed as though he were chewing angrily on something down inside himself.

'What the hell are you doing here, anyway?' I said.

'I got a bad habit, man. I picked it up in the army digging latrines all over Europe for sweet pink assholes. I figure a yard of white shit went into the ground for every shovelful of dirt I turned. When I got out I decided I paid my dues to Mr Charlie's bathroom and I ain't applying at the back door no more for my mop and pail. You know what I mean, man?'

He licked his tongue over his bottom lip, and the scar glistened like a piece of glass. For the second time that day I felt I had nothing to say. Outside, the cicadas were singing in the stillness. I finished my beer and left him at the table, lighting one of my cigars.

I didn't believe that I would be welcome again at the rooming house, so I drove thirty miles to the next town on the river and checked into a motel. I lay on the bed in the air-conditioned darkness with my arm over my eyes, and each time that I almost made it into sleep, broken images and voices would click together in my mind like the edges of a splintered window-pane, and I would be awake again with the veins drawing tight against my scalp. The highway rolled towards me out of the twilight, then the bush axes were raised high in the air once more, glinting redly in the gloom of the toolhouse, and a Chinese private leaned his face down to the sewer grate and spat a long stream of yellow saliva on my head. I sat on the edge of the bed in my underwear and drank half the bottle of Jack Daniels before I fell asleep in the deep whiskey quiet of my own breathing.

The next morning I dressed in a pair of khakis, my old cowboy boots, and a denim shirt (all of which I carried in a suitcase that always stayed in the trunk of the Cadillac), had my hangover breakfast of a steak with a fried egg on top and a slow cup of coffee and a cigar, then started down the road for Pueblo Verde. The sun was white on the horizon, and the washed-out blue sky hurt your eyes to look at it. The green of the citrus orchards, the fields of corn and cotton, and the sear hilltops floated in the humidity and heat. Watermelons lay fat in the rows, shimmering with light, and the cucumber vines were heavy with their own weight. Even with sunglasses on I had to squint against the glare. Hawks circled over the fields, and on some of the cedar fence posts farmers had nailed dead crows, salted and withered in the sun, to keep the live ones out of the corn. In the middle of an empty pasture, far from the roadside, a sun-faded billboard warned that THE COMING IS SOON, LISTEN TO BROTHER HAROLD'S NEW FAITH REVIVAL ON STATION XERF.

Outside Pueblo Verde I pulled into a clapboard country store shaded by a huge live oak. There was an old metal patent-medicine sign nailed to one wall, three pickup trucks parked on the gravel in front, and on the wood porch was a rusted Coca-Cola cooler with bottle caps spilling out of the opener box. The inside of the store was dark and cool and smelled of cheese and summer sausage and cracklings in quart jars. I bought a wicker picnic basket, a tablecloth, two bottles of California burgundy, some peppered German sausage, white cheese, a loaf of French bread, and six bottles of Jax pushed down in a bag of crushed ice. A small barefoot Negro boy, with bluejeans torn at the knees, helped me carry the sacks to the car. Then I turned back onto the highway into the white brilliance of the sun above the Rio Grande.

The high sidewalks in town were crowded with people, and the beer taverns and pool halls were filled with cowboys and cedar-cutters who had come into town to drink every piece of change in their bluejeans. I was always struck by the way that all small Texas towns looked alike on Saturday morning, whether you were in the Panhandle or the Piney Woods. The same battered cars and farm trucks were parked at an angle to the sidewalks; the same sun-browned old men spat their tobacco juice on the hot concrete; the young boys in crewcuts and Sears Roebuck straw hats with health and blond youth all over their faces stood on the street corners; and the girls with their hair in curlers and bandannas sat in the same cafes, drinking R.C. Cola and giggling about what Billy Bob or that crazy Lee Harper did at the drive-in movie last night.

I drove down the dusty street of the Mexican district with the lisping voice of a local hillbilly singer blaring from my radio:

> *I warned him once or twice*
> *To stop playing cards and shooting dice*
> *He's in the jailhouse now.*

Rie was sitting at the table in the front room of the union headquarters with a cup of coffee in her hand. She was barefoot and wore a pair of white shorts and a rumpled denim shirt, and her face was pale with hangover. I went through the screen door without knocking.

'Get in the car, woman. I'm going to do something for that yankee mind of yours today,' I said.

'What?' She looked at me with her hair in her eyes.

'Dinner on the ground and devil in the bush, by God. Come on.'

'Hack, what are you talking about?' Her words were slow and carefully controlled, and I knew she really had one.

'I'm going to introduce you to my boyhood. Goddamn it, girl, get up and stop fooling around.'

'I don't think I can do anything today.'

'Yes, you can. Never stay inside with a hangover. Charge out into the sunlight and do things you never did before.'

'How much did I drink?'

'You just did it with bad things in your mind.'

'I'm sorry about last night. I must have seemed like a real dumb chick.'

'You could never be that.'

She smiled and pushed the hair out of her eyes.

'I'm sorry, anyway,' she said.

'Right now there's a green river about seventy miles from here, and under a big grey limestone rock there's an eight-pound bass with one of my flies hanging in his lip, and unless you get your ass up I'm going down the road by myself.'

'You're a real piece of pie, Hack.'

'No, I ain't. I'm shit and nails and all kinds of bad news. You ought to know that by this time. If you need any references you can contact my brother. I left him yesterday with his ulcer bulging out of his throat.'

She put her fingers to her forehead and laughed, and that wonderful merry flash of light came back into her eyes.

'I'll be out in a minute. There's some chickory coffee and cornbread on the stove,' she said.

'Well, goddamn, for a yankee girl you may be all right after all,' I said, and watched the smooth curve of her hips against her shorts as she walked into the back of the house.

We drove north through the hills and flat farmland of string-bean and corn fields and cow pasture to a wide, green, slow-moving river lined with willow, redbud, and juniper trees, where I had fly-fished as a boy with my father. The river was low from the drought, and the surface was covered with seeds from the juniper trees, but there were still eddies and deep holes behind the boulders in the current, and I knew that I could take all the crappie, bream, and bass that I could put on a stringer. The mudbanks were covered with the sharp, wet tracks of deer and raccoons, and mockingbirds and bluejays flew angrily through the hot shade of the trees. The sunlight reflected off the water, and farther down, where the river turned by a grove of cypress trees, the sandbars gleamed hard and white in the middle of the current. Dragonflies flicked over the reeds and lily pads near the bank, and the bream were feeding in the shade of the willows, denting the water in quiet circles, like raindrops, when they rose to take an insect.

I took my three-piece Fenwick flyrod in its felt cover and the small box of number-eighteen dry flies from the trunk, and we walked through the trees and dead leaves and twigs to the river. Comanche and Apache warriors used to camp here on the banks to cut and shave arrow shafts from the juniper wood, and for a moment my eyes became twenty years younger as I looked for the place where they had probably built their wickiups and hung their venison in the trees over smoking fires. I knew that if I looked long enough I could find their old camp: the fire line a foot or so below the soil, the flint chippings from a work mound, the bone awls and shards of pottery. Since I was a boy I always felt that the land breathed with the presence of those dead men who had struggled on it long before we were born, and sometimes as a boy, particularly in the late evening, I almost felt that they were still living out their lives around me, firing their arrows from under the necks of war ponies at pioneer cabins that had long since decayed into loam. Once when I was plowing a field that we had always used for pasture, I felt something hard and brittle snap against the share and grind into pieces over the moldboard. I felt it right through the vibration of the tractor, and before I had shut off the engine and turned around in the metal seat I already knew that I had scraped across a warrior's grave. The shattered skull and bits of white vertebra were scattered in the furrow, and all of his rose quartz arrowpoints gleamed among his ribs like drops of blood.

We sat under a cypress tree close to the water, and Rie opened the beer and made sandwiches of sausage and cheese while I tied a new tapered leader with one-pound test tippet. I waded out into the warm water and false-cast under the overhang of the trees, pulling out the line from the reel easily with my left hand, and shot the small brown hackle fly into a riffle on the far side of a boulder. The Fenwick was a beautiful rod. It was as light as air in my palm, and it was tapered and balanced so perfectly in its design that I could set the hook hard with one flick of the fingers. The fly drifted through the riffle twice without a strike, but on the third cast a large-mouth bass rose from the bottom of the pool, like a green air bubble floating slowly upwards, and broke the surface in an explosion of light. He took the fly in the corner of his lip, shaking his head violently, his dorsal fin and tail boiling the water, then he dove deep again towards the heavy current. I kept the rod high over my head with my right arm outstretched and let the line run tightly between my fingers. He sat on it once, deep, pointed downstream, and the tip of the rod bent downward until I knew that he was about to break the leader and I had to give him more line. I waded with him in the current, working him at an angle towards the bank, then he rose once more, the hook now protruding close to his eye, and hit the water sideways. He tried to turn his head back into the current, but he was weakening fast, and I started pulling in the line slowly with my left hand. He waved his tail in the shallows, clouding the water with sand, and each time I lifted the rod to bring his mouth to the surface he sat on it again and bent the tip in a quivering arch. I let him spend his last strength against the spring of the rod, then I worked my hand down the leader and caught him carefully under the stomach. He was heavy and cold in my hand, and I slipped the hook out of his mouth, watching the eye, and placed him back in the water. He remained still for a moment, his gills pulsing, then he moved slowly off through the shallows and dropped into the green darkness of the current.

I leaned the rod against the cypress trunk and drank a bottle of Jax with a sausage and cheese sandwich. The Spanish moss overhead looked like wisps of cobweb against the sun, and I could smell the dank, cool odor of the rotted stumps and worm-eaten logs back in the woods. Rie had waded on the edge of the river while I fished, and her bare, suntanned legs were coated with sand. She sat with her arms behind her, looking at the sandbars and stretch of willows on the far side of the river, and I had to force myself from dropping my eyes to her breasts.

'How did you find such a wonderful place?' she said.

'My father used to take me here when I was a boy. In the spring we'd fish the riffle from that rosebud tree down to where the river turns in the shade. Then we'd dig for an old Indian camp. I found my first bannerstone in the bottom of that wash.'

I sat down beside her on the tablecloth and drank

from the beer. A shaft of sunlight struck inside the amber bottle.

'It must be fine to have a father like that,' she said.

'Yeah, he was a good man.'

'Was he a lawyer?'

'He taught southern history at the University of Texas, then he was in Congress two terms during Roosevelt's administration. He took me deer hunting once on John Nance Garner's ranch in Uvalde, but I was too small then to believe that the Vice President of the United States could chew on cigars and spit tobacco juice. My father had to convince me that Mr Jack really did work in an important capacity for the government.'

'Gee, what a great story,' she said.

'I shook hands with Roosevelt once at Warm Springs, too. I wanted to look at the metal braces on his legs, but his eyes were so intense and interested, even in a boy's conversation, that you couldn't glance away from them. I was full of all kinds of pride and sunshine when I realized that my father was a personal friend of this man. I watched them drink whiskey on the verandah together, and for the first time I knew my father had another life that I'd never imagined before.'

I drank the foam out of the bottle and looked at the summer haze on the river. It was a wonderful place. The juniper seeds on the water turned in swirls past the sandbars, and stray seagulls that had wandered far inland dipped and hovered over a dead gar on the mudbank.

'Go on,' she said. Her face was happy and so lovely in the broken shade that I had to swallow when I looked at her.

'I don't like people who show home movies,' I said.

'I do, especially cowboy lawyers that dig up old arrowheads.'

'I told you I'm shit and nails, didn't I? The Lone Ranger with a hangover.'

'You just think you're a bad man.'

'There are probably several hundred people who will disagree with you.'

'You're not even a good cynic.'

'You're taking away all my credentials.'

'Go on. Please.'

'The old man knew Woody Guthrie, too. He stayed at the house once during the war, and every evening I'd sit with him on the front steps while he played that beat-up old Stella guitar and his harmonica. He always wore a crushed felt hat, and when he spoke his words had a cadence like talking blues. He could never talk very long, at least while he had a guitar in his hands, without starting another song. He played with three steel banjo picks on his fingers, and he had the harmonica wired to a brace around his neck. He played Negro and workingmen's beer-joint blues so mean and fine that I didn't want him to ever leave. When we drove him to Galveston to catch a merchant ship my father asked him what the migrant farm workers thought of the movie *Grapes of Wrath*, and he said, "Most of the people I know ain't going to pay a quarter to see no more grapes, and I don't expect they need any more of this here wrath, either." '

'Wow, did your father know anybody else?'

'Those were the best ones. And I'm all out of stories, babe.'

'Your father must have been an unusual man.'

'Yes, he was.' I bit the tip off a cigar and looked at

the haze on the water and the line of willows beyond, and for just a moment, in the stillness and heat of the summer morning, in the time that the flame of my match burned upward in one sulfurous curl, I saw my father lying half out of the chair in the library, the circular explosion of gunpowder on the front of his cream-colored coat, with his mouth locked open as though he had one final statement to make. The pistol had flown from his dead hand with the weight of its own recoil, and his arm had caught behind him at a twisted angle in the chair. His eyes were receded and staring, and his grey hair hung down on his forehead like a child's. As I stood in the doorway, unable to move towards him, with the shot still loud in my ears and Bailey running down the stairs behind me, I thought: *It was his heart. He had to do it. He couldn't let it kill him first.*

'Hey, come in, world,' Rie said.

'The old man had rheumatic fever when he was a kid. All of the things he loved to do put his heart right in a vise.'

She touched the back of my hand with her fingers and looked quietly into my face. Her strands of sunburned hair were gold in the broken light through the cypress tree.

'All right, goddamn, how about opening another beer?' I said.

'You're a special kind of guy, Hack.'

'How did we get on this crap, anyway? Come on, girl. Get the beer open.'

'Okay, kemosabe.' Her eyes went flat, and she reached inside the sack of crushed ice.

'I mean, you're hurting my badass identity.'

She worked the opener on the bottle cap without answering.

'Say, Rie. Come on.'

'You kick doors shut real hard,' she said.

'Look, I behave like a sonofabitch so often that sometimes I don't think about who I'm talking to.'

'You don't like anyone to get inside you, and maybe that's cool, but you ought to hang out a sign for dumb chicks.'

'I'm sorry.'

'It's a swell day and you're still a piece of pie.'

I leaned over her and kissed her on the mouth. I felt her heavy breasts against me, and I slipped my arms under her back and kissed her forehead and her closed eyes and put my face in her hair. She breathed against my cheek and ran her hands under my shirt.

'Oh, Hack,' she said, and moved her whole body into me.

My blood raced and I could feel my heart clicking inside me. Each time I kissed her my head swam, my breath became short, and I felt myself dropping through her into the earth.

She put one leg in mine and held me closer and ran her fingernails up my neck through my hair. When she moved her body against me the dark green of the trees and the summer haze on the river seemed to spin in circles around me.

'I felt you kiss me last night. I didn't want you to stop,' she said. 'All night I wanted to feel you around me.'

'My southern ethic wouldn't let me take advantage of a bombed girl.'

'You have so many crazy things in your head, Lone

Ranger.' She moved her lips over my cheek and bit me on the neck, and then I couldn't stop it.

I put my hand under her shirt and felt her breasts. They swelled out each time she breathed and I could feel her heart beating under my palm. I unzippered her white shorts and touched her thighs and her flat stomach.

'I'm sorry for the woods. I should take you up the road, but you really got down inside me, babe,' I said.

She smiled and kissed me, and her almond eyes took on all the wonderful color and mysterious light that a woman's eyes can have when they make you weak with just a glance.

That evening we drove back through the hills and the baked fields of string beans and corn, and stopped at a roadside restaurant and beer tavern north of Rio Grande City for Mexican food. On the broken horizon the sun was orange behind clouds that looked as though they had been burned purple. The sky seemed so vast and empty in its darkening light that my head became dizzy in looking at it. (Sometimes, at moments like this, I felt a south Texas sunset was so hard I could strike a match against it.)

We finished dinner and drank bottles of Carta Blanca while two drunk cowboys played the jukebox and arm-wrestled with each other at the bar. We had chickory coffee, and I brought in my flask of Jack Daniels from the car and poured a shot into our cups. On the jukebox Lester Flatt and Earl Scruggs rolled out a Blue Ridge song, in their mournful southern accents, of ancient American loves and distant mountain trains:

I can hear the whistle blowing
High and lonely as can be
Each year is like some rolling freight train
Cold as starlight upon the rails.

I don't know if it was the whiskey (I eventually drained the whole flask into my cup), the events and emotional fatigue of the past two days, or my need to confess my guilt of fifteen years ago, or a combination of the three, but anyway I began to talk about Korea and then I told her all of it.

chapter eight

My legs were on fire as we marched the five miles along a frozen dirt road from the freight train to a temporary prison compound. The sky was lead gray, and the dark winter brown of the earth showed in patches through the ice and snow that covered the fields and hills. The few peasant farmhouses, made from mudbricks mixed with straw, were deserted, and at odd intervals across the fields there were old craters left from a stray bombing. Our Chinese guards, in their quilted uniforms and Mongolian hats, walked along beside us with their burpguns slung on straps at port arms, one gloved finger curled inside the trigger guard, hating us not only because we were Occidentals and the enemy but also for the cold and misery in their own bodies. When a man fell or couldn't keep pace with the line or find someone to help him walk he was pushed crying (or sometimes white and speechless in his terror) into the ditch and shot. The Chinese were thorough. Two and sometimes three guards would fire their burpguns into one shivering, helpless man.

By all chances I should have bought it somewhere along that five miles of frozen road. My pants legs were stiff with dried blood, and each step sent the flame in my wounds racing up my body and made my groin go weak with pain. I had never known that pain could be as prolonged and intense and unrelieved. I saw the guards kill six men and I heard them kill others behind me, and I knew that I was going to fall over soon and I would die just as the rest had, with my arms across my face and my knees drawn up to my chest in an embryonic position. But a Marine major from Billings, Montana, a huge man with lumberjack arms, caught me around the waist and held me up, even when I felt my knees collapse entirely and the horizon tilted quickly as in a feverish dream. His right ear was split and crusted with black blood, and his eyes were bright with control of his own pain, but it never showed in his voice and his arm stayed locked hard around my waist.

'Stay up, doc. We're going to need all of our corpsmen,' he said. 'Just throw one foot after another. Don't use your knees. You hear me, son? These bastards won't march us much farther.'

And for the next four miles we went down the road like two Siamese twins out of step with each other. That night the guards put us in a wooden schoolhouse surrounded by concertina wire, and in his sleep the major cried out once and tore open his mutilated ear with his fingernails.

Several months later I heard that he died of dysentery in the Bean Camp.

I was in three camps while I was a P.O.W. Whenever the complexion of the war changed or a new offensive was begun by one side or the other, the Chinese moved us in cattle cars or Russian trucks or on foot to a new camp where there was no chance of our being liberated, since we were an important bargaining chip at the peace talks. I spent two months at the Bean Camp, a compound of wretched wooden shacks used by the Japanese to hold British prisoners during World War II, and for reasons unknown to me, since I had no military knowledge worth anything to the North Koreans or the Chinese, I was singled out with twelve others, including two deranged Greeks, for transfer to Pak's Palace outside of Pyongyang. Major Pak conducted his interrogations in an abandoned brick factory, and each morning two guards led me across the brick yard covered with fine red dust to a small, dirty room that was bare except for two straight-backed chairs and the major's desk. A rope with a cinched loop in one end hung from a rafter, and when everything else failed the major would tie the hands of a prisoner behind him and have him drawn into the air by the arms and beaten with bamboo canes. It was called Pak's Swing, and the screams that came from that room were not like human sounds.

Major Pak's personality was subject to abrupt changes. Sometimes his eyes burned like those of a religious fanatic or an idealistic zealot who revered in the pain of his enemies. His tailored uniform was always immaculate, as though he were born to the professional military, but the wrong answer from a prisoner would make his face convulse with hatred and his screaming would become incoherent. Then moments later his eyes would water, his constricted throat would relax, and his voice would take on the tone of a tormented man who was forced to do things to people who couldn't understand the necessity of his job or the historical righteousness of his cause. The two Greeks suffered most from him, because he was sure that their insane, pathetic behavior was an act. Each night they were returned to our building streaked with blood and moaning in words that we couldn't understand.

The major also had fixations. He threatened to tear out my fingernails with pliers unless I told him where the 101st Airborne planned to drop into North Korea. I infuriated him when I answered that I was a Navy corpsman and that I had spent only six days on the line before capture. He believed that all Americans lied instinctively and looked down upon him as an Oriental of inferior intelligence. He struck me in the head with the pliers and cut my scalp, and as I leaned over with the blood trickling across my eye I waited for him to order the guards to draw me up on the rope. However, he threw a glass of water in my face and pulled my head up by the hair.

'Americans are weak. You can't accept pain for yourselves. You only expect others to bear it,' he said.

Then I realized that it really didn't matter to him whether or not I knew anything about the 101st Airborne. He hated me because I was everything which he identified with the young American archetype portrayed in *The Saturday Evening Post*: I was tall, blond, good-looking, unscarred by hunger or struggle or revolutions whose ideology was just rice. So Major Pak's interest in me was personal rather than of a military nature, and he soon tired of interrogating me in favor of a British commando who had been caught behind their lines, and I was sent back to the Bean Camp in a captured U.S. truck loaded with Australian prisoners.

But my recall deals primarily with Camp Five in No Name Valley, where I spent the greater portion of the war until I was exchanged at Freedom Village in 1953. Also, it was here that I learned that men can live with guilt and a loathsome image of themselves which previously they didn't believe themselves capable of enduring.

The Yalu River was north of our camp, and in the winter the ice expanded against the banks and rang in the cold silence at night, and sometimes we would hear it break up and crash in great yellow chunks at a turn in the current. The wind blew all the time, sweeping out of the bare hills across the river in China, and when there was no fuel in our shack we slept on the floor in a group, breathing the stench of our bodies under the blankets, the nauseating odor of fish heads on our breath, and the excretions of men with dysentery who couldn't control themselves in their sleep.

We were always cold during the winter. Even when we had fuel to burn in our small iron stove the heat would not radiate more than a few feet, and the wind drove through the cracks in the boards and would drop the temperature enough to freeze our jerrycan of water unless we kept it close to the fire. During the day the sun was a pale yellow orb in the sky, and the light was never strong enough through the grey winter haze to cast a hard shadow on the ground. Three men were taken out with a guard once a week to forage for wood, but the landscape was largely bare and the sticks and roots that hadn't already been picked up were now covered by ice and snow. We had one pair of mismatched knitted mittens in our shack, and when the wood detail went out one man would take the mittens and be responsible for gathering the largest share of fuel, as our fingers would often be left cut and swollen or discolored at the tips from frostbite after a day of ripping frozen sticks out of the snow.

There were oil stoves in the camp, but these went to the progressives, those who had signed peace petitions, confessions to participating in germ warfare, or absurdly worded statements denouncing Wall Street capitalists. The progressives were kept in two oblong buildings on the far side of the compound, separated from the rest of us by a barbed-wire fence and a wooden gate that stayed locked with a chain. Many of them were informers, or 'snitches,' and they would have been killed had they been forced to live with the rest of the prisoner population. In the morning they exercised in the yard behind the wire fence, their faces averted so they wouldn't have to look at the rest of us. They received the same diet as we did, bean cakes, millet, and boiled corn, but much more of it, and occasionally they were given some greens and hard-boiled eggs, and they didn't have to worry about beriberi and diarrhea that left your entrails and rectum burning day and night. I should have hated them for the weight on their bodies and the flush of health in their faces, the Red Cross packages they were given by the guards, but I was always too sick, cold, or afraid to care what they did on their side of the fence. Like most of the others I didn't believe that we would ever be liberated or exchanged. New prisoners told us that the Chinese had poured into South Korea, the ROKs had thrown down their weapons and run, and our forces were being pushed into the sea. So even the most optimistic and strong knew that freedom was probably years away, and our death rate in the camp averaged a dozen men a day.

Some died quietly in their sleep under their blankets, and in the morning we found them white and stiff, the skin hard as marble, and we dragged them outside the shack like pieces of stone and left them for the burial squad. Others died delirious with agony, their eyes feverish and rolling white in their heads, their inflamed entrails bulging out the colon like inflated rubber. There was nothing to do for them — no medicine, no priest, not even the option of killing out of mercy.

There were fifteen enlisted men in my shack (the Chinese kept the officers, NCOs, and enlisted men separated from one another so there would be no system of military order or authority among us). We spent our days in boredom or listening to ridiculous lectures by Colonel Ding and a 'group monitor,' one of the progressives whom Ding always brought with him. Ding was a small, thin man, with a harelip and a face that was as lifeless as wax. There were spaces between his front teeth, and when he ranted about imperialism and the American bombing of Pyongyang his disfigured mouth gave his face the appearance of a lunatic's. He was fond of telling us that he had attended the University of California for a year in the thirties, and also that he had been with Mao on the Great March. Many times he would digress from his tirades on the evils of the Western world and slip into a history of his own career, which seemed to give him a special pleasure. Sometimes he would ask where each of us was from, and then show the knowledge that he had of that area, although he often referred to such places as 'San Antonio, Missouri.' The group monitor was usually even more pathetic. He would stand behind the colonel, embarrassed, his gloved hands never able to find a pocket more than a few moments, and sometimes he would light a cigarette nervously, then pinch it out and put it back in the pack when our eyes looked into his. After the colonel had finished, the monitor would read to us from his journal, his self-deluding confession of guilt, and tell us that American troops were waging a war against innocent people and that we were as much victims of the defense industrialists as the people whom we killed. But his face always stayed buried in the notebook, as though he couldn't read his own handwriting, or he stared above our heads at the distant hills. Many times his words faltered and he would look helplessly at the colonel, who would only nod for him to go on. I suppose that I felt more pity towards the progressives than anger. They were cared for and would live, and eventually they would have to face some of us after the peace came.

However, our classes weren't merely an exercise in Marxist buffoonery. The Chinese knew a great deal about the effect of compromise on the individual. The progressives did not end up on the other side of the wire fence simply because they knew that the rations were better there. It was a gradual process, much like the irreversible stages of seduction portrayed in a stag movie. Most of us knew that it was a matter of time before we died of hunger or any of the diseases that accompanied it, and if we volunteered for Ding's classes, although it was never stated, we knew that the guards would put extra bean cakes in our shack's food bucket at night. And once we were in the classes all we had to do was sign a non-political peace petition, asking in the most general terms for an end to the war (supposedly these were sent to the United

Nations), and our millet would include fish heads, which we could boil into broth with roots and give to those who had the worst cases of dysentery. Then if we wanted an occasional hardboiled egg or a package of tobacco for the shack, we could say a couple of sentences against war into a tape recorder without identifying ourselves. Many nights we sat close to the small stove in silence, the honey bucket reeking in the corner, and thought about the next stage in the progression. Sometimes we would discuss the morality of signing a peace petition or whether or not it was all right to do it if you misspelled your name or gave your serial number incorrectly, since someone would surely know that you didn't mean it after all and you had beaten the Chinese at their own game, and I thought of Chaucerian monks debating the virtue of their fornication.

'Fuck it. I'm going to sign what the bastard wants,' one man would say. 'Nobody believes that shit, anyway. It probably don't even go out of camp. Ding gets his rocks off and we get some more chow. It's just a piece of paper. He probably wipes his ass with it.'

We wrote journals for Colonel Ding, confessing imaginary sins and describing the poverty of our lives in America (many times this was done as much to relieve our boredom as it was to earn extra rations). He particularly liked descriptions of slums and sweatshops. Often we would collaborate on one journal and invent accounts of social injustice that would make Charles Dickens pale. Orphans were beaten with whips by Catholic nuns, virtuous young girls were forced into prostitution and infected with venereal disease by fat bankers, southern policemen fired their pistols from car windows into Negro homes, a dismal pall of despair and political oppression hung over the tenement buildings of the working classes while Zionists with faces like sleek pigs filled their bank accounts with the profits of war. We all had committed every type of sin, from sodomy and incest to fornication with sheep. In the candle light at night we revered in our iniquity and wrote detailed histories of ax murders, arson, screwing a dead woman, and male rape in the shower at the Y.M.C.A. No group of men had ever been guilty of greater crimes, and the more depraved the confession the more generous Ding became towards his captives.

We all grew to know each other in the intimate and physical way that men do when in confinement. There was no secret shame or weakness that one of us could conceal from the others for very long. We shared our love affairs, our nights of depravity in Japanese brothels, our memories of a beating by a bully on the elementary school ground, our failures with wives and company bosses. We knew each other's smell, latrine habits, particular nightmares, or when one man was masturbating under the blanket. Through hunger and fear our virtues and inadequacies burned just below the skin. When one man in the shack died and was replaced by a new prisoner, we knew him within a week as well as we had the lifeless piece of stone we had dragged out into the compound for the burial detail.

We were of every background and mental complexion; the helpless who already had the smell of their dying in their clothes; the strong ones, the gladiators, with iron in their bodies, who knew they could live through anything and boiled their fish heads into broth for the sick; the brave and the terrified, the cowards and the Shylocks, the hoarders, the dealers, the religious, and those whose self-sacrifice made them glow, in the hush of their deaths, with the aura of early martyrs. There was Joe Bob Winfield from Baton Rouge, a redneck hillbilly and an ex-convict at nineteen, with leg-iron scars on his ankles and a story about every type of crime and prison caper; Bertie Fast, the house mouse, our one roaring homosexual, who was raped his first week in camp and liked it so much that he went professional; a Sears Roebuck shoe salesman from Salt Lake who wrote endless letters to his wife and children which Ding threw in the garbage can; O. J. Benson from Okema, Oklahoma, a bootlegger who used to run whiskey from Joplin in a bookmobile before the war; a reactivated World War II paratrooper, the oldest man in the shack, who had spent two years in a German concentration camp; Cigarette Williams, the other Navy corpsman, from Mount Olive, Alabama, a six-foot-five country singer who hanged himself during the night because his feet were so frostbitten he couldn't put boots on them; the Australian miner who called Ding a bloody yellow nigger and was strung up all day on a rafter by his hands; and the wild Turk who knew no English, a man on fire, a killer with insane eyes and a bricklayer's kowel hidden in his tick mattress.

There were many others who came and died or were transferred for interrogation, but only two of them from my shack are important in this brief account of my Korean experience. Pfc. Francis Ramos from San Angelo had Indian-black hair, wide-set intense eyes, hard bones in his face, and hands and wrists that could break boards in half. He used to drive a beer truck before he was drafted, and the muscles in his shoulders and chest were as taut and hard as concrete from years of loading and stacking metal beer kegs. There were white scars on his knuckles where they had been mashed on a warehouse ramp, and another thick, raised scar that he had received in a whorehouse brawl ran back in a crooked line through his hair. He had an obsession with escape. He had spent six months in a city stockade once for nonsupport, and he was released only after the jailer became convinced that he was mad, and solitary confinement and beatings with rolled newspapers would not make him less of a threat to the guards and the rest of the prison population. He had been Golden Gloves middleweight champion of Texas in high school, and sometimes when I looked at his huge fists and the swollen veins in his wrists I had nightmarish images of what he must have done to his opponents in the ring.

He couldn't sleep at night. After Sergeant Tien Kwong handed us our food bucket and locked the chain on the shack door, Ramos's eyes flicked wildly across the walls and ceilings, his breathing became deeper, and then he would set about doing dozens of unnecessary things with the frenetic energy of a man on the edge of hysteria. He put fuel into the stove when we were trying to conserve every twig, boiled water to make soup when we had no fish heads, shook out his blankets and folded them so he could unfold them again, restrung his bootlaces, tried to teach the wild Turk English, and eventually sat alone in the darkness after the rest of us had gone to sleep. He would be so tired the next day that sometimes his head would fall on his chest during one of Ding's lectures, which meant one night in the hole under the sewer grate.

Then there was Airman First Class Lester Dixon, captured when the Chinese overran Seoul, a teenage hoodlum from Chicago, one of the dealers, a ten percenter, a poolroom hustler and reefer salesman on the South Side, slick, a kid with a venal mind and an eye for the profit to be made from free enterprise, blue movies, dope, and fifteen-year-old Negro prostitutes. He had tattoos of skulls and snakes' heads on his arms, and his hair had grown out long enough to comb back in ducktails. His colorless face was like the edge of a hatchet. He thought of charity as naïveté, bravery as stupidity, and honesty with others, even in a prisoner of war compound, a fool's venture.

He shared nothing. He stood first in line for his bean cakes and millet, and ate alone from his tin plate in one corner while the rest of us put small bits of our food into the soup pot on the stove for the Australian who was dying of beriberi. He was never ashamed of not sharing, or at least he didn't show it; he ate with his face in his plate, his chopsticks scraping against the metal, as though his whole being were concentrated into one scrap of bean cake that he might miss.

It was a cold, windswept gray morning with hailstones on the ground, and Dixon had just left the shack with the wood detail.

'I think he's a snitch,' Ramos said. 'I seen him eating some vitamin pills in the dark last night.'

We were hunched around the iron stove, bent forward towards the heat. Our breaths steamed out like ice in the silence.

'Are you sure?' I said.

'He took three of them out of his pocket and swallowed them dry.'

'I don't know about no vitamin pills,' Joe Bob, our ex-convict, said, 'but I got something in my pecker that goes off when I get near a snitch, and that boy gives me a real bone.'

'If you're right, what are we going to do with him?' another man said.

'For openers, you better start shutting up about running,' Joe Bob said. His sandy red hair stuck out from under his stocking cap, and he chewed on the flattened end of a matchstick in one corner of his mouth.

'We ice him,' Ramos said.

'Hey, cut that shit, man,' Joe Bob said. 'Ding'll waste the whole shack.'

'No, he ain't,' Ramos said. 'I'll tell Kwong that Dixon's been spitting blood and ask him for some eggs, and then we wait a few days and smother him.'

'I tell you, buddy, they ain't that stupid,' Joe Bob said.

'We got to take him out one way or another,' O. J., the bootlegger from Okema, said. 'If Ding's greasing him, he's got to burn somebody.'

'Yeah, you don't fuck around with guys like this.'

'There's other ways to get a snitch out of the shack,' Joe Bob said. 'We can turn the Turk loose on him, and he'll ask Ding to transfer over with the pros.'

'You're not sure about him, anyway,' I said. 'He could have gotten those pills off of somebody else in the yard.'

'You know that's a lot of crap, too, Holland. He smelled like a snitch when he first come in here,' Ramos said.

'He's a pimp and a wheeler, and that's all he's been his whole life. That doesn't mean he's working for Ding,' I said.

'I'll do it in the middle of the night,' Ramos said. 'There won't be no sound, and he'll look just like every other guy we drug out in the yard.'

'I ain't telling you what to do,' Joe Bob said, 'but you got some pretty amateur shit in your head for this kind of scene. Ding might be a harelip dickhead, but he ain't dumb and he's going to fry our balls in a skillet before you get done with this caper.'

'The sonofabitch has to go. What else are we going to do with him?' O. J. said.

'If you got to ice him, use your head a minute and do it out in the yard,' Joe Bob said. 'Catch him in a bunch during exercise time and bust him open with the Turk's trowel. You'll probably get shot, anyway, but maybe the rest of us won't get knocked off with you.'

'If you don't want in it, just stay out of my face,' Ramos said.

'Like I said, I ain't trying to grow any hairs in your asshole. You just don't know what you're doing. Like this escape caper. I chain-ganged in the roughest joint in the South, and I started to run once myself, but you got to be out of your goddamn mind to try and crack a place like this. You got two fences to cut through, there's a hundred yards of bare ground between both of them, and them gooks up on the platform ain't going to be reading fortune cookies while you're hauling for Dixie. You better get your head rewired before Ding lays you out in the yard like he done to that Greek that took off from the wood detail.'

'If I get nailed I'll buy it running on the other side of

that wire,' Ramos said. 'I ain't going to stay here and shit my insides out till somebody rolls me into the yard like a tumblebug. There's a colored sergeant with a compass and some pliers for the fence, and he figures if we can make it to the sea we can steal a boat and get out far enough for one of our choppers to pick us up.'

'Goddamn, if that ain't a real pistol, Ramos. I once knew a guy that climbed into the back of a garbage truck with chains on, buried himself in the trash, and rode down the highway with the hacks looking all over for him. Except he almost got fried when they unloaded the truck in the county incinerator. But you got him beat, buddy. Running across North Korea with a nigra. Now that's cool. You guys ought to stand out like shit in an ice cream factory.'

Ramos didn't say anything more. He glared at the grey ash in the grate awhile, then paced around the shack, beating his arms in the cold. He didn't have the intelligence or prison experience to argue with Joe Bob, but we knew that he planned to kill Dixon, regardless of what anyone said.

And it wasn't long before Dixon knew it, too. He came in from the wood detail late that afternoon, his face red and chafed with windburn, and dropped a load of sticks and roots by the stove. There was snow in his hair, and his quilted pants were wet up to the knees. In the silence we heard Kwong lock the chain on the door. Dixon pulled off his mittens with his teeth and stuck his hands under his armpits.

'Somebody else is going on that bastard next time,' he said. 'That whole goddamn field's picked clean. I broke two finger-nails digging down to the ground.'

No one answered.

'Shit, look at them.'

We turned our faces away or found things to do that would remove us from the eventual meeting of eyes between Ramos and Dixon. But instead it was O. J. and Bertie Fast, the drag queen, who tore open the wrapper and let Dixon look for just a moment inside the box.

'What is this crap, anyway?' Dixon said. 'Maybe I didn't wipe my ass clean this morning or something. Don't I smell sweet enough to you, house mouse?'

'I didn't say anything,' Bertie said, his voice weak and his eyes searching for a spot on the far wall.

'House mouse, you better not hold out on me.'

'Fuck off, man,' O. J. said. He was sticking twigs into the fire grate, and his jawbones were flat against the skin.

'What's the deal, then?' Dixon said. 'You want me to kick in part of my chow for the soup? Okay. No sweat. Is everybody cool now?'

'Where did you get vitamin pills?' O. J. said.

'Vitamins? You must have a wild crab loose in your brain.' But he was surprised, and there was a flicker of fear in his face.

'Yeah. Like those little red ones Ding gives to the pros,' O. J. said.

'You better see a wig mechanic when you get out of here. You got real problems.'

'You're holding a hot turd with both hands, buddy,' Joe Bob said. 'This ain't the time for none of that smart-ass Yankee jive.'

'You guys have been flogging your meat too much or something. I mean what kind of joint is this, anyway? I spend the whole day digging in the ice with

Kwong jabbing me in the ass, and I come back and you guys got me nailed for a pro.'

'How did you get the pills?' I said.

Everyone was looking at him now. The snow in his hair had melted, and his face was damp with water and perspiration. He held his two bruised fingers in one hand and glanced at the locked door.

'I traded them off a spade in the yard for some cigarettes. All right, so I didn't share them. Big deal. You going to tear my balls out because I want to stay alive?'

'Which spade?' O. J. said.

'I don't know. He's with the NCOs.'

'There ain't but one over there,' Ramos said.

'Maybe he's an enlisted man. What difference does it make? All those boons look alike.'

'Get it straight, cousin. That turd is melting in your hand,' Joe Bob said.

'You guys already want to fry me. It don't make any difference what I say. You've been pissed ever since I come in here because I wouldn't put in my chow for guys that were already dead. All of you got a purple heart nailed right up in the middle of your forehead because you keep some poor sonofabitch alive a few extra days so he can shit more blood and chew his tongue raw. If I buy it I hope there ain't a bunch like you around.'

'Okay, you got the pills off a colored sergeant,' Ramos said. He sat cross-legged on his blanket close to the stove, rubbing his dirt-caked bare feet with his hand. 'That's all we wanted to know. Next time you share anything you get in the yard.'

Dixon stared into Ramos's face, and then realized that he was looking at his executioner.

'Not me, buddy,' he said. 'You're not going to stick my head down in the mattress. None of you pricks are. You find some other cat to hang a frame on. How about Bertie here? He don't keep his ass soft and fat on bean cakes.'

'Quit shouting. There ain't anybody going to bother you,' Ramos said. 'Just don't try to bullshit us next time.'

'No, you're going to ice me. You been wanting to do it a long time, you spick, and now you got these other bastards to go in with you. Hey, Kwong!' He began beating against the wooden door with his fists and kicking his feet into the boards. The chain and padlock reverberated with the blows.

'You get down here. You hear me? I want to see Ding!'

O. J. and Ramos started for him at the same time, but Joe Bob jumped up in front of both of them and stiff-armed them with all his weight in the chest.

'The shit already hit the fan. Just ride it out and stay cool,' he said.

We heard Kwong running through the frozen snow outside. Dixon's face was white with fear, and he brought his knees into the door as though they could splinter wood and snap metal chain after his feet and fists had failed. Kwong turned the lock and threw open the door, with his burpgun slung on a leather strap around his neck and the barrel pointed like an angry god into the middle of us. His squat, thick body was framed against the grey light and the snow-covered shacks behind him, and his peasant face was concentrated in both anger and anticipation of challenge. He grabbed Dixon by his coat and threw him into the snow, then flicked off the safety on his gun.

'Crazy,' Joe Bob said, pointing to his head. 'He had the shits all week. *Shea tu.* Blood coming out his hole.'

We were all frozen in front of the burpgun, each of us breathing deep in our chests, our hearts clicking like dollar watches. I couldn't look at the gun. Dixon got to his knees in the snow and started crying.

'He needs medicine,' Joe Bob said, and held his head back and pointed his thumb into his mouth. 'Shits all the time. Got shit in his brain.'

'You fucked,' Kwong said, and kicked the door shut with his foot, then locked the chain.

He must have hit Dixon with the stock of his burpgun, because we could hear the wood knock into bone, then the two of them crunched off in the snow towards Ding's billet on the other side of the wire.

The next morning at dawn Kwong was back with two other guards. They opened the door and motioned us against the far wall of the shack with their guns before they stepped inside. The fire in the stove had died out during the night, and the room temperature must have been close to zero. We stood in our socks, shivering under the blankets we held around our shoulders, and tried to look back steadily at Kwong while his eyes passed from face to face. He already knew the ones who had been chosen for the first interrogation, but he enjoyed watching us hang from fishhooks. Then he motioned his burpgun at five of us: O. J., Bertie Fast, Joe Bob, the Turk, and me. We sat down in the middle of the floor and laced on our boots, then marched in single file across the yard with the guards on each side of us. The pale sun had just risen coldly over the hills, and as I looked at our dim shadows on the snow I felt that my last morning was now in progress, and that I should have bought it back there in the Shooting Gallery and whoever shuffles the cards had just discovered his mistake and was about to set things straight.

The wounds in my legs had never healed and had become infected, and when I slowed my pace in the snow Kwong jabbed the barrel of his gun into my scalp. I felt the skin split and I fell forward on my hands and knees. Kwong kicked me in the kidney and pulled me erect by my hair.

'You walk, cocksuck,' he said.

I put my arm over Joe Bob's shoulder, my side in flames, and limped along with the others to the yellow brick building that Ding used for his headquarters. Bertie Fast's eyes were wide with terror, and I could see the pulse jumping in his neck. He looked like a chill in his oversized quilted uniform and all the blood had drained out of his soft, feminine face. Even Joe Bob, with scars from the black Betty on his butt, was afraid, although he held it down inside himself like a piece of sharp metal. But the wild Turk showed no fear at all, or possibly he didn't even know what was taking place. His hot black eyes stared out of his white, twisted face, and I wondered if he had the trowel hidden somewhere inside his clothes. His tangled black hair had grown over his shoulders, and he breathed great clouds of vapor, as though he had a fever, through his rotted teeth. He stood immobile with the rest of us while Kwong knocked on the door, and I thought that beyond those hot black eyes there was a furnace instead of a brain.

Ding sat behind his desk in his starched, high-collar uniform with a tea service in front of him. Dixon stood in one corner by the oil stove, his face heavy with lack of sleep, and there was a large, swollen knot above his right eyebrow. His eyes fixed on Ding's desk when we entered the room, and drops of sweat slid down his forehead in the red glow of the stove.

Ding finished his tea, flicked a finger for a guard to remove the tray, and lit a Russian cigarette. He leaned forward on his elbows, puffing with his harelip, his eyes concentrated like BB's into the smoke, and I knew that we were all going to enact a long and painful ritual that would compensate Ding in part for his lack of a field command.

'I know there's a plan for an escape,' he said, quietly. 'It's a very foolish plan that will bring you hardship. There has never been an escape from a Chinese People's detention center, and you're hundreds of miles from the American lines. Now, this can be very easy for you, and it will also help the men who would be shot in trying to escape. Give me their names and you can return to your building, and nothing will be done to the men involved.'

We stood in silence, and the snow melted off our clothes in the warmth of the room. I looked at Dixon, and for a moment I wished that Ramos had killed him as soon as he had come back from the wood detail. The cut in my scalp was swelling and drawing tight, and my legs felt unsteady from fear and the pain in my calves.

'You're not in a cowboy movie,' Ding said. 'None of you are heroes. You're simply stupid. I don't want to punish you. I don't want to see the other men shot. There's no reason for it. This war will be over someday and all of you can return to your families. it's insane for you men to die in trying to escape.'

Our eyes were flat, our faces expressionless, and the

room was so quiet that I could hear Kwong shifting the weight of his burpgun on its strap.

'Do you want me to punish all of the men in your building?' Ding said. 'Do you want to see the sick Australian punished because of a stupid minority? All of you grow up on silly movies about Americans smiling at death. You think the Chinese are busboys in restaurants and laundrymen for your dirty clothes. You believe your white skin and Western intelligence reduces us to fools in pigtails groveling for your tips.'

'We don't know about no escape, Colonel,' Joe Bob said. 'Nobody can crack this joint. Dixon give you a lot of shit last night.'

'You do think we're stupid, don't you?'

'No, sir, we don't. I done time before, Colonel, and I don't want to get burned because some jerk wants to run. Believe me, there ain't no break planned.'

'What do you have to say, airman?' Ding said, and turned towards Dixon.

Dixon's face blanched and he swallowed in his throat. He hadn't thought it was going to be this tough. His eyes looked up at us quickly and then fixed on the desk again. His words were heavy with phlegm. 'It's like I told you, Colonel. They been planning it a long time.'

'How long?'

'I heard them whispering about it in the corner the other night after they blew out the candle.'

'Which ones?' Ding drew in on the cigarette and looked at Dixon flatly through the smoke. He was really tightening the rack now, and he enjoyed tormenting Dixon as much as he did us.

'All of them, I guess. It was dark.'

'You haven't told me very much to earn all those extra gifts.'

Dixon's face flushed and drops of sweat began dripping from his hair.

'You should move away from the stove,' Ding said. 'It's bad for you to become overheated.'

'Colonel, we ain't trying to con you,' O. J. said. 'We got on Dixon because he wouldn't share nothing and he was eating vitamin pills, and he thought we was going to knock him around. He went off his nut and started beating on the door and screaming for Kwong. There wasn't no more to it.'

'Would you like to say something, private?'

'No, sir,' Bertie said. I had to turn and look at him. His voice was high with fear, but I didn't believe the resolve that was there, also.

'Do you want to suffer with these other men?'

'They told you the truth, Colonel. There ain't any break.'

'You haven't spoken. Would you like a turn?' Ding said to me, and at that moment I hated him more than any other human being on earth, not merely for his cruelty but also for the mental degradation that he could continue indefinitely with his physical power over us.

'There's nothing to say, sir. Dixon lied.' I wouldn't let my eyes focus on his face, but he sensed my hatred towards him, anyway, and he smiled with that crooked harelip.

'So the corpsman believes me stupid, too. What are we going to do with you American fighting men? That's how you're called at home, isn't it? What would you suggest if you had my position? Intelligent Western men like you must have suggestions. You're a

Texan, aren't you, corpsman? You must have learned many lines from cowboy movies.'

'They gave it to you straight, Colonel.'

'He was one of them last night,' Dixon said. 'They were going to smother me in my sleep.'

(At the time I would have never guessed that the terrified man in the corner, sweating in the heat of the stove, would one day have his picture on the front page of newspapers all over the world as one of the twenty-two American turncoats who chose to remain in Red China after the peace was signed. However, the photograph would show him with full, clean-shaved cheeks, his cap pointed neatly over one eye, a redblooded enlistee fresh out of the Chicago pool-rooms.)

'Then maybe we should begin with you, corpsman,' Ding said, and motioned Kwong with his hand.

The sergeant slammed me down in the wooden chair in front of the desk. Ding lit another cigarette and dropped the burnt match into a butt can. The room was now close with the smell of our bodies and the cigarette smoke. I could almost feel the cruel energy and expectation in Kwong's body behind me.

'Do you want this to be prolonged, or do you want to talk in an intelligent manner?'

I stared into nothing, my shoulders hunched and my hands limp in my lap. I could hear the Turk breathing through his teeth in the silence. Kwong slapped me full across the face with his callused hand. My eyes watered and I could feel the blood burning in the skin.

'Do you think you're in a movie now, corpsman?' Ding said. 'Are the Flying Tigers going to drop out of the sky and kill all the little yellow men around you?'

I stared through my wet eyes at the wall. The lines in the room looked warped, glittering with moisture, and the oil stove burned brightly red in one corner of my vision. Ding nodded to the sergeant, an indifferent and casual movement of maybe an inch, and Kwong brought my head down with both hands into his knee and smashed my nose. The blood burst across my face, my head exploded with light, and I was sure the bone had been knocked back into the brain. I was bent double in the chair, the blood pouring out through my hands, and each time I tried to clear my throat I gagged on a clot of phlegm and started the dry heaves.

'He don't know nothing, Colonel,' Joe Bob said. 'Sometimes the guys bullshit about escape, but he don't even do that. He knows they're bullshitting and he always walks away from it. He don't have no names to give you.'

'Would you like to give me some names?'

'It ain't nothing but guys setting around shifting each other about a break, Colonel. Anybody in a joint does the same thing, or you start beating your rod with sandpaper after a while. Dixon's a goddamn fish and he couldn't cut it, so he sold you a lot of jive.'

'Your corpsman hasn't been hurt at all. The sergeant can do many other things to him.'

'I know that, sir,' Joe Bob said. 'It just won't do no good. He can't tell you nothing.'

'Then I think you should take his chair,' Ding said.

My hands were covered with blood and saliva, and I was still choking on my breath, but I wanted to go over Ding's desk and get my thumbs into his throat. However, I never got the chance to learn if I was that brave or desperate with pain and hatred, because the

Turk suddenly stopped breathing a moment, his white face filling with dark areas of rage, and his hot, black eyes glared insanely. Then he shouted once, a bull's roar that came out of some awful thing inside him, and he started for Ding with his huge hands raised in fists over his head.

Kwong stepped quickly in front of him and swung the stock of his burpgun upward into the Turk's mouth. I could hear his teeth break against the wood. He reeled backward on the floor, his lips cut open in blue gashes, then Kwong raised his foot back, poised himself, and kicked him in the stomach. The Turk's breath rushed out in a long, rattling gasp, he drew his knees up to his chin, and his face went perfectly white. His mouth worked silently, the veins rigid in his throat, and his eyes were glazed with pain like a dumb, strangling animal's.

Ding was on his feet, shouting in Chinese at Kwong. His waxlike face was enraged, and he kept stabbing one finger in the air at some point outside the building.

'He's crazy, Colonel,' Joe Bob said. 'A stir freak. He probably don't even know where he is.'

'You wouldn't behave intelligently,' Ding yelled. 'You stand there with your confident faces and think you're dealing with comical peasants. You're stupid men that have to be treated as such.'

Kwong pulled me out of the chair by my collar and pushed me towards the door, then he began kicking the Turk in the spine. The Turk's breath came in spasms, and when he tried to suck air down into his lungs the blood bubbled on his lips.

'Pick him up and carry him!'

Joe Bob and O. J. lifted him between them by the

arms. His dirty, black hair hung over his face, and his chest heaved up and down.

'Look, Colonel, we ain't to blame for what some nut does,' Joe Bob said. 'He ain't much better than that with us. We got to watch him all the time.'

Ding spoke again in Chinese to Kwong and the other two guards, and they levered their burpguns at us and motioned towards the door.

'They're going to kill us,' O. J. said.

'Colonel, it ain't fair,' Joe Bob said. 'We never give you no trouble out of our shack.'

'I told you it could have been very easy for you.'

'There wasn't nothing to tell you,' O. J. said. 'Do we got to lose our lives because we give it to you straight?'

'Fuck it,' Joe Bob said. 'They're going to waste us, anyway.'

Kwong hit him in the ear with his fist and pushed us outside. It had started to sleet, and the ice crunched like stones under our feet. The sun was a hazy puff of vapor above the cold hills, and then we saw a lone F-86 bank out of the snow clouds and begin its turn before it reached the Yalu River. It dipped its wings once, as all our planes did when they passed over the camp, and then soared away into a small speck on the southern horizon. We stopped at the work shack, and each of us was given a G.I. entrenching tool. The Turk dropped his in the snow, and Kwong picked it up and punched it hard into his chest.

'You hold, cocksuck,' he said.

Kwong chained the door shut, and we marched across the compound, past the silent faces of the progressives who watched us from their exercise yard, past the few men who had stopped scrubbing out the lice from their clothes under the iron pump, past our own shack and the men inside who were pressed up against the cracks in the wall, and finally into the no-man's-land between the two fences that surrounded the camp.

'Here. You dig hole,' Kwong said.

'Oh, my God,' Bertie said.

'You dig to put in shit.' He kicked five evenly spaced places in the snow, and then raised his burpgun level with one hand.

We folded our entrenching tools down like hoes and started chopping through the ice into the frozen ground. The bridge of my nose was throbbing and the blood had congealed in my nostrils. I had to breathe through my teeth, and the air cut into my chest like metal each time I took a swing. The Turk knelt in a melted depression around him, thudding his shovel into the ground, while large crimson drops dripped from his mouth into the snow. I raised my eyes and saw the compound filling with men. The guards were unlocking all the shacks while Ding delivered a harangue through a megaphone. He had his back to us and I couldn't understand the electronic echo of his words, but I knew the compound was receiving a lesson in the need for cooperation between prisoner and captor. Hundreds of faces stared at us through the wire, the steam from their breaths rising into the air, and I began to pray that in some way their concentrated wills could prevent Kwong from dumping that pan of bullets into our bodies.

He walked back and forth in front of us, his eyes bright, his hand rubbing the top of the ventilated barrel. His face was as tight and flat as a shingle, and when one man slowed in his digging he jabbed the gun hard into his neck. Some of the prisoners said Kwong had been a train brakeman in North Korea before the war and that all of his family had been killed in the first American bombings. So he enjoyed his work with Americans. And now he was at his best, in his broken English, with the loading lever on the magazine pulled all the way back.

'Deep. No smell later,' he said.

We were down two feet, the mud and broken ice piled around us. I was sweating inside my clothes, and strange sounds lifted in chorus and disappeared in my mind. The wind polished the snow smooth in front of me, rolling small crystals across Kwong's boots. His leather laces were tied in knots across the metal eyes. The sleet had stopped, and the shadow of my body and the extended shovel moved about as a separate, broken self on the pile of dirt and ice that grew larger on the edge of my hole.

'I ain't going to buy it like this,' O. J. said. 'I ain't going to do the work for these bastards.'

'You dig deep,' Kwong said.

'You dig it.'

'Pick up shovel,' Kwong said.

'Fuck you, slope.' O. J. breathed rapidly, and the moisture from his nose froze on his lip.

'All stand, then.'

'Mother of God, he's going to do it,' Bertie said.

The sun broke from behind a cloud, the first hard yellow light I had seen since I had come to the camp. My eyes blinked against the glaring whiteness of the compound and the hills. The ice on the barbed wire glittered in the light, and the hundreds of prisoners watching us beyond the fence stared upward at the sky in unison, their wan faces covered with sunshine.

The stiff outlines of the buildings in the compound leaped at me and receded, and then Kwong turned his burpgun sideways so that the first burst and recoil would carry the spray of bullets across all five of us.

'You stand!'

We got to our feet slowly, our clothes steaming in the reflected warmth of the sun, and stood motionless in front of our graves. My body shook and I wanted to urinate, and my eyes couldn't look directly at the muzzle of his burpgun. I choked in my throat on a clot of blood and gagged on my hand. Joe Bob's face was drawn tight against the bone, and Bertie was shaking uncontrollably. O. J.'s arms were stiff by his sides, his hands balled into fists, and there were spots of color on the back of his neck. The Turk's heavy shoulders were bent, his ragged mouth hung open, and the blood and phlegm on his chin dripped on the front of his coat.

'You want talk Ding now?' Kwong said, and smiled at us.

No one spoke. The line of men behind the fence was silent, immobile, some of their heads turned away.

'Who first?'

'Do it, you goddamn bastard!' O. J. shouted. Then his eyes watered and he stared at his feet.

'You first, then, cocksuck.' Kwong raised the burpgun to his shoulder and aimed into O. J.'s face, his eyes bright over the barrel, a spot of saliva in the corner of his mouth. He waited seconds while O. J.'s breath trembled in his throat, then suddenly he swung the gun on its strap and began firing from the waist into the Turk. The first burst caught him in the stomach and chest, and he was knocked backward by the impact into the grave with his arms and legs outspread. The quilted padding in his coat exploded with holes, and one bullet struck him in the chin and blew out the back of his head. His black eyes were dead and frozen with surprise before he hit the ground, and a piece of broken tooth stuck to his lower lip. Kwong stepped to the edge of the grave and emptied his gun, blowing the face and groin apart while the brass shells ejected into the snow. When the chamber locked open he pulled the pan off, inserted a fresh one in its place, and slid back the loading lever with his thumb. The other two guards began to kick snow and dirt from the edge of the grave on top of the Turk's body.

'You next, corpsman. But you kneel.'

The wire fence and the empty faces behind it, the wooden shacks, the yellow brick building where it had all begun, Kwong's squat body and the hills and the brilliance of the snow in the sunlight began to spin around me as though my vision couldn't hold one object in place. My knees went weak and I felt excrement running down my buttocks. The wind spun clouds of powdered snow into the light.

Kwong shoved me backwards into the hole, then leaned over me and pushed the gun barrel into my face. His nostrils were wide and clotted with mucus in the cold.

'You suck. We give you boiled egg,' he said.

I clinched my hands and put my arms over my face. There were crystals of snow, like pieces of glass, in my eyes, and he brought his boot heel down into my stomach and forced the barrel against my teeth. My bowels gave loose entirely, a warm rush across my genitals and thighs, and my heart twisted violently in my chest.

'Good-bye, prick. You no stink so bad later,' and he pulled the trigger.

The chamber snapped empty, a metallic clack that sent all the air rushing out of my lungs.

Kwong and the other two guards were laughing, their faces split in hideous grins under their fur caps. Their bodies seemed to shimmer in the brilliant light. Kwong pushed his boot softly into my groin, pinching downward with the toe.

'I put new clip in and we do again. Each time you guess.'

He spoke to one of the other guards, who handed him a second clip, then he pulled the empty one loose from his burpgun and held them both behind his back.

'Which hand you like, corpsman?'

'You fucking chink. Get it done!' Joe Bob said.

The guard who had given Kwong the clip struck him back and forth across the face with his open hand. Joe Bob's arms hung at his sides while his head twisted and his skin rang and discolored with each slap.

'I pick for you, then,' Kwong said, and he dropped one pan into the snow and snapped the second one into the magazine.

He stood above me, his gun balanced on its strap against his waist, and we went through it again, except this time I curled into a ball like a child, my hands over my face, a sickening odor rising from my clothes, and when the firing pin hit the empty chamber I vomited a thick yellow residue of millet and fish heads out of my stomach.

Then I heard Ding speak in Chinese through the megaphone on the far side of the fence. Kwong's boots stepped backward, and I saw the shadow of his burpgun swinging loose from his body. But I couldn't move. My heart thundered against my chest, my body was drained of any further physical resistance, and I kept my face pressed into the wetness of my coat sleeves. 'You lucky. All go to hole now. Another time we have class.'

I heard Joe Bob, Bertie, and O. J. crunch past me, but I still couldn't lift my head. The other two guards picked me up from the grave by my coat and threw me headlong into the snow. The crystals of ice burned on my face and in my eyes. I got to my feet slowly and stood in a bent position, the compound and the hills shrinking away in the distance and then leaping towards me out of the sunlight. I tried to stand erect, and an electric pain burst through the small of my back and rushed upward into my head. Excrement dripped down my calves into the snow. I looked over at the half-covered body of the Turk in his shallow grave. One glaring eye was exposed through the snow, and his curled fingers extended upward as though he wanted to touch his toes. In seconds it seemed that the others were already far ahead of me, crunching silently between the guards towards the far end of the compound. Kwong pushed me forward between the shoulder blades with his hand, and I stumbled along in the slick, wet tracks of the others, tripping on my bootlaces, to the square of barbed wire and row of holes and sewer grates where Ding put the reactionaries.

One of the guards opened the gate and used an ice hook to pull the grates off four holes. Three occupied holes were still covered with tarpaulins from the night before, the creased canvas heavy and stiff with new snow. Ding pushed me forward with his burpgun at port arms into the first hole and kicked a G.I. helmet in on top of me, then slid the grate back in place. He squatted down and leaned his face in silhouette over me.

'You can play with prick when you get cold tonight,' he said.

The hole was eight feet deep and four feet wide, and the mud walls were covered with a dirty film of ice. The inside of the steel helmet was encrusted and foul from the other men who had used it, and the sour smell of urine had soaked into the floor. I heard the grates dropped heavily into place on the other three holes, then the guards moved away in the snow and chained the wire gate shut.

I spent the next six weeks there, although I lost any concept of time after the first three days. We were each given two blankets, and at night the guards marched a progressive into the wire square, and he emptied out our helmets and handed down our food pans before they covered the grates with the tarpaulins. We had to sleep in a sitting position or with our feet propped up against the wall, and there was always a hard pain in my spine, and sometimes at night I dreamed that I was in a chair car on a train and if I could just stretch my legs out in the right direction the pain would go away. Then I would wake with the blankets twisted around me, the small of my back burning, and I would stand in the darkness until my knees went weak.

During the day we would talk to each other by speaking upward through the iron slits, then our necks would become tired or there wouldn't be anything else to say, and each of us would fall back into his silent fantasies on the floor of the hole. The wounds in my legs had festered and small pieces of lead rose with the pus to the surface of the skin, and many times I slipped off into feverish, distorted scenes that lasted until I heard the ice hook strike the grate at nightfall. Sometimes my eyes stayed fixed on the pattern of iron over my head and the distant, checkered clouds, as though I were staring upward out of a tunnel, and then I would be fifteen years old again in a winter cornfield, the sun bright on the withered stalks, with the single-shot twelve-gauge against my shoulder and a cottontail racing across the dry rows. I aimed just in front of his head and squeezed off the trigger, and when the gun roared in my ears I knew that I had hit him clean, without destroying any of the meat, and that night Cap would deep-fry him in egg batter and flour for supper. Then I would be back in the Shooting Gallery, and I'd feel the heavy weight of the stretcher in both palms while the potato mashers exploded in our wire and the BAR man searched frantically in the bottom of the ditch for another clip. The wounded Marine on the stretcher stared up at me, his eyes full of terror, as I stumbled forward with his weight over the empty ammunition boxes, then the burpguns raked the ditch and knocked men like piles of rags into the walls, and I dropped him and ran. But in one heart-rushing second I saw the expression of helplessness and betrayal in his eyes, and in my feverish dream I wanted to go back and close his eyes with my fingers and tell him that we were all going to buy it, they had already overrun us, and there was nowhere I could have taken him.

Each day I saw the Shooting Gallery again, sometimes in an entirely different way from previously, and the faces of the men in the ditch became confused; their screams when they were hit and their death cries often sounded like a distant band out of tune with itself, and I tried to go back to the winter cornfield and the smell of oak wood burning in the smokehouse and the rabbit racing towards the blackjack thicket. I knew that if I just held that field in the center of my mind, or the smokehouse with a shallow depression in the ground under one wall where my father used to push in the oak logs, I could keep everything intact and in its proper place and I wouldn't let Ding or Kwong make me admit that I was guilty of a wounded Marine's death.

Then on a bright, sun-spangled day I would look up through the slits at the drifting clouds and briefly realize, with a sick feeling in my chest, that they didn't care about the Marine, they only wanted me to inform on Ramos and the Negro sergeant, and eventually I might begin to cry in my sleep, as Bertie sometimes did, and one morning ask Kwong to take me into Ding's office. I heard the voices of other men from our shack farther down the row of holes, and Joe Bob whispered hoarsely up through his grate one day that the World War II paratrooper had been machine-gunned and buried next to the Turk. The temperature began to go above freezing in the mid-afternoon, the melted snow ticked into the bottom of the hole, and the reek from the helmet and my own body often made me sick when I tried to eat my bean cakes. My hair and beard were matted with mud and the thick residue of fish heads that I licked from the bottom of my food pan, and my yellow fingernails had grown out like a dead person's. My ribs felt like strips of wood to my touch, and although I had masturbated my first week in the hole, creating geisha girls under me, with their toy, pale faces and sloe eyes, I couldn't hold the image of a woman in my mind more than a few seconds. Then on a wet morning, with the fog lying close against the ground, I heard the ice hook click against the sewer grates and the hushed voices of O. J. and Bertie as the guards helped them out of their holes.

A day later I was still hoping that they would return. It was too easy now to bang on the grate with my food pan and shout for Kwong to pull me out. Whatever I told Ding now wouldn't have any effect on Ramos and the sergeant, I thought, and it was insane to die for men who possibly were already dead themselves. As the fog rolled over me and drifted through the iron slits I went through all the ethical arguments about surrender, and I discovered that there were dozens of ways to justify any human act, even dishonor. I thought of my grandfather, who had fought the most dangerous man in Texas, and I wondered what he would do if he were here now instead of me. I saw the flashes of Wes Hardin's revolver, and his murderous, drunken eyes, and my grandfather standing in the open barn door with the Winchester in his hands. Then Hardin wheeled his horse and charged, his fingers tangled in the mane, the shotgun banging against the saddle, and Old Hack leaped forward and swung his rifle barrel down with both hands into the side of Hardin's head. But his wars had been fought in a different time, between equally armed men, under hot skies and in dusty Texas streets, and death or victory came in a matter of seconds. He hadn't lived in an age when lunatics locked men in filthy holes and turned them into self-hating creatures that were sickened with their own smell.

So that night, at feeding time, I knew that Old Hack would understand when I held up my hand silently to the progressive and he pulled me over the edge of the hole on my stomach.

I was the eighth man to inform. The Australian died in the hole, and it took another week for Ding to break the three remaining men from our shack. Then on a dripping, grey morning we all stood at the wire and watched Ramos and the Negro sergeant executed and their bodies thrown into an open latrine.

chapter nine

It was dark as Rie and I drove through the sloping hills towards the Valley. Her face was soft in the glow of the dashboard, and she rubbed one hand on my shoulder.

'You've kept all that inside you for fifteen years?' she said quietly.

'There aren't a lot of other places to put it.'

'You weren't to blame for their deaths. The others had already informed.'

'That's the strange thing about a certain type of guilt. When you try to confess it and draw the whips across your own back, there's always someone there to tell you that you're really not guilty of anything. Dixon came back from China a year after the war, and I testified against him at his court-martial. But I didn't care what happened to him anymore. I only wanted to confess before some type of authority and be exposed publicly for cowardice. Each time that I tried to tell them I had informed, I was told to answer the questions directly and they disregarded anything else I had to say. After they gave Dixon five years, officers shook my hand and wished me luck in law school.'

'What happened to the others?'

'Bertie died of beriberi before the truce. O. J. married an Indian girl and was swelling like a balloon with beer fat, and Joe Bob bought a pool hall in Baton Rouge. Four others from the shack testified against Dixon, and the afternoon that he got his five years we all got drunk together, but we found that we didn't have many good things to talk about.'

She slipped her arm across my chest and kissed me behind the ear, and I felt her wet eyelashes against my skin. I wanted her again, more strongly than I had ever wanted a woman in my life, and I pressed the accelerator down and the rolling highway raced towards me in the headlights. We dropped down into the Valley, and I saw the Rio Grande under the moon and the candlelit windows of the adobe houses on the far side. She pressed her breasts close to me, rubbing her curly hair against my cheek, and I turned onto the main highway towards my motel.

I woke early the next morning and leaned over her and kissed her lightly on the mouth. Her sunburned hair was spread on the pillow, and without opening her eyes she put her arms around my neck and pulled me down on top of her. Her body was warm with sleep, and she widened her thighs and ran her hands down my back and moved her lips across my cheek. She breathed softly in my ear, touching the lobe with her tongue, and each time she pressed her stomach into me I felt my skin burn. Then my eyes were closed and I felt my body go weak, the heat gathering like a flame in my loins, and I tried to rise on my elbows and hold it back, but she held her breasts tight against my chest and put her legs in mine and ran her fingers up my neck into my hair.

'Do it now, Hack, and then we'll do it again and again and again.'

She stretched out her legs and flattened her stomach, and then the flame grew more intense and went out of me in a long heart-beating rush.

It had been years since I had slept with a woman whom I really loved, and the experience now was as strange and wonderful as the first time I had made love to a girl in high school. The times of need with Verisa, which she and I had both grown to accept, with our feigned affection in the dark, and the indifference towards one another when it was over, seemed like a sophisticated imitation of a Tijuana film that we had seen so many times we were no longer embarrassed by it.

Rie lay against me with her arm across my chest and her face close to my cheek, and I felt her large breasts and the heat in her thighs, and she told me about the strange world of revolution and political rage that she came from: her father, the University of Madrid professor, who was marked for execution by the Guardia Civil during the Civil War and walked barefoot across the mountains into France before the border was closed; her Irish mother, a member of the I.W.W., who worked years for the release of the Scottsboro Boys during the 1930s, went to jail during World War II in protest against the treatment of the Nisei Japanese, and was blacklisted as a schoolteacher in California during the McCarthy era. Rie joined CORE and the Mississippi Freedom Project when she was nineteen and rode across the country to McComb in an old school bus with a boiling radiator and freedom signs painted in white letters on the sides. They were going to integrate lunch counters, bus depots, and water fountains and sit in front of segregated hotels with their arms locked in a chain and sing 'We Shall Not Be Moved.' Instead, their bus was burned, they were knocked off lunch-counter stools and beaten senseless by clean-cut high school kids, dragged by their hair along sidewalks and thrown into police vans, shocked with cattle prods, spat on by housewives, hit with nightsticks, and crowded into filthy drunk tanks, and some of them ended up on Parchman Farm.

'Most of the people on our bus were middle-class kids who believed southern cops were a creation out of a Paul Muni movie,' she said. 'We were taught how to roll up in a ball with our hands over our heads when they started swinging the clubs, but nobody really thought they would do it. It was just something to talk about on the bus, and everyone was sure that if it really got tight Mr Clean would appear from somewhere with the Constitution in his hand. After it was all over I was able to accept the cops and what they did and the housewives who were having trouble with their period, but there was one scene I couldn't get out of my head for a long time. The first day in McComb we tried to integrate the lunch counter in Penny's, and a thug hit the black guy next to me in the head with a sugar shaker and split his skin. The black guy tried to look straight ahead and hold his head up level, and a blonde chick of about seventeen took the cap off a salt shaker and poured it into the cut.'

I felt her breast rise under my hand, and I pulled her close against me and pressed her face into my neck and kissed her hair. The smooth curve of her back felt like the graceful line of a statue, and when she looked up from the pillow to be kissed again her almond eyes and the slight separation of her lips made my head swim and then the fire began to build inside me again.

Later, we had breakfast in a wood-frame cafe filled with farm and ranch families that had come into town for church, then we drove down the highway under the early sun towards Pueblo Verde. There was still dew on the pastures, and the light breaking across the hills cast a purple haze over the sage and short grass. The air was heavy with the smell of morning and the oak thickets and the churned mud around the wind-mill troughs, and when the breeze changed direction I could smell the horses and cattle in the fields and the burning hickory in a smokehouse. A few clouds were drifting in from the Gulf, and great areas of shadow passed briefly over the cattle and moved across the crest of the hills. For just a moment I thought I could taste rain in the air, and then the sky was clear again and the blacktop highway began to gather pools of light.

There was a union strike meeting and barbecue planned at the Catholic church in the Mexican district that afternoon, and Rie was supposed to provide transportation for the families in the migrant worker camps who didn't have automobiles. Many of them had been brought in on buses from New Jersey, South Carolina, and Florida, and their crew leaders, who contracted the harvest, would do nothing to help the union, and sometimes they refused to take migrants to the next job if they were seen talking with strike organizers. So we waited on the front porch of the union headquarters for a dozen battered cars and pickup trucks to arrive, and then we rolled in a long rattling caravan down a dusty county road to the first of three labor camps.

The land was flat here, without trees, and the weeds in the ditches along the road were covered with dust. The camp was surrounded with a barbed-wire fence, and crude hand-lettered signs were nailed to the cedar posts: NO TRESPASSING, BEWARE OF DOG, TRAILERS FOR COLORED, UNAUTHORIZED PEOPLE STAY OUT. The buildings were made of wood and covered on the sides with red tar paper. The windows didn't have glass or screens, and the wooden shutters were propped open with boards. The corrugated tin roofs reflected brightly in the sun, and I could hear the hum of flies around the community toilets. The yards were bare of grass, and boxes of garbage stood along the dirt lane that ran through the camp. At intervals between every third cabin there was an iron water spigot where the women washed out diapers and cleaned their dishes, but Rie said the handles were often removed by the camp owner because the children left the water running. The showers were located in a grey concrete enclosure without doors or a roof in the center of the camp, and when you passed close to it you could smell the wet reek of the walls and the mold and the sour stench of stagnant water in the bottom of the stalls.

Men and women with towels over their shoulders and toothbrushes went inside together, barefoot brown children in frayed and wash-faded clothes played in the dirt yards, and emaciated dogs with bent spines and mange on their bodies slunk about in the lane. Four dilapidated school buses with broken windows and license plates from several states on them were parked by a tin trailer with an air-conditioning unit in the window and OFFICE painted above the door. Rie walked up on the porch of a cabin and knocked while I leaned against the automobile and smoked a cigar. Mexican men walking towards the shower building looked at me and the Cadillac, and I dropped my eyes to the ground and concentrated on the end of my cigar. I felt the same way that I had when I drove into the penitentiary to see Art. I had intruded into a place where even a courteous nod from me and the world I represented was a form of patronization.

Several children stood ten feet from me and stared at my face and the interior of the car. Their black hair was full of nicks and uneven scissors cuts, and their knees and elbows were covered with dirt. A small girl carried a kitten on her shoulder, and one little boy in cut-off overalls had a broken cap pistol in his hand. I smiled at them, but their faces showed no expression in return. I reached inside and turned on the radio, and the insane, blaring voice of some Baptist preacher roared out of the dashboard.

'Do you kids go to school?' I said. Now that's cool, Holland. Come up with another good one like that.

They looked at me with their silent, black eyes.

'We're going to a barbecue this afternoon. Why don't you ask your folks if you can come along?'

The little girl set the kitten down in the dust and pushed at him with her bare foot. The others continued to stare at the strange man who had just dropped from the stratosphere right on his head. I switched off the radio, closed the car door, stuck my hands in the back pockets of my khakis, and looked off into any direction where I wouldn't have to answer those questioning brown faces. Behind me I heard Rie talking with a woman on the front porch of the cabin, and then a man in a dirty T-shirt, with a swollen stomach, as though he had a hernia, stepped out of the tin trailer and walked towards us.

His bluejeans were bursting just below his navel, his crewcut head was beaded with sunlight in the center, and his fly was only partly zipped. His shoulders were too small for his head, and the bluejeans sagged in the rear. There was a line of sunburn and dandruff where he wore a hat, and his grey eyes went from me to the Cadillac and back again. I took the cigar out of my mouth and nodded at him.

'How do, sir,' he said.

'Pretty fine. How are you today?'

'It's a right nice day, all right.' He ran one hand over his fat hip and looked at a spot over my shoulder. 'I keep the office here, and I'm supposed to take anybody around the camp that wants to see the workers. Sometimes people can't find who they're looking for, and I got all the cabin numbers up in my trailer.'

'Thank you. We're just giving some people a lift to the church.'

He pulled a dead cigar butt from his pocket and put it in his mouth. He lowered his crewcut head and scraped his foot in the dust and rolled the frayed end of the cigar wetly between his lips.

'You see, the soda-pop people that own this land don't like just anybody coming on it. It don't matter to me, but sometimes them union agitators come down here and try to fire up the Mexicans and nigras and shut down the harvest, and I'm supposed to see that nobody like that gets a free run around here. Now, like that Mexican woman up there on the porch. Her husband run off two weeks ago and she's got five kids in there. She can't afford to miss a day's work because some union man won't let her get into the field.'

We talked politely, on and on, while Rie loaded the Cadillac full of children and two huge Negro women. Well, we have a barbecue planned at the church today. I don't think that would bother the soda-pop people. Why don't you have a fresh cigar? Like I don't have nothing against any religion or group of people, but there's a priest down there that's preaching commonism or something at the Mexicans, and it's going to come to a lot of broken heads and people without no paychecks. I can tell you that for a fact, by God. It ain't any skin off my ass, I got that trailer and a salary whether they work or not, but I don't like to see them lose their jobs and get kicked out of their cabins because they listen to people that steals their money in union dues while the citrus burns on the vine. Now, that ain't right. I have a little Jack Daniels in a flask. Would you like a ditch and another cigar before we leave? . . . No, sir, I'm working right now, but tonight when you come back, drop up to the trailer and I'll buy you a shot with a couple of cold ones behind it . . . Thank you. I'm looking forward to it . . . Yes, sir. You come back, hear?

I drove back out the barbed-wire gate and headed down the road past the rows of identical cabins with their shimmering tin roofs. The dust rolled away behind me.

'You ought to do public relations for us, you con man,' Rie said, and smiled at me over the heads of the children sitting between us.

The Catholic church was made of white stucco and surrounded by oak and chinaberry trees. Pickup trucks and junker cars were parked in the side yard, and Negro, Mexican, and a few white families sat on folding metal chairs with paper plates of barbecued chicken in their laps. Their clothes were sun-faded and starched by hand, and many of the women wore flower-patterned dresses that were sewn from feed sacks. A priest in shirt sleeves was turning chickens on the barbecue grill while the Negro from the union headquarters pulled bottles of beer out of a garbage can filled with cracked ice. I parked the car in the shade of a post oak, and the children raced off across the lawn and started throwing chinaberries at each other. In minutes their washed overalls and checkered shirts were stained with the white, sticky milk from the berries.

'Come on. I want you to meet this wild priest,' Rie said.

'I never got along with the clergy.'

'Wait till you catch this guy. He's no ordinary priest.'

'Let's pass.'

'Hack, your prejudices are burning through your face.'

'It's my Baptist background. You can never tell when the antichrist from Rome is going to sail his submarine across the Atlantic and dock in DeWitt County.'

'Good God,' she said.

'You never went to church in a large tent with a sawdust floor.'

'With a box of snakes at the front of the aisle.'

'There you go,' I said.

'Wow. What an out-of-sight place to come from.' She took my hand and walked with me across the lawn towards the barbecue pit.

Two Mexican men sat on a table behind the priest and the Negro, playing mariachi guitars with steel picks on their fingers. They looked like brothers with their flat, Indian faces and straw hats slanted over their eyes. The steel picks glinted in the sun as their fingers rolled across the strings.

'What do you say, whiskey brother?' the Negro said. His eyes were red with either a hangover or the beginnings of a new drunk, and his breath was heavy with alcohol and snuff. He popped the cap off of a sweating bottle of Lone Star and handed it to me. The foam slipped down the side over my hand.

'I guess I have a couple of shots in the car if the smoke gets too much for you,' I said. Then it struck me, as I looked at his cannonball head and remembered the humiliation I had seen in his face the other night, that I had never learned his name.

'I'm cool today, brother,' he said. 'Saturday's for drinking, and Sunday you catch all kinds of sunshine with these church people.'

The priest looked like a longshoreman. His thick arms were covered with black hair, and he had a broad Irish face with a nose like Babe Ruth and a wide neck and powerful shoulders under his white shirt. His black eyes were quick, and when Rie introduced us I had the feeling that he had done many other things before he had become a priest.

'You handled Art's appeal, didn't you?' he said.

'Yes, I did.' I took a cigar from my pocket and peeled off the wrapper.

'His family appreciated it a great deal. The rest of us did, too.

'I knew him in the service,' I said.

'He told me. I saw him before he was sent to prison.'

I chewed off the tip of my cigar and looked away at the line of battered cars and trucks gleaming in the sunlight. Overhead, two bluejays were fighting in the chinaberry tree. Every clergyman has to be so goddamn frank, I thought.

'Have you been here very long, Father?'

'Three months, but I'm being transferred to Salt Lake in September.'

'He's the church's favorite Ping-Pong ball,' Rie said, and laughed. 'He's had five parishes in six years. Kicked out of New Orleans, Compton, California, the Pima reservation in Arizona, and now he's going to turn the Mormons on. I bet those guys will be a real riot.'

'You're not improving my image, Rie.'

'Listen. This was the guy that took black children through those lines of screaming women and thugs when the elementary schools were integrated in New Orleans. He dumped a cop on his ass in the school doorway and said mass in a Negro church the same day in Plaquemines Parish while the Klan burned crosses on the front lawn.'

'Rie's given to hyperbole sometimes, Mr Holland.'

'No, I'm afraid she's pretty exact most of the time, Father,' I said.

'Well, at least it wasn't that dramatic. A little pushing and shoving and a few truck drivers sitting on the curb with more Irish in them than they deserve.'

He filled two paper plates with chicken, rice dressing, and garlic bread, and handed them to us. There were small scars around his knuckles, and his wrists and forearms were as thick and hard as cordwood. He smelled of hickory smoke from the fire, and his balding head glistened with perspiration in the broken shade. Rie was right – he wasn't an ordinary man. I remembered the television newsreels about the priest and ex-paratrooper chaplain who had led terrified Negro children from the buses through the spittle and curses in front of an elementary school in New Orleans in 1961. I also recalled the one short film clip that showed him backing down four large men who had poured beer on the children as they walked up the school steps.

We sat in the shade and ate from our paper plates and drank bottles of Lone Star while the guitar players picked and sang their songs about infidelity, their love for peasant girls in hot Mexican villages, and Villa's raid on a train loaded with *federales* and machine guns mounted on flatcars. The children had established forts behind two lines of folding chairs, and chinaberries flew back and forth and pinged against the metal, and because it was somebody's birthday the Negro climbed up an oak tree, grabbing the trunk with his knees, and hung a *piñata* stuffed with candy from a piece of cloth clothesline. Then he formed all the children into a line, in stair-step fashion, with a foaming beer in his hand, and gave the first child a sawed-off broom handle to swing against the cardboard-crepe-paper horse turning dizzily in the dappled light. The children flailed the *piñata*, and twists of candy showered out over their heads. I borrowed a guitar from one of the musicians and ran my fingers over the strings. The sound hole was inlaid with an Indian design, and there were deep scratches on the face from the steel picks that the owner used.

'Go ahead and boil them cabbages down,' Rie said.

I couldn't be profane in front of the priest.

'I never play too well sober. Wrong mental atmosphere for hillbilly guitar pickers,' I said.

'Will you go ahead?' she said. Her eyes took on that wonderful brightness they had when she was extremely happy.

I tuned the guitar into D and ran a Jimmie Rodgers progression all the way down the neck, then bridged into an old Woody Guthrie and Cisco Houston song while the Negro opened more bottles of Lone Star and the children rolled over one another in the grass after the candy.

Ezekiel saw that wheel a-whirling
Way up in the middle of the air
Tell you what a bootlegger he will do
Sell you liquor and mix it with brew
Way in the middle of the air.

Later, the men on the strike committee pulled two long tables and several benches together in the sun. They sat in the glaring heat, sweat dripping from inside their straw hats over their faces, their browned forearms on the hot wood, as though the sunlight were no different from the shade a few feet away.

The warm beer bottles in their hands were bursting with amber light, and their faces were all of one calm and intent expression while Rie spoke to them in Spanish. Her voice was even and flat while she looked quietly back and forth at the two rows of men, and although my Tex-Mex was good enough so that I could understand most of what she said, I realized she was speaking in a frame of reference that had always belonged in the wretched Mexican hovels on the other side of my property line. As I leaned against an oak trunk, watching them through my sunglasses and sipping a beer, I thought about Art's description of the anglo roaring down the highway in his Cadillac towards the next Holiday Inn, unaware of anything beyond the billboards that flashed by him like a kaleidoscopic vision. So have another beer on that one, Holland, I thought. And polish your goddamn Spanish.

It was late afternoon and hot when the barbecue ended. A dry wind was blowing from the Gulf, and dust devils spun out of the dirt road and whirled away in the fields. We loaded the children and the two Negro women into the car and drove back to the migrant camp. The tarpaper shacks seemed to glow with the heat, and my friend the camp manager was sprinkling the dirt lane in front of his trailer with a garden hose. His clothes were even filthier than they had been that morning, and his face had a red, whiskey flush. He turned off the water and walked over to the car. The fat in his pot stomach bulged against his T-shirt, and his odor was so strong that I opened the door part way to keep him a few feet from me.

'There was a deputy sheriff down here this afternoon, and he says you're working with them union people.'

'Must be somebody else.' I watched Rie on the front porch of one of the cabins.

'He knowed this car, and he described you exactly. Even them cigars.'

'What else did he have to say?'

'He says he's going to lock your ass in jail. And I'll tell you something else, buddy. You come down here and give me a lot of shit about taking them people to a church barbecue. I don't like nobody lying to me when they come on the property, and I got a ball bat up there in the trailer to handle anybody that tries to make my job harder than it is.'

I bit into the soft wetness of my cigar and closed the door carefully. I felt the anger draw tight across my chest, the blood swelling in my temples, and I looked straight ahead at the sunlight beating down on his silver trailer. I coughed on my cigar smoke and picked a piece of tobacco off my lip.

'Well, sir, we should be gone in a few minutes,' I said.

'You better get your luck off that porch and haul it down the road a lot faster than that.'

I opened the door again, hard, so that it hit him sharply in the knees and stomach, and looked into his face.

'You're about two remarks ahead of the game right now, podner,' I said. 'Say anything more and you're going to have problems that you never thought about. Also, if you have any plans about using that baseball bat, you'd better find an apple box to stand on first.'

His red face was caught between angry insult and fear, and the sweat glistened in his brows over his lead-grey eyes.

'You're trespassing, and I'm putting in a call to the sheriff's office,' he said, and walked away in the dust towards his trailer.

Rie got back in the car, and I closed the windows, turned on the air conditioner as high as it would go, and we rolled out the front gate and headed down the county road towards town. There were buzzards drifting high in the sky on the wind stream, and the sun burned white as a chemical flame. The rocks and alkali dust on the road roared away under the Cadillac.

'Say, take it easy, Lone Ranger,' Rie said.

'I've been easy all my life. One of these days I'm going to blow all my Kool-Aid and rearrange a guy like that for a long time.'

She put her hand on my arm. 'That's not your kind of scene, Hack.'

'I'm up to my eyes with rednecks that come on with baseball bats.'

'Hey, man, you're not acting like a good con man at all. What did he say?'

'Nothing. He's defending the soda-pop people.'

'He clicked a couple of bad tumblers over in your brain about something.'

'I burn out a tube once in a while with the chewing-tobacco account. Forget it.'

'I heard him say something about getting your luck off the porch. Was that it?'

'Look, Rie, I was raised by a strange southern man who believed that any kind of anger was a violation of some aristocratic principle. So I turn the burner down every time it starts to flare, and sometimes I get left with a broken handle in my hand.'

'What did he mean?'

The air conditioner was dripping moisture.

'A guy like that doesn't mean anything,' I said. 'The words just spill out of a junk box in his head.'

'Talk straight, Hack.'

'It's a racial remark.'

'Is it important to you?'

I felt my heart quicken, because we both knew now why he had gotten inside me.

'All right, I lived around that shit all my life, and

238

maybe I'm not as far removed from it as I thought. If I was a cool city attorney with *liberal* tattooed on my forehead I would have yawned and rolled up the window on him. But I never could deal with people abstractly, and he stuck his finger in the wrong place.'

The perspiration on my face felt cold in the jet of air from the dashboard. I looked straight ahead at the white road and waited for her to speak. Instead, she slipped close to me and kissed me behind the ear.

'You great goddamn woman,' I said, and hit the road shoulder in a spray of rocks when I pulled her to me.

'Let's go back to the house,' she said, and put her hand under my shirt and rubbed her fingers along my belt line.

'What about those college kids and the Negro?'

'I already asked them to do something else this afternoon.'

She looked up at me with her bright, happy eyes, and I wondered when I would stop discovering things about her.

I bought a bottle of Cold Duck in town, and we drove down the corrugated road through the Mexican district to the union headquarters. The beer tavern was roaring with noise, and fat women sat on the front porches of their paint-blistered houses, fanning themselves in the heat. Rie walked up the path in front of me, lifting her shirt off her breasts with her fingertips. The rusted Dr Pepper thermometer nailed to the porch post read 106 degrees, and the sky was so hot and blue that a cloud would have looked like an ugly scratch on it. Rie opened the screen door and a yellow envelope fell down from the jamb at her feet.

'Hey, buddy, somebody found you,' she said.

I set the heavy bottle of Cold Duck on the porch railing and tore open the telegram with my finger. Flies hummed in the shade of the building.

WHERE THE HELL ARE YOU ANYWAY. HAD TO CANCEL SPEECH LAST NITE IN SAN ANTONIO. SENATOR HAS CALLED THREE TIMES. VERISA QUITE WORRIED. HACK DO YOU WANT IN OR OUT.

BAILEY.

Rie looked at me quietly with her back against the screen.

'It's just my goddamn brother with his peptic ulcer,' I said.

'What is it?'

'I was supposed to make a speech to the Lions or Rotary or one of those good-guy bunches last night.'

'Is that all of it?' Her quiet eyes watched my face.

'Bailey thinks an offense against the business community has the historical importance of World War III.' I folded the telegram and put it in my shirt pocket. 'He's probably swallowing pills by the bottle right now. Do you have a telephone?'

'There's one down in the beer joint.'

'I'll be back in a few minutes. Put the wine in the ice box.'

'All right, Hack.'

'I mean, I don't want the poor bastard to rupture his ulcer on a Sunday.'

'Go on. I'll be here.'

I walked down the road in the hot light to the tavern. Inside, the bar was crowded with Mexican field hands and cedar-cutters, dancers bumped against the plastic jukebox, and billiard balls clattered across the torn, green covering of an old pool table. Cigarette smoke drifted in clouds against the ceiling. I called the house collect from the pay phone on the wall, bending into the receiver away from the noise, then I heard Bailey's voice on the other end of the line.

'Where are you?' he said.

'In a bowling alley. What's it sound like?'

'I mean where?'

'In Pueblo Verde, where you sent your telegram. What the hell are you doing at the house, anyway?'

'Verisa's pretty upset. You'd better get back home.'

'What is this shit, Bailey? You knew why I had to leave Friday.'

'The Senator wasn't very pleasant with her when he called here, and maybe all of us are just a little tired of you not showing up when you're supposed to. They waited the banquet an hour for you before they called our answering service, and I had to drive to San Antonio at ten o'clock and offer an apology for you.'

'Look, you arranged that crap without asking me first, and you knew when I left Austin that I wouldn't be back this weekend. So you hang that bag of shit on the right pair of horns, buddy. And if the Senator wants to be unpleasant with someone, I'll give you this number or the one at the motel.'

'Why do you want to behave like this, Hack? You've got all the easy things right in your hand.'

A pair of drunk dancers knocked against me, and then waved their hands at me, smiling, as they danced back onto the floor in the roar of noise.

'I just want a goddamn weekend free of migraine headaches and Kiwanians and telegrams,' I said. 'I'll be back at the office in a couple of days. In the meantime you can schedule yourself for the next round of speeches with the civic club account.'

But he was already off the phone.

'Hack?' Verisa said.

'Yeah.' I closed my eyes against her voice.

'I'm not going to say much to you. I warned you in Houston what I'd do if you blew this for us. I've got enough to go into court and win almost all of it. I'll take the house, the land, and the controlling share of the wells, and you can start over again with your alcoholic law practice.'

I took a breath and waited a moment on that one.

'I should have called you, but I didn't have time,' I said, evenly. 'I thought Bailey would tell you why I had to leave.'

'Oh, my God.'

I started to answer, and instead looked out at the dancers on the floor.

'Why should he have to tell me anything?' she said. 'You seem to have a strange idea that Bailey should take care of all your unpleasant marital obligations. He was embarrassed enough apologizing for you last night.'

'Well, I'm a little worn out with people selling me by the pound and then telling me how embarrassed they are for me. And it also strikes me that nobody was ever concerned if I was called out of town by a paying client. Maybe some people wouldn't get their ovaries so dilated if I was on another case besides a Mexican farm worker's.'

I heard her breath in the phone, and then, 'You bastard.'

I hung up the receiver softly and walked back outside into the sunlight. The road was blinding in the heat, and the noise from the jukebox and Verisa's voice were still loud in my head. I lit a cigar, sweating, and imagined the stunted rage she was now in. Poor old Bailey, I thought. He would stay at the house the rest of the evening, talking quietly to her while her eyes burned at the wall, and then he would begin to consider all the side streets they could use for my election in November, regardless of what I did in the meantime. He would drink cups of caffeine-free coffee with his ulcer pills, Hicking over the alternatives in his mind, and soon he would forget that Verisa was in the room. Or maybe the Senator would phone again, and both of their faces would focus anxiously, their eyes reflecting into one another across the kitchen table, while Bailey's voice measured out his assurances about my sincerity in the campaign and my deep regret that I wasn't able to be with the Kiwanians (or whatever) last night. Then they would both wonder if we would ever get to that marble and green island of power where you carried a small, stamped gold key in your watch pocket.

Rie was sitting on the front steps with her back against the porch railing and one leg drawn up before her. She had changed into a pair of faded Navy ducks, with the laces on the back, and a rose-flowered silk shirt, and in the shade she looked as cool and beautiful as a piece of dark sculpture. There was an unopened can of Lone Star and a tall, cone glass by her foot. My shirt stuck wetly to my shoulders, and my sunglasses were filmed with perspiration.

'You look like Tom Joad beating his way out of the Dust Bowl,' she said. 'You'd better have one of these.'

I sat down beside her and opened the can of beer. The tin was cold against my hand, and the foam rushed up in the glass and streamed over the lip. I took my glasses off and wiped the perspiration and dust out of my eyes, but I avoided looking at her face.

There was a broken anthill by the edge of the path, with a deep boot print in one side, and thousands of ants were moving over one another in a hot swarm.

'Was everything cool back there?' she said.

'Yeah.' I drank out of the beer – and squinted my eyes into the bright light. 'I'm going to give Bailey a frontal lobotomy team for Christmas. Or a can of alum to drink. He has a remarkable talent for calling up everything bad in a person within seconds.'

I heard her take her cigarettes out of her shirt pocket and rip back the cover.

'He's not a bad guy. He's just so goddamn obtuse sometimes.'

'Hack, I'm not pressing you.'

'Then who the hell is?'

'I don't care what you belong to outside of here.'

I looked at her quiet, beautiful face in the shade.

'I love to be a part of your Saturday morning fishing world and your crazy Indian graves,' she said. 'I'd never ask you about anything back there in Austin.'

I took the cigarette from her hand and drew in on the smoke. The trees in the dirt yards along the street were still and green in the heat.

'I put the wine on a block of ice,' she said.

'Maybe we had better drink that, then,' I said. 'What do you think, good-looking?'

She smiled at me with her eyes full of light again, and we walked into the back of the house and opened the tall, dark bottle of Cold Duck. I chipped off a bowl full of ice from the block in the top of the cooler and set it in front of the fan in the bedroom so the wind stream would blow cool across the bed. The sun burned yellow against the window shade, and across the river in Mexico a calf stuck in the mudflat was bawling for its mother. Rie undressed in the half light and put her arms around my shoulders, and I pressed my face into her neck and felt her smooth stomach and breasts curve against me.

That evening we drove over to the Gulf in the fading, lilac twilight, and just before the highway turned out of the citrus fields onto the coast we could smell the salt in the air and the dead seaweed at the edge of the surf. The water was slate-green, and the white caps crashed against the sand and boiled in deep pools, and then sucked out again with the undertow. Brown pelicans and sea gulls, like fat white cigars, dipped out of the sky over the water, picking small fish from the crest of the waves with their beaks, and in the distance we could see the gas flares and strings of lights on offshore oil rigs and quarter boats. The red sun was as big as a planet on the horizon, and the light broke across the water in long bands of scarlet. The stretch of brown beach and the palm trees were covered with a dark, crimson glow, and then the sun moved deeper into the Gulf, with a strip of black cloud across its flaming edge, and the moon began to rise behind us over the land.

I bought another bottle of Cold Duck and some chicken sandwiches in a restaurant, and a Mexican family camped on the beach sold us two salt-water cane poles with treble hooks and a carton of live shrimp. The sand was still warm from the sun, and we sat behind a dune out of the wind and ate the sandwiches and drank half the bottle of wine, then I baited the three-pronged hooks with the shrimp, slipped the lead sinkers close to the bottom of the line, and we waded into the surf to fish the bottom for channel cat and flounder. The tide began to come in, and the waves broke across the rotted wooden pilings in the jetties, and when the wind shifted across the water we could smell the dead shellfish and baked scales and salt in the pilings. Rie held her cane pole under her arm, with both hands raised in front of her, while the waves swelled against her breasts. The water was splintered with moonlight, and the salt spray in her hair looked like drops of crystal. Then the tip of her pole arched into the water and went all the way to the bottom.

'What do I do now, Lone Ranger?' she shouted.

'Keep his head up or he'll break it.'

She leaned backwards and strained with both hands, and a cloud of sand rose in the swell at the end of her pole. Then the line pulled out at an angle, quivering, and the pole went down again. She looked at me helplessly, her face shining with water and moonlight.

'Walk him into the shore,' I said.

A large wave crested in front of her and broke across her shoulders.

'Hack, you bastard.'

'You have to learn these things to overcome your Yankee childhood,' I said.

She tried to slip the pole back under her arm and raise it again, but the fish had turned into the waves and was pulling hard for the bottom. I waded over to her and picked up the line with both hands at the water and walked backwards with it towards the beach. The line tightened around my knuckles and cut into the skin, and when I reached the shallows I could see the long blue outline of the channel cat shaking his head against the three hooks caught in his mouth. I dragged him up on the sand and placed my fingers carefully around his spiked ventral fins and made one cut with my pocket knife through his gill and across the spine. He flipped quietly in the sand and then lay still.

'God, the things you Southerners do for kicks,' she said.

But I could see the excitement in her face at having caught a large and beautiful blue-black fish under the moon in waves up to her shoulders.

'It's against Texas law to keep this kind,' I said. 'Maybe we'd better flip him back in.'

She stepped down on the top of my bare foot and pinched my arm with her fingernails. I held her close to me and kissed her wet hair and dried her face against my shirt. I could taste the salt on her skin and smell the Gulf wind in her hair, and she put her arms inside my shirt and ran her hands over my back.

We gave the channel cat, the poles, and the remaining shrimp to the Mexican family, and built a fire on the sand out of dried wood and dead palm fronds. The wind caught the flames and sent sparks twisting into the sky, and the fronds, coated with sand, and the polished twists of wood snapped in the fire and burst apart in a yellow blaze. We drank the rest of the wine and sat inside the heat with our clothes steaming. On the southern horizon dark storm clouds were building over the water. The moon was high, and I could see the clouds rolling in a heavy wind off the Mexican coast, and a few large whitecaps were hitting the pilings around the oil derricks. The air had become cooler, and there was a wet smell of electricity in the air. I lit a cigar, stuck the cork in the wine bottle, and threw it end over end into the surf.

'We really get it on tomorrow, don't we, babe?' I said.

She ticked the top of my hand with her finger and looked into the fire.

The wind was blowing in gusts the next morning when we arrived at the cannery and loading platform where the union was setting up its main picket. The sun was brown in the swirling clouds of dust from the fields, and I could still smell the wet electric odor of a storm. Dozens of junker cars and pickup trucks with crude wood shelters on the back were parked along the railway tracks, and Negro and Mexican field workers had formed a long line in front of the platform where the harvest trucks would unload. Their picket signs flopped and bent in the wind, and the sand blew in their faces, while a man in slacks and a tie walked back and forth above them, waving his arms, and told them to get off the company's property. His tie was blown over his shoulder and his glasses were filmed with grit, and after he was ignored by everyone on the picket he went into his office and came back with a camera and began taking pictures. Two Texas Rangers in sunglasses and Stetson hats leaned against a state car, watching with their tanned, expressionless faces. Their uniforms were ironed as stiff as tin. The priest, in Roman collar, stood in the back of a stake truck, with his sleeves rolled over his thick arms, handing out picket signs to the people who had just arrived, and I saw one of the Rangers raise his finger, aim at the priest, and say something to his partner.

'I didn't think this was your kind of scene, whiskey brother.'

It was the Negro from the union headquarters, and

248

he was still drunk. His slick face was covered with dust, and he had a wad of snuff under his lip.

'What the hell is your name, anyway?' I said.

'What's a name, man?' He took a bottle of port wine from his back pocket and unscrewed the cap. 'Sam, Tom, You. People give me a lot of them. But I like Mojo Hand the best. That's a name with shine. It feels good in your mouth just like all these sweet grapes.'

'Put the wine away till later,' Rie said.

'Those dicks ain't going to bother me. They know a nigger can't change nothing around here. They want to strum some white heads.' He drank from the bottle and coughed on the tobacco juice in his mouth.

'They'll use anything they can for the newspapers,' Rie said.

'You know it don't make any difference what we do out here today. It's going to read the same way tomorrow morning. Ain't that right, whiskey brother? They could bust up Jesus with them billy clubs and the people would find out how He started a riot.'

'Let's hang a good one on later,' I said.

'Where you been, man? There ain't going to be no later. These dudes have just been practicing so far.'

'Everything is cool now, isn't it?' I said.

He pulled on the bottle again and laughed, spilling the wine over his lip. 'Out of sight. But you're right. You got to keep thinking cool, cousin. You got to keep a little shine in your name.'

'We don't want a bust this early,' Rie said. 'Stay in the car until the rest of our people get here.'

But he wasn't looking at us any longer. His red eyes stared over my shoulder in the direction of the county road, and I turned around and saw the two black and white sheriff's cars, followed by three carloads of townspeople, rolling towards us in the dust. The whip aerials sprang back and forth on their springs, and muscular, shirt-sleeved arms hung out the windows of the other cars, beating against the door sides. The wind flattened the clouds of dust across the road, and a moment later two Texas Ranger cars closed the distance with the rest of the caravan.

'It ain't cool no more, whiskey brother,' the Negro said.

The line of cars pulled into the gravel bedding along the railway track, and the Rangers and deputy sheriffs walked casually towards the two Rangers in sunglasses who were leaning against their automobile and looking at the priest. The other men stayed behind and formed in a group by a boxcar, their hands in their back pockets, their faces tight, spitting tobacco juice into the rocks, and glaring at the Mexicans and the Negroes. They had crewcuts and faces put together out of shingles, and they wore T-shirts or bluejean jackets with the sleeves cut off at the armpits. There were tattoos of Confederate flags and Easter crosses, Mother and the United States Marine Corps, inscriptions to Billy Sue and Norma Jean, and even the young ones had pot stomachs. They looked like everyone who was ever kicked out of a rural Texas high school.

Then I saw my friend from the sheriff's office. He walked from behind the freight car with a filter-tipped cigar between his teeth, his khaki trousers tucked inside his half-top boots, and his wide leather cartridge belt pulled tight across his flat stomach. He spoke quietly to the men in T-shirts and denim jackets, smiling, his hands on his hips, and then he and the others turned their faces towards me at one time. His green, yellow-flecked eyes were filled with an intense delight, and his lips pressed down softly on the cigar tip.

'Let's get into the picket before it starts,' Rie said.

I walked with her to the back of the stake truck, where the priest was still handing down signs. The wind whipped the dust in our faces, and swollen rain clouds were rolling over the horizon. The air was becoming cooler, and I heard the first dull rip of thunder in the distance. The priest wiped his face on his shirt sleeve and grinned at us.

'How are you, Mr Holland? We can use a good man from the establishment,' he said.

'I know a two-word reply to that, Father,' I said.

'I believe I've heard it.'

'Mojo's drunk. Try to get him into the truck,' Rie said.

'He's not fond of listening to church people,' the priest said.

'There's some badass types back by the freight car, and he's been in a winehead mood since some kids tried to get it on with him the other night,' she said.

'I'll watch him,' he said.

'Watch that bunch of assholes, too. One of the dicks was winding them up.'

The priest looked over at one of the Rangers who was talking into the microphone of his mobile radio.

'Get into the line. They're going to start moving in a few minutes,' he said.

Rie picked up two cardboard signs tacked on laths and handed me one of them. A single, large drop of rain splattered on the black eagle over the word HUELGA.

'Come on,' she said.

'Can I get a cigar lit first, for God's sake?' I said.

'We don't want anybody arrested outside the picket, Hack.'

'All right, goddamn. Just a minute.'

For some reason I hadn't yet accepted the fact that I would be walking on a picket line that Monday morning, or any morning, for that matter. The sign bent backwards in my hands against the wind, flopping loudly, and my knees felt disjointed as I followed her into the slow line of Mexicans and Negroes in their faded work clothes, battered straw hats, and dresses splitting at the hips. Drops of rain made puckered dimples in the dust, and the wind blew cool inside my shirt, but I was perspiring under my arms, and my face was burning as though I had just done something obscene in public. I saw the eyes of the sheriff's deputies, the Rangers, and the poolroom account watching me, and my head became light and my cigar tasted bitter and dry in my mouth. I felt as though I had walked naked in front of a comic audience. A fat Negro woman behind me held her child, in cut-off overalls, with one hand and her picket sign in the other. She wore a pair of rippled stockings over the varicose veins in her legs.

'You don't worry about these children. They ain't going to bother them,' she said.

I looked away from her brown eyes at the man in slacks and tie on the platform. He was still taking pictures, and his face was quivering at the outrage he had seen that day against the principle of private property. Storm clouds covered the sun, and the fields were suddenly darkened and the shadows leaped across the cannery, the freight cars, and the county road. The men in T-shirts and denim jackets were now pulling the caps on hot cans of beer and spilling the foam down their necks and chests.

'How you doing?' Rie said.

'I think my respect for the demonstrator just went up a couple of points.'

'Look, if those bastards move in on us, you have to take it. Okay?'

'That doesn't sound cool.'

'No shit, Hack. They're waiting for reasons to split heads.'

'All right, but when do we finish this caper?'

'We've only been on the picket ten minutes, babe.'

Then I saw a television news car pull into the gravel bedding by the railway track. Two young men got out with cameras attached to half-moon braces that fitted against the shoulder. They walked over to the group of law officers by the squad cars, their faces full of confident foreknowledge about their story, and for the first time it struck me that I had never seen a newsman begin a story any differently; without thinking, they went first to the official source before they considered the people on the other end of the equation.

One of them walked towards the picket and did a sweeping, random shot with his camera, the brace pulled tight against his shoulder. Then he lowered the camera and looked at me steadily, his face as bland and unembarrassed as a dough pan. I threw my cigar away and looked back at him with my meanest, southpaw ninth-inning expression. He walked back to his friend and began talking, and the two of them stared in my direction.

'I believe a couple of kids just earned a pay raise,' I said.

'I bet you're handsome on film,' Rie said.

'Well, here they come. You want to do my P.R. work?'

One of them already had his camera whirring before they were close enough to speak. They had forgotten the cops and the long line of migrant workers; they were both concentrated on the little piece of entrail they might carry back to the station.

'Are you widening your district, Mr Holland?' His voice was good-natured, and he smiled at me in his best college fraternity fashion.

'No, no,' I said, in my best humorous fashion.

Isn't this a delightful game we're about to play, I thought.

'Do you think your support of the union will affect your election?' He held the microphone towards me, but his eyes were looking at Rie.

'I couldn't tell you that, buddy.'

'The farm corporations consider this an illegal strike. Do you have a comment on that?'

'I don't know how it can be illegal to ask for a higher wage.'

'Does the union plan a strike in your area?' He was cocking the rifle now, but his face looked as sincerely inquisitive as a reverent schoolboy's.

'Not that I know of.'

'Does that mean the conditions of the migrant farm workers are better in your area?'

'No, it doesn't,' I said. 'But I tell you what, buddy. I need a cigar real bad right now, and it's hell lighting up in this wind with one hand. So how about holding this sign for a minute, and I can get one of these awful things lit and we can talk all day. That's right, just take it in your hand and fold your fingers around the stick.'

His face went blank, the lath straining in his palm, and his eyes flicked at his partner and the cops by the railway track. I used three matches to light my cigar while he blinked against the raindrops and shifted his feet in the dust.

'I appreciate that,' I said. 'Say, did you interview any of those fellows over by the freight car? I bet that bunch of boys would give you some deathless lines.'

'We just do a job, Mr Holland.'

'I bet you'll get there with it, too,' I said.

'Would you like to say something else, sir?' His face was mean now, the eyes dirty.

'You've got a whole reel of good stuff there, pal.'

He turned away from me and put the microphone in front of Rie. The sky was almost completely dark, except for the thin line of yellow light on the distant hills. His partner moved around behind him so the lens would catch me in the same shot with Rie.

'Do you think the families in the farm camps will suffer because of the strike?'

'Why don't you fuck off, man?' Rie said.

Then one of the men by the freight car threw an empty beer can at the picket line. It missed a Negro woman's head and clattered across the loading platform. The two newsmen backed away from us with their cameras turning. A moment later three more carloads of townspeople arrived and swelled into the group by the freight car, and then one man stepped out from them and started walking towards us, and the rest followed. He wore a tin construction hat back on his shaved head, steel-toed work boots, and denim clothes that were splattered with drilling mud from an oil rig. His eyes had a wet, yellow cast to them, and his front teeth were brown with chewing tobacco. His scrotum bulged in his bluejeans between his heavy thighs, and he stretched out his huge arms, his hands in fists, as though he were just awakening from sleep, and spat a stream of tobacco juice in the dirt.

'Hey, buddy,' he said to me. 'Do you eat Mexican pussy?'

I looked straight ahead, my face burning.

'You better get that chili off your mouth, then,' he said.

'Leave that man alone, J. R. You know a lawyer don't have to eat pussy,' another said.

'This one does. You get your nose right in it, don't you?'

The looming outline of the cannery and the rusted freight cars in silhouette against the light rain seemed to shrink and expand before my eyes. My knuckles whitened on the sign lath, and my breath caught in my throat.

'He might beat you to death with that cardboard, J.R.'

'Do you get to try some of these nigger girls?' the oilfield worker said.

My eyes watered and I felt myself leaping towards him before I had even moved or changed my line of vision, but several men behind him shouted and laughed at one time in a phlegmy roar, and he turned his wide back to me. Mojo had been sitting in the cab of the stake truck with his wine bottle until it was empty, and then had decided to join the picket. His shirt was unbuttoned to the waist, his socks were pulled down over his heels, and he walked towards the line as though his knees were connected with broken hinges. There was a patch of snuff on the corner of his lip, and the drops of rain slid over his cannonball head like streaks of black ivory. An unopened can of beer flew out of the crowd and hit him above the eye. He reeled backwards, still standing, and pressed his hand like a fielder's glove against his head, the blood dripping down from his dark palm. His uncovered eye was wide and rolling with pain and shock.

'Goddamn,' I said.

'Don't, Hack,' Rie said.

'They hurt him bad.'

'Stay in the line,' she said.

Mojo bent forward and let the blood run down his forearm onto the ground, then he started walking towards us again as though he were holding a cracked flowerpot delicately in place. A man in khaki clothes with a green cloth cap on and a Lima watch fob in his pocket stepped into his path and kicked his feet out from under him. Mojo struck the ground headlong, and his face was covered with strings of dust and blood.

'This is too goddamn much, Rie,' I said.

'Don't get out of the line. They'll kill him if you do,' she said.

He pushed himself up from the ground and stood erect, the ragged cut on his head already swelling like a baseball. The wind blew his shirt straight out from his body, and his chest heaved and his nostrils dilated when he breathed.

'You can bust me 'cause I'm winehead now, but you ain't going to beat all these people,' he said. 'They too many for you, and they're going to stand all over this place when you all are long gone.'

The oil-field worker moved towards him, his buttocks flexing inside his bluejeans, but two deputy sheriffs walked up behind Mojo and led him away by each arm towards their automobile. Before they put handcuffs on him, they stripped off his shirt and wrapped it in a twisted knot around his head.

The car rolled off down the road, with Mojo in back behind the wire screen, his blood-soaked shirt like a dark smear against the closed glass.

The priest was next, and they had a special dislike for him as a Catholic clergyman. The man in the khaki clothes shook up a hot beer and sprayed it on him, and the oil field worker put his hot breath in the priest's face and insulted him with every whorehouse statement he could make. Several women had joined the crowd, and they rasped at him with their contorted faces, their eyes shrunken inward at some terrible anger, and then one spat on him. She was small and stunted, her thin arms were puckered and wrinkled at the armpits, and her electric hair was scraped back in a tangle over the thinning places in her head, but she gathered all the energy and juice in her wasted body and spat it in an ugly string over his chest.

He blinked his eyes against the spittle and obscenities, but he kept his face straight ahead, his big hands folded around the sign lath, and never broke his step in the line. His composure enraged the women to the point that they were shouting at him incoherently, their heads bent forward like snakes, the veins in their throats bursting against the skin. Then the deputy sheriff who had arrested me walked to the back of the crowd, put his hand on the oil-field worker's shoulder, and motioned in my direction. Across the railway track I saw two large police vans with cage doors on the back turn off the county road into the cannery gate, and then the crowd came towards me.

Their faces were tight with anger, the lips dry, the eyes hot and receded in the head, as though their own rage had dried out all the fluids in their bodies. In the gloom and swirling patterns of rain their skin looked white and stretched over the bone. Lightning struck against the hills, and the wind was beginning to strip the cotton in the fields.

'We ain't got a lot of time for you, lawyer. So you know what I'm going to do?' the oil field worker said, and put a half plug of tobacco in his mouth. He pushed it into his jaw with his tongue and chewed it into pulp, then cleaned the juice off his lip with his finger. 'I ain't going to touch you with my hand. I'm just going to show you how we treat dip shit around here. Now, when you get tired of it, all you got to do is tear that sign up and walk to your car. There won't nobody hurt you.'

'I'll tell you something, motherfucker,' I said. 'You spit on me and I'll take your head off.'

The man in the khaki clothes with the green cap reached out with his fist, off balance, as though he were leaping at a departing train, and struck me in a downward swing across the nose. His ring peeled back the skin, and I felt the blood swell to the surface. I stared at them all stupidly, with the sign in my hands, while my eyes filmed and burned. The oil worker was grinning at me.

'You want to cut bait, dip shit?' he said.

The woman who had spat on the priest flicked a

lighted cigarette at my face, then I was hit again, this time across the side of the head with something round and wooden. I felt it clack into the bone, and I tumbled sideways, the ocean roaring in my ears, and struck the ground on one knee and an elbow. My ear and the side of my head were on fire, and I looked up through the unshaved legs and denims stained with grease and cow manure and saw a thin, muscular boy of about nineteen with a freight-door pin in his hand. Somebody pulled my shirt loose from my trousers and poured beer down my spine. I felt a cigar burn into my neck, and a woman slapped wildly at my head with a shoe. I tried to raise my arms in front of me, but someone stepped on my hand and the man in khakis tripped in the crowd and fell across my back. I heard Rie's voice shouting outside the circle of people around me, then the deputy sheriff pulled my head up by the shirt collar and started to raise me to my feet, but before he did he flicked out his knee, in a quick, deft motion, and caught me in the eye. Half my vision exploded in dark red and purple circles, and I pressed my hand into the socket as though I had a piece of sandpaper under the lid. But in the swimming distortion I could still see his khaki trousers stuffed inside his low-topped boots, and his cartridge belt and holster welded against his flat stomach and narrow hips. I rose on one knee and put all my strength into a left-handed swing from the ground and hit him in the stomach an inch above the belt. I felt the muscles collapse under my fist, just like you kick open a door unexpectedly. He bent double, his face white and his mouth open in a wide O, and his breath clicked dryly in his throat. His eyes were drowning, and when he fell forward on his knees in the mud, a line of spittle on his cheek, the crowd stepped backwards in silence as though someone had thrown an unacceptable icon at their feet.

Then the Rangers, the city police, and the sheriff's department went to work. They arrested everybody in sight. They handcuffed my arms behind me while the television cameras whirred, gave artificial respiration to the deputy and strapped an oxygen mask to his face, pushed scores of people into the vans with nightsticks until there was no more room, commandeered the stake truck, and arrested the man with the camera on the loading platform by mistake. Two deputies led me by each arm to the van, squeezing tightly into my torn shirt, their faces like hard wax, and the television newsmen were still hard at work with their lenses zooming across my manacled hands and swollen face. The rain was coming down harder now, and the gravel road was covered with wet boles of cotton and leaves stripped from the citrus orchards. The wind was rattling the tin roof on top of the cannery, and the ditches by the road were slick and brown on the sides with the run-off from the fields. I was the last man put in the second van. The deputies took the handcuffs off me, pushed me inside against the crowd of Mexicans and Negroes, and locked the wire-cage doors. The engine started, and we bounced across the railway track and turned through the cannery gate onto the county road.

The men in the van balanced themselves against the walls and each other and rolled cigarettes, or poured Bull Durham tobacco from the pouch between their lip and gums. Somewhere in back a child was crying. I leaned against the cage door and watched the road shift in direction behind the van, while the wind shook the barbed wire on the fences and bent the weeds flat along the irrigation ditches, and then I heard Rie's voice way back in the crush of people. She pressed her way out between several Mexican men, who raised their arms in the air in order to let her pass, and her face and eyes made my heart drop. She put her arm in mine and touched her fingers lightly against the swollen place on my head, then pulled my arm close against her breast and kissed me on the cheek.

'I was very proud of you, Hack,' she said.

'I'm afraid I screwed up your picket. That was an assault and battery caper I pulled off back there.'

She hugged my arm tighter against her breast, and the rain poured down on the fields and began to flatten the long, plowed rows even with the rest of the land, and in the distance I could see the citrus trees whipping and shredding in the dark wind.

chapter ten

The streets in town were half-filled with water when
the vans arrived at the courthouse. Beer cans and
trash floated along next to the curb, and the lawn was
strewn with broken branches and leaves from the
oaks. The deputies, now wearing slickers and plastic
covers on their hats, formed us into a long line, two
abreast, while the rain beat in our faces, and marched
us into the courthouse. The booking room was small,
and it took them three hours to fingerprint everyone
and sort out the shoelaces, belts, pocket change, and
wallets into brown envelopes. Most of the charges
were for trespassing or failure to keep fifty feet apart
on a picket line, but after the deputy had rolled my
fingers on the ink pad the sheriff filled out my charge
sheet personally and he wrote for five minutes. I
dripped water onto the floor and looked at his steel-
rimmed glasses and the red knots and bumps on his
face. His fingers were pinched white on the pencil,
and towards the bottom of the page he pressed down
so hard that he punctured the paper.

Then he picked up a cigarette from the desk and lit
it.

'You want to hear them?' he said.

'I bet you have a whole bunch,' I said.

'Assault and battery on a law officer, obstructing an officer in the line of duty, resisting arrest, inciting to riot, and I'm holding a couple of charges open. You ain't going to get this shifted to no federal court, either. You're going to be tried right here in this county, and maybe you'll find out a lawyer's shit stinks like everybody else's.'

'I have a phone call coming.'

'It's out of order.'

'It rang five minutes ago.'

'Take him downstairs,' he said to the trusty.

I was locked in the drunk tank at the end of the stone corridor in the basement. The room was crowded with men, wringing out their clothes on the concrete floor. Their dark bodies shone in the dim light. There were two toilets crusted with filth, without seats, in the corner, and the drunks who had been arrested during the weekend still reeked of sour beer and muscatel. Through the bars I could see the screened cage where I had talked with Art, and the row of cells with the food slits in the iron doors. The stone walls glistened with moisture, and the smoke from hand-rolled cigarettes gathered in a thick haze on the ceiling. An old man in jockey undershorts, with shriveled skin like lined putty, walked to the toilet and began retching.

Rie had been put with the other women into a second holding room on the other side of the wall. Someone had drilled a small hole in the mortar between the stones, and a Mexican man had his face pressed tightly against the wall, talking to his wife, while a line of other men waited their turn behind him. I wanted to talk with Rie badly, but the line grew longer, and often in the confusion of names and voices the two right people could never get on the opposite sides of the hole at the same time. Twice during the afternoon a deputy, dripping water from his slicker, brought in another prisoner, and each time the door clanged open a tough, bare-chested kid, who was waiting to do a six-year jolt in Huntsville, shouted out from the back of the room, 'Fresh meat!' At five o'clock the trusty wheeled in the food cart with our tin plates of spaghetti, string beans, bread and cups of Kool-Aid, and after the group of men had thinned away from the wall I tried to talk through the hole to a Mexican woman on the other side, but she couldn't understand English or my bad Spanish, and I gave up.

That night I dragged my tick mattress against the door and lay with my face turned towards the bars to breathe as much air as I could out of the corridor and avoid the odor of the open toilets and the sweet, heavy smell of perspiration. I had one damp cigar left, and I smoked it on my side and looked at the row of gray, iron doors set in the rock. Mojo was in lockdown behind one of them, and once I thought I saw the flash of his black face through a food slit. I had never been more tired. I was used up physically the way you are after you've thrown every pitch you have in a ten-inning game. There was a raised water blister on my neck from the cigar burn, and a swollen ridge across the side of my head, like a strip of bone, where the boy had caught me with the freight pin. I fell asleep with the dead cigar in my hand, and I slept through until morning without having one dream or even a half-conscious, nocturnal awareness of where I was, as though I had been lowered through the stone into some dark underground river.

I heard the trusty click the food cart against the bars and throw the big lock on the door. The fried bologna, grits and coffee steamed from the stainless-steel containers, and the men were rising from their tick mattresses, hawking, spitting, and relieving themselves in the toilets, or washing their spoons under the water tap before they formed into line. I had to move my mattress for the trusty to push the cart inside, and when I stood up I realized that I felt as rested and solid as a man in his prime. But it took me a moment to believe the man I saw walking down the stone corridor with the sheriff by his side. He wore yellow, waxed cowboy boots, a dark, striped western suit, with a watchchain hooked on his handtooled belt, a bolo tie, a cowboy shirt with snap buttons on the pockets, and a short-brim Stetson hat on the back of his head. He didn't have an undershirt on, and I could see the hair on his swollen stomach above his belt buckle, and his round face was as powdered and smooth as a baby's. There wasn't another man in Texas who dressed like that. It was R. C. Richardson, all right.

'Hack, have you lost your goddamn mind? What the hell are you doing in here?' he said, in his flat, east Texas, Piney Woods accent.

'R.C., you old sonofabitch,' I said.

'I was down here buying leases, and I come back to the motel last night and turned on the television, and I couldn't believe it. What you trying to do to yourself, boy?'

'Get a bondsman, R.C.'

'I already done that. I got his ass out of bed at midnight, but he wouldn't come till this morning. Do you know the bail they set on you? Ten thousand dollars. I swear to God if you ain't a pistol, Hack.'

'I tell you, Mr Richardson,' the sheriff said, 'if you go this man's bond, you're also going to be responsible for him, because I don't want to see him again.'

'Well, I guarantee you he won't be no trouble,' R.C. said. 'We might shoot on across the border this afternoon and try the chili, then go on back to DeWitt.'

'R.C., are you going to turn the key on me or just drip water on the floor?' I said.

'Hold on, son. That man will be here in a minute,' he said. 'I told him I'd put a boot up his ass if he wasn't here five minutes after I walked through that door.'

'Bail the rest of them out, too,' I said.

'You know that brother of yours is right. The whiskey's getting up in your brain.'

'R.C., how many years have I kept you out of prison?'

'Goddamn, how much money do you think I carry around with me?'

'Enough to buy this county and a couple of others.'

'Hack, I can't do that. There must be fifty people in there.'

'There's more in the next room,' I said.

'And they'll be spread all over Mexico when they're supposed to be in court.'

'Will you stop screwing around and just do it?'

'If you ain't a pistol, the craziest goddamn man I ever met. All right, but I'm going to send your brother a bill for a change, and it's going to bust his eyeballs.'

'Good, and give me a cigar while you're at it.'

The bondsman arrived, and R.C. wrote out a check

on the stone wall for the whole amount. The bondsman, a small man with greed and suspicion stamped in his face, thought he was either drunk or insane. He held the check between his fingers with the ink still drying and looked at R.C. incredulously.

'Call the First National Bank in Dallas collect and use my name,' R.C. said, 'or I'll find me another man right fast.'

We had to wait ten minutes, then the sheriff opened the doors to both holding rooms and the corridor was filled with people, laughing and talking in Spanish. A deputy unlocked one of the cells set back in the wall, and Mojo stepped out barefoot in the light, blinking his red eyes, with his stringless shoes in his hands.

'What happened?' he said. 'The Man get tired of us already?'

A Mexican man put his arm around Mojo's shoulders and pulled him into the crowd walking towards the stairwell. The Mexican spoke no English, but he pointed his thumb into his mouth in a drinking motion.

'There you go, brother,' Mojo said.

The sheriff glared at us all, the red knots on his face tight against the skin.

I came up behind Rie and slipped my arm around her waist, and kissed the cool smoothness of her cheek. She turned her face up to me and I kissed her again and ran my hand through her hair.

'How did you do it, babe?' she said.

'I want you to meet R. C. Richardson,' I said.

R. C. lifted off his Stetson with a slow, exact motion and let it rest against his pants leg, and bent forward with a slight bow and his best look of southern deference to womanhood on his face. He pulled in his stomach and stiffened his shoulders, and for just a moment you didn't notice the bolo tie and the yellow cowboy boots.

'I'm proud to meet you, miss,' he said.

'Rie Velasquez,' she said, and her eyes smiled at him.

'I was just telling Hack I didn't have time to eat breakfast this morning, so why don't we go across the street to the cafe and see if we can get a steak?'

His eyes were looking over Rie's face, and I knew that it took everything in him to prevent them from going further. He stepped aside and let us walk in front of him as we followed the crowd upstairs. R. C. was about to begin one of his performances. He had several roles, and he did each of them well: good-natured oil man when he was buying leases; humble Kiwanian and patriot; friend-of-the-boys with a wallet full of unlisted telephone numbers. But now he was a gentleman rancher, somebody's father, an older friend with his fingers on all the right buttons when you were in trouble. We had to wait for the deputy to find the brown envelopes with our wallets, change, and belts in them. He was young and evidently new to his job, and he had difficulty reading the handwriting of the people who had booked us.

'Snap it up, boy,' R.C. said. 'We don't want to grow no older in this place.'

'R.C., we still have about seventy-five feet to go to the door,' I said.

'You either do a job or you don't,' he said. 'That's what's wrong all over this country. Like that little bondsman back there. He don't spit without sitting down and thinking about it first.'

We signed for our possessions, and R.C. slipped his

slicker over Rie's shoulders. It was still raining hard outside. It came down in curving sheets that swept across the flooded courthouse lawn. Some of the oaks were almost bare, and the leaves floated up against the trunks in islands. Cars and trucks were stalled in the street, the headlight beams weak in the driving rain, and somewhere a horn was stuck and blowing. The neon sign over the cafe and tavern looked like colored smoke in the wet, diffused light.

R.C. opened up a big umbrella over our heads and we splashed down the sidewalk towards the cafe. The air smelled clean and cool, and even the rain, slanting under the umbrella and burning against the skin, felt like an absolution after the day and night in jail. There's no smell exactly like that of a jail, and when you can leave it behind you and walk out into a rain storm you feel that the other experience was never really there.

The water in the street was up to our knees, and R.C. held Rie by one arm and covered our heads with the umbrella while exposing his own. The rain sluiced off the brim of his pearl-gray Stetson, his western suit was drenched, his shirt had popped open more above his belt and his stomach winked out like a roll of wet dough. He was an old crook and a lecher, but I liked him in a strange way – maybe because he had no malice towards anyone, and even in his dishonesty he was faithful to the corrupt system that he served, and his buffoonery lent a little humor to it. Possibly that's an odd reason to like someone, but I had known much worse men in the oil business than R. C. Richardson.

He opened the door for us, and we went inside with the rain swirling through the screen. Men in cowboy boots and bluejeans were drinking bottles of Pearl and Jax at the counter, a Negro was racking pool balls in back under an electric bulb with a tin shade around it, and the jukebox, with cracks all over the plastic casing, was playing a lament about lost women and the wild side of life. R.C. took off Rie's slicker and held the chair for her at one of the tables with oilcloth covers tacked around the sides. In his politeness he was awkward, like a man who had been put together with bad hinges, but it was seldom that he was called upon to show manners above those practiced in the Dallas Petroleum Club.

'R.C., you're not a sonofabitch, after all,' I said.

He looked at me strangely, his thick hands on the table top.

'Well, I hope your brother was wearing his brown britches when he watched the late news last night,' he said, then blinked at Rie, his smooth face uncertain. 'Excuse me. I forget I ain't in the oil field sometime.'

She smiled at him, and he took in his breath and opened his fingers. We hadn't eaten at the jail that morning, and I could smell the pork chops and slices of ham frying on the stove. We ordered steaks and scrambled eggs, with side orders of hashbrowns and tomatoes.

'You must have put your fist plumb up to the elbow in that man's stomach,' R.C. said. 'I've never seen a man dump over that hard. I thought he was going to strangle right there on the ground.'

'The local news boys must have done a good job,' I said.

'They sure as hell did. They got it all. You smiling with handcuffs on and them two cops holding you by each arm. I bet Bailey needed a respirator if he seen

271

that.' R.C. laughed and lit a cigar. 'Goddamn, if I wouldn't mark off all that bail money just to see him trying to get to the phone.'

The waiter brought our steaks and eggs, and set a pot of coffee on a napkin in the center of the table. I cut a piece of steak and ate it with a slice of peppered tomato. R.C. was still laughing with the cigar in his mouth.

'You reckon he's already called the mental ward in Austin?' he said.

'I think it's been a good morning for you,' I said.

'Hack, you and him have been giving me hell all these years, and by God I don't get many chances to bail my lawyer out of jail.'

'How bad is it going to be, Hack?' Rie said.

'I don't know.'

The door opened and the rain swept across the floor. I felt the cool air against my neck.

'Miz Rie, don't worry about Hack losing in court, because he don't.'

'It might be a little more difficult this time,' I said.

'I remember once I was almost chopping cotton on Sugarland farm, and you had the case dismissed in a week.'

I remembered it also – painfully. Four years ago R.C. had drilled into a state-owned oil pool and had bribed three state officials, one of whom went to the penitentiary.

'He walks into court with that white suit, and it don't take him five minutes to have everybody in the jury box watching him.'

Rie looked at me, and I dropped my eyes.

'Once he got a colored man off for raping a white

woman, and I swear to God the jury never even knew why they let him go.'

'It's almost noon. Let's have a beer,' I said.

'You know you ain't going to get any time. Why you let this girl worry?'

'Order some beers.'

'You really think they're going to put somebody from your family in the penitentiary?'

'Would you shut up, R.C.?'

His face was hurt and embarrassed, and Rie touched my hand under the table.

'You're giving away all his secrets,' she said. 'He hates to admit that he's anything but a left-handed country lawyer.'

He looked at her eyes, and his face mended as though a breeze had blown across it. He was in love with her, and if I hadn't been at the table his performance would have grown to absurd proportions.

We finished eating, and R.C. paid the check and left a three-dollar tip on the table. We walked across the flooded street in the rain to his Mercedes, and he opened the car door for Rie and held the umbrella over her head while she got in. The inside panels were covered with yellow, rolled leather, and the black seats were stitched with a gold longhorn design, and on top of the dashboard there was an empty whiskey glass and a compass inside a plastic bubble. We drove slowly out of town while the water washed back in waves over the curbs, and R.C. pulled a pint of Four Roses from his coat pocket and offered it to us.

'Well, that's the first time I ever seen you turn one down,' he said, and he drank from the bottle as though it contained soda water.

The county road that led to the cannery had collapsed in places along the edges from the overflow of ditch water, and the rows in the fields had been beaten almost flat by the rain or washed into humps of mud. The gusts of wind covered the brown water with curls and lines like puckered skin, and the torn cotton and leaves turned in eddies around the cedar fence posts. In the distance I saw a cow trying to lift her flanks out of the mud.

A great section of the cannery roof had been blown away in the storm. The metal was ripped upward in a ragged slash, like a row of twisted knives, and there was a huge black hole where the rest of the roof had been. Picket signs were strewn over the ground by my automobile, and the rain drummed down in a roar on the tin building, the loading platform, and the freight cars. R.C. parked as close as he could to the Cadillac and went around to Rie's side with the umbrella. His western pants were splattered with mud up to the knees, and drops of water ran down his soft face. He closed the door after her and walked around to the driver's side with me, the rain thudding on the umbrella.

'Look, Hack, it's going to take some money to beat this thing,' he said. 'I know you got plenty of it, but if you need any more you only got to call. Another thing. You take care of that girl, hear?'

'All right, R.C.'

'One more thing, by God. I think you flushed your political career down the hole, but I felt right proud of you out there. That boy looked like he had muscles in his shit till you come off the ground. I always told Bailey you was crazy but you're still a goddamn good man.'

He slammed the door and splashed through the mud to his automobile, his face bent downwards against the rain. We followed him out through the cannery gate onto the county road, and I saw the empty whiskey bottle sail from his window into the irrigation ditch. Then he floored the Mercedes and sped away from us in a shower of mud and brown water.

'He's a wonderful man,' Rie said.

'I believe he liked you a little bit, too.'

'Where's he going?'

'Back to his motel room and get sentimentally drunk in his underwear. Then about dark he'll drive across the border and try to buy a whole brothel.'

'Couldn't we ask him over?'

'He'd feel better with the morning intact the way it is. In fact, it would hurt him if he had to continue.'

The collapsed places along the edges of the road were beaded with gravel, and cut back into deepening sink holes in the center. I could feel the soft ground break under my wheels.

'Was he straight about nobody from your family going to the penitentiary?' she said.

'The deputy already has my civil rights charge against him, and if those camera boys were any good they filmed his knee in my eye, and I can make a hard case against the cops. But there's a good chance I'll get disbarred.'

'Oh, Hack.'

I put my arm around her wet shoulders and pulled her close to me.

'Stop worrying about it, babe. My grandfather knocked John Wesley Hardin on his ass with a rifle stock, and Hardin was a lot tougher than the Texas Bar Association.'

'I kept making fun of you about picket lines and the union, and now you might get burned worse than any of us.'

Her back was cold under my arm. I kissed the corner of her eye and squeezed her into me.

'Don't you know that real gunfighters never lose?' I said.

She put her hand on my chest, and I could feel my heart beat against her palm. She looked up at me once, then pressed her cheek against my shoulder the rest of the way back to town.

The dirt yards in the poor district were covered with water up to the front porches, and the waves from my automobile washed through the chicken-wire fences and rolled against the houses. Tin cans, garbage, and half-submerged tree limbs floated in the ditches, and a dead dog, his skin scalded pink by the rain, lay entangled in an island of trash around the base of a telephone pole. Some of the shingles had been stripped by the wind from the union headquarters roof, and the building itself leaned at an angle on the foundation. I took off my boots, and we waded through the water to the porch.

Mojo and a Mexican man were sitting at the table in the front room with a half-gallon bottle of yellow wine between them. They had melted a candle to the table, and Mojo was heating his glass of wine over the flame. The smoke curled in a black scorch around the glass. His eyes were small and red in the light.

'My brother here is teaching me how to put some fire in that spodiodi,' he said. 'You can see it climb up right inside the color. That's what I been doing wrong all these years. Drinking without no style.'

He drank the glass down slowly, and poured it full again. I could smell the wine all the way across the room.

'This telegram was in the door when I got back from the jail, and a man come by in a taxicab looking for you,' he said. 'He didn't leave no name, but he looked just like you. Except for a minute I thought he had to go to the bathroom real bad.'

I tore open the envelope and read the telegram, dated late last night.

I DON'T KNOW IF YOU WILL RECEIVE THIS. I GUESS I DON'T CARE WHETHER YOU DO OR NOT. CALL VERISA IF YOU FEEL LIKE IT. OR SIMPLY TEAR THIS UP.

Bailey didn't bother to sign his name.

'What did the man say?' I said.

'He was going up to the cafe, and then he was coming back,' Mojo said. 'He give me a dollar so I'd be sure to tell you.'

Good old perceptive Bailey, I thought.

'I think we ought to buy that man a glass of this mellow heat when he comes back. He needs it,' Mojo said.

'He needs a new mind,' I said.

Rie went into the back to change clothes. I looked in the ice box for a beer, and then drove the Cadillac down to the tavern and bought a dozen bottles of Jax and a block of ice. I found a tin bucket in the kitchen, and chipped the ice over the bottles. Rie came out of the bedroom dressed in a pair of white ducks, sandals, and a flowered shirt. She had brushed back her gold-tipped hair and had put on her hoop earrings and an Indian bead necklace.

'Hey, good-looking,' I said, and put my arms around her. She pressed her whole body against me, with her arms around my neck, and I kissed her on the mouth, then along her cheek and ear. I could smell the rain in her hair.

'Do you have to leave with him?' she said.

'No.'

'Are you sure, Hack?'

'We'll give him some of Mojo's sneaky pete. That's all he needs.'

She ran her fingertips over the back of my neck and pressed her head hard against my chest.

'Don't feel that way, babe,' I said. 'I just have to talk to him.'

She breathed through her mouth and held me tightly against her. I kissed her hair and turned her face up towards me. Her soldier's discipline was gone.

'I couldn't ever leave you, Rie,' I said. 'Bailey is down here out of his own compulsion. That's all there is to it.'

I hadn't lied to her before, and it didn't feel good. I picked up the bucket of beer and cracked ice by the bail, and we walked onto the porch and sat in two wicker chairs away from the rain slanting under the eaves. The solid grey of the sky had broken into drifting clouds, and I could see the faint, brown outline of the hills in the distance. The Rio Grande was high and swirling with mud, the surface dimpled with rain, and the tall bank on the Mexican side of the river had started to crumble into the water. I opened two beers and raked the ice off the bottles with my palm.

It had been a long time since I had enjoyed the rain so much. The wind was cool and smelled of the wet land and the dripping trees, and I remembered the times as a boy when I used to sit on the back porch and watch the rain fall on the short cotton. In the distance I could see Cappie's grey cabin framed in the mist by the river, and even though I couldn't see the river itself I knew the bass were rising to the surface to feed on the caterpillars that had been washed out of the willows.

'Is he really like you describe him?' Rie said.

'I don't know. Maybe I'm unfair to him. After our father died he had to take care of the practical things while I played baseball at Baylor, and then I quit college to join the Navy, and he had to finish law school and run the ranch at the same time. He can't think in any terms now except finances and safe people, and he usually makes bad choices with both of them. Sometimes I'm afraid that if he ever finds out where he's invested most of his life he'll shoot himself.'

I drank out of the beer and leaned my chair back against the porch wall. Inside, I could hear Mojo singing, 'Hey, hey, baby, take a whiff on me.'

'Do you think that's why people shoot themselves?' she said.

'I never thought there was anything so bad that it could make a man take his life in seconds. But I do know there are other ways to do it to yourself over long periods of time.'

'Bailey sounds like a sad man.'

'He gets some satisfaction from his tragic view. His comparison of himself with me lets him feel correct all the time.'

'Hey, hey, everybody take a whiff on me,' Mojo sang inside.

I saw a taxicab turn into the flooded street and drive towards us, the yellow sides splattered with mud. The floating garbage and tin cans rolled in the car's wake.

'Do you want me to go for a drive?' she said.

'No. I want you to meet him. It will be the best thing that's happened to him in a long time.'

'I feel like I shouldn't be here, Hack.'

'Who the hell lives here, anyway? He doesn't, and I sure didn't ask him down.'

I squeezed her hand, but I saw it made her uncomfortable. The waves from the taxi washed up through the yard and hit against the porch steps. Bailey paid the driver and stepped out the back door into the water. His brown windbreaker was spotted with rain, and the lines in his brow and around his eyes had deepened with lack of sleep. The rims of his eyes were red. In fact, his whole face looked middle-aged, as though he had worked hard to make it that way. He walked up through the water with his head lowered slightly and his mouth in a tight line.

'How you doing, brother?' I said, and took a sip out of the beer.

'I have a plane at the county airport,' he said. He looked straight at me and never turned his head towards Rie.

'Get out of the rain and meet someone and have a beer.'

'We'll leave your car there. You can fly back and get it later,' he said. His voice had a quiet and determined righteousness to it, the kind of tone which he reserved for particularly tragic occasions, and it had always infuriated me. But I was resolved this time.

'It's bad weather for a flight, Bailey. You should have waited a day or so,' I said. I was surprised that he had flown at all, because he was terrified of airplanes.

'Do you have anything inside?' he said.

'Not a thing.'

'Then we can be going.'

He was making it hard.

'Would you sit down a minute, for God's sake?' I said. 'Or at least not stand under the eave with rain dripping on your head.'

He stepped up on the porch and wiped his forehead with his palm. He still refused to recognize Rie. I carried a chair over from the other side of the porch and pulled another beer from the ice bucket.

'There. Sit,' I said. 'This is Rie Velasquez. She's the coordinator for the union.'

'How do you do, ma'am?' He looked at her for the first time, and his eyes lingered longer on her face than he had probably wanted them to. She smiled at him, and momentarily he forgot that he was supposed to be a somber man with a purpose.

I opened the bottle of beer and handed it to him. The chips of ice slid down the neck. He started to put the bottle on the porch railing.

'Drink the beer, Bailey. If you had some more of that stuff, you wouldn't have ulcers.'

'The Senator and John Williams are at the house.'

'John Williams. What's that bastard doing in my home?'

'He was spending the weekend with the Senator, and he drove down with him this morning.'

'You know the old man wouldn't let an asshole like that in our back door.'

'He told me he would still like to contribute money to the campaign.'

'You'd better get him out of my house.'

'Why don't you take care of it yourself? This is my last errand.'

'Do you think we could get that in writing?' I said.

'You don't know the lengths other people go to for your benefit. The Senator is going to stay with you, and so is Verisa, and I wouldn't be here if I didn't feel an obligation to her.'

'What obligation is that, Bailey?' I said.

'I'm going to fix lunch,' Rie said.

'No, stay. I want to hear about this feeling of obligation. What is it exactly, brother?'

His eyes looked quickly at Rie, and he drank out of the beer.

'Don't worry about decorum or people's feelings,' I said. 'Dump it out on the porch and let's look at it. You're doing a swell job so far.'

'I'll be inside, Hack,' Rie said.

'No, goddamn. Let Bailey finish. He's saved this up in his head through every airpocket between here and Austin.'

'All right,' he said. 'For the seven years of disappointment you've given her and the alcoholism and the apologies she's had to make to people all over the state. A lesser woman would have taken you into court years ago and pulled out your fingernails. Right now she's under sedation, but that will probably slide past you like everything else in your life does.'

'What do you mean, sedation?' I said.

'She called me up drunk an hour after the television

broadcast, and I had to go over to the house with a doctor from Yoakum.'

Rie lit a cigarette and looked out into the rain. Her suntanned cheeks were pale and her eyes bright. I didn't know why I had forced her to sit through it, and it was too late to change anything now. The wind blew the rain against the bottom of Bailey's chair.

'How is she now?' I said.

'What do you think? She drank a half bottle of your whiskey, and the doctor had to give her an injection to get her in bed.'

The bottle of beer felt thick in my hand. I wondered what doctor would give anyone an intravenous sedative on top of alcohol.

'She threw away her pills this morning and tried to fix breakfast for the Senator and Williams,' Bailey said. 'She almost fell down in the kitchen and I put her to bed again and refilled her prescription.'

'Don't you know better than to give drugs to people with alcohol in their system?' I said. But he didn't. His face was a confession of moral earnestness with no awareness of its consequence.

'Go back with him, Hack,' Rie said.

'Bailey, why in the bloody hell do you bring on things like this?' I said.

'Don't you have it confused?' he said.

'No. You have this talent for turning the simple into a derelict's hangover.'

'I think you're shouting at the wrong person.'

'You've always got all kinds of cool when you do it, too. Think about it. Isn't it in moments like these that you're happiest?'

'I don't need to listen to this.'

'Hell, no, you don't. You just dump the hand

grenades out on the porch and let other people kick them around.'

'I told you I'm through with this crap, Hack.'

'You've been peddling my ass by the chunk to all buyers and bitching about it at the same time, and now you're through. Is that right, buddy? Frankly, you make me so goddamn mad I could knock you flat out into the yard.'

'Stop it, Hack. Go on back with him,' Rie said. Her face was flushed, and her fingers were trembling on the arm of the wicker chair.

'Should I run a foot race with him down to the airport? Or maybe Bailey can import the whole bunch down here and we can sit on the porch and find out what a sonofabitch I am.'

Rie put her fingers on her brow and dropped her eyes, but I could see the wetness on her eyelashes. None of us spoke. The rain drummed flatly on the shingled roof and ran off the eaves, swinging into the wind. My face was perspiring, and I wiped my forehead on my sleeve and drank the foam out of the bottle. I looked at her again and I felt miserable.

'I'm sorry, babe,' I said.

She turned her head away from Bailey and put an unlit cigarette in her mouth.

'Call me tonight at the beer joint. Somebody will come down for me,' she said.

The wind blew the curls on the back of her neck, and I could see her shoulders shaking. But there was nothing to do or say with Bailey there, and I went inside the screen and asked Mojo to stay with her until I called. When I came back out Bailey was still on the porch.

'I didn't get out the back door on you,' I said.

But he didn't understand; he stood against the railing, with the rain blowing across his slacks, as though his physical proximity was necessary to draw me into the automobile. I started to tell him to get in the car and read a road map and not raise his eyes until he heard me open the door, but he would have had something to say about that and we would start back into it all over again. When we drove away Rie was still looking out into the rain with the unlit cigarette in her fingers.

We didn't speak on the way to the airport. The air conditioner stopped working, and the windows fogged with humidity and the sweat rolled down my face and neck into my shirt. I felt a black anger towards Bailey that you can only feel towards someone you grew up with, and as the heat became more intense in the car I resented every motion that he made. He opened the window and let the rain blow across the leather seats, then he closed it and tried to pull off his windbreaker by the cuffs and hit me against the arm. I turned on the radio and we both listened to a Christian crusade evangelist rant about the communist antichrist in Viet Nam.

The two-engine plane was parked at the end of the runway in three inches of water. The rain beat against the silver, riveted plates of the fuselage, and the wind out of the hills was still strong enough to push the plane's weight against the anchor blocks around the wheels. In the distance the hills looked as brown and smooth as clay.

The cabin had three metal seats in it, spot-welded to the bulkhead, with old military safety straps, and when the pilot turned the ignition, the electric starter on the port engine wouldn't take hold. Then the propeller flipped over stiffly several times, black exhaust blew back across the wing, and the whole plane vibrated with the engines' roar. The backwash from the propellers blew the concrete dry around the plane, and the pilot taxied out slowly on the runway with the nose into the wind. Bailey kept wiping the rain water and perspiration back through his hair, and his other hand was clenched tightly on his thigh.

'I'm going to jump it up fast,' the pilot said over his shoulder. 'There's bad down drafts over those hills.'

Bailey reached under his seat and took out a half-pint bottle of sloe gin in a paper sack. He didn't look at me while he drank. The plane gained speed, the brown water blowing off the sides of the runway, and the wet fields and the few silver hangars flashed by the windows, then we lifted off abruptly into the grey light, the plane shaking against the wind and the strain of its own engines. The crest of the hills swept by below us, and in moments I could see the whole Rio Grande Valley flatten out through the window. The fields were divided into great, brown squares of water, the orchards that hadn't been destroyed by the storm were dark green against the land, and the river had almost covered the willow trees along its banks. There were dead cattle and horses in the fields, their stiff legs turned out of the water, and the barbed-wire fences had been bent down even with the road. Milking barns had been crushed over sideways, and some farmhouses had lost their roofs, and from the air I felt that I was looking down into something private, an arrangement of kitchens and bedrooms and family eating tables, which I had been unfairly allowed to see.

Bailey's face was white, and he pulled on the bottle

again and coughed. He hated for me to see him drink, but his terror of the plane was greater than any feeling he had about personal image or even his ulcerated stomach.

'We'll be there in an hour,' I said. 'He's above any bad currents now.'

Bailey was rigid in the metal seat, the safety belt strapped across his stomach. His fingers were pressed tight across the flat side of the bottle, and the perspiration was still rolling down his face.

'I don't know what kind of agreement you'll come to with Verisa and the Senator, but you and I are going to have one with our practice,' he said. His voice was dry, and his accent had deepened with his fear.

'Why do I have to come to an agreement with anyone?' I knew all the answers he had, but he wanted to talk or do anything to forget the plane and the distance from the ground.

'Because you're holding a big I.O.U. to other people,' he said.

'Did it ever strike you that the Senator is a bad man who never did anything for anyone unless his own ass was buttered first? That for thirty years he's served every bad cause in this country? Or maybe that he needs me much more than I needed him?'

He sipped out of the sloe gin, and the cap rattled on the bottle neck when he tried to screw it back on.

'I've already told you, you say it to him,' he said. 'I don't give a goddamn where your paranoia takes you this time, because tomorrow I'm going to write a check for your half of the practice.'

'Okay, Bailey,' I said, and watched him hold in all

his anger and bent ideas about a correct world and the correct people who should live in it.

I had thought we would land at one of the small airstrips in Yoakum or Cuero, but Bailey had told the pilot to put the plane down in the empty pasture behind my house. The land was flat and cleared of stones, and ten feet above the riverbed, but even from the air I could see the pools of water that had collected in the Bermuda grass. We circled over the ranch once, the wings tilting in the wind currents, and I tapped the pilot's shoulder and leaned against the back of his seat.

'There's armadillo sinkholes and a lot of soft dirt in that field,' I shouted over the noise of the engines.

He turned sideways briefly and nodded, then began his approach over the river. The fields of corn, tomatoes, and cotton rushed towards us, the stalks and green plants pressed into the earth by the wind, and I saw the natural gas wells pumping up and down and the windmill ginning like a flash of light in the thin rain, the grey roof of the stable and the weathered smokehouse leaning into the depression where we put the oak logs, and then the white house itself with the latticework verandah and the rose bushes and poplar trees along the front lane. We dipped suddenly over the post oaks by Cappie's cabin and hit the pasture in a spray of mud and grass across the front windows. The wheels went deep into the wet ground, the tail lifted momentarily into the air, and the pilot gunned the engines to keep us in a straight line across the pasture, although he couldn't see anything in front of him. Water and mud streaked across the side windows, then one wheel sunk in a soft spot and we spun in a sliding half circle, with one engine feathered, against the white fence that separated my side lawn and the pasture.

The pilot feathered the other engine and wiped his face on his sleeve. Bailey had spilled the bottle of sloe gin over his slacks.

'Do you have a hard drink inside?' the pilot said.

'If you drink Jack Daniels,' I said.

I opened the cabin door, and the rain blew into our faces. We climbed over the white fence and ran across the lawn through the oak trees to the front porch. The Senator's limousine with the tinted windows was parked on the gravel lane. The poplar trees were arched in the wind, and magnolia leaves and rose petals were scattered across the grass. One of Verisa's large earthen flowerpots had fallen from the upstairs verandah, and the soft dirt and cracked pottery lay in a pile on the front steps. It seemed a long time since I had been home; maybe the house looked strange to me because the Senator's car was parked in front, but even the worn vertical line of bullet holes in the porch column seemed new, as though Wes Hardin had drilled them there only yesterday.

I took the pilot through the front hall into my library and opened a bottle of bourbon for him and filled a silver bucket with ice cubes. He sat in my leather chair, his wet cigarette still in his mouth, and poured the glass half full without water.

'I usually stay on a formal basis with my passengers,' he said, his face fatigued over the raised glass, 'but are you guys on a kamikaze mission or something?'

I closed the door behind me without answering, and walked into the living room. The Senator was sitting in the deer-hide chair by the bar, dressed in blue slacks and a gray golf shirt with a highball balanced on his crossed knee (the whiskey was just enough to color the water). His tan was darker than when I had seen him last, and his mowed, white hair moved slightly in the soft current from the air conditioner. John Williams leaned against the bar with his sunglasses on, tall, the face pale and as unnatural-looking as smooth rubber, and his tan suit hung on him without a line or crease in it. Verisa sat on the couch in a sundress she had bought three weeks ago at Neiman-Marcus, and if she had a hangover from the alcohol or the sedation she had done a wonderful job of burying it inside her. Her auburn hair was brushed back against her shoulders, the makeup on her face made her look fresh and cool, and she lay back comfortably against the cushions with the stem of her wineglass between her fingers as though she were at a D.A.R. cocktail party. But there was also a quick glint in her eyes when I walked into the room, and I knew she was looking forward to a painful retribution on my part.

The Senator rose from his chair and shook hands with me. His blue eyes wrinkled at the corners when he smiled, and his hand was as square and hard as a bricklayer's.

'You've had an eventful weekend,' he said.

'It was probably exaggerated by the television boys,' I said.

'I don't believe there was any camera distortion there. Do you?' The acetylene-blue eyes wrinkled again so that it was impossible to read them. 'But, anyway, you know John Williams.'

'Mr Holland,' Williams said, and raised his glass. 'Hi.'

'I'm enjoying your taste in bourbon.'

'Help yourself to a bucket of it,' I said.

'Thank you. I think I will,' he said, and smiled somewhere behind his sunglasses.

'In fact, take a case with you. I have a crate of limes on the back porch to go with it.'

The room was silent a moment. Bailey looked at the floor, his brown windbreaker dark with rain, then went behind the bar and raked a mint julep glass through the ice bin.

'You want water in it, Hack?' he said.

'Give it to Mr Williams. I'm changing my taste in bourbon.'

'Maybe I had better wait on the porch,' Williams said.

'There's no need for that,' the Senator said, and his blue eyes moved onto my face again.

'Hell, no,' I said. 'That's a real storm out there, Mr Williams. Enough to short out all the electric circuits on an ICBM.'

I despised him and what he represented, and I let him have a good look at the anger I felt towards his presence in my home. He finished his drink and clicked his glass on the bar.

'I think it's better, Allen,' he said.

'Fix John another drink,' the Senator said to Bailey.

'Get some limes, too, Bailey,' I said.

'For one afternoon would you talk without your histrionics?' Verisa said.

'I haven't had much of a chance to talk today. Bailey has spent the last two hours giving me the south Texas sonofabitch award.'

'This doesn't have to be unpleasant, Hack,' the Senator said.

'Talking reasonably is beyond him,' Verisa said. 'It violates some confirmed principle he has about offending other people.'

'Give Mr Williams a drink, Bailey,' I said. 'See about the pilot, too. I think he's getting plowed.'

'Well, we won't drag it out then, Hack,' the Senator said. 'The state committee called last night and asked me if we should drop you and run a boy from Gonzales. I told them that we would still carry the district no matter who runs, and I want you in the House in January.'

'That's good of you, Senator, but I wonder why we all have this intense commitment to my career,' and I looked right through the wrinkled light in his eyes.

'Because I feel an obligation to your father, who was a good friend to me. I think what you've done is irresponsible, but with time you'll probably make a fine congressman.'

'I'm afraid that I'm through with political fortunes.'

'That's a lovely attitude at this point,' Verisa said.

'I believe Hack is still a little angry with Rio Grande policemen,' the Senator said. 'Actually, we may have picked up more of the union vote, and your arrest won't hurt you with the Negroes and the Mexicans. The important factor is that we make use of it before the Republican gentleman does.'

'Sorry. I think that boy from Gonzales would be a better bet.'

'You're everything I expected today,' Verisa said.

'How about the car planted against the fence?'

'You're lovely just as you are. It couldn't have been more anticipated,' she said.

'I want to finish this, Hack,' the Senator said. 'I

plan to talk to the committee this afternoon and give them your assurance about the rest of the campaign.'

'I don't think you should do that, Senator.'

'The assault charge can be taken care of,' he said. 'It will probably involve a small appointment in Austin, but it's a simple matter.'

He had still chosen not to hear me, and I felt the anger rising inside me.

'Don't you realize what's being done for you?' Bailey said from behind the bar. 'Try to think about it a minute. You committed a felony yesterday that could get you disbarred or even sent to jail.'

'No, I don't realize a damn thing, because I have an idea that all this investment in me isn't out of good will and old friendships. What do you think, Mr Williams?'

He sipped from his fresh drink with a sprig of mint leaves in it, rested his arm on the bar, and looked at me from behind his sunglasses. The texture of his skin was the most unnatural I had ever seen on a human being.

'I think it would save time if the case were explained to you a little more candidly,' he said.

The Senator looked at Williams, and momentarily I saw the same uncomfortable flicker in his eyes that I had seen on the trip to Washington when I had realized that predators came in various sizes. He paused a moment, then turned back to me before Williams could speak again, his fingers pressed on the highball glass.

'Possibly your alternatives aren't as clear or easy as you might believe, Hack,' he said. 'I've made some commitments in this election that I intend to see honored.'

'It's a matter of votes on a House bill to rescind the oil-depletion allowance, Mr Holland. Although Allen doesn't run again for two years, it's been necessary to promise several oil companies that the right people will be on a committee to prevent anyone from lowering the twenty-seven-and-a-half-percent allowance that we now have. As you know, it involves a great deal, and so a few people have pressed Allen rather hard on winning support.'

Williams was enjoying the Senator's discomfort, but I didn't care about either of them then. I felt light inside, like a high school athlete who had been told he was needed to pick up the towels in the locker room.

'Did you know about this shit, Bailey?' I said.

'No.'

'You sold my ass all over the state and you never guessed what it was about.'

'I didn't know, Hack.'

'Well, you saw me coming, Senator,' I said.

'Are we going to enjoy a melodrama about it now?' Verisa said.

'No, I think I just finished the ninth inning, and you can have the whole goddamn ball park.'

'I believe you're being overly serious about this. The oil-depletion allowance is in the interest of the state,' the Senator said. 'Also, every holder of office pays some kind of personal price to represent his constituency.'

'I'd call that boy in Gonzales. Let me have a beer, Bailey.'

'Maybe you should tell Mr Holland about the rest of his alternative now,' Williams said. He raised his drink slowly to his mouth.

'I thought you'd been saving something special out,'

I said. Bailey handed me the beer in a glass, and I took a cigar from the oakwood box on the coffee table. The Senator sat down in the deer-hide chair and crossed his legs with his highball in his hand, but his eyes didn't look at me.

'I don't like to do this, but there's a man named Lester Dixon in Kansas City and he's made a deposition about the time he spent with you in a North Korean prison camp,' he said. His eyes looked at the end of his shoe, thoughtful, as though he were considering a delicate premise before he spoke again.

Verisa took a cigarette from her pack and put it in her mouth. Her arm lay back against the couch, and her breasts swelled against her sundress when she breathed.

I lit my cigar and stared into the Senator's face.

'What did Airman First Class Dixon have to say?' I said.

'I don't believe we have to talk about all of it here,' he said.

'I think you should, Senator. I imagine that Lester's deposition was very expensive.'

'Two men from your shack were executed after they were informed upon.' He raised his eyes into my face and tried to hold them there, but I stared back hard at him and he took a drink from his glass.

'Did he tell you how it was done?' I said.

'I never met him.'

'He's an interesting person. I helped send him to prison for five years.'

'The statement is twenty pages long, and it's witnessed by two attorneys,' he said. 'It's been compared for accuracy with the transcript from his court-martial, and I don't think you'll be able to contest what he says about your complicity in the deaths of two defenceless men.'

'The telephone is in the hall, Senator. Next to it is a list of numbers, one of which is *The Austin American*. No, instead finish your drink and let Verisa get the city desk for you.'

'It will be done more subtly than that. Possibly a leak from someone on the state committee, a small rumor at first, and then a reporter will be given the whole thing.'

'You probably have ways I've never dreamed about.'

'That's true, but the outcome will be the same in this case.'

'Then I guess we can all say good-day to each other.'

'No, there's one more thing,' he said, and his eyes took on the same expression they had before he drove the tennis ball into my nose. 'Right now you're enjoying your virtue. With an impetuous decision you've become a Spartan lying on his shield, and I'm sure you'll need this image for yourself during the next few weeks. But I want to correct a couple of your ideas about integrity in political office. Negotiation and compromise are part of any politician's career, and your father learned that lesson his first term in Congress.'

'What do you mean?'

'He accepted a fifteen-thousand-dollar contribution to sponsor the sale of public land to a wildcat company in Dallas. The land sold for fifty dollars an acre.'

'Bailey, do you want to tell these men to get out, or you want to wait on me?'

He looked down at the bar, his forehead white.

'Bailey,' I said.

The balding spot on his head was perspiring, and I could see the raised veins in the back of his hands.

'Just look at me,' I said.

'I'm sorry, Hack. I didn't know they were going to do this.'

'Then you tell them to get out.'

He leaned on his arms, his face still turned downwards, and I felt my head begin to grow light, as though there were no oxygen in my blood.

'Goddamn it, you're not going to bring these men into my home to do this, and then stare at the bar,' I said.

'He was going to lose the ranch, Hack. He knew heart disease was killing him, and he was afraid he'd die and leave us nothing.'

The rain blew against the windows, and I could hear the oak branches sweeping heavily back and forth on the roof. Outside, the light was grey in the trees, and the stripped leaves stuck wetly against the trunks. My dead cigar felt like a stick between my fingers.

'You and this man will leave now, Senator,' I said.

'Thank you for the drink, Mr Holland,' Williams said, and set his glass on the bar. 'You have a nice home here.'

'Thank you, too, Verisa,' the Senator said. 'I'm sorry if we've made the day a little hard for you.'

The three of them rose and walked together to the front hall. They could have been people saying goodbye after a Sunday dinner. Verisa's sundress fit tightly against her smooth back, and she had a way of holding herself at a door that made her look like a little girl. Williams raised his hand once to me, backwards, the way a European would, and smiled again somewhere behind those black-green glasses.

'Good-bye, Hack,' the Senator said.

I lit my cigar and didn't look back at him, then I heard the door click shut as I stared down into the flame.

'I'm sorry,' Bailey said.

'Forget it and give me one hard one.'

'I wouldn't have brought you back for this.'

'I know that. Just make it about three inches and a little water.'

He poured into a tall shot glass and let the whiskey run over the edge. He started to wipe off the counter with a towel, and then knocked the glass into the sink.

'Christ, Hack,' he said.

'I'm all right,' I said, and poured the shot glass full myself and drank it down neat.

'You goddamn fool,' Verisa said.

'Leave him alone,' Bailey said.

'You're going to pay for it with every stick and nail in this house,' she said.

I walked away from them towards the hall. The hum of the air conditioners and the heavy sweep of the oaks against the eaves were loud in my head, and the boards in the floor seemed to bend under my boots. I could feel something important begin to roll loose inside, in the way that you pull out a brick from the bottom of a wall. I opened the door to my library and took the cigar out of my mouth. The pilot still sat in my leather chair with the half-empty bottle of Jack Daniels in his lap. His face was colorless, and he had dropped a lighted cigarette on the rug.

'Do you think you can get it up again today?' I said.

'Yeah, buddy, if you don't mind flying drunk,' he said.

We walked out into the rain, crossed the lawn, and climbed over the fence to the plane. The air was sweet with the smell of the wet land and the dripping trees and the ruined tomatoes that had been pounded into the furrows. The chain on the windmill had broken and the water was spilling white over the lip of the trough into the horse lot. I could see the willows on the river bank bending against the sky, and the deep cut of the drainages on the distant hills and the thin line of sunlight on the horizon's edge. My two oil wells glistened blackly in the rain, pumping up and down with their obscene motion, and the weathered shacks of the Negro and Mexican farm workers stood out against the washed land like matchboxes that had been dropped from the sky at an odd angle.

The pilot wiped the plane's windows clean of mud and grass with his windbreaker, and we took off across the pasture in a shower of water from the backdraft of the propellers. Just before we reached the river the pilot pulled back on the stick and gave the engines everything they would take, and we lifted over the trees into the sky and turned into the wind. The river, the willows, the post oaks and Cappie's cabin dropped away below us, and then the house and the deep tire imprints of the Senator's limousine on my gravel lane, and finally the small whitewashed markers in the Holland family cemetery.

epilogue

No one won the strike, not the growers or the farm companies or the field workers, because the storm didn't leave anything to win. After the water had drained from the fields, the ruined citrus lay on the ground and rotted under the humid sun until the air was heavy with the smell of the cantaloupe, watermelon, and grapefruit that dried into cysts and then burst apart. The cotton rows were washed flat and the sweep of mud through the fields baked out hard and smooth in the late August heat as though nothing had ever been planted there.

I withdrew from the election, and one of the Senator's aides released Lester Dixon's deposition to a state news service, but no one was particularly interested in it. A reporter from *The Austin American* telephoned me and asked if I had seen it, would I like him to read it to me over the phone, and I answered that I wouldn't and would he do several things with it of his choosing, and I never heard about it again. Since then I've come to believe that one's crimes and private guilt, those obsessions that we hide like that ugly black diamond in the soft tissue of the mind, are really not very important to other people.

Bailey acted as my defense lawyer at my hearing in

Pueblo Verde, and had the assault charge dropped after he promised the district attorney we would file our own charges against the sheriff's department (there were several lovely frames in the news film that showed the deputy's khaki knee bending upward into my eye). I was even proud of Bailey. He was a better criminal lawyer than I had thought, or at least he was that day, and even though the court was hostile to us and the judge stared hotly at Bailey when he addressed the bench, he was determined that I wouldn't get any time and he made the county prosecutor stumble in his wording and contradict himself. I was given a year's probation for resisting arrest and disturbing the peace, and we went across the street to an outdoor barbecue stand and drank beer for three hours in the warm shade of an oak tree. Two weeks later I received a letter of reprimand from someone in the Texas Bar Association, and I refolded it in the envelope and returned it with a pass to the Houston livestock show.

Verisa divorced me and took the Cadillac, eighty acres I owned up in Comal County, and the two natural gas wells, but I held onto the ranch and the house and my thoroughbred horses. She went to Europe for six months, and occasionally her name was mentioned on the society pages of *The New York Times* (a reception at the American embassy in London, dancing with a member of the Kennedy entourage in a Paris nightclub), then she returned to Dallas, where she had been born, and bought a penthouse apartment overlooking the city's skyline and the green hills beyond. She entertained everyone, and from time to time I heard stories about what a radiant hostess she was and how many unusual and interesting people she managed to have at her parties. She sent me an invitation to her wedding, and at first I didn't recognize the groom's name, then I remembered meeting him once at a Democratic cocktail party in San Antonio. He had inherited the controlling stock in a newspaper, and he had turned the paper's editorial page into a right-wing invective against everything liberal in the state. But I remembered him most for the fact that he didn't drink and his cleancut chin was always at an upward angle when he turned his profile to you. I sent them a silver service with a one-line note of best wishes on a card inside. Four months later he was killed with another woman in an automobile accident on the Fort Worth highway. Verisa inherited the newspaper, and after a period of mourning the parties began again at the penthouse and her picture appeared regularly on the society pages with a young district attorney who rumor said might run for governor in two years.

Rie and I were married right after the divorce, and the next fall we had twin boys. They were both big for twins, and I named one Sam for my father and the other Hackberry, since I felt there should always be one gunfighter in the Holland family. Bailey bought out my half of the law practice, although he argued against it in his emotional way and wanted to continue the partnership, but I was through with the R. C. Richardson account and dealing with oil company executives. I didn't practice for seven months, and spent the winter and early spring working on the ranch. I dug fence holes and strung new wire on the pasture, reshingled the barn roof that had been stripped by the storm, put a new water well down, and plowed and seeded sixty-five acres of corn and tomatoes. And each time I twisted the posthole digger in the ground or drove a six-penny nail down flat in the wood, I could feel the last drops of Jack Daniels sweat out through my pores and dry in the wind, and a new resilience in my body that I hadn't felt since I pitched at Baylor. I worked hard each morning, with the sun low over the willows on the river bank, and through the day until late evening when the shadow from the tractor fell out across the rows and the purple light drew away over the horizon. And when I had pulled the seed drill over the last furrows against the back fence I could already smell the land beginning to take hold of new life, and after the next shower small green plants would bud one morning in long, even lines.

Rie and I took my best three-year-old up to Lexington that spring and raced him at Keeneland. Each afternoon we sat in the sun with mint juleps and watched the horses break from the starting gate on the far side of the field, with the jockeys like toy men on their backs, and move in a tight formation down the back stretch, the lead horses pushing hard for the rail, then into the far turn as the roar of their hooves grew louder, their bodies glistening with sweat, and Rie would be on her feet with her arms wrapped tightly in mine, the quirts whipping down into the horses' flanks and the sod flying into the air, and then there was that heart-beating rush when they came down the homestretch with the jockeys pouring it into them, and the thunder against the turf was louder than the shouting of the crowd. We won a thirty-five-hundred-dollar purse in one race, and placed in two others, and the evening before we left for Texas I took Rie on a long drive through the bluegrass and the

Cumberland Mountains. The limestone cliffs rose straight up out of the hollows, and the tops of the white oaks and beech trees were covered with the sun's last light. I was tired and quiet inside after the two weeks of racing, and the rolling hills stretched away towards Virginia in a violet haze, but a sense of time and its ephemeral quality began to weigh on me, as when you give yourself too long a period of restoring things that you hurt through indifference or cynicism in the first place.

Two days after we returned home I drove to San Antonio and became a trial lawyer for the A.C.L.U.

It's summer again now, and the corn is green against the brown rows in the fields, and I irrigated my cotton acreage from the water well I put down and the bolls have started to come out white in the leaves. In the evening I can smell the dampness of the earth in the breeze off the river, and the wet sweetness of the Bermuda grass in the horse pasture, and just before dusk the wind flattens out the smoke from Cappie's cabin and there's just a hint in the warm air of oak logs burning in a wood stove. I built a large, circular crib around a chinaberry tree in the side yard for the boys to play in, and every afternoon while I sit on the verandah and try to outline a defense for impossible cases, I'm distracted by the spangle of sunlight and shade on their tan bodies. They're both strong boys and they don't like being inside the crib, and they show me their disapproval by throwing their stuffed animals out on the grass. Sometimes after their nap they shake the side of the crib so violently that Rie has to bring them up on the verandah and let them play in all the wadded paper at my feet. When I look at them I can see my father and Old Hack in their faces, and I try not to look over at the white markers in the cemetery or I would have to grieve just a little on that old problem of time and loss and the failure of history to atone in its own sequence.

Mi.. ..d ..r u li .. ..d..., ... a ... ..
prof..sion who started writing after the Second World War, beginning with light essays written for *Punch* and other journals. She then wrote on educational and country matters and worked as a scriptwriter for the BBC. Miss Read was married to a schoolmaster for sixty-four years until his death in 2004, and they had one daughter.

Miss Read was awarded an MBE in the 1998 New Year Honours list for her services to literature. She was the author of many immensely popular books, including two autobiographical works, but it was her novels of English rural life for which she was best known. The first of these, *Village School*, was published in 1955, and Miss Read continued to write about the fictional villages of Fairacre and Thrush Green for many years. She lived near Newbury in Berkshire until her death in 2012.

Return to Thrush Green

* * *

Miss Read

Illustrated by J. S. Goodall

An Orion paperback

First published in Great Britain in 1978
by Michael Joseph Ltd
This paperback edition published in 2008
by Orion Books,
an imprint of The Orion Publishing Group Ltd,
Orion House, 5 Upper St Martin's Lane,
London WC2H 9EA

An Hachette UK company

3 5 7 9 10 8 6 4

A CIP catalogue record for this book is available
from the British Library.

ISBN 978 0 7528 8236 9

Typeset at the Spartan Press Ltd,
Lymington, Hants

Printed and bound in Great Britain by
Clays Ltd, St Ives plc

The Orion Publishing Group's policy is to use papers that
are natural, renewable and recyclable products and
made from wood grown in sustainable forests. The logging
and manufacturing processes are expected to conform to
the environmental regulations of the country of origin.

www.orionbooks.co.uk

To
Sir Robert Lusty
whose early encouragement
began it all

CONTENTS

* * *

PART THREE

Safe Arrival

Epilogue

PART ONE

Travelling Hopefully

* * * *

1. SPRING AFTERNOON

The finest house at Thrush Green, everyone agreed, was that occupied by Joan and Edward Young. Built of honey-coloured Cotswold stone, some hundred or so years ago, it had a beautiful matching tiled roof, mottled with a patina of lichen and moss. It looked southward, across the length of the green, to the little market town of Lulling hidden in the valley half a mile away.

The house had been built by a mill owner who had made a comfortable fortune at the woollen mill which straddled the river Pleshey a mile or two west of Lulling. It was large enough to house his family of six, and three resident maids. A range of stone-built stables, a coach house and tack room, stood a little way from the house, and at right angles to it. Above the stable was the bothy, where the groom-cum-coachman slept, and immediately above the bedroom was the stable clock.

The Youngs often wondered how on earth people managed without such storage space. Nowadays, the buildings were filled with furniture awaiting repair, lawn-mowers, deck-chairs, tea-chests full of bottling equipment or archaic kitchen utensils which 'might come in useful one day', two deep freezers, a decrepit work bench and an assortment of outgrown toys, such as a tricycle and a rocking horse, the property of Paul Young, their only child. Everything needing a temporary home found its way into the stable and then became a permanency. Sagging wicker garden chairs, shabby trunks, cat baskets, camping stoves, old tennis racquets, fishing waders, and Paul's pram, unused for nine years, were housed here, jostling each other, and coated with dust, bird droppings and the debris from ancient nests in the beams above.

'If ever we had to move,' said Edward to Joan one sunny afternoon, 'I can't think how we'd begin to sort out this lot.'

He was looking for space in which to dump two sacks of garden fertilizer.

'Those new flats in Lulling,' he went on, 'have exactly three cupboards in each. People seem to cope all right. How do we get so much clobber?'

'It's a law of nature,' Joan replied. 'Abhorring a vacuum and all that. However much space you have, you fill it.'

She pushed an unsteady pile of old copies of *Country Life* nearer to a mildewed camp bed.

'I suppose we could set a match to it,' suggested Edward, dragging the first sack to a resting place beside some croquet mallets. There was a rustling sound and a squeak.

'That was a mouse!' said Joan, retreating hastily.

'Rats, more like,' commented Edward, heaving along the second sack. 'Come on, my dear. Let's leave them to it. I'm supposed to be meeting Bodger at two-thirty and it's two o'clock already.'

Together they made their way back towards the house.

When her husband had gone, Joan sat on the garden seat to enjoy the spring sunshine. Cold winds had delayed the opening of many flowers. Certainly no daffodils had 'come before the swallow dared to take the winds of March with beauty'.

Here we are, thought Joan, surveying the garden through half-closed eyes, in mid-April, and the daffodils and narcissi are only just in their prime. Would the primroses be starring the banks along the lane to Nidden, she wondered? As children, she and her sister Ruth had reckoned the first outing to pick primroses as the true herald of spring.

How lucky they had been to have grandparents living at Thrush Green, thought Joan, looking back to those happy days with affection. She and Ruth lived most of the year in Ealing, where their father owned a furniture shop. They lived comfortably in a house built in King Edward's reign. The garden was large for a town house. The common was nearby, and Kew Gardens a bus ride away. But to the little girls, such amenities were definitely second-best.

'It's not *the country*!' they protested. 'Why can't we live in *the country*? Why don't we go to Thrush Green for good?'

'Because my living's here,' said Mr Bassett, smiling. 'There are four of us to keep, and the house and garden to care for, and your schooling to be paid. If I don't work, then we have nothing. You must think yourselves lucky to be able to go to Thrush Green as often as you do.'

He too adored Thrush Green, and when his parents died, it became his. Barely fifty, he intended to continue to live and work in Ealing. By this time, Joan had married Edward Young, an architect in Lulling known to the Bassetts since childhood, and the young couple had lived in the house ever since.

'But the day I retire,' Mr Bassett had said, 'I'll be down to take over, you know!'

'I'll build a house in readiness,' promised Edward. That was over ten years ago, thought Joan, stretching out her legs into the sunshine, and we still have not built it. Perhaps we should think about it, instead of drifting on from day to day. Father must be in his sixties now, and had not been well this winter. The time must come when he decided to retire, and only right that he should come to Thrush Green to enjoy his heritage. They had been wonderfully blessed to have had so long in this lovely place.

The telephone bell broke in upon her musing, and she left the sunshine to answer it.

Some two hundred yards away, the children of Thrush Green Village School were enjoying the first really warm and sunny playtime of the year.

Squealing and skipping, jostling and jumping, they celebrated the return of spring with youthful exuberance. Little Miss Fogerty, teacup in hand, watched their activities with fond indulgence. She had coped with playground duty now for over thirty years. The mothers and fathers of some of these screaming infants had once cavorted here under her kindly eye. She lifted her wrinkled face to the sun, and watched the rooks flying to the tall trees on the road to Nidden. Two of them carried twigs in their beaks. It was good to see them refurbishing their nests, she thought, and better still to note that they were building high this year. A sure sign, old countrymen said, of a fine summer to come. Well, it could not be too hot for her old bones, thought Miss Fogerty. She must think about looking out her cotton dresses. What a blessing she had decided not to shorten them last year! Hems were definitely mid-calf this season, and very becoming too after those dreadful miniskirts which were downright improper, and must have given many a fast young man ideas of the worst sort.

A windswept child pranced up to her. 'Finished, miss? Give us yer cup then!'

Miss Fogerty held her cup and saucer well above the child's head, and looked sternly at his flushed face.

' "May I take your cup, *Miss Fogerty*," is the way to ask, Frederick,' she said reprovingly. 'Just repeat it, please.'

'May I take your cup, Miss Fogerty,' repeated Frederick meekly. 'And I never meant no harm, miss.'

Miss Fogerty smiled and put the empty cup and saucer into his hands.

'I'm quite sure of that, Frederick dear, but there is a right and wrong way of doing everything, and you chose the wrong way first.'

'Yes, miss,' agreed Frederick, holding the china against his jersey, and setting off across the playground to the lobby where the washing up was done.

Miss Fogerty glanced at her wrist watch. Only three minutes more and she must blow her whistle.

There would be nice time for *The Tailor of Gloucester* before the end of the afternoon. She thought, with pleasure, of the scores of children she had introduced to Beatrix Potter. How many times, she wondered, had she carried the little picture showing the embroidered waistcoat round the room, watching each child's face rapt with wonder at the smallness of the stitches and beauty of the design.

And her new classroom was so pleasant! For years she had worked in the infants' room to the right of the lobby in the original village school building. Now the new classroom at the rear of the school was hers alone, complete with its own washbasins and lavatories, so that there was no need for any of the babies to brave the weather when crossing the playground, as in the old days.

The new room was a constant delight to her. The big windows faced south-west across the valley towards Lulling Woods. Bean and pea seeds, as well as mustard and cress growing on flannel in saucers, flourished on the sunny windowsill, and it was delightful to stand, back against the glass, and feel the hot sun warming one's shoulder blades through one's cardigan.

It had been good of Miss Watson, her headmistress, to let her have the room. She could so easily have appropriated it for her own class had she wished. But there, thought loyal little Miss Fogerty, Miss Watson would never do a thing like that! There could not be a better headmistress in the whole of the United Kingdom! It was a privilege to be on her staff.

Miss Fogerty fished up the whistle from the recesses of her twin-set and blew a loud blast. Three-quarters of the playground pandemonium ceased. Miss Fogerty's grey eyes, turning like twin lighthouse beams round her territory, quenched the last few decibels of noise.

'You may lead in, children,' she called. 'My class last this time.'

And as the school filed indoors, she followed the youngest children across the playground to the beautiful new terrapin building where *The Tailor of Gloucester* was waiting on her desk.

From her bedroom window across the green, Winnie Bailey watched Miss Fogerty at her duties. Since her husband's death, she had found herself observing other people with an interest which she had not had time to indulge during the years of the doctor's last illness.

She missed him more than she could say. The fact that their last few months together had involved her in nursing Donald day and night, made their home seem even more lonely now that he had gone.

The tributes she had received at his death, and still received daily from those who had known him, gave Winnie Bailey much needed comfort. He had been a dear man all his life, and a very handsome one when young, but it was his complete dedication to the task of healing which had endeared him to the people of

Lulling and Thrush Green. Every day, Sundays included, Donald Bailey had visited Lulling Cottage Hospital, until infirmity had overtaken him. His young partner, Dr Lovell, married to Ruth, Joan Young's sister, knew how lucky he was to have watched and learnt from such a splendid man as his senior partner.

'Never appear to be in a hurry,' the old man had said to him. 'Listen to their tales, no matter how irrelevant they may seem at the time. You'll learn more that way about your patient than any number of tests at the clinic. Mind and matter are interwoven to an extent that none of us truly appreciates. If you are going to expect exactly the same reaction to the same treatment in every case, then you might just as well become a mechanic.'

Dr Lovell's car backed cautiously away from the surgery into the road. He looked up and saw Winnie at the window, and waved cheerfully. He had probably called for medicines, thought Winnie, and was off to pay a few afternoon calls before evening surgery.

A bent figure was hurrying across Thrush Green from the church. It was Albert Piggott, sexton and so-called caretaker of

St Andrew's, and he was obviously intent upon waylaying the unsuspecting doctor.

His cracked voice floated up to Winnie at the window.

'Doctor! Doctor! You got somethin' for me choobs? They've gone again!'

Dr Lovell wound down the car window and said something which Winnie could not hear. She moved away hastily, not wishing to appear inquisitive, and made her way downstairs, where Jenny, her maid and friend for many years, was getting the tea-tray ready.

I am a lucky woman, thought Winnie, to be able to continue to live at Thrush Green among old friends, to have Jenny with me for company, and to see Donald's work carried on so conscientiously by John Lovell and his new young assistant. How pleased Donald would have been!

Albert Piggott, returning from, his foray upon the doctor's car, looked upon the closed door of The Two Pheasants and thought sadly how far distant opening time was. They did things better abroad, he believed. Opened all day, so he'd heard. Now we were all in this Common Market perhaps we'd follow the foreigners' good example.

At that moment, the landlord of The Two Pheasants struggled through the wicket gate at the side of the public house, bearing two hanging baskets.

'Well, Albert,' said Mr Jones, depositing the baskets at his feet, 'how's tricks?'

'Chest's bad,' said Albert flatly.

'Always is, ain't it? Time you was used to it.'

'That's right,' growled Albert. 'Show plenty of sympathy!' He surveyed the two baskets. 'You being fool enough to put them geraniums out already?' he continued. 'I s'pose you know we're due for plenty more frost.'

'They won't hurt under the eaves,' said the landlord. 'Got some shelter, see?'

'Might well get one tonight,' went on Albert, with every appearance of satisfaction. 'My choobs have been playin' up somethin' cruel. Went to see the doctor about 'em.'

'Ah! I saw you,' said Mr Jones. 'Holding up the poor chap when he was just off to see them as is really ill.'

Albert did not reply, but commented by spitting a flashing arc towards the churchyard wall.

The landlord pulled out the wooden bench and began to mount upon it.

'Wouldn't want to give me a hand-up with the baskets, I suppose?'

Albert looked at him sourly. 'You supposes right,' he said. 'I've got work of me own to do, thank you.'

He shuffled off towards his cottage which stood next door.

'Miserable old faggot,' said Mr Jones dismounting, and making towards the baskets. He made the comment quietly, but just loud enough to carry to Albert's ears as he opened his front door.

After the fresh air of Thrush Green, even Albert noticed that his kitchen seemed stuffy.

The general opinion of his neighbours was that Albert's home was absolutely filthy and smelt accordingly. No one had ever seen a window open, and the door was only opened long enough to allow the entry or exit of its master's unwashed body.

Albert sat down heavily in the greasy armchair, and began to unlace his boots. He removed them with a sigh of relief, and lay back, his gaze resting upon a pile of dirty crockery which littered the draining-board. He supposed he would have to tackle that sometime, he thought morosely. And get himself a bite to eat.

He became conscious of his hunger, and thought of Nelly, his wife, who had left him over a year ago to share life with the oil man somewhere further south.

'Nothin' but a common trollop!' muttered Albert aloud. 'But, golly, she could cook!'

He thought of the succulent steak and kidney pies which had emerged steaming from the now cold and dusty kitchen range. She made a fine stew too, remembered Albert, his gastric juices working strongly, and liver and bacon pudding with haricot beans. As for her treacle tarts, and rice puddings with a nice brown crinkly skin of butter and nutmeg on top, they were real works of art.

She had a way with mashed potatoes too, beating an egg into them so that the saucepan was full of light fluff, slightly creamy in colour and texture. He could do with a plateful of Nelly's cooking at the moment, he thought wistfully.

He rose from the chair and went to the cupboard where he found a piece of bread. He spread it with a dollop of dripping from a stone jam-jar, and began to munch disconsolately. It wasn't right that a man had to find his own vittles, especially one who was delicate, One with ailing tubes, like himself, for instance.

Still, cooking wasn't everything, Albert told himself, wiping his hands down his trousers. She might be a good cook, his Nelly, he would be the first to give you that, but what a Tartar too! What a temper! And sly with it! Look at the way she'd been carrying on with that blighted oil man behind his back! He wished him joy of her, the wicked hussy. He hoped he'd had a lashing from her tongue by now, so that he'd see what he'd taken on, and what her lawful wedded husband had had to put up with.

He filled the kettle and put it on to boil. By the time he'd washed up, and had a snooze, it would be near enough time to go and lock up the church and see that all was straight for the night.

And after that, thought Albert, The Two Pheasants would be open!

Life suddenly became warmer and sunnier as Albert advanced bravely upon the sticky horrors piled in the sink

2. DOCTOR'S PRESCRIPTION

While the children of Miss Fogerty's class listened to the story of *The Tailor of Gloucester*, and Albert Piggott awaited opening time, Joan Young was busy preparing a salad.

As she washed lettuce and cut tomatoes her thoughts turned time and time again to her parents and her old home in Ealing. She was vaguely puzzled by this. She had an uncomfortable feeling that perhaps something was wrong, and tried to persuade herself that the fact that she had been thinking of her father's heritage, after Edward's return to work that afternoon, simply accounted for this present preoccupation.

But somehow she was not convinced. She was the last person to be telepathic, or to believe in such nebulous things as thought-transference. Nevertheless, the malaise continued, and for two pins she would have left her salad-making and rung her parents there and then.

'What nonsense!' she told herself. 'They would think I'd gone mad. I should have heard soon enough if anything were wrong!'

She began to slice cucumber with swift efficient strokes.

Some sixty miles away, Joan's father, Robert Bassett, listened to some very unwelcome truths spoken by his doctor.

'These X-rays show that that chest of yours needs a lot of care. And I'm not happy about your heart. I'm not suggesting that you should consider yourself an invalid, but frankly it's time you gave up work.'

'But it's quite impossible—' began his patient, and was interrupted by a violent spell of coughing.

The doctor watched gravely until the attack had passed. He said nothing, but continued to look steadily at the older man.

'Dammit all,' wheezed Robert, 'it's only this confounded cough that makes me so tired! I'm fine otherwise. Look here, I've a business to run, you know.'

'Someone else will have to run it anyway in a few months,' said the doctor soberly.

He rose from the bedside and went to look out of the window at the neat suburban garden. Robert Bassett, shocked by the last few words, addressed the doctor's straight back.

'You don't mean that?'

The doctor swung round. 'I do indeed. All the tests we have done, these X-rays, and my knowledge of you over the last six years show that you are running yourself into the ground at an alarming rate. You need rest, cleaner air and more quiet than Ealing can give you, and a complete removal from sight and sound of your work. If you refuse to take my advice, I don't give you twelve months. It may sound brutal, my old friend, but that's the position.'

There was a short silence. Somewhere in the distance, a train hooted, and nearer at hand a lorry changed gear and ground away up the hill outside.

'I just can't take it in,' whispered the sick man.

'You own a house somewhere in the west, don't you? Can you go and stay there for a time?'

'Now do you mean?'

'Not immediately. You're going to have a week or two in that bed, with a daily visit from me. It will give you time to get used to the idea of moving, and to put things straight this end.'

'But what about my business?'

'Surely, there's someone there who can take over?'

'I suppose so,' said Robert slowly. 'It's just that I've never really considered the matter.'

The doctor patted his patient's hand, and rose to go. 'Well, consider it now, and cheer up. You'd like to go to this country house of yours, I take it?'

'Of course I would,' said Robert. 'I've always promised myself a retirement at Thrush Green.'

'Good, good! That's grand news.'

He picked up his case, and smiled at his patient.

'What's more,' said Robert, 'I've a son-in-law who is the doctor there.'

'Better still! I'll be in touch with him, no doubt, when the time comes. Meanwhile, you stay here and get some sleep. I'll be in tomorrow.'

He closed the door behind him, leaving his patient in mental turmoil.

'Sleep!' muttered Robert crossly. 'What a hope! I must get Milly to ring the office straight away and get young Frank to come over.'

He sat up suddenly, and was reminded of his weakness by a severe pain in the chest. Rubbing it ruefully, he thought of further arrangements to be made.

'We'd better warn Joan and Edward, poor dears, that they may have a convalescent father on their hands in the near future.'

Nevertheless, the thought of Thrush Green in spring sunshine, gave comfort to the invalid in the midst of his trials.

In Miss Fogerty's classroom *The Tailor of Gloucester* had been returned to the shelf, the children had stacked their diminutive chairs upon the table, leaving the floor clear for the cleaner's ministrations later, and now stood, hands together and eyes closed, waiting for their teacher to give the note for grace.

> Now the day is over,
> Night is drawing nigh,
> Shadows of the evening
> Steal across the sky.
> Now the darkness gathers
> Stars begin to peep,
> Birds and beasts and flowers
> Soon will be asleep.
>   Amen.

They sang much too loudly for Miss Fogerty's peace of mind. It sounded irreverent, she felt, but she had not the heart to reprove them, knowing how eagerly they were looking forward to running home through the first of the really warm days of spring.

She thought, not for the first time, that this particular closing hymn was not one of her favourites. That line 'Stars begin to peep', for instance, was a little premature at three-thirty, except in December perhaps, and in any case the word 'peep' seemed a trifle coy. But there, Miss Watson wanted the children to use that hymn, and she must fall in with her wishes in these little matters.

'Hands away! Good afternoon, children!' said Miss Fogerty briskly. 'Straight home now, and no shouting near the school windows. The big girls and boys are still working, remember.'

They streamed from the room comparatively quietly, and across the playground towards Thrush Green. Daisies starred the greensward, and the sticky buds of the chestnut trees were beginning to break into miniature fans of grey-green. The children raced happily to meet all the glory of a spring afternoon.

All except Timmy Thomas, always a rebel, who saw fit to stand beneath Miss Watson's window, put two fingers into his mouth and produce an ear-splitting whistle.

He was gratified to see his headmistress's face appear at the window. She shook her head at him sternly and pointed towards the gate. Miss Fogerty had emerged from her classroom, and also exhorted him to depart immediately.

Grinning, he went.

'That boy,' said Miss Watson later, 'will become a very unpleasant leader of students, or some such, as far as I can see!'

'He might make a happy marriage,' observed Miss Fogerty, more charitably, 'and settle down.'

'It seems a long time to wait,' commented her headmistress tartly.

One of the first of Miss Fogerty's pupils to reach home was young Jeremy Prior who lived just across Thrush Green at Tullivers, a house as venerable as the Youngs', although not quite so imposing.

Jeremy enjoyed life at Thrush Green. His mother Phil had

married for the second time, and his stepfather, Frank Hurst, was a man whose company he enjoyed. His own father had been killed in a car crash, but before that had happened he had left home to live in France with another woman, so that the child's memories of him were dim. Frank had given him the affection and care which he needed in his early years, and Jeremy flourished in the happy atmosphere surrounding him at Thrush Green.

Now, as he opened the gate, he was conscious of his mother talking to friends in the garden. One was Winnie Bailey, their next-door neighbour. The other was Ruth Lovell, the doctor's wife, and clutching her hand was Mary, her two-year-old daughter.

As soon as the toddler saw Jeremy she broke away from her mother and charged over the flower beds to greet the boy, babbling incoherently, fat arms outstretched.

'*Mary!*' shouted Ruth. '*Not* over the garden!'

But she was ignored. Her daughter by now had Jeremy's legs in a rapturous embrace which nearly brought him to the ground.

'Is it as late as that?' exclaimed Winnie. 'I must get back. Jenny has gone down to Lulling, and I'm supposed to be keeping an eye on a fruit cake in the oven.'

She hurried away and they heard the click of the next-door gate as she returned to her duties.

'How are things working out there?' asked Ruth.

'Very well, I gather,' said Phil. 'It was a marvellous idea to invite Jenny to live with her. At one stage I was afraid that Winnie might think of moving into a smaller house, perhaps near her sister. We should have missed her horribly, and I think she would have been lost without Thrush Green.'

'I'm sure of it. We're lucky to live here. Joan and I always thought it was the best place on earth when we were children. I can't say that my opinion has changed much.'

She walked towards her daughter who was rolling over and over on the grass, being helped by Jeremy.

'Come along, Mary. We're off to see Aunt Joan.'

'No! Stay here,' said Mary, stopping abruptly, her frock under her armpits and an expanse of fat stomach exposed to view. Her expression was mutinous.

'No nonsense now! We've got to collect the magazines.'

'Why not let her stop here while you see Joan?' suggested Phil, in a low tone. 'Jeremy would love to play with her for a while.'

'That's so kind. I won't be more than a few minutes.' She turned towards the gate. 'Do you mind, Jeremy?' she called.

'I'll show her my new fort,' said Jeremy enthusiastically. 'It's got Crusaders and Saracens, and lots of flags and horses and swords.'

'Mind she doesn't swallow them,' advised Ruth. 'You don't want to lose any.'

She waved to the potential sword-swallower and made her way across the green to her sister's.

Joan Young was sitting in the hall when Ruth arrived. She was listening intently to the telephone, her face grave.

Ruth was about to tiptoe away, but Joan covered the mouth-piece with her hand, and motioned her sister to take a seat.

'It's mother. Tell you in a minute.'

Ruth perched on the oak settle, and fell to admiring the black and white tiles of the floor, and the elegant staircase, which always gave her pleasure.

'Do you want a word with Ruth? She's just dropped in.'

Silence reigned while Joan listened again.

'No, no. All right, darling. I'll tell her, and you know we'll look forward to seeing you both. Yes, *any time*! Give him our love.'

She replaced the receiver and looked at Ruth.

'Poor Dad, he's pretty weak evidently. Bed for a week or two, and then his doctor wants him to come here for a rest.' She stood up abruptly. 'Come in the garden, Ruth. I've left a cookery book on the seat, and I probably shan't remember it until it pours with rain in the middle of the night.'

'How bad is he?' asked Ruth, following her.

'Mother was calm about it, but sounded anxious. It seems he's had this bronchial trouble most of the winter, but wouldn't give up. I'll be glad to get him here. Mother must need a rest too. Dash it all, they're both around seventy.'

They sat down on the garden seat, and Joan nursed the cookery book.

'Shall we go up tomorrow to see him?' said Ruth.

'Mother says not to. He's not in any danger, but the doctor wants him to be kept quiet.' She began to laugh. 'Poor Mum, trying to stop him working! As it is, she's had to ring Frank to give all sorts of messages about the office.'

'It's time he retired,' agreed her sister. 'Perhaps this will make him think about it.'

'Funnily enough,' said Joan, 'they've been in my mind a lot today. Probably because Edward said something about moving. It's about time we built a house of our own. We may have to now. Heaven knows we've been lucky to stay here so long.'

'Dad won't let you move,' said Ruth shrewdly. At times she saw more clearly than her older sister, who usually led the way.

'But he'll have to!' replied Joan, beginning to look slightly agitated. 'If he's to have a quiet life from now on, then it's only right that he should come back to his own home.'

'Maybe,' agreed Ruth. 'He'll be willing to come to Thrush Green, I have no doubt, but he won't let you give up your home, you'll see.'

'But where else is there for him? We've always known that they would retire here.'

'Don't forget that Dad hasn't yet said he will retire. So far, he's simply having a short convalescence here. I shouldn't take too many leaps ahead, Joan. Things will work out, you'll see.' She rose to her feet. 'I came for the magazines really, and then I must collect Mary before she drives Jeremy Prior mad. Noble boy, he's showing her his fort. I tremble to think how much of it is broken already.'

They made their way back to the house, and collected the pile of magazines from the hall table. A dozen or so inhabitants of Thrush Green had begun this communal magazine effort during the war, each contributing one journal and passing the collection from one to the other, and the custom had continued.

'I'll walk across the green with you,' said Joan. 'It's marvellous to feel the sun really warm again after months of shivering.'

They paused at the roadside and Joan gazed across the grass towards the church.

'Do you realize that we shall have the Curdles' fair here on

May the first? Only another week or so. Won't it be lovely to see Ben and Molly Curdle again? I still miss her.'

'The only comfort is that she's a lot happier with her Ben than she was with that ghastly father of hers, Albert Piggott. Isn't that him over there in the churchyard?'

'Looks like it. Waiting for The Two Pheasants to open, no doubt.'

'Mary is going to the fair this year,' said Ruth. 'Perhaps we could make up a party with Jeremy and Paul?'

'Yes, let's. Though I may have the parents here by then, of course.'

They exchanged troubled glances.

'I shall ring Mother later on this evening,' said Ruth, 'and we'll keep in touch about developments.'

A yell from across the road drew her attention to her daughter who was struggling to climb over the Hursts' gate.

'I must be off,' she said hastily, and dashed to the rescue.

Joan returned thoughtfully to the garden. Of course, as Ruth said, the parents were only coming for a short stay. But this was a reminder that the future must be faced. When Edward came home they must have a serious talk about plans. They really must think of the years ahead.

The family cat met her at the door, and rubbed round her legs, mewing vociferously.

'Poor old puss! I've forgotten your lunch and tea,' said Joan remorsefully. 'It's all this thinking ahead that's done it.'

The cat led the way purposefully towards the kitchen. As far as he was concerned, the next meal was as far ahead as he was prepared to consider.

3. PROSPECTIVE LODGERS

If the Youngs' house was acknowledged to be the most beautiful at Thrush Green, the rectory, it was admitted ruefully, was the ugliest.

Unlike its neighbours, its Cotswold stone walls had been clad by some Victorian vandal in grey stucco. It was tall and bleak. It faced east rather than south, and the front door opened upon a long dark corridor which ran straight to the back door, thus creating a wind tunnel which worked so successfully that unlucky dwellers there needed a fortune to keep the house warm.

Despite the fuel bills, the present inhabitants of the rectory were not unhappy. The Reverend Charles Henstock and his wife Dimity considered themselves exceptionally lucky in their marriage, and in their work at Thrush Green. Material matters did not affect them greatly, and the fact that their home was cold, shabby, dark, and difficult to clean bothered Charles not at all, and Dimity only occasionally, and then mainly on her husband's behalf.

For years she had lived only some fifty yards from her present home, at a snug thatched cottage on the other side of the road. Her companion then had been a stalwart friend, called Ella Bembridge, who still lived there and spent her spare time in creating textile designs, which she sometimes sold, and a great variety of handicrafts which she did not.

Not that these products were wasted. Ella's cupboards and drawers were stuffed with handwoven ties, raffia mats, cane basketwork, mirrors decorated with barbola work, wobbly teapot stands, and a number of unidentifiable objects, all of which were destined for Christmas presents or given to charitable institutions, preferably those concerned with animals. Ella rated the animal race rather more deserving than the human one, and who can blame her?

The cottage had been warm, Dimity was the first to admit. It faced south, and was sheltered by the hill which rose steeply from Lulling to Thrush Green. Furthermore, Ella enjoyed a fire, and never returned from her walks without some firewood or fir cones with which to create a cheerful blaze in the evenings. It was not until Dimity had spent her first winter at the rectory that she realized quite how bleak was her present abode.

'The trouble with this barn of a place,' said Ella one morning towards the end of April, 'is that it faces the wrong way. You get no sunshine at all, except in the kitchen. Frankly, I'd live in there.' She thrust a bunch of daffodils at Dimity. 'Here, these should cheer things up a bit. They're some you planted years ago near the gooseberry bushes.'

'Thank you, dear. They are simply lovely. I shall put some on Charles's desk. The study does tend to be a little dark. Have some coffee?'

'Yes, please. I tried some jasmine tea yesterday that I'd dried myself, but can't say it's really palatable. Probably be better as potpourri. Pity to waste it.'

'You've heard about Mr Bassett, I suppose?' said Dimity, setting out cups upon a tray.

'No? Dead, is he?'

'No, no, Ella! I know he's been far from well, but he's nowhere near dead yet.'

'Sorry, sorry. What's, the news then?'

'He's coming down for a rest after a rather nasty illness. Mrs Bassett too, of course.'

'Good. A nice pair. Might get a game of bridge. I miss dear old Donald Bailey for that.'

'I miss him for a lot of things,' replied Dimity. 'And so does Charles.'

At that moment, her husband entered, advanced upon Ella as though about to kiss her, remembered she did not like to be kissed, hastily stood up again, and contented himself with energetic hand-rubbing.

'Yes, they're due next week, I gather,' said Charles, 'but I'm afraid they'll miss the fair. A pity really. I always enjoy the Curdles' fair.'

'Not the same without the old lady,' said Ella, taking out a battered tin and beginning to roll one of the noisome cigarettes for which she was renowned. 'I like young Ben, but I shouldn't be a bit surprised if he didn't give up the job one day.'

'But he can't!' cried Dimity. 'Why, it's a sacred trust!'

'Not *sacred*, my dear,' corrected the rector mildly. 'He may have a *loyalty* to the business and to the memory of his grand-mother, but that's not quite the same thing.'

'Well, I can't imagine May the first at Thrush Green without the Curdles' fair blaring and gyrating for hours,' said Ella, putting a match to the ragged end of the very thin cigarette which drooped from her lips. 'But, come to think of it, why on earth should Ben Curdle want to give up a perfectly good living?'

'I very much doubt,' said Charles, pushing an ashtray towards his friend, 'if the fair really does bring in much these days. People demand rather more sophisticated pleasures than our forebears did. And of course there's television to contend with.'

At this moment, the milk rose with a joyous rush to the brim of the saucepan and was about to drench the stove, when Ella, with remarkable speed for one so bulky, leapt towards it, removed it from the heat, and blew heavily across its surface. The milk sank back obediently, and Dimity expressed her gratitude.

She did so with some inner misgivings. She could not feel that Ella's smoke-laden breath could be truly hygienic in contact with milk, but common civility forbade her from pouring it down the sink and starting again. Putting aside her qualms, she poured coffee for the three of them at the kitchen table.

'That smells good!' said Ella, sniffing greedily. 'I'm rationing myself with coffee since it's become so expensive. I did try ground acorns which Dotty said were almost as good, but I found them revolting.'

'Does Dotty really use ground acorns?' asked Charles. 'She hasn't offered me acorn coffee yet. At least, I don't think she has. I must admit that Dotty's coffee always tastes a little – well – er, peculiar.'

'Dear old Dotty is the prize eccentric of all time,' said Ella, 'and I love her dearly, but I try not to eat or drink anything of her making ever since I was laid up for three days with Dotty's Collywobbles after drinking her confounded elderberry wine, D'you remember, Dim?'

'Indeed I do. It stained the kitchen sink a deep purple, I remember. One of Dotty's more potent brews.'

'To come upon Dotty at her cooking,' went on Ella, 'is rather like looking in on the three witches in *Macbeth*. You know, "tongue of bat and leg of frog", or whatever it is. I certainly saw her fish a fat spider out of the milk jug before making a rice pudding. It's a wonder she doesn't suffer from her own creations.'

'Hardened to it, no doubt,' said Dimity.

'You are not being very charitable,' reproved the rector.

'Whatever her funny little ways, she has a heart of gold. I hear she has taken on a poor dog which some callous brute abandoned at the side of the main road.'

'Good for Dotty,' cried Ella, 'but how will she manage? That place of hers is crammed with animals already. It must cost her a fortune in food for them. It beats me how she copes. I find it hard enough. In, fact, I'm thinking of getting a lodger to help out.'

Her friends looked at her in amazement.

'Are you serious?'

'Well, nothing's definite yet, but there's your old room empty, Dimity, and it seems a shocking waste when the Third World is being rammed down your throat whenever you switch on the television. Besides, a few pounds a week would certainly help with the food bills. I haven't quite got to Dotty's stage of searching the hedgerows for my lunch.'

'Don't do anything too hastily,' warned Dimity. 'I mean, you might get a dreadful man who turned out to be violent or dishonest—'

'Or a drunkard,' put in the rector, retrieving the ashtray, which had not been touched, and putting it resignedly on the windowsill again. Ella's saucer was holding the stub of the pungent cigarette, and ash sprinkled the table.

'Or simply someone with *designs* on you,' went on Dimity earnestly. 'There really are some terribly wicked men about. He might even make suggestions.'

'That'll be the day,' said Ella robustly. She stood up and dusted the rest of the ash to the floor. 'Don't worry. It may never come to pass, and in any case I don't want to be cluttered up with a man as a lodger. He'd want too much done – socks mended, shirts ironed, and all that razmatazz. No, a nice quiet woman is what I had in mind. Do for herself, and be no bother.'

'Well, just don't *rush* into anything,' pleaded Dimity. 'It's better to be poor and happily solitary, than rich with unpleasant company.'

Ella patted her friend's thin shoulder. 'I promise not to be rash. And now I must get back to the garden. You can't see my lettuce seedlings for groundsel.'

She vanished down the dark passage to the front door, and crossed the road to her own snug abode opposite.

Dotty Harmer lived about half a mile from Thrush Green, in a cottage which stood beside the track leading to Lulling Woods.

For years she had kept house for her martinet of a father, a local schoolmaster, feared by generations of Thrush Green and Lulling boys for his iron discipline. On his death, Dotty had sold the house in Lulling and bought this secluded cottage where she lived very happily, quite alone, but for a varied menagerie ranging from goats to kittens.

Whilst Ella, Dimity and Charles were imbibing coffee, Dotty was sitting on a fraying string stool in her hall, telephoning the local police station. At her feet lay a golden cocker spaniel, its eyes fix trustingly upon her.

'Yes, yes,' Dotty was saying testily, 'I am quite aware that I gave you full particulars when I telephoned two days ago. The purpose of this call is to find out if there have been any more inquiries.'

There was the sound of rustling paper.

'Well, ma'am, there doesn't seem to be any message about a lost dog. A golden cocker, you said?'

He remembered that Dotty was unmarried, elderly and perhaps rather prim. He broached his next question with some delicacy. 'Would it be a lady or a gentleman?'

'It's a *bitch*, officer,' said Dotty, who spoke plain English. 'A bitch of about six months old, I should say. Rather thin, and with sore feet – obviously had travelled some way along the main road to Caxley. No collar, of course, but a very nice little dog.'

'Would you want us to take it – her, I mean – to the kennels for you, ma'am?'

'No, indeed. Excellent though I'm sure they are. No, the little thing has settled in very well since Friday, and I am quite prepared to adopt her if she is not claimed.'

'Thank you, ma'am. In that case, I'll make a note to that effect.'

'But, of course, you will telephone immediately if the owner comes forward? I should not wish to deprive anyone of their own

animal, although I have the strongest suspicion that this one was purposely abandoned, in the most callous fashion. You are perhaps studying that side of this affair?'

'We're doing everything possible,' said the constable earnestly, eyeing a mug of tea which had been placed at his elbow by a fellow policeman. 'We'll let you know if anything comes of our inquiries.'

'Very well, officer. I shall let you return to your duties. I know how hard-pressed the force is.'

'Thank you, ma'am,' said the constable, replacing the receiver with a sigh, and picking up the mug.

'Chuck over the paper, Ted,' he called to his colleague. 'Haven't had a minute to look at the headlines yet. All go, innit?'

Dotty replaced her receiver, and surveyed her new charge with affection.

'Good little Floss,' she said kindly. 'Good little dog.'

She was rewarded with a frantic lashing of Floss's fine plumy tail.

'It might be a good idea,' continued Dotty, rising from the disreputable stool, 'to give you a little walk today. On the grass, of course, with those tender feet. Perhaps a gentle stroll up to the green? We could take Ella's goat's milk to her, and save her a trip.'

She made her way into the kitchen, closely followed by the dog. A vast iron saucepan bubbled on the stove, cooking the hens' supper. Floss looked at it hopefully, and barked.

'I think not, dear,' said Dotty, 'but I have a bone for you in the larder. Take it under the plum tree while I get ready.'

The bone was located under an old-fashioned gauze cover in the pantry. On the slate shelf beside it were a number of receptacles holding food suitable for Dotty's varied family – corn, bran mash, chopped lettuce leaves, crusts of bread, tinned cat food and the like. The provisions for Dotty seemed non-existent.

Dotty watched Floss gnawing the bone in the shady garden. A fine little animal! Very intelligent too, and very nice to have another Flossie after so many years.

She was eight years old when she had been given the first Flossie as a birthday present. That little bitch had been another cocker spaniel, but black with mournful eyes, and a sweet and saintly expression which quite belied its destructive nature. Rugs, slippers, upholstery and Dotty's beloved dolls all fell prey to those sharp teeth, but still the whole family forgave her, including Dotty's stern father.

She was named after a great aunt of Dotty's. Aunt Floss had been christened Florence, after the famous Florence Nightingale, but she lacked her namesake's vigour, and retired to her red plush sofa when she was a little over forty.

Dotty could remember being taken to see her on the family's visits to London. Aunt Flossie's house was in the Bayswater Road, a dark gloomy establishment, and the drawing-room where she lay in majesty seemed to be the most depressing room of all.

The heavy chenille curtains were always half drawn. They were edged with woollen bobbles, looking like the seed pods which dangled from the plane trees on the other side of the window.

Aunt Floss's legs were always covered by a tartan rug. Not that Aunt Floss ever used the word *legs*. 'My *extremities*,' she would say plaintively, 'are very susceptible to draughts.'

A bamboo table stood beside the sofa, laden with medicine bottles and pill boxes, a carafe of water and the latest novel from the lending library. The room reeked of camphor, and to the young Dotty, used to the Cotswold air of Lulling, the stuffiness of this apartment was unendurable.

Aunt Flossie had a long sad face, and wore her hair parted in the middle, and gathered into bunches of ringlets, rather in the style of Elizabeth Barrett Browning. She certainly had a spaniel-like appearance, and when Dotty's father, in a rare mood of frivolity, suggested 'Flossie' for the name of her birthday puppy, the family agreed with much hilarity. Aunt Flossie, of course, never met her namesake, and would have thought the whole thing most indecorous had she ever heard about it.

Armed with an old-fashioned metal milk can with a secure lid, and with Floss-the-second on a long lead, Dotty emerged into the sunshine, and into the meadow at the end of her garden.

The footpath lay across rich grass, used for grazing cattle most of the year. At the moment, the fields were empty, starred with daisies and a few early buttercups. Soon there would be sheets of golden flowers, thought Dotty happily, all ready to

> Gild gloriously the bare feet
> That run to bathe . . .

Rupert Brooke, thought Dotty, might be out of fashion at the moment, but he had supplied her with many felicitous phrases which had given her joy throughout her life. She remained grateful to him.

Floss padded ahead at the end of the lead, keeping to the grass, and pausing now and then to sniff at some particularly fascinating scent. In ten minutes they had reached Thrush Green, and Dotty sat down upon a bench, in order to change the milk can from one hand to the other, and to admire the glory of spring flowers in the gardens.

The hanging baskets outside The Two Pheasants won her

approval, and the bright mats of purple aubretia and golden alyssum hanging from the low stone walls. Through the gate of the Youngs' house she could see a mass of daffodils and narcissi under the trees, and a particularly beautiful copper-coloured japonica was in full bloom against Harold Shoosmith's house. Even Albert Piggott's cottage had a few bedraggled wallflowers close to his doorstep.

'A time of hope,' commented Dotty to Floss who was busy licking a paw. 'We must remember that, Flossie dear. Let's trust that it augurs well for us too.'

Refreshed by her brief rest, she collected milk can and dog again, and made her way to see her old friend Ella Bembridge.

4. April Rain

Meanwhile, at Ealing, Robert Bassett's mood changed from stunned shock to querulous fury, and finally to philosophic resignation. Milly, his wife, bore all with patience.

'The firm won't automatically crumble, my dear, just because you are away from the office,' she told him. 'Frank knows the ropes as well as you do, and has always coped during the holidays perfectly well. That old saying about no one being indispensable is absolutely true, so just stop worrying.'

Frank Martell had been with the firm all his working life, starting as office boy at a wage of twenty shillings a week, and soon promoted to thirty shillings a week when Robert Bassett had seen the boy's capabilities. He was now a man in his mid-forties, quiet, conscientious and absolutely trustworthy. To Robert he was still 'young Frank' despite the sprinkling of grey hairs round his ears, and Robert found it difficult to have to face the fact that he would have to give him full responsibility for the business during his own absence.

He felt better about the whole affair after Frank had spent an afternoon by the bedside going through a file of letters and orders. His grasp of affairs surprised Robert. Frank had never said much, and Robert had always been too busy to realize quite how much Frank knew of the running of the firm. His quiet confidence reassured the invalid, and when Milly returned to the bedroom, after seeing Frank out, she found her husband breathing more easily and looking very much more relaxed.

'He's done you good,' she commented. 'You'll sleep better tonight.'

'I believe I shall,' agreed Robert.

Milly brought him an omelette at half-past seven, and for the first time since the onset of his illness he emptied his plate.

When she had gone, he lay back upon the pillows contentedly. The door was propped ajar, and darkness was beginning to fall. He felt as he had as a child, secure and cosseted, with the door left open for greater comfort, and access to grown-ups in case of emergency.

His gaze roamed over the shadowy room. How little, over the past years, he had noticed the familiar objects around him! He looked now, with renewed awareness, at these old inanimate friends. There, on the dressing-table, stood the shabby oval leather box containing the two splendid hair-brushes which his father had given him on his twenty-first birthday. They were still in daily use, but had far less hair to cope with these days.

Nearby stood the photograph of Milly as he first saw her, hair parted demurely in the middle, eyes upraised soulfully, and never a hint of a double chin. To his mind, she was better looking now, plump and white-haired, her complexion as peach-like as when they first met, and the tranquillity, which had first attracted him, as constant as ever. He had been lucky in his marriage, and lucky to have two beautiful daughters.

On the wall opposite the bed hung a fine print of the Duomo of Florence. They had spent their honeymoon in that city, staying at a quiet hotel which had once been an ancient family home, not far from the cathedral. They had always promised themselves a return visit to that golden city, but somehow it had never happened.

'If I get over this,' said Robert aloud, 'I'm damned if we don't do it. That's the worst of life. One is everlastingly putting things off until it's too late.'

He smoothed the patchwork bedspread. Here was another

reminder of the past, for Milly and the two girls had made it together, before marriage had taken them away from home to Thrush Green. Robert had teased them, he remembered, about ever finishing it. They must have spent three winters on the thing, he thought, now tracing the bright hexagons of silk with a finger.

Most of the furniture had come from his own shop, but the bedside table had stood beside his parents' bed. He remembered it well, at the side of his widowed mother during her last long illness, laden with medicine bottles, books and letters, much as it looked now, he thought, with a mild feeling of shock. Well, it had served the generations loyally, and no doubt would continue to be used by his children and grandchildren. There was something very comforting in this quality of permanence. It put into perspective the brief frailty of man compared with the solid works of his hands.

Yes, here, all around him stood the silent witnesses of his life. He was glad to have had this enforced breathing space to acknowledge his debt to faithful old friends.

He slid farther down the bed, sighing happily. When his wife came with hot milk at ten o'clock, she found him in a deep sleep, and crept away again, with a thankful heart.

The last few days of April brought torrential rain to Thrush Green. It drummed on the tarmac of the roads and the school playground, with relentless ferocity, so that it seemed as though a thousand silver coins spun upon the ground. It cascaded down the steep Cotswold roofs, gurgled down the gutters, and a miniature river tossed and tumbled its way down the steep hill into Lulling High Street.

At the village school, rows of Wellington boots lined the lobby, and mackintoshes dripped from the pegs. Playtimes were taken indoors. Dog-eared comics, incomplete and ancient jigsaw puzzles, and shabby packs of cards were in daily use, much to the children's disgust. They longed to be outside, yelling, running, leaping, fighting, and generally letting off steam, and would willingly have rushed there, despite the puddles and the downpour, if only their teachers had said the word.

Miss Fogerty, rearranging wet and steaming garments on the

radiators, was thankful yet again for the comfort of her new classroom. At least her charges were able to pay their frequent visits to the lavatories under the same roof. In the old building it had been necessary to thread a child's arms into its mackintosh sleeves (invariably needing two or more attempts) before allowing it to cross the playground during a deluge. Really, thought Miss Fogerty, life was now very much simpler.

Next door to the village school, Harold Shoosmith, a middle-aged bachelor, struggled to locate a leak which had appeared in the back bedroom. He stood on a ladder, his head in the loft and a torch in his hand, while Betty Bell, his indefatigable daily help, stood below and offered advice.

'You watch out for bats, Mr Shoosmith! They was always partial to that loft. I remember as a girl the old lady as lived here then used to burn sulphur candles to get rid of them. Can you see any?'

'No,' came the muffled reply.

'You want a bucket for the drips?'

'No. I can't see a damn thing.'

'You want another light? A candle, say?'

There was no answer, but Harold's trunk, then his thighs, and lastly his well-burnished brogues vanished through the trap-door, and thumps and shuffles proclaimed that the master of the house was surveying the highest point of his domain.

Betty Bell transferred her gaze from the gaping hole above her to the view from the streaming window. Rain slanted across the little valley at the back of the house, where Dotty Harmer's cottage glistened in the downpour. The distant Lulling Woods were veiled by rain, and the grey clouds, barely skimming the trees, told of more to come. She was going to have a wet ride home on her bike, that was sure.

'Found it!' came a triumphant call from above. 'It's running down one of the rafters. Get a thick towel, Betty, and a bucket, and I'll fix up a makeshift arrangement.'

'Right!' yelled Betty. 'And I'll put on your dinner. You'll need something hot after mucking about up there.'

She descended the stairs and caught a glimpse of a very wet

Thrush Green through the fanlight of the front door. Across the expanse of puddles Winnie Bailey was battling her way towards Lulling with her umbrella already dripping.

'Never ought to be out,' thought Betty, 'at her age, in this weather! She'll catch her death.'

But Winnie was quite enjoying herself. There was something very pleasant in splashing along under the shelter of Donald's old umbrella. It was very old, but a beautiful affair of heavy silk and whalebone, and a wide band of solid gold encircled the base of the handle. It was certainly far more protection from the rain than her own elegant umbrella, which was smaller and flatter, and which she resolved to keep for ornament rather than use in future.

There were very few people about, she noticed, as she descended the hill to Lulling. Hardly surprising in this weather, but what a lot they were missing! The stream of surface water gushed and gurgled at her side. Silver drops splashed from trees and shrubs, and a fresh breeze whipped the colour into her cheeks. It was an exhilarating morning, and she remembered how much she had loved a boisterous day when she was a child, running with arms thrown wide, mouth open, revelling in the buffeting of a rousing wind.

She was on her way now to visit three old friends, the Misses Lovelock, who lived in a beautiful Georgian house halfway along the High Street. Here they had been born, and the outside and the inside of their home had altered very little, except that there were far more *objets d'art* crowded inside than in their childhood days.

They were making plans for one of Lulling's frequent coffee mornings, and although Winnie tried to dodge as many of these occasions as she could, the proposed effort was for a cause very dear to her heart, and that of her late husband's, the protection of birds.

If the three sisters had been on the telephone, Winnie might have been tempted to ring up and excuse herself on such a wet morning, but she was glad that the Lovelocks considered a telephone in the house a gross extravagance. She would have missed this lovely walk, she told herself, as she approached their door.

The sisters were, in fact, very comfortably off, but they thoroughly enjoyed playing the part of poverty-stricken gentlewomen. They were inveterate collectors, and rarely paid much for any new acquisition. Their house was full of furniture, porcelain, fine glass and silver objects which would have made the gentlemen at Sotheby's and Christie's pink with excitement. A great many of these exquisite items had been begged for by the mercenary old ladies who had brought the art of acquiring other people's property, for nothing or almost nothing, to perfection. They were a byword in Lulling and Thrush Green, and newcomers were warned in advance by those luckless people who had succumbed in a weak moment to the sisters' barefaced blandishments.

Winnie had been invited to coffee, and was quite prepared for the watery brew and the one Marie biscuit which would be presented to her on a Georgian silver tray.

She was divested of her streaming mackintosh and umbrella in the hall, the Misses Lovelock emitting cries of horror at her condition.

'So brave of you, Winnie dear, but *reckless*. You really shouldn't have set out.'

'You must come into the drawing-room at once. We have *one bar* on, so you will dry very nicely.'

Miss Bertha stroked the wet umbrella appreciatively as she deposited it in a superb china vase which did duty as an umbrella stand in the hall. There was a predatory gleam in her eye which did not escape Winnie.

'What a magnificent umbrella, Winnie dear! Would that be *gold*, that exquisite band? I don't recall seeing you with it before.'

'It was Donald's. It was so wet this morning I thought it would protect my shoulders better than my own modern thing. As you can guess, I treasure it very much.'

'Of course, of course,' murmured Bertha, removing her hand reluctantly from the rich folds. 'Dear Donald! How we all miss him.'

The ritual of weak coffee and Marie biscuit over, the silver tray and Sèvres porcelain were removed and the ladies took out notebooks and pencils to make their plans.

'We thought a Bring and Buy stall would be best for raising money,' exclaimed Violet. 'We can use the dining-room, and Bertha took a lot of geranium and fuchsia cuttings last autumn which should sell well, and Ada has made scores of lavender bags from a very pretty organdie blouse which was our dear mother's.'

'Splendid,' said Winnie, stifling the unworthy thought that these offerings would not have cost her old friends a penny.

'And Violet,' chirped Ada proudly, 'has made dozens of shopping lists and jotters from old scraps of paper and last year's Christmas cards. They really are *most* artistic.'

Violet smiled modestly at this sisterly tribute.

'And we thought we might ask Ella for some of her craft work. She has managed to collect a variety of things, I know, over the years. Would you like to ask her to contribute? It would save us calling in.'

'Of course,' said Winnie, 'and Jenny and I will supply all the home-made biscuits to go with the coffee, if that suits you.'

The Misses Lovelock set up a chorus of delight. Pencils moved swiftly over home-made notebooks and all was joy, and comparative warmth, within, as the rain continued to pelt down outside.

Albert Piggott, standing in the church porch with a sack draped cowl-wise over his head, gazed at the slanting rain with venom. He took the downpour as a personal affront. Here he was, an ageing man with a delicate chest, obliged to make his way through that deluge to his own door opposite. And he had a hole in the sole of his shoe.

When Nelly had looked after him, he thought, she had always kept an eye on such things. She'd washed his shirts, brushed the mud off his trouser legs, darned his socks, sewn on all them dratted buttons that burst off a chap's clothes, and took his shoes down to Lulling to be mended when the time came.

No doubt about it, Nelly had had her uses, hussy though she turned out to be.

'I bet that oil man's found out his mistake by now,' said Albert to a spider dangling from a poster exhorting parishioners of Thrush Green to remember their less fortunate fellows in darkest Africa.

He hitched the sack more firmly round his shoulders, and made a bolt across the road. Which should it be? Home or The Two Pheasants? The latter, of course, won.

'Lord, Albert, you're fair sopped!' cried the landlord. 'Been digging up the graves or something?'

Albert ignored the facetious remark, and the titters of the regulars. 'Half a pint of the usual,' he grunted, 'and I wouldn't mind a look at the fire, if it ain't asking too much of you gentlemen.'

The little knot of customers, steaming comfortably by the blaze, moved a short distance away, allowing Albert to enter the circle.

'Terrible weather,' said one, trying to make amends for any offence given.

Albert maintained a glum silence.

'Bashing down the daffodils,' said another. 'Pity really.'

Albert took a swig at his beer. He might have been an ageing carthorse taking a drink at the village pond for all the noise he made. The customers avoided each other's eyes.

'You getting your own dinner, Albert, or d'you want a hot pie here?' asked the landlord.

'How much?'

'Same as usual. And as good as your Nelly ever made, I'm telling you.'

Albert cast him a sharp look. 'There's no call to bring my wife into it. But I'll have a pie all the same, daylight robbery though it is, you chargin' that amount!'

'Daisy!' shouted the landlord through an inner door. 'Hot pie for Albert, toot-der-sweet.'

Uneasy silence fell upon all as Albert waited, mug in hand. A sudden gust of wind shook the door, and a little trickle of rainwater began to seep below it and run down the step into the bar.

'Blimey!' said one of the men. 'We're goin' to be flooded out.'

'Can't go on much longer,' said his companion, retrieving the doormat before it became soaked. 'Rain this heavy never lasts long.'

'It's been on for two days,' remarked Albert, accepting his hot pie. 'Don't see no sign of it letting up either.'

The landlord bustled forward with a mop and bucket. 'Here, stand away and I'll clear up.' He began to attack the rivulet. 'Let's hope it stops before the month's out,' he puffed, wielding the mop energetically. 'Be a pity if Curdle's Fair gets this sort of weather.'

'Always gets a change afore the beginning of May,' announced one aged regular in the corner. 'You mark my words now.' He raised a trembling forefinger. 'I never knowed old Mrs Curdle have a wet day at Thrush Green. We'll get a fine day for the fair, that I knows. You just mark my words!'

'S'pose he's forgot the old lady died years ago,' whispered one customer to his neighbour.

'No, I ain't forgot!' rapped out the old man. 'And I ain't forgot

36

as young Ben runs it now, and pretty near as good as his grandma.'

The landlord shouldered his mop and picked up the bucket. 'Shan't see you in here next week for hot pies then, Albert. I s'pose your young Molly will be cooking your dinner for you while the fair's here?'

Albert thrust the last of his pie into his mouth, and turned towards the door. 'Ever heard of mindin' your own business?' he asked sourly. 'First me wife, and now me daughter. You talks too much, that's your trouble.'

He opened the door, and a spatter of rain blew into the room. The newly dammed river gushed joyfully over the step again, and Albert departed.

'That miserable old devil was *grinning*!' said the landlord, and went into action once more, sighing heavily.

5. The Coming of Curdle's Fair

The rain was still lashing down on the last day of April, as Ben Curdle and his wife Molly, *née* Piggott, approached Thrush Green with the fair.

They were the cheerful young couple, happy in their marriage, and proud of their little boy George, who was now four years of age.

The child sat between them as they towed their caravan at a sedate pace through the streaming countryside. Molly's spirits were high for she was returning home, and although Albert Piggott was never a particularly welcoming father, yet she looked forward to seeing him and the cottage where she had been born.

She was well aware that she would have to set to and do a great deal of scrubbing and general cleaning before the little house was fit for them all to live in for their few days' stay, but she was young and energetic and had never feared hard work.

She was looking forward, too, to seeing the Youngs again. She had worked in their beautiful house for several years before going to the Drovers' Arms where Ben Curdle had come a-courting.

Joan Young had been a great influence and a good friend to the motherless young girl, and had taken pleasure in training such as a bright and willing pupil in the ways of housewifery.

Molly had also acted as nursemaid to Paul Young when he was a baby, and had treasured the postcards and letters which the boy, now at school, sent from time to time. The happiest of her memories of Thrush Green were centred on that house, and working for the Youngs had been the highlight of her life. They had provided a haven from the dismal cottage across the green, and from the continuous complaining of her sour old father.

Ben Curdle's spirits were not quite so high. For one thing, he disliked his father-in-law, and resented the fact that his wife would have to work so hard in getting the neglected house together. But he was a sensible young fellow, and kept his feelings to himself. It was good to see Molly so happy, and he was wise enough to make sure that she remained so.

But he had another cause for worry. The fair was bringing in far less than when his redoubtable old grandmother had run it. Now that petrol and diesel oil had supplanted the shaggy-hoofed horses of her day, the cost of moving the fair from one place to the next was considerable. Takings too were down.

It was not only the counter-attraction of television in almost every home. That was one factor, of course, and who could blame people for staying comfortably under their own roofs, especially when the weather was as foul as it was today? No, it went deeper than that, Ben realized.

The fact was that most people wanted more sophisticated entertainment. The children still flocked to the fair, accompanied by adults. But the number of people who came without children was dwindling fast. In his grandmother's time, everyone virtually attended the great Mrs Curdle's Fair. It was something to which farmers, shop-keepers, school teachers, as well as their pupils, looked forward from one May Day to the next. Those grown-ups came no more, unless it was to bring their children or grand-children for an hour's frolic.

And then, his fair was so small, and likely to get smaller as the machinery wore out, for replacements were becoming prohibitively expensive. Ben himself was a good mechanic, and conscientious about keeping everything in apple-pie order, but as parts became worn and more and more difficult and costly to replace, he saw clearly that some of the attractions would have to be withdrawn. As it was, the famous switchback, which had delighted so many generations at Thrush Green, would not be erected on this May Day. It was altogether too shaky, and Ben was not the sort of man to take chances.

The thing was, what should he do? He was used to travelling the country and sometimes wondered if he could ever settle down in one place, even if he should be fortunate enough to find a congenial job.

And then, he was devoted to the fair and had never known any other way of living. His grandmother he had adored. She had brought him up from early childhood, for his father had been killed and his mother had married again. The old lady's upright and staunch principles had been instilled into this much-loved grandchild, and Ben had repaid her care with loyalty and respect. Not a day passed but he remembered some word of advice or some cheerful tag of his grandmother's, and to give up the fair, which she had built up so laboriously, smacked of treachery to the young man.

But there it was. Something would have to be done, and soon. He turned his mind to an offer which had been made to him some weeks earlier by Dick Hasler, the owner of a much larger concern.

This man had three large fairs touring the country. Over the years he had bought up many a small business, such as Ben's, and combined them into a highly-efficient organization. He was astute, and could foresee possibilities which a slower man would not. He was not liked, for there was a strain of ruthlessness in him without which he could not have succeeded, but there was grudging respect for his ability, and it was agreed that he treated fairly those whom he employed, as long as they worked well.

Ben felt pretty sure that he would be offered a job if he decided to sell. But would he like working for a master after being his own for so long? And what about his fellow workers? He had little respect for some who had sold up and gone to work for

Dick Hasler, and he had heard of some underhand transactions which disgusted him. No, if he had to make the break, it would be a clean one, and he would nave a complete change. Surely, there must be something he could do to earn a living? His old grandmother always said he had the most useful pair of hands in the business. What honest living could he earn with them? Perhaps a job in a garage somewhere? He brooded silently, as windscreen wipers flashed to and fro hardly keeping pace with the torrent.

'Soon be there,' cried Molly. 'Look out for the river, Georgie! Once we're over that we're nearly home.'

Ben watched their excitement with a smile. So far he had said very little about the fair's diminishing profits, but Molly must have some inkling, and the time would soon come when they would be obliged to have a straight talk about the future.

The steep hill to Thrush Green was just ahead. Ben sighed, and changed gear. Slowly they came abreast of St Andrew's church, and drew to a halt outside Albert Piggott's cottage. From the joy which lit Molly's face, you might think it was Buckingham Palace, thought Ben wryly.

'Here we are,' she cried, 'home again!'

Ella Bembridge saw the Curdles arrive from her bedroom window. She had gone upstairs to rummage through drawers and cupboards to find some contributions to the Lovelocks' Bring and Buy stall, and Dimity was with her.

'They'll have to look slippy if they want the fair to be ready by the morning,' commented Ella. 'Don't envy them that job in this weather.'

'What about this cushion cover?' inquired Dimity, holding up a square of hessian embroidered in thick wool.

'It's a peg bag,' said Ella. 'Rather fine, isn't it? Bold, you know. Plenty of pure bright colour.' She looked at the enormous flowers of scarlet and gold with affection. 'Too good for a Bring and Buy. Put it back, Dim. It'll do for a Christmas present.'

'What are they, dear?' Dimity was studying the blossoms, with some distaste. 'Zinnia? Red hot pokers? I can't quite recognize them.'

Ella gave her booming laugh. 'They're no known species. I just made 'em up as I went along. You know, three threads up, four down, and all that. Effective, isn't it?'

'Very,' said Dimity, folding the object carefully and returning it to the drawer.

'Here, they can have this magnolia talcum powder. I'll never use that. Can't think who thought I'd relish magnolia scent. Do I *look* like magnolia?'

'Well, no, Ella. Not really.'

'And this useless handkerchief sachet, and this idiotic comb case. Here they come.'

Ella was now ferreting in the drawer like some eager fox terrier in a rabbit hole. Objects flew from her towards the bed, and Dimity did her best to sort them out.

'But Winnie said they wanted things you'd made,' she pointed out, fielding a crocheted bobble cap rather neatly.

'They can have these as well,' replied Ella, head well down. A long string of plastic beads, pretending to be jet, swung through the air, Dimity added it to the motley collection.

'Right,' said Ella, slamming the drawer back. 'Now let's look in the cupboard.'

One turn of the handle burst open the door. Out from the depths sprang a snarl of cane and raffia, and a few objects made from similar material. Ella bent to retrieve them.

'Two waste paper baskets, and three bread roll holders! What about that?'

'Lovely,' said Dimity faintly.

Ella looked at her handiwork approvingly. 'I was thinking of decorating them with raffia flowers,' she mused. 'But what d'you think?'

'They are just right as they are,' replied Dimity firmly. 'No need to gild the lily, you know.'

'Yes, you're right. Somewhere at the back there are some teapot stands. Push over the chair, Dim, and I'll have a look.'

She clambered up with surprising agility for one of her bulk, and began to scrabble at the back of a high shelf. Dimity drifted to the window and looked out at rain-washed Thrush Green.

Ben Curdle was carrying a large suitcase into Albert Piggott's cottage, and young George was capering beside him, glorying in the puddles.

'Got 'em!' came Ella's triumphant call. 'Catch!'

Dimity caught about half a dozen wooden teapot stands, edged with cane and beadwork, wrapped in a polythene bag, and added them to the pile.

'There!' said Ella, stepping down heavily. 'That's a pretty good haul, isn't it? Do them a good turn, and me too, come to think of it. If I ever take a lodger I shall have to clear out all the shelves and drawers in this room. Made a start anyway.'

'So you're still thinking about it?' said Dimity, following her old friend downstairs.

'Oh, I honestly don't know,' replied Ella, settling in a chair and fishing in her pocket for the battered tobacco tin which contained her cigarette factory. She began to roll one of her deplorable cigarettes. She looked pensive.

'It's like this,' she began, blowing out a cloud of acrid smoke. 'I can do with the money and I've got plenty of spare room, but I'm wondering if I should find a lodger congenial.'

'Anyone in mind?'

'Not really, although I believe Winnie Bailey's nephew Richard is looking for somewhere to stay, but no doubt Winnie would put him up.'

'Are you going to advertise?'

'I think not. I've decided to see if I hear of anyone – personal recommendation, that sort of thing. I don't want a stream of folk banging at the door.'

'Well, I must say I'm relieved to know you are not doing anything too hastily. I know Charles has mentioned it in his prayers.'

Ella patted Dimity's thin arm gratefully. 'You're a good pair. It's plain to see your religion is the mainspring of your lives. Lucky old you!'

'It could be yours too.'

Ella shook her head sadly. 'You know me, Dim. Full of honest doubts. Whenever I read "Thanks to St Jude" in the personal column I think: "How do they know St Jude reads this paper?"

It's no good, I'm afraid. What I can't see I can't believe in. I suppose you find that pathetic?'

'Not at all. Someone as honest as you are is never pathetic. But I grieve for all you are missing. If you are a believer then you have so much to look forward to.'

'Bully for you,' said Ella cheerfully, 'but time alone will tell. Here, let's brew a cup of something, and let the future look after itself.'

Within an hour of his arrival, Ben and his workmates were hard at it erecting the various attractions of Curdle's Fair. A knot of interested spectators had assembled, and at playtime the railings of the village school were thick with pupils eager to see what was afoot.

Little Miss Fogerty, patrolling the wet playground, and thankful for a clearing sky at last, determined to make 'The Fair' a subject for the afternoon session, and only hoped that she had enough paper to supply the class with adequate artistic material.

Joan Young, making up beds in the room intended for her parents, noted the preparations outside with approval. Still more encouraging were the patches of blue sky which were appearing over Lulling Woods, and the gentle movement of low clouds moving away to the east, and giving way to high ones from the west. It certainly looked as though the fair would have its usual fine weather.

She smoothed the bedspreads and then went to the window. Leaning out she felt the soft breeze lift her hair. The avenue of chestnut trees still shed an occasional drop into the puddles below, and their stout trunks were striped with little rivulets of water, but there was a warmth in the air which spoke of better weather to come.

The daffodils and narcissi, which had taken such a battering in the last few days, were beginning to lift their heads again, and the wallflowers, their velvety faces still wet, were giving out a heady fragrance.

Tight buds beaded the cherry tree nearby, and soon would burst into dangling snow, and the lilac bushes, massed with pyramids of buds, would soon be adding their perfume.

Tomorrow was May. Ever since she could remember, May the first had meant the coming of Curdle's Fair and the real beginning of summer. Her spirits always rose with the advent of May, 'loveliest of months', as the poet truly said.

Even now, she thought, with a great many problems ahead, her heart leapt to greet the fair, the flowers, the coming of summer, and the knowledge that Thrush Green would soon be gilded with sunshine, and aflutter with birds and butterflies.

It was good to know that her father would be with them at the most beautiful time of the year. Thrush Green could not fail to restore him to health. Of that she felt positive, as she ran downstairs full of hope.

By the time the children ran home from school, a watery sun was shining, sparkling upon the drying roofs and the wet grass of Thrush Green. The air was filled with the clashing of hammers on metal, and the thump of mallets on wood, as the massive equipment of the fair was assembled.

Ben walked purposefully from one site to the next, followed by the diminutive figure of young George clad in duffle coat and wellingtons. He was a sensible child, and obedient to his father's directions. He knew that if he did not do as he was told, and keep out of harm's way, then he would be dispatched back to his mother without further ado.

Back at the cottage, Molly was making a cup of tea for Albert. She had scrubbed the kitchen table, the draining-board and the cupboard tops, and thrown away several revolting remnants of food in various crocks and saucepans.

After the teabreak she resolved that she would get her father to depart across the road to his church duties, while she had an energetic session with soap, hot water and the scrubbing-brush on the filthy kitchen floor. There was no doubt about it, Albert Piggott's standards of cleanliness grew lower and lower as the years passed.

She looked across at him now, as he sat sipping his tea noisily. It was not just the house which he neglected. The man himself looked half-starved, sickly and dirty. Molly's kind heart was stirred. He had never been a good father, but after all, blood

was thicker than water, and she wanted to see him in better shape
than this.

It was a pity that Nelly, her stepmother, had ever left him,
although she could not blame her. Admittedly, Nelly was
avaricious, flighty and coarse. Nevertheless, she was warm-
hearted and lively, and the little cottage had never been so clean
and wholesome as when Nelly had cared for it. And Albert had
always looked spruce and well-fed, his linen spotless, his shoes
polished. He looked now, thought Molly, as if he needed a
thorough scrubbing and a completely new set of clothing from
top to toe.

'I'd best take me tablets with me tea,' said Albert, rising to run
a hand along the mantelpiece. The movement triggered off a
vicious bout of coughing.

Molly watched with alarm as the old man rested his forehead
on the shelf, his thin frame racked with the cough. It ended at
last, and Albert sat down again, medicine phial in hand, and drew
great noisy breaths.

'You didn't ought to be about, Dad,' said Molly earnestly,

'with that chest of yours. What about havin' a day in bed? I could ask Dr Lovell to come and see you.'

'He's seen me,' retorted Albert, 'and a fat lot of good that be! If I takes these tablets it do seem to help a bit.'

He rammed one in his mouth, and sent it down his throat with a mouthful of tea.

'What you want,' went on Molly, 'is a good hot bath. The steam'd do them tubes good, you know. Then a day or two resting in bed. You're properly knocked up, and I don't believe you ever feed yourself, do you?'

'I gets a hot pie next door when I'm clemmed,' muttered Albert.

'And plenty of drink to go with it, I don't doubt,' remarked Molly with spirit. 'And that don't do you a ha'porth of good. You could do with a regular dosing of Nelly's cooking.'

'And you could do with minding your own business,' said Albert nastily. 'I manages all right, and I won't have that trollop crossing my doorstep again.'

He rose shakily, and took down his deplorable jacket and cap from the peg on the door.

'Best see to the church, I suppose, while I've got me strength.'

He slammed the door behind him. Molly shook her head sadly and filled the kettle again, ready for her onslaught on the kitchen floor.

It was all very well for him to tell her to mind her own business. As a daughter, his welfare *was* her business. If he went on as he was at present, he would very soon find himself back in hospital, or in one of Lulling's almshouses. The thought of either filled Molly's mind with horror.

She was half inclined to try to get in touch with Nelly. After all, legally she was his wife, even if she had left him for the charms of the oil man. On the other hand, Albert had every right to refuse to have her back. It was his house. She had treated him shabbily, and no doubt the two would fight like cat and dog, if they were ever brought together again.

Lord, what a to-do it all was, thought Molly! She would have to see what Ben could do about it. Perhaps he could persuade her father to have at least one decent meal a day. Someone might come in to cook it, or The Two Pheasants might provide it regularly. They could leave the landlord some money in advance.

Meanwhile, she determined that her father was going to be got into a bath, by hook or by crook, and she would burn those filthy clothes herself, and face the storm afterwards.

Much refreshed by these brave plans, she attacked the kitchen floor, and rejoiced in the shadowy pattern on the linoleum which gradually reappeared as the result of her energy.

6. THE FIRST OF MAY

May the first fell on a Thursday, and it was Ben's intention to stay at Thrush Green until the middle of the following week. Most of his takings would come on Friday night and Saturday. He might pick up enough to cover expenses early in the following week, if the weather held, but he was not due at his next stand for a full week, and he wanted Molly to have time to see all her Thrush Green friends and to get her father's domestic arrangements straightened out.

Not that they could do anything to satisfy that curmudgeonly old fellow, Ben realized. He was a real problem, and likely to become worse as the years passed. He disliked the idea of living near the old man, and yet he had begun to wonder if that might have to be, as his father-in-law's health failed. Of one thing he was quite positive – he would never live under the same roof with him. It was bad enough to watch Molly wearing herself out, once or twice a year. To see her slaving for that old tyrant, day in and day out, would be impossible, and he was not going to stand for that, whatever the future held.

The day of the fair dawned with a respite from the rain, but no one could truthfully call it 'Mrs Curdle's weather'. The old lady had always seemed to bring sunshine and cloudless skies, but this particular morning was overcast, with only a few shreds of blue sky among the grey mass to give hope of better things to come.

During the day, Ben completed the preparations to his satisfaction, and gave the men an hour or two off. The fair would open at four o'clock, and most of the trade would come from mothers with young children for the first two or three hours.

After that, with any luck, a good crowd of adults would arrive, willing to spend and out to enjoy some boisterous fun. At ten-thirty the fair must close, so that Ben earnestly hoped that the rain would hold off for the next few days, and particularly during those few vital hours each day when he hoped to recoup some of his outlay.

He was determined to try and get Molly alone for an hour during the afternoon, out of earshot of her father, and to tell her a little about his fears for the future of the fair. Not that she was completely ignorant of its diminishing returns. It was she who kept the rudimentary accounts, and she who helped at one of the stalls whenever she could. It did not need a vast intelligence to see that the crowds were thinner than before, and that takings were down, but Ben feared that she did not realize how dangerously low their resources were. She knew nothing of the offer made by Dick Hasler, and Ben wanted to know how she felt about it.

A fine brown steak and kidney pie dominated the table at midday, and they all did justice to Molly's cooking. Even the old man, Ben noticed, tucked in, and grunted his appreciation in a grudging fashion.

'Now, you go and have a lay down, Dad,' said kindly Molly, 'while we wash up. Do you good to have a nap, and I'll wake you in time to go over to the church.'

Albert departed aloft and the young couple went to the sink. George was busy with his bricks at the table before going for his own brief rest. Now, thought Ben, was the time to broach the delicate subject. But Molly forestalled him.

'How d'you think Dad seems?'

'Not too bad. Ate two platefuls of pie, so he can't be at death's door yet. You worry overmuch about him, and he plays up to you.'

'That's not wholly true. His breathing's that rattly it scares me. He'll be back in hospital if he don't take care, and he's no more likely to do that than young George there.'

'He's a grown man. You can't expect to do everything for him.'

'And that ain't all,' went on Molly. 'His underclothes is in rags. I've torn up most of 'em for dusters as I've washed 'em, and I've taken a set of yours for him to keep the old fellow going until I can get down to Lulling to set him up.'

'Thanks,' said Ben laconically. 'And who pays for the new clobber?'

'Well, he will. I'll see to that. He's got a bit put by in the Post Office, and it's time he took some out for a few decent warm clothes. He don't know yet, but I had a bonfire of some of the worst this morning.'

Ben looked startled, and nearly dropped the pie-dish he was wiping.

'Watch it, girl!' he cried. 'He can be real nasty when he's roused. Lord knows the sparks'll fly when he finds out.'

'Then they must fly,' said Molly flatly, tipping away the washing-up water. 'I'm going to sort him out before we move on next week. And what's more, he's going to be given a good hot bath tonight, come what may!'

'Well, you can face that fight while I'm over the fair,' said Bert. 'And good luck to you!'

He watched her militant face as she shepherded George upstairs for his rest. This was not the time, he thought sadly, to introduce the subject of their own troubles.

That would have to wait.

Harold Shoosmith was busy weeding among the wallflowers by his front gate. He viewed the fair with mixed feelings. A peace-loving man who had retired to Thrush Green because of its tranquillity, he personally loathed the noise which Curdle's Fair generated, and for that reason would rejoice when the great trailers and caravans departed, leaving the green to recover from the scars.

On the other hand, he was amused and impressed by the ardour with which almost all the older inhabitants greeted May the first. The rites of spring had nothing on it, thought Harold, removing a worm which had become entangled in his shoelace. He dropped it nearby, and was roundly scolded by a robin who had been looking forward to snapping up this delectable morsel, but did not dare to come too close.

It was natural that the children should be excited, but surprising to find Joan Young and her sister Ruth Lovell so exhilarated at the thought of going on the swingboats and roundabouts as though they were still about ten years old. Even dear old Charles Henstock had rubbed his hands gleefully, and had said how good it was to see the fair again.

He straightened his creaking back and observed Phyllida Hurst coming out of her gate, across the green, letter in hand. He waved to her and she waved back, and after putting the envelope in the pillar box at the corner of the green, she walked over to talk to him.

She grew prettier than ever, thought Harold. There had been a time when he had fancied himself in love with this attractive young widow, but she had married his good friend Frank and, on the whole, he was relieved to find himself still a bachelor.

But now and again he had a twinge of regret. It must be very comforting to come home to find a pretty woman there, to have someone to talk to, to laugh with, and to share one's problems.

'That's exactly what I should be doing,' observed Phil, pointing a toe at the bucket of weeds, 'but I had a horrible story to alter this morning, and it's put me back in the day's programme.'

'How's the writing going?'

'Oh, slowly. I've about four or five magazines who take stuff regularly, but I'm thankful to say I don't have to worry so dreadfully about making money.'

'I'm very glad to hear it,' said Harold. 'You've quite enough to keep you happily occupied, and that's what matters.'

'Are you going to the fair?'

Harold noticed that the girl's eyes were sparkling as brightly as Joan's and Ruth's.

'Well, no! I'm a bit long in the tooth for all that whizzing round.'

'Rubbish!' said Phil. 'It does your liver a world of good! I'm taking Jeremy as soon as he comes out of school, and if Frank gets home in time, I hope I can persuade him to come too later on.'

'You'll manage that,' Harold told her with conviction.

She laughed, and moved away. 'Change your mind,' she called. 'Do come if you can. It's tremendous fun.'

He smiled, but made no reply. He had no intention of getting mixed up with a noisy, shouting throng of people, of being deafened with the brazen notes from those dreadful hurdy-gurdys, and of tripping over coils of cable on the wet grass of Thrush Green.

But how easy it would have been to say 'Yes' to that invitation.

Lucky Frank, thought Harold, turning again to his digging.

Promptly at four o'clock the strident music of Curdle's Fair rent the air. Outside the booths stood the showmen, shouting their wares. The swingboats began their delectable movement up and down, and the galloping horses moved steadily round and round and up and down, their barley-sugar brass supports gleaming like gold.

Most of the patrons were the children from the village school, with a few mothers. Jeremy, in company with some schoolfellows and his mother, Phil, was astride the horses and ostriches within five minutes of the fair's opening. If all his customers were as thrilled as this small boy, thought Ben, then this year's visit to Thrush Green might be well worth while.

His thoughts flew back to his wonderful old grandmother whose grave was behind him in the churchyard. She had always looked upon Thrush Green as her true home, the one place where she felt that she could rest, largely because of the affection she felt for Dr Bailey, who had looked after her, so many years ago, at her confinement with George, her son, father to Ben.

Ben too had this feeling of affinity with Thrush Green, partly because of his grandmother's loyalty to the place, partly because she now rested there for ever, and partly, of course, because he had found his dear Molly here, and heard about it from her almost daily, wherever they happened to be.

Yes, he supposed Thrush Green would be the obvious place to settle if the fair had to go. He sighed at the thought. What would the old lady have said?

Guilt flooded him, but within a minute it had given way to a comforting thought. Mrs Curdle had always been a realist. If one stall did not pay its way, she was quite ruthless in scrapping it.

When she had discovered her nephew Sam stealing the takings, she had not hesitated to banish him from the fair. If now she had been alive and had to face the sad fact that the business was not thriving, she would do as Ben was thinking of doing, cut her losses and start afresh, with courage and a stout heart.

It was a warming thought, and Ben felt better as he watched the spinning roundabout and the gaudy booths. She would have understood, and so would Molly when he broke the news.

'Roll up! Roll up!' he shouted with vigour, hoisting a four-year-old into a swingboat, and setting it into movement with a cheerful shove.

Some hours later, Winnie Bailey surveyed the scene from her bedroom window. By now it was dark. A few stars pricked the clearing sky, but it was difficult to see them against the blaze of light from Curdle's Fair.

'It's even better at night,' Winnie murmured to herself, watching the moving figures, silhouetted against the glare of the bright lamps. She had a great affection for the fair. The bond between Mrs Curdle, of hallowed memory, and Donald and herself had endured for decades. Every year the old lady had made a magnificent bouquet of artificial flowers for her Thrush Green friends. If she had kept them all, thought Winnie, she must have had several dozen.

They were glowing gaudy blossoms, made of finely-pared wood, and dyed in bright shades of orange, pink and red. Winnie still had one of these offerings in a vase on the landing, a constant reminder of a faithful friend.

'A fine family,' commented Winnie, closing the window.

Tomorrow she would seek out Ben and Molly, and hear all their news. The girl must enjoy coming home again and seeing Albert.

As it happened, at that very moment, Molly was confronting her incensed father across a zinc bath half full of steaming water.

The kitchen was snug and steamy. The kitchen range was alight, and on its gleaming top stood a large kettle and the biggest saucepan the cottage could boast.

'Never!' shouted Albert, his face suffused with wrath. 'I ain't gettin' in there, and that's flat.'

'You are,' replied Molly. 'You're plain filthy. You smell somethin' chronic, and you can get them rags off of your back for me to wash, or burn maybe, and get soaping. I'll be upstairs, sorting George's things out, so nobody's going to stare at you.'

'Never!' shouted Albert again. 'Never 'eard such cheek!'

Molly looked at him grimly. 'D'you want me to get the *District Nurse*?'

Albert's bravado cracked. 'You wouldn't dare! Besides, it's not decent. That young woman? Why, she ain't even married!'

'She's coming tomorrow, if you don't do as I says, then we'll both get you into the tub. So take your choice.'

Slowly the old man fumbled with the greasy scarf about his scrawny neck. He was muttering crossly to himself.

'That's right,' said Molly, reaching for the kettle. 'I'll just top up the water, and you can have a good soak in front of the fire. See here, I'll spread the towel over the back of the chair. Warm it nice, that will, and keep the draught off of you.'

Her ministrations done, she mounted aloft, leaving the staircase door ajar in order to hear that the old man attended properly to his ablutions. Once he was in, she intended to return to scrub his neglected back, modesty or not. Heaven alone knew when Albert's body had last seen soap and water! Not since his last trip to hospital, Molly suspected.

Albert stepped out of the last of his dilapidated underwear. He put one toe reluctantly into the steaming water.

'Women!' muttered Albert, and braced himself for semi-immersion.

7. New Hopes

As Miss Fogerty was on her way to school on Monday morning, she espied Willie Bond, the postman, pedalling towards her.

She waited at the end of the chestnut avenue. Willie was fat, and never hurried. However, Miss Fogerty was in good time as usual, and observed while she waited the fine sticky buds of the chestnut trees which were beginning to put forth little green fans of leaves.

'Morning, miss,' puffed Willie, dismounting. He studied a handful of letters and handed over two, much to Miss Fogerty's delight. She did not expect to get more than one or two in a whole week. Two in one day was quite an excitement.

She thanked Willie, and turned right between the trees, opening her first letter. It was a printed message from Messrs Ames and Barlow who, so their heading said, were Drapers, Milliners & Mantle Makers of 82 Lulling High Street, established 1862. They thanked Miss Fogerty for her esteemed order, and begged to inform her that the goods awaited collection at her earliest convenience, and they remained her obedient servants.

Miss Fogerty felt a little glow of pleasure. Her new lightweight mackintosh, ordered at Easter, would be a very welcome addition to her modest wardrobe. She might need to withdraw some money from her Post Office account, but it was a comfort to think that she could face the expense.

The other letter was from her dear friend Isobel, and she resolved to read it at her leisure when she arrived at school. She and Isobel had first met at college, many years ago. Isobel was so pretty and clever, and rather better dressed than the majority of girls. It had always surprised young Agnes Fogerty that they had become such firm friends. It had begun when the two discovered that they both came from the Cotswolds. Isobel's father was a bank manager at Stow-on-the-Wold, while Agnes's father was a shoemaker in Lulling.

Visits had been exchanged in the holidays, and Agnes had attended Isobel's splendid wedding. Marriage had taken her to Sussex where her husband owned several shops dealing in antique furniture.

The two girls kept in touch, although distance and Isobel's young children meant that they saw each other rarely. But whenever Isobel paid a visit to her parents at Stow she called to see Agnes, and the two picked up the threads of their friendship immediately.

When Isobel's husband died, Agnes had persuaded her to stay a few days at Thrush Green. Mrs White, her landlady, had a spare room then, and was glad to put it at the disposal of Agnes's old friend in her trouble.

Since then Agnes had spent several spells at Isobel's comfortable Sussex home. The children were now out in the world, and Isobel seemed glad of company. This letter, Miss Fogerty surmised, studying the envelope, might well contain another kind invitation to stay. In which case, it was a good thing that the new mackintosh 'awaited collection at her earliest convenience'. Isobel was always so beautifully dressed, and although she could never aspire to such elegance, at least she could look *respectable*.

She decided to enjoy reading the letter later and tucked the blue envelope into her handbag, and crossed the playground, nodding and smiling at the early arrivals who rushed to greet her. The asphalt, she noticed with her experienced teacher's eye, was quite dry again. Thank heaven, the children would be able to play outside! She entered her splendid new classroom in good spirits.

Albert Piggott, on that Monday morning, was certainly not in good spirits. He had woken with a sharp pain in his chest and a severe headache. He had no doubt about the cause of these symptoms. It was that dratted bath that his fool of a daughter had bullied him into – and he told her so.

'Don't talk soft, Dad,' Molly said tartly at breakfast, but secretly she felt a little guilty. Could he have caught a chill? In any case, it was absolutely necessary for him to be cleaned up, and she did not regret burning his disgusting garments.

'Well, wrap up when you go out,' said Molly. 'And I'll get you some cough mixture when I go down to Lulling.'

The old man continued to grumble throughout the day, and certainly by tea time, was flushed in the face and breathing heavily. Molly, trying to hide her alarm, persuaded him to go to bed early.

'He's not right,' she told Ben. 'I'm going to get the doctor to him if he's no better in the morning. Sometimes I wonder if we oughtn't to settle here. He needs looking after, and there's no one but me, now Nelly's gone. And another thing, we'll have to be thinking of George's schooling soon. It's not fair to send him here, there and everywhere, for a week or so at a time, as we move around. He won't learn nothing that way.'

Ben nodded understandingly. 'I've been thinking too. I reckon we've got to face staying put, and if you want that place to be Thrush Green, then that suits me. But not in this house, love, and not until we can get a place of our own.'

'But when will that be?' cried Molly, in despair. 'All we've got is the fair, and would you ever want to give it up?'

'It looks as though I might have to,' said Ben slowly, and began to tell her the problems and plans which had been plaguing him for the last few months.

She listened in silence, and then put her hand on his. 'You did right to tell me. You shouldn't have kept all this to yourself, Ben. We'll put our heads together and work out what's best to be done, and find out more from Dick Hasler too. You see, something'll turn up.'

A heavy thumping came from the bedroom above them.

'That's Dad,' said Molly. 'I promised him a cup of tea, and clean forgot it.' She crossed to the sink. 'You go and earn some honest pennies over the fair there,' she smiled at Ben. 'We're going to need 'em in the future.'

Some sixty miles away, Robert and Milly Bassett were rejoicing in the doctor's verdict that a journey to Thrush Green could be undertaken at any time.

'But watch it!' he warned. 'Keep those tablets in your pocket, and don't ignore any warning signs. I have been in touch with your son-in-law, Dr Lovell, and I know you will be well looked after.'

'And I intend to do the driving,' said Milly. 'Not on the motorway though. We'll take the old road, and stop at our old haunts on the way.'

'Good idea. But he's quite fit to drive, you know, as long as he stops if he feels the least bit tired.'

'I shall ring Joan tonight,' said Milly, when the doctor had gone. 'Won't it be lovely to see Thrush Green again?'

'I can't get there fast enough,' confessed Robert. 'Now that I know the business is safe in Frank's hands I have just given up worrying about it completely. It's wonderful to look forward to something. That's been half the trouble, I realize now, thinking about what one has done, or ought to have done, instead of looking ahead with hope. Thrush Green is going to set me up, and I'm not going to be such a fool as to jeopardize my health again. Life's too good to waste.'

'Come on Friday,' Joan said, when her mother telephoned. 'Everything's waiting, and everyone here wants to see you. Don't be surprised if all the flags are out!'

As it happened, Isobel's letter was not opened until after dinner time, for when Miss Fogerty entered her classroom she found that the fish tank had sprung a leak, and that the three goldfish (named Freeman, Hardy and Willis by the adoring class), were gasping in a bare inch of water.

Miss Fogerty rushed for a bucket of water, and the net to catch the luckless fish, and spent a busy ten minutes on this errand of mercy and mopping up the floor and cupboard.

The children were entranced at the mess and added to the confusion by trying to help with their handkerchiefs, hastily removed socks, and any other unsuitable piece of material which they could press into service. The amount of water which had come from one small tank was prodigious, and seemed to spread right across the room as well as flooding the cupboard below it. Naturally, it was the cupboard holding piles of new exercise books, the term's supply of coloured gummed squares, now living up to their name, tissue-paper, drawing paper, and thick paper used for painting. It was all most vexatious, and Miss Watson would not be pleased when she had to beg for more supplies, thought poor Agnes, wringing out the floor-cloth.

She took her class across the playground, to the main building for morning prayers, and was obliged to postpone her account of the disaster until after assembly. Usually, she and Miss Watson had a minute or two together before Miss Fogerty seated herself at the ancient upright piano. Neither Miss Watson, nor any other member of the staff over the past ten years, seemed to have learned to play the piano, so that Miss Fogerty was obliged to face the music every morning.

Today Miss Watson was called to the telephone, and arrived a few minutes late. However, she stood in front of the children with her usual calm smile, and prayers began.

Miss Fogerty noted that the hymn was not one of her favourites.

> Raindrops are our diamonds
> And the morning dew,
> While for shining sapphires
> We've the speedwell blue.

What was more, the thing was in four flats, a key which Miss Fogerty detested. However, she did her best, noticing yet again how sharp the older children's voices became towards the end of the hymn.

As the children were led away to their classrooms, Agnes told her headmistress of her misfortune.

'How tiresome,' said Miss Watson, 'and it would be dreadfully wasteful to have to throw away so much good material! I think you had better spread out the sheets separately, Agnes dear, and dry them as best you can. We simply can't waste things.'

And easier said than done, thought Agnes rebelliously, as she crossed the playground. There were mighty few places to spread hundreds of sheets of wet paper in her classroom, and every time the door opened they would blow to the floor, and the children would rush to collect them, as well Miss Watson knew. There had been a chiding note too in her headmistress's voice, which annoyed her usually submissive assistant. Did she think that she had purposely damaged the fish tank? Good heavens, surely she wasn't being accused of wilful damage, or even of neglect? It was simply an act of God, well, perhaps not of God, thought Agnes hurriedly. He cared for all creatures after all, and must grieve for those poor fish who had been almost literally at their last gasp. No, it was a Complete Accident, she told herself firmly, and the only thing to do was to borrow another tank immediately for the poor things, and to endeavour to get her excited children into a calmer state of mind, ready for a good morning's work.

Consequently, it was not until cold mutton with jacket potatoes, followed by pink blancmange, had been dispatched that Miss Fogerty was at liberty to take out Isobel's letter in the peace of her empty classroom and read the news.

It gave her much food for thought, and distracted her attention for a while from her damp surroundings.

She was contemplating a move, Isobel wrote. Now that she was alone, it seemed silly to keep up such a large house. The fuel bills alone were horrifying. The garden was far too big, and dear old Bates, who had come twice a week for more years than she cared to remember, had just told her that he must give up.

She would like to return to the Cotswolds, and proposed to look out for a small house, preferably in the Thrush Green area. Not that she was going to *rush* things. If possible, could kind Mrs White put her up for, say, a week while she got in touch with local estate agents? She would much prefer to stay there, in

Agnes's company, than put up at The Fleece in Lulling. Hotel life was rather noisy at night, and The Fleece had no really quiet lounge during the day. Also it was a good distance from Agnes's house, and it was she that Isobel wanted to see, of course. But perhaps Agnes could find out if Mrs White would be agreeable?

Little Miss Fogerty shook her head sadly when she read that paragraph. Mrs White, she knew, would not be able to accommodate her old friend, for an ailing aunt now occupied the spare bedroom and looked like remaining there for some time to come.

The main news, of course, was wonderfully exciting. To think that Isobel might one day be her neighbour! It would be lovely to have her so close. She knew several people in Thrush Green and Lulling, and it was not very far from the Stow area where some of her relations still lived. How she hoped that Isobel would soon find somewhere suitable! She would help her with the move, of course. Perhaps next summer holidays?

Agnes's mind ran ahead happily, anticipating the joys to come. The only snag was this visit in the near future.

Where could she lodge? Mentally, Agnes reviewed the accommodation available near at hand. The Two Pheasants would never do. If Isobel thought The Fleece noisy, she would find The Two Pheasants insupportable, and there had been occasions when men had emerged *drunk* at closing time. Miss Watson, who lived so close to it, had told her so, and said how disagreeable it was.

She toyed with the idea of asking Miss Watson if she could put up her friend for a week. The two ladies had met, and enjoyed each other's company. But Agnes was not at all sure that Miss Watson deserved to have the honour of having Isobel as a paying guest, after her heartless handling of this morning's mishap. Besides, Miss Watson had a brother who occasionally called unexpectedly, and the room might be needed for him.

And then little Miss Fogerty had a brainwave. She would call on the dear rector and see if he knew of likely lodgings. He and Dimity knew Isobel quite well, and had invited her to tea and bridge on several occasions. They would know the sort of place which would suit her. Somewhere in the parish there must be someone who would like to let a room to a charming, considerate lady like dear Isobel.

Out in the playground a whistle shrilled, and the children's roaring, whilst not actually stilled, was certainly diminished in volume.

Miss Fogerty put away her letter and her private problems, and went out to meet her class.

By mid-week, Albert Piggott was considerably worse, and was confined to his bed.

Dr Lovell said that it would be wise for him to stay indoors for the rest of the week. His breathing was giving him pain, and he was seriously under weight, the legacy of a year or so's catering, or rather non-catering, for himself.

The wind had veered to the north-east, and Albert himself had forecast that it would stay in that quarter until Whitsun.

'You mark my words, gal,' he wheezed. 'We shan't have no more rain for a bit, but just this pesky dryin' wind to keep the buds from openin'. Won't get no bees venturing out in this cold weather.'

'Nor you, Dad,' said Molly, tucking in the bed clothes. 'You stay there, and I'll do my best to feed you up, like Dr Lovell said.'

'It's no good,' she told Ben later. 'I'll have to stop here at least until the end of the week. You'll have to go on to Banbury alone. He's not fit to be left yet.'

Ben was philosophical about it. This had happened before, and was likely to happen again. It brought home to both of them the necessity to find a house and a job somewhere near the old man.

'One thing, our George isn't at school yet. Won't hurt him to stay here a few days. He's better off with you in the warm, than following me around, in this wind.

Albert Piggott was not a good patient. He never ceased to remind poor Molly that it was the unnecessary bathing which had reduced him to his present plight. He toyed with the food which Molly so carefully prepared, pouring contumely upon such dainties as steamed fish and egg custard which he dismissed as 'damn slops'. Molly had to stand over him to make sure that he took his medicine every four hours. He took to throwing off the bedclothes, complaining of heat, and occasionally hung out of the window in his flimsy pyjamas 'to get a breath of air'.

Molly was sometimes in despair. Only the threat of calling in the district nurse or, worse still, getting the old man into Lulling Cottage Hospital, kept her irascible patient in some sort of submission.

The fair was due to go on the Thursday. She spent the time washing and ironing Ben's clothes and packing the caravan with groceries and homemade pies and cakes.

'Lord!' commented Ben. 'How long am I supposed to be alone? I'll be back for you and George next Monday, I reckon. I'll never get through that lot in a month of Sundays.'

'You never know,' said Molly. 'You give me a ring Monday morning at The Two Pheasants. I've fixed it with Bob. Then we can see how things are.'

That afternoon she remembered, with shame, that she had not called to see the Youngs where she had worked so happily. She left her father asleep, took George by the hand, and walked across the green to the lovely old house.

The buds of May were being violently assaulted by the rough

wind. Dry leaves of last autumn were flying pell-mell across the grass, and a great roaring came from the branches of the chestnut trees. Little eddies of dust whirled like miniature sand storms in the road, and the smoke from a bonfire in Harold Shoosmith's garden blew in a rapidly moving cloud towards the distant Lulling Woods.

It was a thoroughly unpleasant afternoon, and Molly was glad to gain the shelter of the walled garden. She made her way to the back door, and rang the bell. Joan opened it and enveloped her in a warm hug.

'Wonderful to see you. I meant to call, but heard Albert wasn't well, and thought you might be rather busy. Tell me the news.'

The two sat at the kitchen table where Joan had been ironing and gossiped happily. Molly looked with affection at her old place of work. Nothing much had changed, and she commented on it with pleasure.

Joan told her about her parents' visit. Molly, in turn, told her about their hopes to find a settled job one day.

'I'll keep my ears open,' Joan promised her. 'I know how clever Ben is with his hands. It shouldn't be difficult to find a job. The house business will be more difficult, I suspect, but I won't forget, and if I hear of anything I shall get in touch.'

Molly left a forwarding address before she went, and promised to look in before Ben claimed her again.

'No, I best not stay for a cup of tea, thank you,' she said, in answer to Joan's invitation. 'Dad's medicine's got to be got down him within half an hour, and that'll take some doing.'

She made her farewells, and set off again to face the biting wind. The children were streaming out of school, followed by Miss Fogerty.

To Molly's surprise, the little figure did not take a homeward path through the avenue, but struck across Thrush Green towards the rectory. Going to collect the parish magazine? Offering to help Miss Dimity with a bazaar or some such? Taking a message from Miss Watson about the hymns? Such surmises are part of the pleasures of country living.

But this time Molly had guessed wrongly, for Miss Fogerty's errand concerned dear Isobel, a lady whom Molly had never met.

Still wondering, she opened the door of Albert's cottage and went to collect the medicine.

8. More News of Lodgers

Dotty Harmer's new lodger, Flossie, had settled in very well, and the fact that nothing had been heard from her last owner was a great relief to Dotty, who had grown much attached to the young spaniel.

The dog followed her everywhere, as if, having been abandoned once, she feared that it might happen again. Dotty was moved by this affection, and returned it tenfold. The two grew very close and the sight of Dotty, shadowed by the faithful golden cocker, became a familiar sight in Lulling and Thrush Green.

On a windy afternoon the two descended the hill to Lulling High Street. Dotty carried a basket in each hand, with Flossie's lead intricately entangled with one of them. They made steady progress against the biting east wind, which reddened Dotty's nose and sent Flossie's ears streaming behind her.

Their destination was the Misses Lovelock's house. Dotty was bearing a collection of contributions for the bazaar, and was glowing with the comfortable feeling of doing good.

'Why, Dotty dear, how kind!' cried Bertha, on opening the door. 'Do bring them in. We'll put them straight on the table. Everything's in the dining-room.'

That gloomy apartment was certainly transfigured. The mahogany table had been covered by an enormous white damask cloth, a relic of some Victorian linen cupboard, and upon it there jostled an odd collection of objects.

Dominating all were Ella's colourful contributions. Dimity had supplied a dozen or so dried flower-and-grass arrangements which the Misses Lovelock wondered if they could sell, as everyone in the district was addicted to making such things, and the market might well be saturated. However, they had been accepted with cries of delight, and one could only wait and see.

More normal contributions, such as soap, handkerchiefs, pots of jam and other preserves were among the rest, and would obviously be snapped up, and Dotty began to put her contributions among them.

'Four pots of preserved boletus, the *edible* kind, naturally,' gabbled Dotty, placing four sinister looking jars on the table. Through the murky fluid could be seen some toadstools of venomous appearance. Ada's jaw dropped, but she remained silent, with commendable control.

'And six pots of hedgerow jelly,' continued Dotty, diving into her basket. 'It's a mixture, you know, of sloes, blackberries, rosehips, elderberries and any other nourishing berries I could find. I thought "Hedgerow Jelly" on the label would cover it nicely.'

'Yes, indeed,' said Ada faintly, noting the sediment at the bottom of the jars, and the hint of mildew on the top.

'Not much room to write all the ingredients on the label, you see,' said Dotty, standing back to admire the imposing array. 'But I'm sure people will understand.'

'I'm sure they will,' agreed Violet bravely. But whether they would actually *buy* a jar of something which looked certain to give the consumer Dotty's Collywobbles – a disease known to all Dotty's friends – was another matter.

'You are so generous, Dotty dear,' quavered Bertha, averting her gaze from the jars. 'And now you must stay and have some tea. Ada has made some delicious scones with wholemeal flour which we ground ourselves in Father's old pestle and mortar.'

'Exactly the sort of thing I love,' said Dotty. 'And Flossie too, if she may have a crumb or two?'

The old ladies made their way to the drawing-room for this modest repast and a great deal of genteel gossip in which a number of Lulling residents' characters would be shredded finely, in the most ladylike fashion.

That same afternoon, Dimity had crossed the road to her old home to broach a subject which she and Charles had discussed thoroughly since Miss Fogerty's visit. Charles had been wholly in favour of suggesting that Isobel Fletcher should spend the proposed week's visit with Ella.

'They both get on very well,' he said. 'Much the same age. And then Thrush Green is so central for the little trips she may wish to make for viewing places. I'm sure she would be perfectly happy.'

Dimity had some private doubts.

Everyone liked Isobel. She was kind, charming, and elegant. Ella had always spoken warmly of her, and admired her quick brain. But Isobel was used to comfort. Her husband had been a prosperous man, and his wife was provided with a beautiful home and everything she could possibly desire. Could she stand the rough-and-ready hospitality which Ella would provide? And what about that all-pervading tobacco smoke? And the lack of punctuality in producing meals?

The meals themselves gave Dimity no fears. Ella had a surprisingly good way with food, and was meticulous about its preparation. The house might be a little dusty and untidy, but Ella's cooking arrangements could not be faulted. The snag was that she might well decide to make a chicken terrine at eleven in the morning, and hope to have it cold, with salad, at one o'clock. Ella never seemed to have mastered the time factor in all her activities.

However, she was now on her way to put the proposition to her old friend. She found her sitting by the window doing the crossword puzzle.

'Funny minds these chaps must have,' said Ella, putting aside the paper. 'This clue "Makes waterproof" is "*Caulks*", and the next one is "Sea travel" which is "*Cruise*", so that makes "Corkscrews", d'you see?'

'No, I don't, dear, but I've something to tell you, and I must get back to take the cat's supper out of the oven, so I mustn't linger.'

'And what is that spoilt animal having this evening?'

'Just a little rabbit. Nothing very special.'

'Lucky old cat! Well, come on, what's bothering you?'

Dimity launched into the account of Isobel Fletcher's need of lodgings for a week while she consulted agents about the possibility of buying a house in the neighbourhood. She explained Miss Fogerty's dilemma. Mrs White would not be able to put her up, as she had done. She *could*, of course, stay at The Fleece, but if Ella were willing . . . ? The question hung in mid-air among the blue smoke from Ella's cigarette.

'Of course I'm willing,' replied Ella. 'I'm very fond of Isobel, and should be delighted to have her here. The only thing is, would she be comfortable?'

Trust dear Ella to come directly to the point, thought Dimity, with some relief.

'I'm sure she will be,' said Dimity bravely. 'If you like, I'll come over and help you make up the spare bed, and empty the cupboards, and so on.'

And give an expert eye to Isobel's comfort, she thought privately.

'When will it be? Any idea?'

'None, I'm afraid, but fairly soon, I imagine. Shall I let Agnes Fogerty know, or will you? I know she wants to write very soon.'

'I'll catch her after school,' said Ella. 'One thing though, I'm not letting Isobel pay me. It'll be a pleasure to have her here.'

'Well, you must sort that out between you,' said Dimity rising to go. 'It will be so nice to see her again, and I do so hope she finds somewhere to live nearby.'

'Unless she gets snapped up by somebody in Sussex before

that,' said Ella shrewdly. 'She's eminently marriageable, from all viewpoints.'

'Oh, I don't think that will happen,' replied Dimity, slightly shocked. 'She's still grieving for her husband, you know. They were quite devoted.'

She opened the door to see a few children straggling across the green from the village school.

'Out already?' cried Ella. 'Here, I'll cut across now and see Agnes. No time like the present, and she can catch the afternoon post if she looks slippy!'

Ben Curdle had departed on his way to Banbury, and Molly was left to cope with George and Albert as best she could.

The old man's temper did not improve. The doctor forbade his going outside in the bitter wind, which still prevailed, and Albert worried about the church and the way in which it was being looked after.

The rector had asked one of the Cooke boys to take on Albert's duties temporarily. The Cooke family was numerous and rather slap-dash, but there was no one else free to lend a hand and Jimmy Cooke had agreed to keep an 'eye on things'.

'And that's about all he will do,' growled Albert. 'And I won't be surprised to find me tools missing. Light-fingered lot them Cookes. Always on the look-out for somethin' to pinch.'

Molly tried to turn a deaf ear to the old man's constant complaining. How right Ben was to insist that they did not live with her father! Whatever the future held, that was certain. Look after him she would, as best she could, but to see dear Ben and young George suffering the gloomy and insulting behaviour of the miserable old fellow, was more than she could bear.

'If that's what old age brings you to,' thought Molly, attacking some ironing, 'I hopes as I dies young!'

Not that all old people were as trying as her father, she had to admit. Dear old Dr Bailey, for instance, had always been a happy man, even in his last long illness, and Mr Bassett, who would be arriving for his holiday that very afternoon, always had a cheerful word for everyone.

Perhaps education helped? Molly pondered on this as she

ironed a pillowslip. If your mind was full of knowledge, then perhaps you did not worry overmuch about your body and its ills? It brought her again to the question of George's future. A sound schooling he was going to have, come what may, and he could not do better than start at Thrush Green School with Miss Watson and Miss Fogerty. He was going to have a better start in life than his father. Poor Ben, she remembered, had been unable to read and write, with any competence, when they first met, and she herself had acted as teacher. She had certainly had a willing – even amorous – pupil, and within a month or so he had mastered his difficulties. But he had never forgotten the humiliation of having to confess his ignorance for so many years, and he was as determined as Molly that George should never suffer in the same way.

Well, the next step was to look out for a suitable job for Ben. Once the Bassetts were settled in, she would have another talk with Joan Young, and perhaps walk down to that new Job Centre in Lulling to see if there were any openings for a hard-working man like her dear Ben.

Whoever employed him, thought Molly loyally, would be lucky. There was no one – simply no one – like her Ben.

There was a splendid sunset as Molly finished her ironing. Bands of gold, scarlet and violet clouds transfigured the western sky, and the dark mass of Lulling Woods was silhouetted against the blaze of glory.

The rooks were flapping homeward, their black satin feathers catching the light. Albert Piggott's cat sat on the sun-warmed wall of The Two Pheasants and enjoyed the last of the daylight.

Betty Bell, who was cleaning Miss Fogerty's schoolroom, stopped her ministrations to admire the spectacle. Just like a jumper she'd knitted once! All different bands of colour, she remembered, and no end of trouble with the vee neck. But what a gorgeous sight!

Miss Harmer would have a good view from her cottage, and Mr Shoosmith, next door to the school, would see that sunset even better from the bedroom she had done out that morning. Did you a power of good to see something pretty like that, thought Betty, returning to her desk-polishing, much refreshed.

A car drew up outside the Youngs' gate, and before the doors were opened, Joan ran out to set the gates open.

Slowly the car drew into the drive. Out stepped Milly Bassett, to be enveloped in her daughter's embrace, and then, rather more slowly, Robert emerged. He looked pale and rather shaky, but he stood erect and took in great breaths of fragrant air. His face was alight with pleasure.

'Just what I've been longing for,' he told Joan, holding out his arms. 'To come home again!'

PART TWO

Change at Thrush Green

* * * *

9. Visitors to Thrush Green

There now began for Robert Bassett a period of intense joy.

It was as if all his senses had been sharpened by the shock of his recent illness. He saw, with fresh awareness, the small beauties around him, and marvelled that he had not enjoyed them before.

The lilac was beginning to break in the garden, each fragrant plume composed of hundreds of exquisite flowerets. Grape hyacinths spread a carpet of vivid blue beneath the burgundy-red stems of the dogwood bushes. He came across a thrush's nest, cleverly hidden in the crutch of the hawthorn hedge, and admired the smooth mud lining, as beautifully rounded as the speckled breast of the bird that sat so patiently upon the four turquoise blue eggs.

Everything delighted him. He ventured from the garden to Thrush Green, observing the pattern of blue smoke from cottage chimneys which matched the distant blur of Lulling Woods. He sat on the seat near the statue of Nathaniel Patten and gloried in the warmth of the sun upon his face, the droplets spangling a spider's web, the timid advances of Albert Piggott's cat whose curiosity had overcome her fear, and the rough comfort of the blackthorn walking stick in his hand.

How right W. H. Davies had been, thought Robert, when he wrote:

> What is this life,
> If full of care,
> We have no time
> To stand and stare?

This was the first time, in a long life, that he had savoured to the full the pleasures of his senses. He remembered the extraordinary sensations he had felt, when bedbound, on his sudden awareness of the inanimate objects in the bedroom. That had been the beginning of his new response to his surroundings, although weakness then had blurred some of the pleasure. Now, with ever-growing strength, he gave thanks for the miracles around him, and his ability to recognize them.

Sickness, reflected Robert, changed a man. He thought of the invalids he had known. How often he had dismissed their querulousness and complaints as the outcome of self-pity! He knew better now.

It was not only with themselves and their pain that the sick were concerned. They worried for others. They grieved for the work they were causing, for the disruption of other people's lives, the sapping of their energy, the tensions within a family, and the awful possibility of increasing helplessness.

He had been lucky, he thought soberly. Lucky to have had his darling Milly as constant support, a doctor he trusted, and a loving family. Lucky too, to have realized this further truth, that the sick are sad, not only for themselves, but for those they love. He would never forget it.

And luckiest of all, thought Robert, gazing around him, to be at peace in Thrush Green on a bright May morning.

Albert Piggott had thrived under Molly's care, and Dr Lovell assured the girl that her father could cope perfectly well without her presence.

'I'll keep an eye on him,' he promised her. 'I gather from Bob Jones that you've arranged for a midday meal for him at The Two Pheasants. He should do well now that the weather's warmer.'

Molly told him of her fears that he would need more care as the years passed, and of their plans to settle within easy distance of the old man.

'Well, it happens to us all,' agreed the doctor. 'But don't completely upset your lives for Albert. He's by way of being a bit of a fraud, you know.'

He laughed to soften his words, and Molly smiled too.

'Oh, we knows him well enough, Doctor! But it don't alter the fact that he's gettin' an old man. I wish his Nelly hadn't left him. She took good care of him.'

'They weren't exactly turtle-doves,' commented the doctor. 'It was plain that it couldn't last.'

'I know she was a right trollop in her ways,' agreed Molly earnestly, 'but she kept that house spotless, and her cooking was just beautiful. Dad was lucky to get her. After all, you can't expect *everything* in marriage.'

Dr Lovell tried to hide his amusement as he drove off on his rounds. There was something very refreshing about Molly's attitude to the wedded state. Obviously, good housewifery was rated rather more highly than fidelity in Molly's scale of reckoning. Her own marriage, he knew, was an outstanding success. So, he thought, was his own to Ruth. They were both lucky to have found the right partners. It did not look as if Albert would find another to give him companionship in his old age.

Ah well! What could he expect? He was a thoroughly selfish old man, and he only hoped that Molly would not put her marriage in jeopardy by trying to live with Albert Piggott.

Not that it was likely, thought Dr Lovell, turning his car into the village of Nidden. Ben would see to that.

The early days of May followed each other with increasing warmth and fragrance. Spring cleaning was finished in a spurt of energy. Blankets blew upon clothes-lines, carpets were beaten, curtains and bedspreads washed, and good housewives congratulated themselves upon the amount of work which could be accomplished, given bright sunshine and fair winds.

Dimity had kept her word and helped Ella to prepare for Isobel's arrival. The spare-room awaited her, with cupboards and drawers emptied and relined with clean paper, furniture glossy with polish, and a vase of pheasant-eye narcissi on the bedside table.

'D'you think she'll be comfortable?' asked Ella, unusually anxious.

'Of course,' replied Dimity reassuringly.

'I'm not sure just when she'll arrive,' went on Ella, 'so I thought

I'd whip up an omelette for this evening. There's plenty of salad. I wonder if that will be enough?'

'Isobel was always a small eater,' said Dimity. 'And no doubt you've plenty of fruit, and cheese.'

'Dotty brought me some goat's cheese this morning,' said Ella, 'but I'm not putting *that* on the cheese board. Don't want the poor girl struck down with Dotty's Collywobbles while she's here.'

'No, indeed,' agreed Dimity. 'Now, I must get back to Charles. He has a diocesan meeting at six, miles away, and I want to make sure that he has a good tea.'

She hurried across the road to the bleak rectory, leaving Ella to survey her preparations with a critical eye.

'Ah well,' she said at last. 'Can't do any more now. Time I had a cigarette before dear old Isobel arrives.'

She settled down on the window seat, and began to roll a pungent cigarette. But before she had a chance to light it, a small pale-blue glossy car stopped at the gate, and Isobel emerged.

Throwing the cigarette into the battered tobacco tin, Ella hurried to open the gate, enfolding Isobel in a great bear-hug on the way.

'Wonderful to see you,' she boomed. 'Had a good trip? My word, this looks a handsome vehicle!' She surveyed the car with much admiration.

'It's an Alfa Romeo,' said Isobel, 'and it certainly got me here in record time today. Traffic was amazingly light, and I know my way so well, of course, there was no need to stop for map-reading or asking people.'

'All "strangers in these parts" anyway, I find,' said Ella, helping with Isobel's case which was as sleek and elegant as the car. 'I'm going to put on the kettle. It can boil while I show you your room. That is, if you'd like a cup of tea?'

'More than anything in the world,' said Isobel, following her hostess.

The arrival of the beautiful Alfa Romeo had been noted by Harold Shoosmith who was walking across the green to call upon Charles Henstock.

Harold loved cars, and was beginning to think that it was high time that he parted with, the ancient Daimler which had served him so well for years. But what to buy in its place? All through his life he had bought cars made in Britain. In the long years abroad, his succession of British cars had been a precious link with home, and a source of admiration to friends overseas. Now he found himself looking in vain for the sort of small, distinguished and well-finished vehicle which he wanted.

Parking in Lulling High Street was no easy task with the gallant old Daimler. Its petrol consumption grew as the years passed. The time had come, Harold knew, with sadness, when he must part with it. There were several foreign cars on the market which attracted him, but loyalty to British makers made him hesitant to look at overseas models. But Isobel's pale blue beauty was certainly an eye-catcher. He looked it over, from a distance, as he waited for someone to come to the rectory door.

Charles greeted him and took him into his study.

'Dimity's gone to take some magazines to Dotty Harmer,' he told his friend. 'Do sit down.'

'I won't keep you long,' replied Harold. He was thinking how dark and cold this room always seemed. Today, with the warm May sunshine flooding the world with golden light, it seemed incredible that this bleak study remained untouched by its ambience.

'I came for the sweep's address,' said Harold. 'Betty Bell tells me that we should have had the chimneys done a month ago. She can't remember the new chap's name, and neither can I, of course.'

'Surely you have Potter from Lulling?'

'He died last year, I'm told.'

The rector looked shocked. 'I'm truly grieved to hear that. He was not one of my parishioners, of course, but I should like to have called on him during his last illness.'

'He didn't really have one, according to Betty,' answered Harold. 'Dropped down on someone's hearth with the flue brush still in his hand, so she says. "A lovely way to go," was her comment, "but made a terrible mess of the carpet." I'm sorry to have brought bad news.'

'Not at all. Not at all,' replied the rector, pulling himself together. 'But about this new man. I'm sure we are as nonplussed as you are, as we always had poor Potter. Have you any clues?'

'Betty tells me that he lives at the other side of Lulling Woods. He clears cesspits and farm drains, does a bit of poaching, has had three wives and rears ferrets.'

'John Boston, without a doubt,' said the rector immediately. 'Rather a rough diamond, but a very useful member of the community, when he's not in prison. I have a soft spot for John, I must admit. I'm sure he'll do your chimneys beautifully.'

He reached for a piece of paper, and wrote down the address.

'It might be best to call on him, Harold. I doubt if he can read very well.' He handed over the slip of paper.

'Many thanks, Charles. I'll do that. Now, tell me, whose is that dazzling little car outside Ella's?'

'It must belong to Isobel Fletcher,' responded the rector. 'I know she was expected today, but I imagined she would arrive later than this. A charming woman. Have you met her?'

'No, I'm afraid not.'

'Then you must,' said the rector firmly, accompanying his visitor into the sunshine of Thrush Green. 'She's here for a week, I know, and may settle here permanently if she finds a suitable house.' He looked about him with some surprise. 'Why, it's quite warm out here! I think I shall leave my paperwork and do a little gardening instead.'

'A very sound idea,' agreed his friend.

Albert Piggott, partially restored to health, was doing a little light gardening himself in the churchyard, Harold noticed, as he returned to his own home. These days, the churchyard was very much easier to maintain than it had been when Harold first came to Thrush Green some years earlier.

It had been his idea to clear the whole area, to put the gravestones round the low wall which surrounded the plot, and to level the ground so that a motor mower could be used. There had been some opposition to this scheme, but there was considerable pride in the improved tidiness of Albert's domain, and certainly the little church of St Andrew's was more attractive now in its very spacious setting.

Albert Piggott was the last person to admit that his labours had been rendered considerably lighter by the new layout. From the first, he had refused to touch the motor mower, and the Cooke boy, who had been acting as locum during Albert's illness, had taken on the mowing from the start, and proved remarkably reliable.

Albert's job consisted of a certain amount of hoeing and weeding, the upkeep of the gravel path round the church, and the pruning of the shrubs.

On this particular afternoon he was plucking groundsel from the gravel. It was about the easiest job he could find outside in the sunshine. Also he was in full view of the rectory, should the rector wish to see him at work, and very handy for The Two Pheasants.

He had demolished a helping of steak and kidney pie, with mashed potatoes and tinned peas, at that hostelry, some two hours earlier, paid for by Ben and Molly in advance.

'Not a patch on Nelly's cooking,' he had grumbled to the landlord, who affected deafness. If he took note of all Albert's whinings, he told himself, he'd be in the local loony bin in next to no time. Best to ignore the old misery!

Now, with bending, Albert was suffering from indigestion, and feeling more than usually sorry for himself. Visions of Nelly's pies and roast joints floated before his eyes. No doubt about it, you never got a ha'p'orth of heartburn after Nelly's cooking!

He collected a few more handfuls of groundsel, threw them on to the compost heap, hidden in a remote corner of the churchyard, and wandered across the road to his cottage.

He rummaged in a jam-jar which served as his medicine chest, discovered an indigestion tablet, and sat sucking it morosely as he surveyed the kitchen.

Nothing had been done to it since Molly had left, apart from a little desultory washing of crockery and cutlery. The stove was dingy. The floor was dirty. The windows were misty with grime, and dust lay everywhere. It needed a woman's hand, thought Albert sentimentally. Here he was, an invalid, with no one to look after him, deserted by his wife and daughter, left to fend for himself in his old age. It was enough to bring tears to your eyes, that it was!

His thoughts turned again to Nelly. She wasn't everybody's

choice, of course. For one thing, she must have turned the scales at sixteen stone, and she had a laugh that fairly made your head throb. Then she was a stickler for cutting down on the drink – a bad thing for a man who enjoyed the occasional glass. She was a nagger too, when the spirit moved her. No, she had been lucky to have found someone like himself to put up with her ways, decided Albert.

But there – she was a real stunner of a cook, and could be very loving when she wanted anything. Money, for instance. She wasn't above taking a pound note out of his wallet on the sly, if he didn't pass it over when requested.

And then that flirting with the oil man! That was enough to turn anyone's stomach, remembered Albert. And finally, to leave a good husband and home to live with the fellow! It was unforgivable.

Albert's indigestion grew worse at the very thought of Nelly's infidelity. What if she was a wonderful cook, and a superb housewife? Her morals were no better than an alley cat's. Come to think of it, an alley cat probably behaved more circumspectly than his wife, he decided, rubbing the pain in his diaphragm.

He was better off without her, dirt, indigestion and all. He stumbled across to the sink, and filled the kettle. A cup of tea might settle his tempestuous inside. Nothing like a cup of tea for comfort! Sniffing slightly with self-pity, Albert fumbled among the dirty dishes on the draining-board and found himself a relatively clean cup.

The golden May day ended in a blazing sunset. The rooks flew home to Lulling Woods, and children pleaded to stay up to play. The bronze statue of Nathaniel Patten on Thrush Green caught the last of the light, glinting like gold. Lilac, narcissi and early stocks breathed out a heady fragrance, and all was at peace.

Two miles away, a train drew out of Lulling Station. Only one passenger had alighted, and the ticket collector tried to hide his amazement as he took the ticket in his hand. No words were exchanged, but he watched the traveller out of sight with the greatest excitement.

Purposefully, the large figure waddled towards the town. In one hand it carried a case. In the other, a handbag and a bag of groceries.

For better or for worse, Nelly Piggott was returning to Thrush Green.

10. ELLA'S PARTY

For little Miss Fogerty, the arrival of her friend Isobel spelt happy excitement.

Modest and retiring by nature, the very fact that she was immured in the classroom all day, and that her lodgings were a little way from the centre of Thrush Green, meant that she had made few friends in the neighbourhood.

> Be civil to all,
> But familiar with few,

was a precept hung upon the shop wall of her father, the shoe-maker. It certainly summed up his attitude to his customers and to his chapel acquaintances. There was little entertaining done. It was not only that money was short. It was an inherent timidity which restrained the shoemaker from giving cause for comment or ridicule. He was a great one for 'keeping himself to himself', and Agnes took after him.

The inhabitants of Thrush Green were fond of her. Many of them remembered her from their schooldays, and always with affection and respect. But Agnes Fogerty was not the sort of person in whom one could confide – or, for that matter, in whom one could arouse laughter or rage. Always kind, always ladylike, shiningly honest and conscientious, these very attributes seemed to surround her with an invisible guard which no one had completely penetrated.

Except Isobel. Perhaps it was because they had first met when they were both young and vulnerable, thrown together in the alien world of college, and grateful for the common memories of their Cotswold background. This friendship had survived the years, the changes of fortune and the many miles between them.

To Isobel it was a source of comfort and quiet pleasure. To Agnes it was much more. She never ceased to wonder that Isobel, so much cleverer, so much more beautiful, so much more prosperous, could still enjoy her own, limited company. Their friendship was an inspiration to the quiet school teacher, and did much to mitigate the fact that she had so few friends at Thrush Green.

Of course, she counted her headmistress, Miss Watson, as a friend, and was glad to hear her confidences and hopes. In times of stress, Agnes knew that she had been of real help, and the thought warmed her. But that inherent timidity, inculcated by her father, made her careful of overstepping the bounds of propriety.

Miss Watson was *The Head*. She was *An Assistant*. Nothing could alter those two facts, and Agnes was careful to keep a certain distance between them, as was only right and proper. Although, sometimes, she had a pang of regret.

It seemed so silly that two grown women, both single, both

lonely at times, should not become closer in friendship. And yet, any overtures must, of course, come from Miss Watson. It would look *pushing* if she herself made the running.

Miss Fogerty remembered how much she had enjoyed being of use to Miss Watson on one or two occasions when accident or ill-health had indisposed her headmistress. She was always so grateful for any little kindnesses done, thought Agnes, and for this generosity of spirit it was worth ignoring the minor pinpricks which daily companionship sometimes brought, such as the wounding words on the recent occasion of the leaking fish tank. Perhaps she was over-sensitive about these things? Or perhaps she was getting prickly in her old age?

Well, whatever the cause, the fact that Isobel was in Thrush Green for a week, wiped out any unhappy feelings. For the next few days she intended to see her old friend as often as her duties would allow.

The May sunshine which warmed Thrush Green only increased the inner glow of little Miss Fogerty's heart. An invitation to drinks from Ella was 'accepted with the greatest pleasure' and, in this case, with perfect truth.

Robert Bassett's returning strength was noted with much relief at Thrush Green. Already he had spent an evening playing bridge at Winnie Bailey's in the company of his wife, the Hursts who lived next door at Tullivers, and Charles and Dimity Henstock.

His daily walk grew a little longer, and he began to plan a walk downhill to Lulling in the near future.

Joan and Ruth and his son-in-law Dr Lovell were beginning to congratulate themselves upon the patient's well-being when something happened to jog them out of their complacency.

Robert had gone out on his own along the quiet lane to Nod and Nidden. Milly was going to catch him up, but a phone call delayed her, and it was some ten minutes later that she left the house.

To her horror, she discovered her husband flat on his face, his head upon the grass verge, and his legs in the road. His breathing was laboured, his lips blue, and his hands were cold. She whipped off her jacket and flung it over the prostrate form and, luckily, at that moment, Willie Bond, the postman, came along on his bicycle.

'Lor!' was his comment. 'Has he croaked?'

'Of course not!' retorted Milly, with understandable asperity. 'Could you run to the Youngs and get help, Willie?'

'Ah! That I will,' responded Willie, throwing a fat leg over the saddle with maddening slowness.

He pedalled off, and Milly felt in her husband's waistcoat pocket for the magic tablets which Dr Lovell had prescribed. She could not find them, and had to content herself with chafing the cold hands, and putting a scarf under her husband's head.

A minute later, Joan arrived, flushed with anxiety. 'John's on his way with the car,' she said. 'Luckily, he was still in the surgery.'

Robert's eyelids began to flicker, and he attempted to lift his head. 'I'm all right,' he murmured. 'I'm all right. I'm all right. I'm all right.'

But the two anxious women knew that he was not, and saw with relief that Dr Lovell's car was approaching.

Within twenty minutes Robert Bassett was back in bed, and the hopes of all had plummeted.

The inhabitants of Thrush Green were united in their sadness when the news broke. But prognostications of what might happen differed, of course.

Betty Bell told Harold Shoosmith that her uncle went just the same way. First time, recovered. Second, snuffed out!

Albert Piggott was of the opinion that a new heart put in might be the answer. Why, that chap in South Africa – Christine Someone, wasn't it? – had put a whole hatful of hearts in dozens of poor souls like Mr Bassett. To his mind, it was worth trying. He only wished this Dr Christine did lungs as well. Pity he lived such a long way off.

Dotty Harmer told Dimity Henstock that she feared that Robert Bassett had eaten far too much animal fat during his life, and this was the consequence.

'I tried, time and time again, to wean him on to a vegetable diet, but with no success,' sighed Dotty. 'Men are very obstinate.'

Naturally, it was a subject of general interest at Ella's small party.

Miss Fogerty had dressed with care. As chief visitor's friend she felt that she owed it to Isobel to appear in her best. She wore a brown silk frock with a small ivory-coloured lace modesty vest let into the front, and her mother's cornelian brooch. She had spent some time trying to decide if her seed pearls could be worn as well, but a horror of being overdressed decided her against them. The brooch was quite enough.

As the weather was so dry and warm it was unnecessary to wear a coat, but Miss Fogerty folded an Indian shawl and put it prudently in her brown leather handbag. It might be chilly later.

She set out from her lodgings in innocent excitement. Outings were rare occasions, and to be the acknowledged close friend of dear Isobel, among her Thrush Green neighbours, meant a great deal to Agnes.

The Henstocks, Winnie Bailey and the Hursts were already there when she knocked timidly at Ella's front door. Isobel came forward to kiss her, and the assembled company greeted her warmly.

'Now, what's it to be?' inquired Ella. She was dispensing drinks with her usual forthright confidence. Some women would have delegated the job to one of the men, but not Ella.

'Tio Pepe? Or a sweet sherry? Gin and lime? Gin and tonic? Dubonnet? Or I've tomato juice and pineapple juice if you like the soft stuff.'

'The dry sherry, please,' said Miss Fogerty. Her dear father had approved of a little dry sherry, she remembered, and despised those who preferred a fruitier variety. Not that sherry had played much part in the shoemaker's house. At Christmas time there might be a bottle of sherry in the cupboard, but it was certainly looked upon as a luxury.

'Can't think what's happened to Dotty,' said Ella. 'Anyone seen her?'

'She was picking greenstuff for the rabbits,' said Winnie. 'I noticed her when I called to see if I could do anything for the Bassetts.'

'Hope she hasn't forgotten,' said Ella. 'And how was poor old Robert?'

'In bed, resting. I didn't go up. He seems to be sleeping quite a bit.'

'It's too bad, after the marvellous progress he was making,' said Dimity. 'I do hope he won't try to get back to that business of his. Time he retired.'

'I agree,' said Charles. 'I take it that the Youngs won't be coming here this evening?'

'No, they cried off,' said Ella.

'Coo-ee!' called a voice.

'Dotty!' exclaimed Ella, hurrying to the door.

They heard voices and footsteps, and in came Dotty, accompanied by Harold Shoosmith.

'We thought you might have forgotten,' said Dimity.

'Good heavens, no!' replied Dotty. 'Why, I went up to change a full hour ago.'

'My fault entirely,' broke in Harold. 'I waylaid her, and took her to see my tulips. Just showing off really.'

'Well, come and meet Isobel Fletcher,' said Ella, leading him across the room.

Harold found himself standing in front of an extremely pretty woman. There was a gentle serenity and poise about her which immediately appealed to him.

'How do you do?' said Isobel holding out her hand, and as Harold held it, he was suddenly reminded of something which he had read recently. Ellen Terry, if he remembered aright, had talked of 'a holy palmer's kiss, a sympathy of the skin', when some hands met in a clasp. For the first time, he was conscious, of it, and was strangely stirred.

They talked of Thrush Green, and of her efforts to find a home nearby.

'I used Williams & Frobisher,' Harold told her, 'when I was seeking a house here. I'd tried four or five other estate agents, but they would keep sending me details of derelict oasthouses and windmills, or manor houses with twenty-two bedrooms and no bath, until I was nearly driven insane. I must say Williams & Frobisher were much more practical.'

'I'll try them tomorrow,' promised Isobel. 'And now I see Ella beckoning to me, so you must excuse me.'

She made her way towards her hostess, and Charles Henstock took her place at Harold's side. If his old friend appeared slightly bemused, the good rector was not conscious of it.

'An excellent party. Ella is so good at this sort of thing, and I always enjoy coming to this house. Something very snug about a low ceiling. The rectory could do with the ceilings lowered by a yard or so. But how would one begin?'

'That's beyond me,' confessed Harold. 'Tell me, how long is Miss Fletcher staying?'

'*Mrs* Fletcher, Harold.'

'Oh, I'm afraid I didn't catch that when we were introduced.'

'I never catch *anyone's* name,' admitted the rector. 'It is a great disability, particularly if one is a parson.'

Harold was looking thoughtful.

'Are you feeling all right?' asked the rector. 'Not finding the room too warm?'

'No, no!' said Harold. 'I'm quite well. An excellent party, as you say. Is Mrs Fletcher's husband here somewhere?'

The rector's chubby face grew sad. 'I am sorry to say that he died last year. A great blow for dear Isobel. They were a devoted couple. It's one of the reasons for the move, I gather. Her present house is really too big now.'

Despite the melancholy news of Isobel's husband's demise, Harold's spirits appeared to revive at once.

'More sherry?' asked Ella, swimming into their ken.

'Thank you, thank you,' said Harold heartily, proffering his glass.

Across the green, as dusk fell, and the lights began to shine from cottage windows, Joan Young and her husband were looking ahead.

Upstairs, Robert Bassett slept fitfully, with Milly sitting in an armchair beside him. Her hands were busy with knitting, her mind busy with plans for the future.

John Lovell, her doctor son-in-law, knew her good sense and had answered her questions honestly. It would be best to face retirement now, to wind up the business, and to find an easily run place near the family at Thrush Green, he had said.

'Would you want to come back to this house?' he asked. 'It's lovely, I know, and it's Robert's, but you'd need resident help, wouldn't you? Have you and Robert ever discussed it?'

'Only very lightly,' admitted Milly. 'We've always had the idea of coming back here to end our days—' Her mouth quivered suddenly, and she looked down quickly.

John patted her shoulder. 'Don't upset yourself. He's got a good few years yet, you know, if he takes care. We'll work out something together.'

Downstairs, Edward was putting forward a suggestion or two.

'I've been thinking about this for some time. Ever since we had a good look at the stables the other day. They would convert into a beautiful little house of one or two floors, ideal for the parents.'

'But this house is theirs!' protested Joan. 'We're the ones who should move out!'

'I agree absolutely,' said Edward, 'but it would have to be altered. The ground floor would make a splendid flat for them, and we could move up to the first floor and open up the attics for bedrooms, if that would suit everyone better than the stable plan.'

'Would it cost the earth?'

'Well, the architect's fees won't need to be found,' said Edward, smiling, 'and I'm sure we could get a loan for this work. After all, we're thinking of providing homes for two families, aren't we?'

Joan looked at him with affection. 'You've been thinking about this for a long time, haven't you?'

'For years,' confessed Edward. 'I've been longing to convert the stables for some time now, and this seems to be the moment to have a go.'

'We can't do anything until Father's over this attack,' said Joan. 'But we'll have a word with Mother in a day or two, just to prepare the ground. I must say, I should be much happier if they were under our eye. They've been so good to us always.'

'Well, it's their choice, of course. All this is theirs, and, if need be, we must go house-hunting ourselves.'

'Somehow,' said Joan, 'I don't think it will come to that.'

Agnes Fogerty had been invited to supper after the guests had gone, and very enjoyable she had found this meal. Afterwards, the three women washed up and between them achieved a degree of unusual tidiness in Ella's kitchen.

That done, Isobel accompanied Miss Fogerty along the road to her home. The air was soft and balmy, auguring well for another beautiful spring day on the morrow.

'No, I won't come in,' Isobel replied in answer to Agnes's invitation. 'I know you've things to get ready for school tomorrow, and I must get back to Ella's.'

They parted affectionately at Agnes's gate, and Isobel retraced her steps.

How snug it all looked at Thrush Green, she thought! The houses sat as comfortably as cats before a fire. If only she were lucky enough to find one before long! Well, tomorrow she would go to see Williams & Frobisher, as recommended by that nice sensible man who lived across the green.

She looked at his house now, a secure bulk dimly visible against the night sky. In a downstairs window, a reading lamp was alight. It looked as though he might be happily settled in there.

She only hoped that she might be as lucky with Williams & Frobisher as he had been, Isobel thought, as she opened Ella's gate.

11. VILLAGE GOSSIP

As Nelly Piggott (*née* Tilling) plodded along Lulling High Street from the station, she looked ahead, with some trepidation, to the kind of welcome she might expect from her husband, Albert.

She had parted from him after a fierce quarrel, but this was only the culmination of weeks of disgust with Albert. He was mean, he was dirty, he was bad-tempered. He drank, he grumbled, he swore. Why she had ever married him, Nelly wondered, shifting her case to the other hand, heaven alone knew.

Well, to be honest, she admitted to herself, she did know. She needed a home. Her own cottage had been sold by the owner, and she had turned down those on offer at the time. Ted and Bessie Allen at the Drovers' Arms at Lulling Woods, had put her up for a few weeks, and she had enjoyed scrubbing out the bar for them.

But a woman needs a place of her own, and Lulling Woods was too quiet for Nelly's taste. Thrush Green seemed just the right setting for a woman of Nelly's sociable habits. The fact that the village school needed a cleaner, just at that time, was another advantage.

And then there was Albert Piggott. Or rather, Albert Piggott's cottage. It was handy for the school, and the bus to Lulling, and looked out on the green where there was always something going on.

Moreover, the cottage was filthy, and Nelly longed to get at it with plenty of hot water, soap and a stout scrubbing-brush. It was a challenge. Dirt was always a challenge to Nelly, and she responded to this one with energy and courage. Within a week the place was transformed, and looking back upon those early days Nelly realized she had been happy, not because of Albert, but because of the satisfaction of cleaning his house.

Not that he was unappreciative. He was particularly grateful for the magnificent meals she cooked, and the fact that she was obliged to curb her art when the doctor told Albert to eat less rich food, was one of the reasons for Nelly's growing resentment. It had culminated in Albert's throwing his helping of Christmas pudding at the wall.

Another factor, of course, was the oil man. He was not every woman's idea of an attractive man, but his sleek black hair and dark beard appealed to Nelly. He had a glib tongue too, and was adept at flattery. It did not need much to woo Nelly away from her husband, and she went to join him with every confidence. She saw now that his charms were superficial. She had never been so short of money in her life, and she strongly suspected that there were several other women in his life.

Things had gone from bad to worse, and one solitary evening, as she ironed her companion's shirts, she worked out just how little he gave her for housekeeping, and how much she had been obliged to subtract from her Post Office account during her stay. The results frightened her.

Here she was, getting on, not likely to get a job easily, and no future with Charlie as far as she could see. He was a bad bargain. The best thing to do was to cut her losses, return to Thrush Green, where she was more likely to get a job, and to throw herself on Albert's mercy – at least for a time. After all, she was his lawful wedded wife, and plenty of husbands had to turn a blind eye to their wives' little weaknesses, Nelly told herself.

Nelly was a realist. She finished the ironing, and went upstairs to pack. The next day she left a note for Charlie, collected some useful groceries from the larder, including a couple of chops which would do nicely for Albert's supper, and made her way to the station.

'Once I've got Albert sweet,' she thought to herself, as she faced the steep hill to Thrush Green, 'I'll pop along to Miss Watson and see if my old job's still open. If not, she'll know someone who could do with a bit of cleaning, I don't doubt.'

Puffing heavily, Nelly Piggott returned to Thrush Green.

On the morning after Ella's party, Winnie Bailey, the doctor's widow, made her way next door to Tullivers.

The May sunshine gilded the green. Daisies spangled the grass, and a lark's song fell from the blue, as clear and pure as a cascade of mountain water. How Donald loved a day like this, thought Winnie, tapping at the door. But there was no point in grieving. It was the last thing he would have wanted, and since his death she had learnt to savour each day as it came, to count her many blessings, and to try to put sadness behind her.

Phyllida and Frank Hurst had helped enormously, she thought. What a comfort good neighbours could be!

Phil's head appeared at a bedroom window above her. 'Oh, do just walk in, Winnie dear. I'm coming down now.'

'I promised you some pansy plants,' said Winnie. 'I haven't brought them in case it's a busy time for you, but they're all ready next door whenever you need them.'

'Lovely!' said Phil. 'Come in and sit down, or shall we sit in the garden?'

'The garden,' said Winnie. 'It's much too gorgeous to stay indoors.'

They sat on the garden seat, facing the sun. A border of pinks nearby was beginning to break into flower, and the roses were in bud.

'You are going to have a fine show this summer,' commented Winnie.

'I know. The sad thing is that we shall miss most of it this year.'

'Not leaving Thrush Green?'

'Good heavens, no! But we only heard this morning that Jeremy and I can go with Frank to America in June.'

'The lecture tour you told me about?'

'That's right. It was all arranged, as you know, last autumn for Frank, but getting accommodation for Jeremy and me was the difficulty. Now we've heard that a publishing friend in Boston can put us up for the whole three months, if need be, or part of that time. I didn't think it right to drag Jeremy from place to place, but this arrangement will be perfect. Isn't it marvellous news?'

'It is indeed. And don't forget that I shall look forward to keeping an eye on the place for you.'

'You are kind. And Harold has offered to keep the garden in trim, so we feel that we can go with an easy conscience.'

'I hope you'll let me look after the cat too. She'll be much happier staying at Tullivers, I'm sure, and anyway she knows she is welcome next door if she feels lonely.'

'I *was* going to ask you about that,' admitted Phil. 'As a matter of fact, she virtually lives in the garden in the summer, so that she shouldn't be too much of a bother.'

Winnie rose to go. 'Now I must do some telephoning. Ella first. What a good party that was! I do hope Isobel finds a house soon. She'll be a great asset to Thrush Green, won't she?'

'Indeed she will. I heard her say that she intended to see if Williams & Frobisher have anything on their books. They're pretty reliable. What about her present house? Is it the sort that will sell easily?'

'I gather so. An ideal family house in a nice part of Sussex, and with a good train service to London. It should find plenty of buyers.'

'Well, I wish her joy of moving,' said Phil. 'It nearly killed me looking at houses and trying to sell the old one, all at the same time. It's usually so horribly *urgent*. People dying to get in before you are ready to get out, while you are waiting to see the colour of their money, and wondering if you can possibly afford all the alterations you will need in the new place. Heavens, what a terrible undertaking! I'm *never* going to move again!'

'And I'm delighted to hear it!' replied Winnie as she took her leave.

Betty Bell, Harold Shoosmith's voluble daily help, found her employer remarkably vague in manner that morning. She began to wonder if he had heard all the titbits of news which she enjoyed imparting.

'I was saying,' she repeated loudly, flicking a feather duster over Harold's treasured Coalport cottages, 'as Miss Fogerty's a different person now her friend's here. They was always close, you know, ever since they was young girls, and Mrs Fletcher don't act no different now she's rich, to what she did before.'

Harold, now listening, felt some impatience. Why must gossip fly as soon as a newcomer appeared? It had been just the same when Phil Hurst had arrived.

'Why should she?' he commented shortly.

'Well, some does, you must allow,' replied Betty, glad to have his attention at last. 'And that Mrs Fletcher did do well for herself after all. Pots of money, and a husband as worshipped her—'

'I wish you wouldn't tittle-tattle so, Betty,' snapped Harold. 'No one's safe from gossips' tongues, it seems, at Thrush Green. I can well remember what poor Mrs Hurst had to endure when she first appeared here.'

Betty Bell's mouth dropped open in surprise, but she soon rallied, flicking the duster with alarming bravado.

'If you lives in a village, as you should know by now, new

94

people gets talked about because they're *interesting*. Why, when you first come here I heard you'd been growing cocoa from Miss Ella, and coffee from Miss Dotty, and tea from Miss Dimity. And how many wives you'd had was nobody's business.'

'Good Lord!' exclaimed Harold, reeling from the attack.

'And what you'd *done* with them all kept everyone on tenter-hooks, I can tell you,' went on Betty. 'So it's no good you trying to muzzle people in a village. They *likes* guessing about other people. It's better than a story in a book, or on the telly.'

'Yes, I do understand that, Betty, but I still think it is insuffer-able to pry into other people's affairs. Particularly unprotected people, like Mrs Fletcher who is still grieving for her husband.'

'She won't need to grieve for long,' said Betty shrewdly. 'She'll be snapped up by some man who's got eyes in his head and some sense too.' She opened the door. 'Liver and bacon suit you? And a couple of tomatoes?'

'Lovely,' said Harold mechanically. It was funny, but his appetite seemed to have gone.

With Betty's departure to the kitchen, Harold set himself to the task of finishing the letters he had been writing before her arrival. It was almost noon before he walked across Thrush Green to the post-box, his eyes straying towards Ella's house at the head of the hill.

He felt strangely disturbed by Betty's remarks about Isobel's probable remarriage. The damnable thing was that she was probably right in her forecast. She *was* an attractive woman, there was no doubt about it. The effect that handshake had had upon him was quite extraordinary. And yet she was completely without guile and those flirtatious ways which he so much detested in older women.

No, it would be no surprise to hear one day that she was going to marry. A very good thing, of course.

He dropped his letters in the box thoughtfully.

So why did he mind so much? He had only just met the woman, and yet she filled his mind. Did she remind him of earlier loves?

He thought of Daphne, fair and calm. And Lucy, who was a flirt and had married a fighter pilot who was killed. Then that red-haired minx, whose name he couldn't remember for the life of him, and her friend, who jolly nearly proposed to him when he wasn't on his guard.

At that moment, a car hooted, and there was the beautiful Alfa Romeo emerging from Ella's gate. Isobel saw him and waved.

With his heart pounding ('Like some fool boy of sixteen,' thought Harold crossly), he hurried along the road to greet her.

She held up a sheaf of papers. 'Williams & Frobisher are doing their stuff,' she told him. 'I picked these up this morning, and John Williams is taking me to see two houses south of Lulling.'

'Well done,' said Harold happily. The sun seemed extra warm and bright, the flowers twice as fragrant, and Isobel prettier than ever.

He patted the car. 'When you've time, would you tell me how you find this particular model? I think I shall have to change my car soon, and this looks as though it would suit me very well. How does it hold the road?'

'Very well indeed. I haven't had it long, but I tell you what. Why don't you drive it yourself? I want to look at another place somewhere between Minster Lovell and Burford tomorrow afternoon, and if you are free I should love to be driven, if you like the idea?'

'Like the idea! You adorable woman!' sang Harold's heart, but he heard himself thanking her politely and saying how very much he would like to try the car, and tomorrow afternoon was absolutely free, and he was entirely at her service.

'Then shall we say two o'clock tomorrow?' said Isobel, giving him a smile which affected his heart in the most peculiar but delightful way. 'I'll hoot outside your gate.'

She waved, and drove off down the hill to Lulling, leaving Harold to cross the green on legs which had suddenly weakened.

'Here I am,' he said to himself in wonderment, 'in my sixties, a confirmed bachelor, and dammit, I'm in danger of falling in love!' It was a disturbing thought. Another, even more disturbing, followed it. 'She'll hoot outside my gate at two o'clock! That'll make Thrush Green talk!'

He suddenly felt intensely happy, and went home, whistling.

*

The children at the village school were just emerging into the playground, after demolishing school dinner consisting of cold lamb and salad, pink blancmange and red jelly. They were, as always, in tearing high spirits and rushed about yelling happily, making such a fearful din that Miss Watson, who was on playground duty, only just heard the telephone ringing.

Agnes, of course, was in her new classroom across the playground, busy cutting up paper ready for her painting lesson that afternoon. The third teacher, a young probationer, would never dare to answer the telephone while her headmistress was at hand, so Miss Watson herself hurried round the side of the building to the lobby door.

Here stood a gigantic metal door-scraper which coped admirably in winter with the sticky Cotswold clay which the children brought along on their boots. In the summer, of course, it was scarcely needed, and Miss Watson had often thought that it should be taken up and stored somewhere during the fine months. It certainly constituted a hazard, and many a child had sustained a grazed knee by tripping over the thing.

On the other hand, where could it be stored? Like most old-fashioned village schools, Thrush Green's was short of outhouses and storage space in general. Such a large, rigid intractable object was impossible to store. Consequently, it remained *in situ* all the year.

In her haste, the telephone bell shrilling its urgency, poor Miss Watson caught her sensibly-shod foot against the edge of the scraper and fell sprawling into the lobby.

A few children hastened to her aid, and Miss Watson began to attempt to regain her feet and her dignity, but realized immediately that something was seriously amiss. It was going to be impossible to stand up. She began to feel faint.

'Get Miss Fogerty,' she told the children, as the playground whirled round and round amidst increasing darkness. The children fled towards the new classroom, and the young teacher appeared.

'Oh dear,' she cried. 'Here, let me help you up.'

She put strong arms about Miss Watson's shoulders and began to heave.

'No, no!' screamed poor Miss Watson. 'Don't move me, please.'

At that moment Agnes Fogerty arrived and took command, marshalling her memories of First Aid, learnt only last winter at Lulling.

'She's quite right,' she said. 'We mustn't move her. But quickly get her coat and a cushion, and then run across to Dr Lovell.'

The girl fled, and Agnes knelt beside her headmistress.

'Poor Dorothy,' she said, all thoughts of protocol vanishing in her anxiety. 'We're getting help. We'll soon have you more comfortable.'

She took the coat and cushion from her fellow teacher, covered the prone form and tucked the cushion gently under Miss Watson's head. Her face was very pale and her eyes were closed, but she managed to smile her thanks.

Fortunately, Dr Lovell was still at his surgery, and hurried across. Within minutes he had rung for an ambulance, put the patient into a more comfortable position, and complimented Agnes on her grasp of the situation.

'They'll have to take her to Dickie's,' he said, using the local term for St Richard's Hospital in the county town. 'They've got all the right equipment there, X-rays and so on. It's the hip joint all right. One thing, they've some marvellous chaps there to put it right.'

Miss Fogerty would have liked to have accompanied her old friend to the hospital, but she knew where her duty lay.

'I'll come and see you as soon as possible,' she promised, as the stretcher was put into the ambulance, and Miss Watson nodded wanly.

'Mind the school,' she managed to whisper, as the doors shut.

Agnes watched the ambulance until it vanished down the hill and turned back, shaken in body, but resolute in spirit, to carry out her headmistress's last command.

12. House-Hunting

When Nelly Piggott finally arrived at her own doorstep, she dropped her heavy case and grocery carrier and paused to take breath. The brass door handle, she noticed, was badly tarnished, the step itself, thick with footmarks. Behind the sparse wall-flowers was lodged a collection of crisp bags, ice-lolly sticks and cigarette cartons which had blown there from the public house next door, and which Albert had failed to remove.

Time I was home, thought Nelly to herself, and opened the door.

'What's going on?' growled Albert thickly. 'Who's that, eh? Get on off!'

There was the sound of a chair being shifted, and Albert still muttering, approached. Nelly swiftly heaved her luggage inside and followed it nimbly, shutting the door behind her.

Albert confronted her. His eyes and mouth were round Os of astonishment, but he soon found his voice.

'None of that, my girl! You're not comin' back here, I'm tellin' you. Clear orf! Go on, you baggage, clear orf, I say!'

He began to advance upon her, one threatening fist upraised, but Nelly took hold of his thin shoulders, and guided him swiftly backwards towards the chair. He sat down with a grunt, and was immediately overtaken by a prolonged fit of coughing.

Nelly stood over him, watching until the paroxysm spent itself.

'Yes, well, you see what happens when you lose your temper,' she said calmly. There was a hint of triumph in her voice which enraged Albert. He struggled to rise, but Nelly put him down again with one hand. 'Just you be reasonable, Albert Piggott.'

'*Reasonable!*' choked Albert. 'You walks out! You comes back! You expects me to welcome you, as though nothink 'as 'appened? You can go back to that so-and-so. Or 'as he chucked you out?'

'Certainly not,' said Nelly, putting the carrier bag on the table, and feeling for the chops. 'I came of my own accord.'

'Oh, did you? Well, you can damn well go back of your own accord.'

99

Nelly changed her tactics. 'You may not like it, Albert Piggott, but you'll have to lump it. Here I am, and here I stay, at least for the night, and you can thank your stars as I've brought you some nice chops for your supper. From the look of you, you can do with a square meal.'

Albert lay back. Exhaustion kept him from answering, but the thought of a return to Nelly's cooking, however brief, was a pleasant one.

Nelly began to busy herself about the kitchen, and Albert watched her through half-closed eyes.

'And when did this place last get a scrub up?'

'Molly done it lovely,' whispered Albert, defending his family.

'And not been touched since,' said Nelly tartly, filling the kettle. 'This frying-pan wants a good going over before it's fit for use.'

She whisked about, unpacking the chops, and some tomatoes and onions. For all his fury, Albert could not help feeling some slight pleasure at the sight of her at her old familiar ploys.

He roused himself. 'Seein' as you've pushed yourself in, you'd best stay the night, I suppose. But it'll have to be the spare bed. You ain't comin' in with me.'

'Don't flatter yourself,' said Nelly shortly, investigating dripping in a stone jam-jar.

She scoured the pan, and then set the food into it. Once the cooking had begun to her satisfaction, she took up the heavy case and began to mount the stairs.

Albert heard her thumping about above. The fragrant smells of frying onion and chops wreathed about the kitchen, and Albert settled back in his chair with a happy sigh.

As Harold Shoosmith had foreseen, a number of interested spectators focused their attention on the Alfa Romeo at his gate on the afternoon in question. He felt more amusement than embarrassment as Isobel emerged elegantly from the driver's seat, and let him take her place.

They drove slowly along the chestnut avenue in front of the Youngs' house and then turned right to descend the hill. The sun was warm and the flowering cherries were beginning to break into a froth of pink in the garden which faced south. They headed westward through the outskirts of the town and were soon on the windy heights. On their right lay the valley of the Windrush, its meandering course marked by willow trees already showing tender leaves of greenish gold.

'Heavenly afternoon,' commented Isobel. Harold agreed. It was not only the balmy spring weather which made it heavenly for him. Isobel's presence was the main source of his contentment, but he had to admit that the smooth performance of the little car also contributed to his pleasure.

'Can we spare time to drop down to Minster Lovell?' he asked. 'If The Swan still does teas we could call on our way back, if you'd like that?'

'Very much, thank you. But I think we'll be lucky to find anywhere that provides teas these days. Isn't it sad? Tea's such a nice meal.'

'My favourite. After breakfast,' smiled Harold.

They took a turning to the right, and ran down the hill to Minster Lovell. Harold stopped the car outside the beautiful old pub, and got out to speak to a woman who was cleaning the windows.

'No, dear,' she said. 'No call for teas much. And it's getting staff as is difficult. Besides, people don't want tea these days.'

'We do,' said Harold.

'Ah well, dear, "Want must be your master", as my old gran used to say. You going near Burford? You'd get some there, no doubt. You see, there's coaches and that pulling up there, and there's more call for teas then.'

Harold thanked her, and returned to the car.

'I think,' said Isobel dreamily, 'that is one of the loveliest villages in England. How I long to get back here! Sussex is beautiful, but it's here I belong.'

'Then we'd better push on to see this house,' said Harold practically, letting out the clutch.

It was not easy to find. The little blue car nosed its way through narrow lanes, between steep banks starred with late primroses and early stitchwort. They passed sign posts to Burford, to Astall Leigh, to Swinbrook, to Witney, and were beginning to wonder if the house really existed when they saw the 'For Sale' sign.

The house was built on the side of a hill, and a steep path went from the lane to the front door. It was a substantial dwelling of honey-gold Cotswold stone, and a scarlet japonica covered the side wall.

'Would you like to come in?' asked Isobel.

'I won't, many thanks,' said Harold. 'It's easier for you to ask questions, and take in what the owners tell you, if you are on your own. I'll wait a little farther down the road, where it is wider.'

'Fine,' said Isobel, collecting her bag and papers. Obviously she was expected, for at that moment the front door opened, and a woman peered out.

Harold watched the two meet, and then drove to the arranged parking place. Here he got out, leant upon a conveniently sited five-barred gate, and surveyed the pleasant scene spread out below him.

He could well understand Isobel's longing to return. His own affection for the area grew with every year that passed. He had never regretted, for one instant, his decision to settle at Thrush Green. He had made many new friends, not an easy thing to accomplish when one was a middle-aged newcomer to a small community, and the countryside was a constant delight.

His own domestic arrangements were also satisfying, although of late he had begun to wonder if the years ahead would prove lonely. He had never regretted his bachelor state. After all, it was of his own choosing, and very contented he had been with it. But observing the happiness of the rector, Charles Henstock, in his second marriage had given Harold cause for thought.

Not that one should contemplate matrimony solely for the betterment of one's lot. Such selfishness would be a sure way to disaster. A true marriage, to Harold's mind, should be a joyous partnership, and if it were not to be so then it were better to remain single.

He had a healthy distrust of strong emotions, and viewed his own present disturbance with mingled amusement, pleasure and caution. But he recognized a deeper feeling towards Isobel which he felt that time would confirm. He hoped that she would soon be living nearby, and that time would prove him right as he grew to know her.

He walked down the lane between the hawthorn hedges shining with new leaf. The sun was warm, some lambs gambolled in the water meadow below, and a thrush sang as it bounced on a flowering spray of blackthorn above him.

When he returned, Isobel was waiting in the car.

'Any luck?' he asked, as he climbed into the driver's seat.

Isobel shook her head. 'Too much needs to be done. It would cost a fortune. And it's dark, and faces north-east. A pity, because the rooms were nice, and my stuff would have looked well there.'

Harold patted her hand. 'Never mind, there'll be others.'

'But I haven't much time. Only two more days. I think I must try and come again later on, when I've sorted things out at home.'

'Must you go this week?'

'I'm afraid so. There are various bits of business to attend to in the next two or three weeks, and I certainly hope to have a few offers for my house to consider.'

Harold nodded. At least it was some comfort to know that she planned to return in the near future.

'Will you stay with Ella again?'

'No, I think not. It's not really fair to her. There's The Fleece, though I'm not keen on staying at hotels. The evenings drag so. But don't let's bother about all that now. Who knows what the next two days may bring? And anyway, what about that cup of tea?'

'Burford may be crowded. What about having tea with me? I can offer you Earl Grey, or Lapsang Souchong, or plain Indian.'

'The last will suit me beautifully,' replied Isobel, with a smile which turned Harold's heart somersaulting.

'Thrush Green it is then,' he replied, letting out the clutch. And the conversation on their homeward way consisted exclusively of the merits, or otherwise, of the Alfa Romeo.

Dotty Harmer, with Flossie in tow, had just delivered the goat's milk to Ella, when they both noticed Isobel's car outside Harold's gate.

'They must be back,' said Ella, stating the obvious. 'I wonder if she's had any luck today?'

'But why is she at Harold's?'

'Search me,' said Ella carelessly. 'Popped in to borrow a map or a book, I daresay. She may be staying with me for a week, Dotty dear, but that doesn't mean she's not free to visit whenever and whoever she pleases.'

Dotty ruminated, her hand stroking Flossie's satin head. 'But why *Harold*?'

'He was trying out her car, that's why. And now, Dotty, to business. I've been paying you five peas for years now. I'm sure the milk should be more. That hogwash from the dairy – so-called – has gone up about six times since we fixed things. What about eight peas?'

'Is that more than a shilling?'

'Lord, yes! More like one and six.'

'Then I refuse to take it. One shilling is ample, Ella. I really wish this pea business had never started. There are so many things I find that muddle me today. Metres and litres and grammes. So bewildering. And what's all this voluntary aided tax I keep finding on my bills?'

'*Taxes*,' replied Ella severely, 'are neither voluntary nor aided, as you should well know! VAT stands for *value added tax*.'

Dotty considered the information, her eyes fixed unseeingly on the distant Alfa Romeo. 'If anything,' she remarked at last, 'it sounds sillier.'

Ella rummaged in her purse and handed Dotty a silver five-penny piece.

'It's not enough, Dotty, but if that's how you want it—'

'It is indeed. I put all the goat's milk money in a special tobacco tin, and it's surprising how it mounts up. I bought a large bag of dog biscuits with it last time, for dear old Floss.'

'Well, she looks pretty fit on it,' agreed Ella, opening the gate for her departing friend.

Dotty hurried away across the green, her stockings in wrinkles as usual and the hem of her petticoat showing a good two inches below her skirt.

Ella watched her go with affection, and turned to carry in the milk. Her eye was caught by Isobel's car again. 'Quite old enough to know what she's doing,' thought Ella, 'and anyway, none of my business.'

Not all the Thrush Green residents were as tolerant.

Bob Jones, landlord of The Two Pheasants, noticed that the dashing blue car was over an hour outside Harold's house, and to his mind, 'it looked bad'. What if Mr Shoosmith and Mrs Fletcher were both middle-aged? Also, they were both unattached, and it was indiscreet, to say the least, to lay themselves open to comment.

Winnie Bailey's faithful maid Jenny also noticed the car and, although she said nothing, she pursed her mouth primly as she set about some ironing in her top flat. Winnie herself was incapable of distinguishing Isobel's car from the milkman's delivery van, and so remained unperturbed by the private tea party.

Albert Piggott was probably the most censorious, but since Nelly's return he was in such a state of turmoil, and his indigestion seemed so much worse now that he was tempted by Nelly's rich food, that it was not surprising.

'No better than she should be,' he told Nelly. 'I could see she be a proper flighty one as soon as I set eyes on that flashy car of hers.'

'Well, I don't know the lady,' said Nelly roundly, 'but I knows Thrush Green and the tongues as wags round it. I'll bet my bottom dollar she's as innocent as I am.'

'As you are!' echoed Albert derisively. 'Some innocent! And talking of that, when are you gettin' back to that Charlie you're so fond of?'

Nelly folded a tea towel with care. 'See here, Albert. Let's jog on a bit longer, shall we? I've said I'm sorry for that last little upset and you know you needs a woman in this place. What about me stoppin' on and gettin' my old job back? I thought I might call on Miss Watson this evening.'

Albert snorted. 'Then you'll have a long way to go, my gal. She's in Dickie's with a broken leg or summat. It'll be Miss Fogerty in charge now, and for all I knows Betty Bell's doin' the cleanin', and makin' a good job of it, too.'

Nelly did her best to look unconcerned at this unwelcome piece of news.

'No harm in asking anyway,' she said, tossing her head. 'Maybe Miss Fogerty'd prefer me to Betty Bell. I always done my best at the school before, and Miss Watson told me so. "Never seen it so clean," was her very words.'

'Go your own way,' growled Albert. 'You will anyway, but don't come grizzling to me when you find there ain't no job there for you, my gal.'

He hobbled to the door, took down his greasy cap from the peg, and began his journey across to the church.

The Alfa Romeo gleamed in the afternoon sunshine, and Albert saw Isobel emerge from Harold's front door, closely followed by her host. They both looked extremely happy.

'The baggage!' muttered Albert. He picked up a clod of earth from the church porch. 'Women!' he added viciously.

He threw the clod spitefully towards an adjacent tomb stone, and was mollified to see that it bespattered one 'Alice, Dutiful Wife and Mother, An Example of Pious Womanhood'.

'Women!' repeated Albert, opening the church door. 'All the same! Dead or living. All the same!'

13. Miss Fogerty Carries On

Miss Fogerty rang the hospital in the early evening expecting to hear that her headmistress was either 'comfortable', which no one could be in Miss Watson's condition, or 'as well as could be expected', which was one of those ominous expressions guaranteed to set one choosing hymns for the funeral.

But to her surprise a remarkably kind sister answered the telephone and assured Miss Fogerty that the patient had stood the operation well, and that, although she had not yet come round, she would be certain to enjoy a visit the next evening.

'Can you tell me,' asked Miss Fogerty diffidently, 'I mean, are you *allowed* to tell me, exactly what was wrong?'

One did not wish such a nice woman to break the oath of Hippocrates, if, of course, she had ever had to take one, but one really must know more.

'A dislocated hip joint, with some damage,' said the sister. 'These days it's quite simple to pop it back.'

She made it sound as easy as returning a cork to a bottle top, but Miss Fogerty shuddered sympathetically in the telephone box.

'Thank you for telling me,' she said sincerely. 'Please give her my love. Just say "Agnes rang". And I will call tomorrow evening.'

While she was there, she telephoned Miss Watson's brother and left a message with his wife. She seemed an emotional woman, and her voice came wailing down the line.

'Oh dear, what a catastrophe! What will Ray say? I'll tell him the minute he gets in. He's so devoted to Dorothy. I expect he'll want her to come here as soon as she's out of hospital, and I really can't see—'

The wailing died away.

'That's looking rather far ahead,' said little Miss Fogerty. 'But let me give you the hospital's number, and then you can keep in touch.'

That done, she rang off, and went across to the schoolhouse to make sure that all was locked up safely.

It did not look as though poor Dorothy would have her convalescence with her brother.

'And probably all for the best,' thought Miss Fogerty. 'She'll be better off in her own home.'

Ella Bembridge said goodbye to Isobel after breakfast on a sunny morning a few days later. She watched the little blue car descend the hill, gave one last wave, and turned back to the empty house.

'I'm going to miss her,' thought Ella, fumbling for the tobacco tin which housed the materials for making cigarettes. She sat on the window seat and surveyed the view across Thrush Green, as she rolled herself a cigarette.

The house was very quiet. A frond of young honeysuckle tapped against the window, moved rhythmically by the light breeze. Ella drew in a satisfying lungful of tobacco smoke, and exhaled luxuriously.

'Quiet, but nice,' she said aloud. 'After all, it's what I'm used to. Nothing like a bit of solitude now and again.'

The sound of a door shutting made her swivel round. Dimity was coming across from the rectory, and Ella stumped to the front door to welcome her.

'Don't say she's gone!' exclaimed Dimity, surveying the empty drive. 'I thought Isobel said "after lunch".'

'After *breakfast*,' replied Ella.

'What a pity! I'd brought her a pot of my bramble jelly.'

'Well, ten chances to one she'll be back again in a few weeks.'

'Staying here?'

'I'd like her to, but from one or two things she said, I think she'll put up at The Fleece. Seems to think it's *imposing* on me, or some such nonsense.'

'She's a very considerate person,' said Dimity. 'We're going to miss her.'

Betty Bell echoed these sentiments as she attacked Harold's kitchen sink.

'I see Mrs Fletcher's gone home. Miss Fogerty will miss her, though no doubt she's got enough to do with that school on her hands. Pretty woman, isn't she?'

'Who?' asked Harold, purposely obtuse.

'Why, Mrs Fletcher! Mind you, it's partly her clothes. Always dressed nice, she did. That's what money does, of course. It's nice for her to have a bit put by, even if she does marry again.'

Harold snorted, and made for the door. This everlasting tittle-tattling was too irritating to bear. As he gained the peace of his hall, he saw the rector at the door, and gladly invited him in.

'I've just come from Ella's,' said Charles, 'and she's given me Isobel's address. She thought you might want it.'

Harold was taken aback. 'Isobel's address?'

'In case you heard of a house, I think Ella said. I know she's got the estate agent working here, but really bush telegraph some-times works so much more swiftly, and who knows? You *may* hear of something.'

'Of course, of course,' replied Harold, collecting himself. 'Ella will miss her, I expect.'

'A truly *womanly* woman,' commented the rector. 'Who was it said: "I like a manly man, and a womanly woman, but I can't bear a boily boy"?'

'No idea,' said Harold. 'Have a drink?'

'No, no, my dear fellow. I have a confirmation class this evening, and must go and prepare a few notes. And there's poor Jacob Bly's funeral at two, and Dimlty wants me to help sort out the boots and shoes for the jumble sale.'

Harold was instantly reminded of another parson, James Wood-forde, who had written in his diary, two hundred years earlier, of just such an incongruous collection of activities in one day. The duties of a parson, it seemed, embraced many interests as well as the care of the living and the dead, no matter in which century he lived.

'Then I won't keep you,' said Harold. 'Thank you for the address, and if I hear of anything I shall get in touch with Isobel, of course, although I think that the chances are slight.'

Little did he realize that he would be invited to write to the address in his hand, within a few days.

Agnes Fogerty was indeed too busy to miss dear Isobel as sorely as she might have done. She was now Acting Headmistress, a role which filled her with more misgiving than pride.

Apart from the day to day responsibilities, there was a profusion of forms from the office which had to be completed and returned, 'without delay' as the headings stated with severity. Agnes, conscious of her duties, spent many an evening struggling with them in her bed-sitting room.

Then there was the supply teacher sent by the office to help during Miss Watson's absence.

Miss Fogerty found her unnerving, and her discipline nonexistent. It worried Agnes to see the children talking when they should have been working. She disliked the way Miss Enderby's charges wandered freely about the classroom, in theory collecting their next piece of work, in practice giving a sly clout to anyone in their path. Either Miss Enderby did not see what was going on, which was reprehensible, or she *did* see and condoned it, which was worse. Eventually, Agnes spoke of the matter and had great chunks of some dreadful report or other quoted to her. To Agnes, the report seemed quite irrelevant to the matter in hand, but Miss Enderby seemed to cling so fiercely to the findings of whatever-committee-it-was responsible for this half-inch thick treatise that Agnes decided to retire temporarily from the field of battle. No doubt there would be other occasions when a word of advice could be offered.

There were. There were many occasions, and brave little Miss Fogerty did her best to put things politely but firmly. She found Miss Enderby's attitude quite mystifying. Throughout her teaching career, Miss Fogerty had worked on the principle that children did as they were told. One did not ask them to do anything *impossible*, of course, or *wrong*, or *beyond their powers*. But open defiance, or the complete ignoring of orders given, had never been countenanced in Agnes's classroom, and all had gone on swimmingly.

What was the good, Agnes asked herself, in reading all those papers and reports with terrible titles like: 'The Disruptive Child and Its Place In Society' or 'Where Have Teachers Gone Wrong?' if at the end of it one still could not *teach*? It was quite apparent that the class now under Miss Enderby's care (one could not say 'control') had learned practically nothing since her advent. That it was dear Miss Watson's class made it even worse.

Miss Enderby, it was clear, was a theorist, but one quite incapable of putting theories into practice. The children would not allow it. They were having a field day enjoying themselves without stricture. In a rare flash of insight, Agnes Fogerty saw that her unsatisfactory supply teacher clung to the theories which she so avidly imbibed, and quoted, because they were all that she had to get her through each day's teaching.

Agnes prayed nightly for her headmistress's return to health and Thrush Green School. She was to come home from the hospital after a fortnight, and Agnes had offered, very diffidently, to stay at the schoolhouse if it would help.

'It is more than kind of you, Agnes dear,' Dorothy had said, 'but I expect Ray will want me to convalesce with them. I shall see him one evening this week.'

Agnes had murmured something non-committal, and repeated her willingness to help in any way, but Dorothy seemed to be quite sure that she would be looked after by her brother and his wife.

'I wonder,' thought Agnes, hurrying through driving rain to the bus stop. 'Poor dear Dorothy! I wonder!'

Robert Bassett made slow but steady progress after his second attack, but it was quite apparent that his confidence was shaken.

'He's suddenly become an old man,' said Joan sadly. 'I hate to see it. He doesn't look ahead as he always did. All the *spunk* seems to have gone out of the poor old boy.'

She was talking to her brother-in-law, John Lovell, after one of his visits to the patient.

'It's nature's way of making him rest. You'll see, he'll pick up before long. Meanwhile, there's one good thing to emerge from this setback.'

'And what's that?'

'He's quite given up the idea of going back to the business, and that's as it should be. In a way, I think he's glad that this blow has settled things for him. He's now coming to terms with the idea.'

'He said as much to Mother, I know, but he hasn't said anything very definite to us. I believe he worries in case we feel that he wants his own house back!'

'If I were you,' said John, 'I should broach the subject your-selves. Tell him Edward's plans for the conversion, and let him toy with the idea. I believe it will do him good to have something to look forward to and to occupy his mind.'

After this conversation, Joan and Edward took John's advice, and spoke frankly about their plans to the parents. Milly had known what was afoot for some days, but to Robert it came as a complete surprise. To the Youngs' delight, he seemed excited and pleased at the ideas put forward, and studied Edward's rough sketches with enthusiasm.

'Leave them with me, dear boy,' he said. 'Milly and I will have a proper look at them, and we may even make one or two suggestions. I can see that you two have been hatching up this little plot for some time, and I am really very touched.'

He smiled a little tremulously, and Joan rose swiftly to put him at his ease.

'I'm off to find us something to eat. Come and give me a hand, Edward,' she said, making for the door.

'Bless his old heart,' said Edward, when they reached the kitchen. 'He's as pleased as Punch! How I like satisfied clients!'

'Don't speak too soon,' warned Joan, busy at the stove. 'He may not be satisfied. Besides, he's every right to turn us out, you know.'

'He won't,' said Edward, dropping a basket of bread rolls on the floor, and bending to retrieve them. 'He's the most unselfish soul alive.' He picked up the rolls, dusted each down the side of his trousers, and put them carefully in the basket again.

Her husband, thought Joan, might be a talented architect, but his grasp of culinary hygiene was nil.

In the Piggotts' household an uneasy truce was being carried on. Nelly was content to live from day to day, gradually cleaning the cottage until it satisfied her own high standards, and cooking succulent meals which Albert secretly enjoyed. Wild horses would not have dragged thanks from him, under the circum-stances, and the frequent bouts of indigestion which afflicted him kept him as morose as usual.

There was no doubt about it, thought Nelly, as she attacked

the filthy cooker one afternoon with plenty of hot soda water, Albert did not improve with age. As soon as she could get a job, she would be off again. But jobs, it seemed, were hard to find.

She had called on her old friends at the Drovers' Arms, but they were already well-staffed, and in any case, were not inclined to do anything to upset Albert. She had come back of her own accord, they felt, and it was up to her to do what she could to look after the old man, curmudgeonly though he might be. Work at the Drovers' Arms meant that Nelly would be away from home for a considerable part of the day.

Undeterred by the news that Betty Bell now cleaned the school, Nelly called one evening at Miss Fogerty's lodgings.

Mrs White, Miss Fogerty's landlady, opened the door, and was somewhat taken aback by the flamboyant figure on the doorstep. She knew quite well who the visitor was, but as she strongly disapproved of Nelly, and her morals, she feigned ignorance.

'Someone to see you, Miss Fogerty,' she called up the stairs. 'If you would like to go up?' she said to Nelly, standing back against the flowery wallpaper.

Miss Fogerty looked even more alarmed than her landlady had been at first sight of Nelly puffing up the stairs. She showed her into her bed-sitting room, and closed the door.

Nelly, seating herself in the only comfortable armchair, looked about her. She noticed the faded carpet, the thin curtains, and the bedspread which was not quite large enough to cover the divan bed. But she noticed too, in that first swift glance, that everything was clean – beautifully clean.

The furniture was well polished, the shabby paintwork and the mottled tiles of the hearth were spotless. Miss Fogerty's small array of toilet things stood in a tidy row on a glass shelf over the corner washbasin. Her books stood neatly, row by row in the bedside bookcase. Only a pile of exercise books, in the process of being marked, gave any clue to the present activity in Miss Fogerty's modest abode.

On the mantel shelf stood two shining brass candlesticks, one at each end. A china cat stood by one, and a china spaniel by the other. A small travelling clock stood dead centre, and on each side stood a photograph.

One showed Miss Fogerty's shoemaker father looking stern. His right hand rested on the shoulder of his wife, sitting on an ornately carved chair in front of him. Agnes's mother looked meek and submissive. Her hair was parted in the middle. Her eyes were downcast. Her hands were folded in the centre of her lap. A fine aspidistra at the side of the couple seemed to display far more vitality than the photographer's sitters.

But it was the second photograph which engaged Nelly's attention. It was framed in silver, and showed the likeness of a fair young man in army uniform. He was smiling, showing excellent teeth, and he wore his hair *en brosse*. Could he be a sweetheart, Nelly wondered? Could colourless, shabby little Miss Fogerty ever have inspired love in someone so obviously lively? You never knew, of course. Still waters ran deep . . . She looked from the photograph to her reluctant hostess, who was now seated in an uncomfortable chair which she had turned round from the dressing table.

'I expect you are wondering why I've come,' began Nelly, removing her scarf.

'Naturally,' replied Miss Fogerty with truth, and just a touch of hauteur. She disliked Nelly, and had never been happy about her appointment as cleaner at the school. She accepted the fact that Nelly was excellent at her job, but she thought her a vulgar creature and not a suitable person to be among young children. She had deplored the fact that it was Miss Watson who had taken on Nelly, and could only put it down to her headmistress's kind heart, and the paucity of applicants for the post at that time.

'Well, I was hoping that my old job might be going still. Always enjoyed it, I did, and I know Miss Watson was satisfied. Pity she's away. Is she going on all right?'

'Yes, thank you,' said Agnes shortly. She did not propose to discuss dear Dorothy's condition with this woman. 'And the post is already filled, Mrs Piggott. Betty Bell is with us now, so that I'm afraid I can't help you.'

'She suit you all right? That Betty Bell?'

'Perfectly,' said Agnes firmly. She rose to indicate that the meeting was ended, but Nelly remained firmly wedged in the armchair.

'I hear she works at Mr Shoosmith's too,' she remarked. 'I wonder she finds time to do two jobs. *Properly*, that is!'

The implications of this snide observation were not lost upon Agnes. Really, the woman was insufferable, and there were all those essays waiting to be marked, and her hair to wash, and the hem of her skirt to be repaired where she had caught it as she had tidied the bottom of the handiwork cupboard. What a nuisance Nelly Piggott was, to be sure!

'She is a very hard-working girl,' said Miss Fogerty sharply, 'and manages her various jobs excellently. Not only does she go to Mr Shoosmith, I think you'll find she helps Miss Harmer as well, and we are all quite satisfied with her work.'

Agnes remained standing, and Nelly, facing defeat, struggled from the armchair.

'Wouldn't take much to satisfy Miss Harmer from what I hear,' said Nelly, 'but there it is. If there's nothing I can do at the school, I'll have to look elsewhere.' She began to arrange the scarf around her fourth chin. 'Don't know of anyone, I suppose, as needs help?'

'I'm afraid not,' replied Agnes, a trifle less frostily now that she saw her visitor departing. She opened the door to the landing and ushered Nelly through it.

'Well, if you do hear of anything you know where I live,' said Nelly, descending the stairs heavily.

'I will bear it in mind,' promised Agnes, now opening the front door.

'Ta ever so, dearie,' said Nelly, sailing down the path.

Shuddering, Miss Fogerty returned to her interrupted peace.

14. COMINGS AND GOINGS

It was Charles Henstock who first told Harold Shoosmith that Phil was accompanying Frank on his trip to the United States.

'I knew Frank was off, and said I'd keep an eye on the garden for him, but I didn't realize that Phil could go too. Do them both good to have a change, and Jeremy will enjoy being off school.'

'They come back early in September, so the boy won't miss much,' replied Charles. 'It will be strange to see Tullivers empty.'

'Empty!' echoed Harold, a splendid idea bourgeoning. He decided to visit Frank and Phil Hurst that very evening, and found them in the garden when he did so.

June had come in with what the Irish call 'soft weather'. Skies were overcast, but the air was mild and the wind gentle. Frank's roses were beginning to make a fine show, and both he and Phil were hoeing round the bushes. They put down their tools to greet Harold.

'Don't let me stop you,' he said.

'Thank God you've come, and given us an excuse to have a break,' replied Frank feelingly. 'I'll get drinks.'

He vanished into the house, and Harold and Phil seated themselves on the grass. A robin, matchstick legs askew, watched them with his head on one side.

'I suppose you realize that you are doing that poor chap out of his worm supper, now that you've stopped hoeing?'

'He's had enough already,' said Phil. 'It's a wonder he doesn't pop.'

Frank arrived with the drinks. 'Heard that Phil and Jeremy are coming with me?' he asked, smiling.

'I have indeed. Wonderful news. Charles told me.'

'So we'll be even more glad than before to know you are keeping an eye on things,' said Frank. 'I don't like leaving the place empty, but there it is. Luckily, we've got good neighbours, like you and Winnie, to look out for any baddies around.'

Harold put down his drink carefully. 'It's that really which brings me over this evening.'

'How do you mean? Are you going away, too?'

'No. I shall be here. I just wondered if you would consider Isobel Fletcher having the house for part of the time. She intends to come back towards the end of June, I gather, unless she's fixed up beforehand.'

'Sounds splendid,' said Phil enthusiastically. 'But would she want to be bothered?'

'Frankly, I've no idea,' confessed Harold. 'It was just a thought. I know she doesn't want to impose on Ella any further, and doesn't particularly relish staying at an hotel. Anyway, perhaps it's cheek of me to suggest it.'

'Not at all,' said Frank heartily. 'I should feel much happier if someone were staying in the place, and I can't think of anyone more suitable. Shall we let you know definitely tomorrow? Then you can get in touch with Isobel, or we will, if you'd rather we did.'

'That's fine,' agreed Harold. He picked up his glass with a satisfied sigh. 'Of course, she may have found something already, but I doubt it. It would be marvellous to have her here, right on the spot.'

Phil looked at his blissful expression with sudden awareness.

'So convenient for the house-hunting,' explained Harold hastily, 'and I'm sure she would be a most careful tenant while you are away.'

'It was a very good idea of yours,' said Frank, 'and now come and have a look at the jasmine you gave us. It's nearly reached the roof.'

Phil collected the glasses and carried them indoors.

'So that's how the land lies,' she said to herself. 'Now who would have thought it?'

Later that evening, when Jeremy was safely asleep upstairs, Phil told Frank about her suspicions. Predictably, he was scornful.

'Old Harold? And Isobel? Rubbish, my dear, you're imagining things! Why, I've known Harold for donkey's years, and he's always been the happiest of confirmed bachelors. He's not likely to change now. Why should he?'

'I don't suppose there's any particular *reason* why he would give up his bachelordom, but I'm sure I'm right about this. After all, you were getting on perfectly well on your own when we first met, but you embarked upon matrimony without a qualm.'

'That's different. You are a most attractive woman.'

'So is Isobel. I can quite understand Harold's change of heart.'

'You're incurably romantic, my darling. It comes of writing for all those women's magazines, I expect. So you are all in favour of enticing Isobel here to further the course of true love?'

'I am indeed. To be honest, that's only the secondary consideration. I'd like someone to be in the house basically.'

'And you've no scruples about leaving defenceless Isobel to Harold's amorous bombardment?'

It was Phil's turn to snort. 'I should think Harold's ardour has subsided to manageable levels in his sixties. And Isobel must have had plenty of experience in warding off unwanted suitors in her time.'

'So you think Harold will be unwanted? Poor old Harold!'

Phil reflected. 'I can't speak for Isobel, of course. She may not want to marry again. She has no family to consider now, and she has lots of friends and a comfortable income. She may well turn down any offer from Harold. That's the pity. I'm afraid he would be very upset.'

'I expect he's taken harder knocks than that in his time,' commented Frank.

'Maybe,' agreed his wife, 'but you know what Jane Austen said? "It is always incomprehensible to a man that a woman should ever refuse an offer of marriage."'

Frank laughed. 'I'll let you, or rather, Jane Austen, have the last word. One thing I've learnt in life is that a man is no match for a woman in affairs of this sort. So, we invite Isobel?'

'We invite Isobel,' agreed Phil.

The sun was slowly dispersing the clouds as Frank walked across to Harold's the next morning. The chestnut avenue was now in full leaf, and the white and pink candles were in flower. Outside The Two Pheasants Bob Jones's hanging baskets made a brave show, the geraniums quite untouched by those frosts which Albert Piggott had forecast earlier.

A yellow Mermaid rose was in full bloom on the sunny side of Harold's house, and the borders on each side of his path glowed with violas, pinks and double daisies. It all looked remarkably spruce, thought Frank. Surely, Harold could want no more than this for happiness? He had made a perfect life for himself in the place of his choice. Was it likely that he would embark on the complications of married life?

He had no need to knock at the door, for Betty Bell, with Brasso and duster in hand, burst out as he approached.

'Lor!' she said, clutching the Brasso to her heart. 'You fair frit me, you did!'

'Sorry, Mrs Bell,' said Frank. 'Is Mr Shoosmith in?'

'Down the garden, by the bonfire. Shall I give him a holler for you?'

'No, no. I'll go and see him.'

Sure enough, Harold was tending a small bonfire, whose smoke was drifting in the leisurely breeze towards Lulling Woods. Looking at him, with his wife's surmises in mind, Frank had to admit that Harold was wearing very well, and was still remarkably good-looking. And tidy too, thought Frank, a little enviously. Harold always looked immaculate, even when tackling a messy job, as he was doing now. He himself, Frank knew, would be crumpled and smeared with smuts, his hands black, and his gardening clothes deplorable. Phil despaired of him at times. She had often told him so.

Harold turned to replenish his fire and saw his old friend.

'Hullo, there! What's the news?'

'Unanimous approval of your bright idea! Will you get in touch with Isobel? Or shall we?'

Harold looked a trifle discomfited. 'I think you should deal with her directly, Frank. By all means say I thought of it, if you like, but I'm sure it's best to have a word with her yourselves.'

'Very well. I'll write today, and perhaps she can ring me when she's studied the suggestion, and we can fix up things then.'

'Fine, fine!' replied Harold. He looked as though he might say more, thought better of it, and changed the subject. 'And when do you fly? Do you want a lift to the airport? I'm a free man, you know, and only too pleased to take you.'

'In just over a fortnight, and it would be marvellous if you can take us to Heathrow. You're sure about this?'

'Positive – or nearly so. Come inside, and we'll have a look at the diary. In any case, it will only be one or other of these damn committees I seem to have dropped into. I shouldn't be missed.'

Betty Bell was busy setting out cups upon a tray as they went through the kitchen.

'I'm getting you two gents a nice cup of coffee,' she said. 'Here, or in the study?'

'In the study, Betty,' said Harold hastily. 'We've something to look up.'

When alone, Harold usually took his elevenses with Betty, allowing her incessant chatter to flow over him. Today he felt that it would not be fair to inflict all the local gossip on his old friend.

'Okey-doke,' said Betty, to their retreating backs.

The diary for the week in question read: Monday, Vestry meeting 7.00. Wednesday, Dentist 10.30. Scouts' Concert 7.30. Thursday, Remember B and B. Friday and Saturday were clear.

'I wonder what "Remember B and B" means?' pondered Harold.

'What's B and B? Bed and Breakfast?'

'Hardly,' said Harold, his brow puckering with concentration.

'Betty and Someone Else beginning with B?' hazarded Frank.

Harold shook his head.

'If you were Irish,' went on Frank conversationally, 'I should suggest "Remember the Battle of the Boyne", but I suppose that's no help?'

'None,' said Harold. 'However, to get back to our muttons. You said Friday, June 23rd, I believe? Well, that's completely free, so count on me as a willing taxi-man.'

At that moment, Betty came in, bearing the tray with two steaming cups and a plate with gingernuts on it.

'Ah, Betty!' cried Harold. 'Put it here, my dear, and tell me something. Why have I got to remember "B and B" on June 22nd?'

'Coffee morning at the rectory,' said Betty promptly. 'Bring and Buy stall. You promised something to Mr Henstock when he came last week.'

Harold smiled his relief. 'I don't know what I'd do without you,' he told her, as she turned towards the door. 'Every home should have a Betty Bell.'

'Or a wife,' commented Frank. But Harold made no response, except to pass the coffee cup.

*

A day or two after this meeting, little Miss Fogerty paid another visit to the hospital.

Miss Watson was propped up on a bank of snowy pillows, surrounded by flowers and 'Get Well' cards. She was wearing a pale pink bed jacket, knitted by Agnes as a Christmas present a year or two earlier, that lady was pleased to see. That feather-and-shell pattern had been remarkably difficult to master, she remembered, but it certainly looked most attractive.

'It's so light and warm, Agnes dear,' said Dorothy, stroking the garment. 'And much admired by the nurses.'

Miss Fogerty grew pink with pleasure. 'I'm so glad. But, tell me, how are you getting on? And when will you be able to come home?'

'I *could* come out on Sunday next, but I think I shall stay a few days longer.'

She began to pleat the top of the sheet, and looked very near to tears, Agnes was horrified to see.

'You see, Ray came yesterday. Poor Kathleen was in bed with one of her migraine attacks.'

And very convenient those migraine attacks could be, thought Agnes tartly.

'So that she couldn't come, of course,' went on Dorothy. 'And it seems that they had arranged a holiday for the next two weeks, so that they can't have me there.'

'Come home,' urged Agnes. 'You know that I can help, and the district nurse would call daily. I'm sure we could manage.'

Miss Watson sniffed, and then blew her nose energetically. 'I do hope I'm not getting a cold,' she said, muffled in the handkerchief. Miss Fogerty was not deceived.

'You are the kindest soul on earth,' said Dorothy, recovering her composure. 'I've done quite a lot of thinking since Ray came, and if I stay here for another few days, gaining strength, I think I really will be able to manage at home. Perhaps someone could slip in at midday and get me a light lunch?'

Agnes thought at once of Nelly Piggott, but decided not to mention her just yet.

'If you would let me stay at the schoolhouse,' said Agnes diffidently, 'I could be with you at night, and bring you breakfast before going over to the school.'

'Oh, Agnes dear,' cried Miss Watson, the tears returning and now rolling down her cheeks unchecked. 'Oh, Agnes dear, *could* you? Would you mind? There's nothing I should like more.'

'I should love it,' said Agnes truthfully. 'We'll have a word with Sister and arrange a day next week.'

'And get the taxi from Lulling,' said Dorothy, already becoming more like her efficient, headmistress self. 'And we'll go back together. What a wonderful day it will be!' She sighed happily, and wiped away the tears without subterfuge. 'It's only the relief, Agnes dear, and being so wobbly, you know. I can't begin to tell you how grateful I am to you, my dear. It's at times like this that one realizes who one's true friends are.'

'Then that's settled,' said Agnes, 'and as soon as the doctor says you may leave, we'll go back to Thrush Green.'

'I can't wait! And now, Agnes dear, tell me how it's all going at school? Are the children behaving well? Is that washbasin mended yet? Have those Cooke boys really got the mumps? Are there many forms from the office? How's the supply teacher managing? And has the piano-tuner been this term?'

Miss Fogerty was still answering questions when the nurse arrived to take Miss Watson's temperature.

'It's up a bit,' she commented as she shook the thermometer.

'I'm not surprised,' said her patient. 'It's excitement, of the nicest kind, that's done it.'

15. Early Summer

The quiet mild weather which had ushered in June, now turned to a spell of gloriously hot sunshine.

Miss Fogerty looked out her sensible cotton frocks and Clark's sandals. Dotty Harmer spread sacks over the chicken run to provide her charges with extra shade. The rector took his light-weight clerical grey from the wardrobe, and Dimity hung it on the line to remove the faint smell of moth-balls. Winnie Bailey and Jenny erected the swing seat, and agreed that although the cretonne was shabby it 'would do another year'.

And, across the green, Nelly Piggott embarked on a mammoth washing spree, hauling down curtains, whisking off blankets and bedspreads, and even snatching up rugs from the floor to thrust into the soap suds.

Albert loathed it all, but recognizing an irresistible force when he met it, resigned himself to the tornado of energy which whirled about him, and took advantage of the sunshine to do a little light tidying of the churchyard. Here, at least, there was peace.

He was engaged in picking a few weeds from the top of the stub wall which surrounded the graveyard when Dotty Harmer stopped to speak to him.

She was an arresting sight at the best of times, but today's summer outfit appeared to consist of a straight low-waisted frock, style circa 1920, made, it seemed, of deck-chair material, and ending just above the knees. A conical straw hat, like a coolie's, surmounted her thatch of grey hair, and lisle stockings, heavily wrinkled, led the eye down to a pair of grass-stained tennis shoes. She was accompanied by the faithful Flossie, now the picture of canine good health.

'I heard,' said Dotty, coming straight to the point, 'that your wife is looking for work. I wonder if she has heard that the Miss Lovelocks need temporary help?'

'Well, no, miss,' said Albert. He took off his greasy cap and scratched his lank hair. 'She ain't said nothin'. Maybe you'd like to tell her? She be washin'.'

'I can't stop now, I'm afraid. I have to meet the bus, at the bottom of the hill, but perhaps you would pass on the message?'

'Very well, miss,' said Albert, unusually respectful. She might look a proper clown, but she was a lady for all that. Got a touch of her old dad about her, that made you mind your manners, he thought.

He watched her figure receding into the distance, and turned back to the wall again. Yes, he'd tell Nelly when he went into dinner. Nice bit of cold fat bacon he had seen in the larder. A slice or two of that with pickled onions was something to relish, whatever the doctor said. It was a comforting thought.

The sun warmed his back as he pottered about his leisurely activities. He dwelt, with pleasure, upon the possibility of Nelly bringing in more money to the household. But best of all was the thought that he would be free of her company for a few hours. He only hoped that they would occur during opening time.

Edward Young had been busy with plans for converting the stable block into a roomy bungalow, and also for altering the top floor of their house into a self-contained flat.

The latter was a fairly straightforward job, for the attics had been divided into three good-sized bedrooms just before the 1914–1918 war. Old Mr Bassett remembered that his nurse had slept in one and, in those spacious days, the cook had had another, while two housemaids shared the third.

There was water already there, and the large dormer windows looked out upon splendid views. It could provide a lovely home for a single person, or perhaps a young couple. It was a conversion which Edward had had in mind for some time, and he submitted both plans together to the local planning committee.

The Bassetts preferred the stable block. For one thing, it was a ground floor abode, and for another, they were at a short distance from Joan and Edward, and both households could be independent, although close enough in an emergency to help each other.

Dr Lovell's surmise that his patient would be stimulated by the plans now afoot, was fully justified. Robert took on a new lease of life, and pottered out to the stables with his foot-rule, planning where favourite pieces of furniture could be placed, how wide the windowsills could be, and other pleasurable activities. He now took a little exercise, or dozed in the sunny garden. His appetite improved and Milly and the family watched his return to health with the greatest satisfaction.

As soon as he was really fit, he and Milly proposed to return to Ealing to settle their affairs and to dispose of the business and the house. Meanwhile, it was enough to enjoy the sunshine of Thrush Green, and to know that the future looked bright with hope.

Isobel Fletcher had replied with gratitude to the Hursts' letter, and said that she would not be free to accept their kind offer until early July, as prospective buyers seemed to be numerous, and there were several matters to arrange with her solicitor and the bank manager.

Williams & Frobisher had sent only one possibility, and it so happened that it was a house in which an old friend of her mother's had once lived. It had a long drive and far too much ground, and Isobel had turned it down as its upkeep would be too expensive. She hoped that she would have better luck while she was staying at Tullivers.

It was arranged that Winnie Bailey would keep the key, until Isobel was free to come, and that she would order milk, bread and groceries for her temporary next-door-neighbour.

Isobel rang Harold, as well as the Hursts, when she had made her decision.

'It was such a kind thing to think of,' said Isobel. 'What put it into your head?'

Harold could hardly say: 'The strongest desire to have you nearby,' but said that Frank had expressed some doubts about leaving the house empty, and knowing that she intended to return to her house-hunting, the two thoughts had gone together, and he hoped sincerely that it had not been a liberty.

'Far from it,' said Isobel warmly. 'I am terribly grateful to you, and I shall look forward to seeing you again before long.'

'And so shall I,' responded Harold, from the heart.

Nelly Piggott lost no time in calling upon the Misses Lovelock in Lulling High Street. The sun was still warmly bathing Thrush Green in golden light when she set out from her home. It was half past six, and Albert was already next door at The Two Pheasants, despite Nelly's protestations.

From berating him, Nelly had turned to more womanly tactics, and on this particular evening, dressed in her finery for the forthcoming interview, and fragrant with attar of roses, she bestowed a rare kiss upon Albert's forehead.

'Just to please me, Albert dear,' she said, in her most seductive tones.

But Albert was not to be wooed. 'That soft soap,' he told her, shaking her off, 'don't cut any ice with me.'

With this splendid mixed metaphor as farewell, he then

departed next door, leaving Nelly to collect her handbag and go off in the opposite direction.

She was not particularly upset by her failure to wean Albert from his beer. Nelly took a philosophical view of marriage. All men had their little weaknesses. If Albert's had not been liquor, it might have been wife-beating, or even infidelity, although Nelly was the first to admit that, with Albert's looks, a chance would be a fine thing.

She sailed down the hill and along Lulling High Street, relishing the evening sunshine and her own aura of attar of roses. Reaching the Lovelocks' fine house, Nelly pulled lustily at the old-fashioned iron bell pull at the side of the door, and Bertha opened it.

'I've come about the place, miss,' said Nelly politely.

Bertha's mind, somewhat bewildered, turned to fish. Had they ordered plaice? Perhaps Violet . . .

'I heard you was needing help in the house,' continued Nelly. 'But perhaps you're already suited?'

'Oh, *that* place!' exclaimed Bertha, light dawning. 'No, not yet. Do come in.'

She led the way into the dining-room which, despite the heat of the glorious day, struck cold and dark.

'If you'll sit down, Mrs Er?'

'Mrs Piggott,' said Nelly, sitting heavily on a delicate Sheraton chair. It creaked ominously, and Bertha felt some anxiety, not only for the chair's safety, but also at her visitor's identity. For, surely, this was the sexton's wife whose conduct had been so scandalous? Hadn't she run away with another man? Oh dear! What would Ada say?

'I will just go and tell my sisters that you are here. You do undertake housework, I suppose?'

'Yes'm. And cooking. I fairly loves cooking.'

'Yes, well – I won't be a moment.'

She fluttered off, leaving Nelly to cast a disparaging eye on the gloomy oil paintings, the heavy velvet curtains and the mammoth sideboard laden with half a hundredweight of assorted silverware. The work the gentry made for themselves!

Bertha, breaking in upon Ada's crochet work and Violet's

tussle with *The Times* crossword puzzle, gave a breathless account of their visitor.

Her two sisters lowered their work slowly, and surveyed her with disapproval.

'But why invite such a person into the house?' asked Ada.

'But can she undertake housework?' asked Violet, more practically.

'Because I didn't know who she was,' cried Bertha, answering Ada, 'and she can certainly do housework. I remember Winnie Bailey telling me what a marvellous job she made of Thrush Green School,' she went on, turning to Violet.

The three sisters exchanged glances of doubt and indecision.

'And another thing,' continued Bertha, 'I've just remembered that she is a first-class cook. It was Winnie who told me that, too.'

Ada sighed. 'Well, I suppose we'd better see this person now that she's here.'

She rolled up her crochet work in an exquisite silk scarf, and put it on one side. Violet placed *The Times* on the sofa.

Together the three sisters advanced upon the dining-room. Nelly struggled to her feet as they entered, the chair creaking with relief.

'Do sit down,' said Ada graciously. The three sisters took seats on the other side of the table, and Nelly lowered herself again into the long-suffering chair, and faced them.

'Let me tell you what we require,' said Ada. 'Our present helper is looking after her daughter who is just about to be confined. She will probably be home again in six weeks or so.'

'Yes'm,' said Nelly, surveying the three wrinkled faces before her. Never seen three such scarecrows all together before, she was thinking. Why, they couldn't weigh twenty stone between 'em!

'Two mornings a week, one of them a Friday, but any other morning which would be convenient for you would be quite in order with us.' She glanced at her sisters who nodded in agreement.

'Tuesday would suit me best,' said Nelly, thinking of washing day on Monday.

'And I hear that you are an excellent cook, Mrs Piggott.'

Nelly smiled in acknowledgement.

'Perhaps, very occasionally, you might prepare luncheon for us?'

'I'd be pleased to,' said Nelly. She waited to hear about payment.

'Have you brought any references?' inquired Ada.

'Well, no,' confessed Nelly. 'But Miss Watson would speak for me, and the Allens at the Drovers' Arms.

There was a whispered consultation between the three sisters, and much nodding of trembling heads.

'Very well,' said Ada. 'As this will only be a temporary arrangement we will waive the references. When can you start?'

Nelly decided that she must take a firm stand. 'I should like to know the wages, ma'am, before saying "Yes" or "No".'

'We pay fifty pence an hour, Mrs Piggott, and should like three hours each morning. You would receive three pounds a week.'

Fifty pence! thought Nelly. It was the least she had ever been offered, but it would be useful, and the job looked like being one after her own heart.

Ada, seeing the hesitation, added swiftly: 'You would be paid extra, of course, if you prepared a meal while you were here. Another fifty pence, Violet? Bertha?'

'Oh, yes, indeed,' they quavered obediently.

Nelly rose. 'Then I'll come next Tuesday,' she said. 'Nine o'clock?'

'I think nine-thirty,' said Ada. 'We breakfast a little late, now that we are approaching middle age.'

She rose too, and the three sisters ushered Nelly out of the front door into Lulling High Street.

'Approaching middle age,' repeated Nelly to herself, as she set off for Thrush Green. 'That's a laugh! They must be over eighty, every one of them! Well, I shan't make a fortune there, but it'll be a nice change from cleaning Albert's place.'

It was on one of these cloudless June days that the Hursts flew to America.

Harold, as promised, drove them to Heathrow airport. The sun was hot through the glass and all were in high spirits. Neither Frank nor his wife were anxious travellers, Harold was glad to see. Much travelled himself, he had always felt slightly irritated by his fellow companions who were constantly leafing through their wallets to check that they had passports, licences, tickets and all the other paraphernalia of travelling, or turning to each other with agitated queries, such as: 'Did you turn off the electricity? The water? Did we leave a key with Florrie? Did you remember to tell the police we would be away? Do you think Rover will *like* those new kennels?'

Frank seemed to have everything in hand, and was looking forward to visiting the United States again, and to introducing Phil to his friends there. He loved the warmth and generosity of American hospitality, and the enthusiasm of his audiences. It made one feel young again. He hoped that Jeremy would pay many visits there as he grew older.

That young man was full of excited chatter. Harold let the boy's commentary on the passing scene flow in one ear and out at the other. He was remembering another trip he had taken to Heathrow, with Phil, some years before. Then she had sat, white and silent, beside him, for the news had just come through of her first husband's death in a car crash in France, and Harold had driven her straight to the airport. How bleak the outlook had seemed then! Harold's heart had been sore for her, so young and defenceless, with the added responsibility of bringing up a young child on her own. Thank God she had met Frank, and this second marriage had turned out so well.

His mind turned to Charles again and his happy marriage. And then, naturally enough, to the pleasant thought of Isobel coming to stay at Tullivers before long. Would the future hold marriage for him, he wondered?

He turned into the road leading to the airport.

'Here we are! Here we are!' carolled Jeremy. 'And there are thousands of planes! Look, look! Don't you wish you were coming too, Uncle Harold?'

'In some ways,' replied Harold circumspectly, 'but I think I'd just as soon stay at Thrush Green for a while.'

16. Problems for the Piggotts

Miss Watson came home from hospital on a Saturday, which meant that Agnes Fogerty could collect her in the taxi, as arranged, and see her settled at the schoolhouse.

Apart from looking pale and rather shaken, Dorothy Watson had come through her ordeal very well. She leant heavily on two sticks, but managed to get into the taxi without much trouble, and was in fine spirits.

'To be out again, Agnes dear,' she cried. 'To feel fresh air on one's face, and to see children *running*! I can't tell you how lovely it is!'

Agnes had put some early roses in Dorothy's bedroom, and everything that could be done by loving hands awaited the invalid. The bed was turned down, a hot bottle was swathed in a fresh nightgown, and that day's newspaper and letters awaited reading on the bedside table.

Miss Watson, who had been looking forward to having lunch

downstairs, saw that she must give way graciously to Agnes's ministrations. Nevertheless, she insisted on limping round downstairs, admiring the care which had been lavished on all her possessions.

'And Betty Bell has made you a sponge cake,' said Agnes. 'It's from Mr Shoosmith, with his love.'

'His love?' echoed Dorothy. 'How kind! He's such a reserved man, I should have been more than gratified with "kind regards". A sponge cake, and *love* as well, really touches me.'

'He's a very thoughtful person,' said Agnes. 'Yesterday he sent Piggott round to tidy the garden here instead of his own, and he has inquired many times about you.'

Miss Watson made her way slowly to the kitchen window at the rear of the house, and gazed with pleasure at the garden. Her roses were beginning to break and the violas edging the beds were gay with blue, white and yellow blooms. A harassed blackbird, followed by four babies larger then itself, scurried to and fro

across the newly-mown lawn, snatching up any morsel available and returning to thrust it down the clamorous throats.

She opened the window and leant across the sill. All the scents of summer drifted in upon the warm air, the mingled potpourri of the jasmine on the wall, the old-fashioned crimson peonies nearby, the freshly-cut grass, and the hay field beyond which stretched to the distant greenery of Lulling Woods.

There, in the distance, was Dotty Harmer's cottage, sitting as snugly as a golden cat in the fold of the meadow. Near at hand, glowing just as effulgently in the sunshine, was the bulk of kind Harold Shoosmith's home, and her own beloved little school.

She drew in her breath, overcome by the bliss of being at Thrush Green again, and suddenly realized how tired she was.

She turned to Agnes. 'Wonderful to be back, my dear. And now I'm going to that lovely bed, if you will help me with my shoes and stockings.'

She mounted the stairs slowly, attended anxiously by little Miss Fogerty, and as soon as she entered the bedroom went to gaze upon Thrush Green from the front windows.

There were the chestnut trees in pride of leaf. There were the homes of her friends and neighbours, sturdy, warm and welcoming. Nathaniel Patten gleamed upon his plinth, and gazed benevolently upon the children playing on the swings and see-saw nearby. A pale blue cloudless sky arched over all, and somewhere, close at hand, a blackbird trilled.

Miss Watson turned back into the room. 'What a perfect day, in all ways!' she commented. 'But, best of all, Agnes, to have you here with me. I am a very lucky woman!'

One sunny afternoon, soon after Miss Watson's return to her home, although not yet to her school duties, she noticed a familiar figure entering the gate of the Youngs' house.

'Now what can Molly Piggott – I mean Molly Curdle – be doing in Thrush Green?' she wondered. She had always been fond of the girl. She had been a rewarding pupil, keen to learn and polite in manner, despite her deplorable old father.

Miss Watson had watched her progress as mother's help at the Youngs, with the greatest interest and approval, and her marriage to young Ben Curdle had won everyone's blessing at Thrush Green.

Joan Young was as surprised to see Molly as Miss Watson had been, but welcomed her warmly. She led her visitor into the garden and they sat in the shade of the ancient apple tree which Molly knew so well. Young Paul's swing had hung there, and she had spent many hours pushing her charge to and fro beneath spring blossom, summer leaf and autumn fruit.

In the heat of the day the dappled shade was welcome, and Molly pushed her damp hair from her forehead.

'That hill gets steeper,' she smiled. 'Or I'm getting older.'

Her eyes roamed to the stable block. Preliminary clearing had begun, in the hope of planning permission being granted, and a stack of assorted and cumbersome objects, ranging from derelict deck-chairs to an equally decrepit cupboard, leant against the wall.

'That's a heavy job,' commented Molly. 'You planning to use the place as a garage?'

'Not a garage,' said Joan. 'Something more ambitious than that.'

She told the girl about her parents' retirement, and the conversions that they hoped to make. Molly nodded enthusiastically.

'I'm glad they're coming back at last to Thrush Green,' she said. 'It's only right that Mr Bassett should be here. Are they here now?'

'At the moment they are at the Henstocks having tea. Which reminds me, Molly, I've offered you nothing – which is shameful. What can I get you?'

'Nothing, thank you. Well, perhaps a glass of water?'

'I'll bring you some home-made lemonade. The same recipe you used to make up when you were here, remember?'

'Indeed I do. I'll come and help.'

They went back into the cool kitchen to fetch their drinks, and Joan wondered what had brought the girl to Thrush Green.

As if guessing her thoughts, Molly spoke.

'Friends of ours had a bit of business to do today over here, and offered me a lift. Ben's minding George, so I thought I'd look in and see Dad, and you, and anybody else as remembered me.'

'We all remember you,' cried Joan, leading the way with the tray back to the garden seat.

They sipped their lemonade, the ice clinking against the glass. Above them a starling chattered, his dark plumage iridescent in the sunlight. A fat thrush ran about the lawn, stopping every now and again, head cocked sideways, to listen for a worm beneath the surface.

'I wondered,' said Molly, breaking the silence, 'if you'd heard of anything for Ben to do?'

Joan felt a pang of guilt. She had certainly made inquiries, and mentioned the matter to several friends, but the advent of her parents, and the anxiety over her father's health had limited her search.

'I haven't done as much as I had hoped to do,' she confessed. She outlined her efforts, and promised to make amends.

'The thing is,' said Molly, 'Dick Hasler has offered us a good sum for the fair, and Ben thinks he'll have to accept. There's no end of expense that we can't face. I left him patching up two swingboats. The timber alone cost a mint of money, and there's a limit to the time Ben can spare for repairs. We've faced it now. We'll have to give up, and although it grieves my Ben, we know the fair's day's done – at least, as we ran it. Dick's got plenty behind him, and if he loses on one thing he can make it up on another.'

'In fact, what he loses on the swings, he gains on the round-abouts?' smiled Joan.

'That's it exactly. And this is where we'd like to be for the future, as you know.'

'You're quite right. There's your father to consider too, although I expect I know that Nelly's back?'

'Yes, indeed. One look at that place showed me that. I can't say I take to Nelly,' she went on, in a burst of confidence. 'She's too bold for my liking, but she do keep a house clean.'

'And keeps Albert well fed.'

'But for how long? D'you think she'll stay? In some ways, I hope she will. It would be a relief to us to know Dad was being looked after. But they're not happy together, as you know. I can't see it lasting.'

'Frankly, neither can I,' agreed Joan.

St Andrew's church clock chimed four, and Molly put down her glass hastily.

'I'd best be getting down to the crossroads. I'm being picked up at a quarter past, and I must drop into Dad's again, to say goodbye.'

'Now, I promise to do my best to find something for Ben,' said Joan, taking the girl's hands in hers. 'When would he be free to start?'

'Any time,' said Molly. 'We could stay with Dad until we found a place of our own. Anything to get back to Thrush Green, and to start afresh. It's been a sad time for us lately, particularly for Ben. The fair's always been his life, as you know.'

'Something will turn, up, I'm positive,' Joan assured her. 'I will write to you very soon.'

She watched Molly cross the grass to go to Albert's cottage. The children were streaming out from school, and Joan thought how lovely it would be when Molly and Ben were back, and George himself would be coming home from Thrush Green school.

Nelly Piggott missed seeing Molly by a mere half hour, as Albert pointed out.

Nelly had been shopping after her bout of housework, and her first attempt to cook lunch for the three sisters. She was hot, tired and cross. Her corsets were too tight, and so were her shoes. She took scant notice of Albert's remarks, as she filled the kettle at the sink, and Albert resented it.

'I said that our Molly'd called,' he repeated loudly.

'*Your* Molly, not ours,' replied Nelly. 'She's nothing to me.'

'No need to be so white and spiteful,' grumbled Albert. 'Specially as she said how nice the place looked.'

'No thanks to her,' rejoined Nelly, struggling to take off her shoes. 'Fat lot she does for her old dad, I must say.'

'They sends me money, don't they?' demanded Albert. 'Regular.'

'And where does that go? Down your throat, the bulk of it. I tell you straight, Albert, I shan't be stopping here long if you don't give me more housekeeping.'

'Well, you've left here before, and I shan't stop you clearing off again. When, you gets into these tantrums I'd sooner see the back of you, and that's that!'

Nelly reached for the teapot. Things were going a little too fast for her. 'Want a cup?' she asked, more gently.

'May as well.'

'Don't strain yourself,' said Nelly, spooning tea into the pot. She set out cups upon a tray, and poured the tea. They sipped in silence.

Albert was weighing up the pros and cons of life with Nelly, an exercise which he undertook frequently.

Nelly was reviewing the situation which she had taken on at the Lovelocks. Could she, she asked herself, continue for six whole weeks, albeit only twice a week, in the present frustrating circumstances?

It was the *meanness* of the three ladies which infuriated Nelly. It was one thing to find that the dusters provided consisted of squares cut from much-worn undergarments, but quite another to be denied the tin of furniture polish.

Miss Violet had undone the lid, selected one of the deplorable squares, and scooped out about a teaspoonful of the polish upon it.

'That,' she told Nelly, 'should be *quite* enough for the dining-room.'

Seeing Nelly's amazed countenance, she had added swiftly: 'Come to me again, Nelly, if you need more, although I hardly think you will find it necessary.' She had swept from the room, tin in hand, leaving Nelly speechless.

All the cleaning equipment was handed out in the same parsimonious style. A small puddle of Brasso in a cracked saucer was supposed to cope with the many brass objects in the house. Vim was handled as though it were gold-dust. Washing-up liquid was measured by the thimbleful. It was more than Nelly could stand, and she said so.

Her complaints brought very little improvement, and Nelly retaliated by cleaning all that she could, and leaving the rest as soon as the rations for the day ran out. But she resented it bitterly. She *liked* to see things clean, and never stinted cleaning agents in her own home. However, she comforted herself with the thought that it was only for six weeks, maybe less. Surely, she could stick it out for that time, especially as nothing else had cropped up to give her alternative employment?

The memory of the lunch she had been obliged to cook made her shudder. Nelly respected food, and always chose the best when shopping. It was no good being a first-class cook, as she knew she was, if the materials were poor. You might just as well try to paint a portrait with creosote.

When Miss Bertha had fluttered into the kitchen that morning, and had asked her to cook that day's luncheon, Nelly's spirits had risen. She had visions of rolling out the lightest of pastry, of whipping eggs and cream, of tenderising steak or skinning some delicate fish cooked in butter.

'And you will stay to have some too, Nelly, I hope.'

'Thank you, ma'am,' said Nelly, envisaging herself at the kitchen table with a heaped plate of her own excellent cooking. Albert had been left with a cold pork-pie, some home-made brawn, strong cheese and pickled shallots, so Nelly had no qualms on his behalf. She had told him that she intended to shop in the afternoon. Really, things had worked out very well, she told herself, and this would save her going to the Fuchsia Bush for a cup of coffee and a sandwich, as she had planned.

Miss Bertha vanished into the larder and appeared with a small piece of smoked fillet of cod. It was the tail end, very thin, and weighed about six ounces. To Nelly's experienced eye it might provide one rather inferior helping, if eked out with, say, a poached egg on top.

'Well, here we are,' said Bertha happily. 'If you could poach this and share it between three, I mean, *four*, of course.'

'Is this all?' inquired Nelly flabbergasted. 'Why, our cat would polish that off and look for more!'

Miss Bertha appeared not to hear, as she made her way back to the larder, leaving Nelly gazing at the fish with dismay.

'You'd like poached eggs with this, I take it?' said Nelly.

Bertha put two small eggs carefully beside the fish.

'We prefer scrambled eggs, Nelly. These two, well beaten, should be ample for us all.'

'There won't be enough,' said Nelly flatly.

'We add a little milk.'

'Horrible!' protested Nelly. 'Should never be done with scrambled eggs. Butter's all you need, and a little pepper and salt.'

'Not *butter*!' gasped Bertha. 'We always use margarine in cooking. *Butter* would be *most* extravagant!'

Nelly began to see that she would certainly need to visit the Fuchsia Bush to supplement the starvation diet being planned.

'Vegetables?' she managed to ask.

'Plenty of spinach, Nelly, in the garden, and I thought some rhubarb for pudding. There is still some growing by the cold frame. I will leave out the sugar for you.'

'Very well, ma'am,' she said as politely as her outraged sensibilities would allow.

She finished drying the breakfast things, and went, basket in hand, to fetch the spinach and rhubarb. On her return, she found half a cupful of granulated sugar awaiting its union with the rhubarb, and about half an ounce of margarine.

Nelly left the spinach to soak, and wiped the thin sticks of rhubarb. They were well past their best, and showed rusty marks when she chopped them. For the rest of the morning she seethed over the appalling ingredients which were to make a lunch for four people.

'Not enough for a sparrow,' she muttered to herself, as she went about her chores. 'And all windy stuff too. If those old scarecrows is doubled up this afternoon, it won't be my fault, and that's flat!'

She cooked the food as best she could. It grieved her to be using margarine instead of butter, but there was nothing else to use, and mighty little of that.

Miss Violet had set the table. The heavy Georgian silver gleamed, the glasses sparkled, and handmade lace mats lay like snowflakes on the polished mahogany.

Nelly carried in the dish of fish and scrambled egg and placed it before Miss Ada at the head of the table. Her face expressed scorn.

'I took the liberty, ma'am,' said Nelly, 'of picking a sprig of parsley to garnish it.'

Miss Ada inclined her head graciously. 'You did quite rightly,' she said. 'It all looks delicious.'

Nelly returned to the kitchen and surveyed the teaspoonful of food upon her plate. At that moment, the cat leapt through the window.

'Here,' said Nelly, handing down the plate, 'try your luck with that.'

Delicately, with infinite caution, the cat sniffed at the food. A rose petal tongue emerged to lick the fish tentatively, then the cat shuddered slightly, and turned away.

'And I don't blame you,' said Nelly. She threw the scraps out of the window, and watched a gaggle of sparrows descend upon them.

'What I could do to a nice fillet steak!' mourned Nelly, preparing to carry in the dish of sour rhubarb, unadorned by any such rich accompaniment as cream or custard.

Later, when Nelly had washed up and had been complimented upon her cooking by the three old ladies, Nelly tried to forget the whole shocking experience. Never again, she told herself, never again! Not if they went down on their brittle old bended knees would she be party to such a travesty of cooking! It was more than flesh and blood could stand.

It was hardly surprising that Albert found her exceptionally snappy that evening. Nelly had suffered much.

PART THREE
Safe Arrival

* * * *

17. Living Alone

Miss Watson's enforced rest gave her plenty of time to think. Not that she did not think in her normal state, but this was thinking at a different level.

She was a healthy busy woman, who ran her school and her home with competence. Her mind was always occupied with such diverse matters as ordering fresh stock, arranging a parents' evening, supervising the new probationer-teacher, as well as remembering to order an extra pint of milk because the Henstocks were coming to coffee, to send the spare-room bedspread to the laundry, and to ring the hairdresser to see if she could fit in a permanent wave on a Saturday morning.

These day to day activities left little time for such things as general reading, although she conscientiously tried to keep abreast with present-day writings on education. She rarely visited the theatre in term time, and her travels had been limited to less expensive areas in Europe. She kept up with a few old friends, and saw Ray and Kathleen several times a year, but this was the first occasion when she had been thrown upon her own resources and had experienced solitude, without activity, for hours at a time.

In this present vague post-operation daze, she found reading irksome, and radio and television equally tiring. She was content to lie back and let her mind dwell upon a great many aspects of life which, until now, she had largely ignored.

It was something of a shock to realize that one was not completely self supporting. So far in her life, she had managed her affairs without needing to ask for any help, other than such specialized aid necessary for coping with tax affairs and other money matters, or the occasional legal problem which dear old Justin Venables in Lulling managed with easy experience.

She had never before suffered such physical weakness as now engulfed her, and it was unnerving to find that she needed help to cope with such everyday matters as bathing, dressing and moving about the house. She felt confident that she would be back to normal in a few weeks, but then how could one be sure that other similar accidents might not occur, as one grew older? It was a sobering thought. If the present mishap had occurred when the school had closed, and she had been alone, how long, she wondered, could she have lain there unattended?

Thank heaven for dear Agnes! It would have been impossible to return to her own home without Agnes's help. She dwelt now upon the sterling qualities of her staunch assistant. Her presence in the house, particularly at night, when she felt at her most vulnerable, was wonderfully consoling, and although she had been careful not to disturb Agnes's much needed slumber, it was a great comfort to know that she was there if the emergency arose.

Soon, of course, she must face the fact that Agnes would return to Mrs White's. But need she?

Miss Watson toyed with the idea of inviting dear Agnes to share her home permanently. It would be to their mutual advantage, she felt sure. The only thing was the uncomfortable fact that Agnes might not want to give up the independence she so much enjoyed.

Miss Watson turned over the problem in her mind, with unusual humility. What right had she to expect Agnes to want to live with her? She had been more than fortunate to find a friend so unselfish that she was prepared to look after her for these few weeks. It was asking too much of her to expect that she would want to remain.

And yet Agnes would be the perfect companion! She grew fonder of her as the years passed. She was a fine person, loyal and kind, much more noble, in every way, than her headmistress, thought Dorothy sadly.

No, it would not be fair to ask her, she decided, with a sigh. Agnes might well agree simply because she felt that she was needed to help, ignoring her own feelings. She was so unselfish. It was very uplifting to live with a saint, but it had its problems.

*

Next door, Harold Shoosmith was also in a state of turmoil. Isobel would soon be arriving, and he hoped that he would be able to greet her without showing the real depths of his feelings. It was quite alarming to find how often his thoughts turned to her, and he was beginning to fear that the observant residents of Thrush Green might guess the cause of his preoccupation.

He was about to cross the green one morning, to mow the grass at Tullivers, when Dotty Harmer appeared, looking even more agitated than usual.

'You haven't seen Flossie, by any chance?' she called, hastening towards him.

'Flossie?' queried Harold.

'My dog. My little spaniel. She's run off, you see.'

'No, I'm sorry. I will keep an eye open for her.'

'It's so upsetting,' continued Dotty, hitching up a stocking with a claw-like hand. 'I fear she must be on heat, and I hadn't realized it.' She peered at Harold sharply. 'I don't embarrass you, I trust?'

'Not in the least,' responded Harold. 'I have been aware of the facts of life for some years now.'

Any gentle sarcasm intended was lost upon Dotty, in her present state of perturbation.

'Of course, of course! But it is so annoying. She may have gone along to Nidden. There is a collie dog there, at the farm, to whom she is rather partial. The results of such a liaison would not be acceptable to the Kennel Club, I fear, but there it is.'

'Well, I'll certainly keep a look out, but it might be as well to call at the rector's, or Miss Bembridge's. They might catch her before she gets into the traffic at Lulling. Would you care to use my telephone?'

'You are most kind! Most kind! But I think I will walk across while I'm here. Besides, I am disturbing your activities.'

'I was only going to cut the grass at Tullivers,' said Harold.

Dotty's wrinkled countenance lit up with pleasure. 'All ready for Isobel? She will be grateful, I'm sure.'

She fluttered off in the direction of Ella's house, leaving Harold to his thoughts.

*

Betty Bell, always exuberant, seamed to bring Isobel Fletcher's name into the conversation more frequently than Harold could have wished, but he had the sense to hold his tongue on these occasions. There was no point in adding fuel to the fire, he told himself.

But, one morning, Betty arrived in a rare state of indignation.

'D'you know what?' she demanded. 'That fat Nelly Piggott's been trying to get my job off of me!'

'What, here?' asked Harold, alarmed.

'No, no! I'd see you was looked after,' said Betty, as though indulging a backward child. 'No need for you to worry. No, that besom – excuse my French – has been crawling round Miss Fogerty, I hear, and would have gone in to see Miss Watson too, if Miss Fogerty hadn't put her foot down. The very idea!'

'She wasn't successful, I take it,' ventured Harold.

'I should hope not!' snorted Betty. 'Why, I keeps that place *beautiful*! *Beautiful*, I tell you! Toffee papers, squashed chalk, bubble gum and all. You could eat your dinner off of the floor when I've done with it.'

'I'm sure you could,' Harold agreed, wondering why anyone should be expected to want to eat dinners from floors or, for that matter, why it should occur to anyone to *serve* dinners in such a peculiarly uncomfortable position.

'And if I sees her about,' went on Betty wrathfully, 'I shall give her a piece of my mind!'

'I shouldn't bother,' said Harold, alarmed at the prospect of a noisy row on Thrush Green.

'Or the flat of my hand,' added Betty, and flung out of the room.

There was sudden activity at the Youngs' house. Edward's plans had been passed with unusual rapidity, and the builders, whom he had alerted earlier, were beginning to move in with all their paraphernalia.

Milly and Robert decided that they would make their way back to Ealing.

'I've no excuse for lingering,' said Mr Bassett. 'Thrush Green has put me on my feet again, and we shall only be in your way with the building going on. It's time we went back and put our affairs in order.'

'We shall miss you,' said Joan, 'but you'll be back for good before long. What a marvellous thought!'

'For us too,' said Milly. 'We've been blessed with two wonderful daughters. This would have been a terrible time for us without you to help.'

A week later, Edward drove them to Ealing in their own car, with Joan following behind. They settled the parents in the house, and were relieved to find that Frank had taken an hour or two off work to welcome them home, and to give Robert the latest news of the business.

'I shall be relieved to have them near us,' said Joan, as they drove back to Thrush Green together. 'How long do you think it will be before the stable block is ready?'

'Quicker than builders usually are!' promised Edward. 'I'll see to that!'

It was mid-July before Isobel was freed from her affairs in Sussex. She arrived on a sunny afternoon, and spent an hour with her new next-door neighbour, Winnie Bailey, before unlocking the door of Tullivers.

Isobel looked tired, Winnie thought, as she poured tea for them both, but then she had had a long journey and probably a good deal of worry in the last few weeks.

'No, still nothing definitely settled,' said Isobel, in reply to her query. 'You know how it is with selling a house. If my present would-be buyers can sell their own, all's well. But they're waiting to see if *their* buyer can sell *his*. How far back the queue stretches, heaven alone knows.'

'And it only needs one to default, I suppose, for the whole chain to collapse?'

'Exactly. Never mind, here I am, and Williams & Frobisher have sent me four possibilities, so I shall go ahead and enjoy looking at them. Better still, it's lovely to think I have so much more time to spend in Thrush Green. Tell me how everyone is.'

Winnie told her about the Youngs' plans.

'Lucky Bassetts! I envy them the stable conversion. If I didn't

want a small house and garden, I think I'd rush across and plead for the top floor flat! Someone's going to have a nice home there.'

Winnie went on to tell her about Ben and Molly Curdle, the Henstocks, Ella and, finally, Harold.

'He's worked so hard in the garden,' said Winnie. 'The lawn looks immaculate, and the roses at Tullivers are the best at Thrush Green.'

'Let's go and see it,' cried Isobel jumping up. 'I feel a new woman after that tea. Once I've unpacked, I shall go to see Harold. He must have been working so hard.'

'I'm sure it was a labour of love,' said Winnie.

But Isobel, leading the way, did not appear to hear.

Now that Isobel had arrived, Harold's happiness grew daily, but he was anxious not to call too frequently at Tullivers, and so lay open the unsuspecting Isobel to the wagging tongues of Thrush Green.

Isobel, as it happened, was not so unsuspecting as Harold imagined. She was used to the admiration of men, and liked their company. An exceptionally happy marriage and a wide circle of friends had given her ease of manner with the opposite sex, and Harold's feelings, although carefully concealed, were guessed by the sympathetic Isobel. In such a small community it was inevitable that they saw each other frequently, and they enjoyed each other's company more and more.

Isobel took Harold to see some of the places which she had known well in her girlhood around Stow, north of Thrush Green, and he accompanied her to look at one or two of the houses which Williams & Frobisher had recommended.

On the whole, it was a dispiriting job. The houses which were large enough to house the furniture which Isobel wanted to keep, were usually much too large, with endless corridors, high ceilings, and a formidable number of stairs. Those which were of manageable proportions were sometimes thatched, which Isobel disliked, or the rooms were small and stuffy.

'What I want is something in between,' sighed Isobel, as they emerged from one such cottage, Harold almost bent double to miss striking his head on the porch. 'I'm beginning to wonder if I shall ever find what I want.'

'Cheer up,' said Harold. 'I went through all this too when I was looking. It's disheartening for you, but I must confess I'm thoroughly enjoying myself.'

Isobel laughed. 'Well, I should have given up long ago if you hadn't been such a support. It's made all the difference to have some company.'

Harold seemed about to speak, thought better of it, and opened the door of the Alfa Romeo for her.

'Are you feeling strong enough to face "a bijou residence set like a gem amidst panoramic views"?' asked Isobel, consulting her papers.

'I can face any amount of them,' replied Harold bravely.

'Right,' said Isobel, letting out the clutch. 'It's about three miles from here.'

'And after that,' said Harold, 'I'm taking you to lunch at The Fleece. You need to keep up your strength when house-hunting.'

Little Miss Fogerty was as delighted as Harold to have Isobel at Thrush Green, and visited Tullivers frequently.

Miss Watson was now back at school, limping about her duties with a stick, and thankful to be of some use again. Agnes was very anxious about her, and insisted that she returned to her bed for a rest after school dinner and this Miss Watson agreed to do, with surprising meekness.

Now that she was back, the supply teacher departed, much to the relief of all.

'I'm quite sure she did her best,' Agnes told Dorothy earnestly. 'She was very *sincere* and *conscientious*, and most diligent in reading reports, and the leaders in *The Times Educational Supplement*, but I think she found the children rather a nuisance.'

'A case of putting the cart before the horse,' agreed Dorothy.

'It's good to be back on our own.'

It also meant that Agnes had more time to see Isobel, and the two old friends had much to talk about. It was clear to Isobel that Agnes still worried about Miss Watson being alone in the house.

'She's still very unsteady,' she told Isobel. 'One stumble, and she'd be quite helpless, you know.'

'You must let her do as she wishes,' comforted Isobel. 'After all, it could happen anyway, whether you were in the house or not. I'm sure she will be sensible. Lots of women have to live alone. Look at me!'

'But do you *like* living alone? I mean, I'm quite glad to know that the Whites are under the same roof as I am when I go up to bed. It makes me feel safer.'

'No, I can't say that I like living alone,' said Isobel thoughtfully. 'But then I'm not used to it yet.'

'Perhaps,' ventured Agnes, 'you might, in time, of course, marry again.'

'I can't imagine it,' said Isobel. 'At our age, Agnes dear, one doesn't think about it. No, I think I shall be quite happy if I can find a little house here, and know that I'm safely among friends. One really can't ask for more.'

The hot weather continued, one blazing day following the other. Harold Shoosmith reverted to his practice of taking a siesta, as he had throughout his working life overseas, and most of Thrush Green did the same. The nights seemed to be as hot as the days, and when the full moon shone through Harold's window, he flung off the sheet which was his only covering, and wandered about the house.

A field of corn stretched towards Nidden, and ran hard by his boundary hedge. He leant from the window, relishing a faint breeze that ruffled his hair refreshingly. In the moonlight the corn was silvered, glowing with an unearthly sheen. In the heat of the day, he had heard the ripe ears crackling under the fierce sun. The harvest would be early this year, although the farmers were already predicting a light yield. What would be in the field next, he wondered? And would Isobel be here by then to see it?

An owl's cry trembled upon the air, and soon he saw the bird swoop silently from a lone oak, sailing downwind upon its rounded wings. What a vast number of lovely things one could see at night, normally missed by having one's head on the pillow! A restless night had its compensations, he decided.

He crossed the landing, and went to see Thrush Green from the window of the front bedroom. The moonlight was so bright that he could see all the houses clearly. It gleamed upon Nathaniel Patten's bald bronze pate, and edged the folds of his frock-coat with silver. A cat was sitting on the plinth at his feet, washing its face.

Harold's eye travelled from Ella's cottage on his far right across the grass, along to Winnie Bailey's, and then next door to Tullivers where, he hoped, Isobel was having a less wakeful night. She had been to see yet another house that afternoon, although on this occasion she had gone alone.

Harold felt deeply sorry for her in this fruitless search, and his mind turned, once again, to the problem that concerned him. How much simpler it would be if she would marry him and live here! But would she want to? And could he ask her, so soon after her husband's death?

He had no doubts now about his own feelings. More than anything in the world he wanted to marry Isobel, and he could think of nothing else.

Harold sighed, and returned to his restless pacing about the house. He knew his own feelings well enough, but what were Isobel's?

18. Hope for the Curdles

Joan Young, mindful of her promise to Molly about looking out for an opening for Ben, now set about the task with extra zeal.

With her parents back in Ealing, she had more time to devote to her own affairs. She heard of several jobs, but somehow none seemed quite right for Ben. She was beginning to despair, and told Edward so.

'I'm seeing Tim Collet this afternoon,' he said. 'I'll have a word with him.'

Collets was a family firm of agricultural engineers in Lulling. It had been in existence for over a hundred years. Originally a blacksmith's, such simple tools as scythes, bill-hooks, horse ploughs and pig troughs figured largely in the early years of the firm. More sophisticated equipment such as threshing machines and harvesters soon came along, giving way eventually to the complicated monsters, costing thousands of pounds, which modern farming demanded.

The business was now run by two Collet brothers, Tim and Bob. They were shrewd and hard-working, and employed a dozen or so skilled men. It was the sort of work which Ben would enjoy and would be capable of carrying out. Joan only hoped that there might be a vacancy.

Luck was with them. Tim Collet told Edward that the man in charge of the yard was leaving at Michaelmas, and he was promoting another employee to take his place, so that there would be a job available.

'I was going to advertise it,' said Tim, 'but if young Curdle wants to apply tell him to come and see me as soon as possible. I knew the old lady pretty well, and Ben too. You could trust him anywhere, which is more than you can say for some of 'em these days.'

When Edward told Joan this news, she broached another subject which had been in her mind for some days.

'Edward,' she began, 'if Ben gets this job—'

'Could they have the top flat?' finished Edward for her, and then laughed.

'You're too clever by half,' said Joan.

'Not really. I thought of it when I was talking to Tim. It would be a great help to us if Molly were here to give you a hand. There's bound to be more to do when the parents live here, and I'm sure she would want to have a little job too.'

'I'll write tonight and tell them the position. We certainly couldn't have better tenants,' agreed Joan. 'But will the flat be ready by September?'

'Pretty well, I think. If not, we can put them up, I'm sure. Unless Ben insists on sleeping at Albert's, of course!'

'Poor Ben! We'll make sure that doesn't have to happen. And in any case, I expect Nelly's in the spare bed.'

'She'd be a fool if she wasn't,' said Edward.

As it happened, at that moment Nelly was a long way from the spare bed, but busy in the Misses Lovelocks' kitchen washing up greasy plates.

The end of her six weeks' sojourn was in sight, and Nelly had heard, with considerable relief, that the usual help was returning to her duties before long.

She had sworn privately never to cook another meal in that house. However, she had been prevailed upon to cook 'a nice little piece of lamb', which turned out to be an extremely fatty breast of that animal, with peas and new potatoes from the garden.

It was apparent from the infrequent entertaining that was done that this would be the last occasion when Nelly would be called upon to demonstrate her art, so she swallowed her pride and set about making the best of a cut of meat which she despised.

Winnie Bailey, Ella Bembridge and Dotty Harmer were coming to lunch, and the amount of meat available, in Nelly's opinion, would just about feed two, rather than six. She herself had said swiftly that she was obliged to have something light, and would prefer a dry biscuit and a small piece of cheese if that was all right?

Miss Ada graciously gave her consent, and with her own hands put two water biscuits and about a quarter of an ounce of desiccated Cheddar cheese on a plate, and put it in the larder for Nelly's repast.

Nelly contrived to make a substantial stuffing of onions, bread crumbs and herbs, and rolled the breast of lamb, hoping that the guests had had large breakfasts.

'And welcome they are to *that*,' said Nelly, to the attentive cat, as she thrust the meat tin into the oven, and then set about making a bread pudding, sparsely furnished with a few sultanas which Miss Ada had counted out earlier.

As she handed round the vegetables at lunch time, she listened to the conversation with much interest. Dotty Harmer's dog, Flossie, was the subject of much questioning.

'I'm afraid so,' said Dotty. 'The vet said she could be aborted, but I don't like the idea.'

'Of what?' asked Miss Violet, who was slightly deaf.

'Of *abortion*,' shouted Dotty.

'*Pas devant la bonne*,' murmured Miss Ada, but Dotty was in no mood for such niceties.

'Why not?' she demanded. 'Abortion is a perfectly normal medical fact. Not, as I said before, that I approve of it. I told the vet that Flossie must just go ahead and have them. I am quite capable of looking after her, and her offspring, and I'm sure I shall find good homes for them.'

She cast speculative glances upon her fellow guests, who quailed. Dotty, with animals to place, was rightly feared by all Lulling and Thrush Green.

'I'm quite sure you will,' said Miss Bertha soothingly. 'If we weren't so near the road, and were more capable of giving a puppy exercise, I'm sure we might have offered to have one.'

'But as it is,' chimed in Miss Ada, 'it is quite out of the question.'

'Indeed it is,' agreed Miss Violet.

'The pudding, Nelly. Would you see if it is ready?' requested Miss Ada, and Nelly was obliged to leave this fascinating conversation and return to the kitchen.

'It's like a mad house in there,' she confided to the cat. 'Well-bred they might be – all six of 'em – but they sound half-barmy to me, the things they talk about!'

At the village school, unconfined joy reigned. It was the last day of term.

In Miss Fogerty's new classroom the cupboards were packed to bursting point with books, folders and boxes belonging to the children. Other, less obliging shapes, such as hanks of raffia, snarls of cane and balls of wet clay swathed in damp dishcloths, were also tidied away, with considerable difficulty, into their allotted place.

As always, just as Miss Fogerty, breathless with lodging the last object into the last space, was about to congratulate herself on finishing an awkward and arduous job, one of the children drew her attention to half a dozen large flower vases which should be stowed away.

'They will have to stay on the windowsill,' decreed Agnes. 'Stand them by the fish tank, dear, and you, Jimmy Todd, may go early with the goldfish so that your bucket isn't jogged by anyone on the way home.'

Jimmy Todd, the envy of the class, had a fish tank of his own, and was to look after Freeman, Hardy and Willis for the entire holiday.

155

'I *hope*,' little Miss Fogerty had confided to Miss Watson, 'I *sincerely hope* that the boy is trustworthy. He is inclined to be a trifle irresponsible at times.'

'He is only seven,' pointed out her headmistress. 'But there's no need to think that he is not perfectly capable of caring for the fish. He has sensible parents, and a little responsibility may work wonders for him.'

Miss Fogerty had her doubts. Secretly, she deplored handing out responsible jobs, such as fish-minding and blackboard-cleaning, to those who had not earned the honour by worthy and decorous behaviour, but as Jimmy Todd was the only child with a spare fish tank she bowed to the inevitable.

He was sent on his way ten minutes before the others, plastic bucket in hand and fervent protestations of concern for his charges on his lips. Miss Fogerty's last glimpse of him was at the school gates where he had stopped to peer anxiously through the butter muslin which Miss Fogerty had tied over the top of the pail.

She gave a sigh of relief. 'I'm sure they will be quite safe with Jimmy,' she said aloud.

'Jimmy Todd,' said a child in the front row, 'has got three cats as likes fish.'

Miss Fogerty quelled her with a glance.

'All stand. Hands together. Close your eyes. *Close* them, I said, Billy Bates, not *cross* them! Any silly nonsense like that, and you stay in, last day of term or not!'

Fortunately, Miss Fogerty's discipline held, and prayers were said reverently. It was as well, she thought, bidding the children goodbye, as she was due to go to tea with Isobel in five minutes' time.

The hot weather continued, day after day, week after week. The heat was almost overpowering as Agnes made her way to Tullivers, thankful of the deep shade of the chestnut avenue.

'One could really do with a parasol,' she said to Isobel, when they were seated in the shade with the tea-tray before them. 'My grandmother had a beautiful cream one, with lace and frills, I remember. Those Victorians had some excellent ideas.'

'My grandmother,' said Isobel, 'had a dove-grey silk one, and the knob on the handle was of pink china, with a tiny picture of Brighton Pier at the top. I wonder where that went eventually?'

'To a jumble sale, no doubt,' responded Agnes, accepting a teacup.

'And now tell me what you are doing this holiday,' said Isobel. 'I know you have been invited to go to the sea with Miss Watson. Is that soon?'

'She goes next Saturday. Her brother and his wife are taking her down, and staying for a week in this nice quiet hotel that Dorothy likes at Barton-on-Sea. Then I'm going down for the next week, while Ray goes with Kathleen to her sister's, and then they are bringing us both back here.'

'It will do you good to have some sea air, especially if the weather holds.'

'It will do Dorothy good, too. There are some nice flat clifftop walks which she can manage now, and easy paths down to the sands.'

'And after that?'

'I shall have a week or so here catching up with all sorts of things I've been meaning to do, and then I shall spend a few days at my cousin's at Cheltenham.'

'And I hope a few days with me if you can spare the time,' said Isobel. 'As far as I can see, I shall be going back before long, and this may be the last time I can offer you hospitality in Sussex. With any luck, I shall have found something near here very soon, and it will be a joy to be near you permanently.'

'I should love to come,' said Agnes, and meant it. Isobel's home was as luxurious as her own bed-sitting-room was spartan. Not that she was discontented with her lot. She had been with the Whites now for a number of years, and appreciated their high standards of cleanliness and responsibility, and the kindness on the rare occasions when she had been obliged to stay in bed because of ill-health.

But it was good to exchange her skimpy bedclothes for Isobel's fluffy blankets and fat eiderdown. It was bliss to have a soft bath towel large enough to envelope her whole body, and wonderful to have exquisite meals served on Isobel's pretty china, instead of on the thick white plates from Mrs White's kitchen.

And then there was the warmth of Isobel's company to enliven her. There had never been anyone quite so dear to her as Isobel, and she enjoyed every minute of her company. Indeed, it had crossed her mind once, when Isobel had first mentioned that she wanted to live near Thrush Green, that she might be invited to share Isobel's home. But, on the whole, she was glad that the matter had not arisen.

Isobel had so many friends already at Thrush Green, and would soon make many more. Agnes did not want her to feel obliged to invite her to meet them, as no doubt Isobel would do. It would be a *strain*, thought Agnes, to have to be sociable when one arrived home, jaded from school, longing simply for a rest with one's feet up, and a quiet cup of tea. Besides, it had to be faced, Isobel's circle of friends was not quite her own. No, it was far better as it was – to visit Isobel in her own home, when she had found it, and to remain in her own modest lodgings which suited her very well. Of course, she was lonely at times, she admitted, but then one simply had to get used to it. There were plenty of single women in the same circumstances and, on the whole, they were certainly better off than those poor unfortunate women who had made unhappy marriages, she told herself stoutly.

But then she was more fortunate than most. The future looked bright. Dear Dorothy was fast returning to health and mobility, and she would always be grateful to her for giving her this lovely week's holiday which lay ahead. 'A small return, Agnes dear, for more kindness than I can ever repay,' is how she had put it.

And then, beyond that, lay the happy prospect of having Isobel actually living at Thrush Green!

Little Miss Fogerty lay back in her deck-chair, and gazed at Tullivers' flowers shimmering in the heat. She was at peace with the world.

Joan Young soon had a reply to her letter. There was nothing they would love more, wrote Molly, than to live in the top flat of the house which had always seemed like home to her.

Ben could not believe in such luck, and was now waiting to hear from the Collets which day they would like to interview him. Reading between the lines, Joan gathered that he was in a high state of tension, poor fellow, and hoped that his ordeal would soon be over. So much depended upon it, he was bound to be nervous.

He did not have to wait long. About ten days later, Molly, Ben and young George arrived at Lulling. Molly and George went to Albert Piggott's gloomy cottage while Ben, dressed in his best blue serge suit, and his dark hair brushed flat against his head, went to see Tim Collet, his heart beating nineteen to the dozen.

Nelly was at her Lulling job, and Molly prepared midday dinner for the three of them, her mind engrossed with what was happening at Lulling. As soon as they had eaten, and she had washed up, she took George out of the way, before Nelly returned, and sat on one of the many seats on Thrush Green.

The excessive heat had scorched the grass, and even the fully-grown trees were beginning to look parched and dusty. But there were a few daisies about, and a friendly collie dog, and these kept young George happily engaged, leaving Molly free to ponder on the joys that might be ahead.

From where she sat, she had a clear view of the top of the hill, and longed to see their old van arrive with Ben at the wheel.

To her left lay the golden bulk of the Youngs' house, beyond the chestnut trees and the railings which ran along the front of the house. She could hear the noise of the builders at work, the chink of metal on stone, the rumble of a wheelbarrow, and an occasional voice as one workman shouted to another.

If only they could live there! If only Ben had landed this job! She began to tremble at the thought of failure. It would be like getting to the gate of heaven and being turned back. There was nowhere in the world that she wanted to be more. This was home. This was her element, as necessary to her as air to a bird, or water to a fish. Without it she would be nothing, simply an adjunct to Ben's life, going where he went, and making the best of any of the places in which he settled.

But here, at Thrush Green, life would be rich and vital. She and Ben would flourish like plants in a sheltered garden, and George would grow up in perfect surroundings, heir to all the joys of Thrush Green.

The sound of the van chugging up the hill sent her flying across the grass, followed by young George.

There was no need to say anything. Ben's glowing face said it all.

'Oh Ben!' cried Molly, clinging to him, and struggling to control tears of relief.

Ben patted her shoulder. 'There! Let's go straight across to Mrs Young, Moll, and tell her the good news.'

19. Miss Fogerty has a Shock

Nelly Piggott faced her last day's work at the Lovelocks with mingled relief and apprehension.

The job had been a frustrating one. It was not only poorly paid, but the parsimony of her employers had tried Nelly's patience to breaking point. It had been a considerable effort to hold her tongue under such extreme provocation, and only the thought of the comparatively short time she needed to endure it, had kept her from outspoken rebellion. No, she would not be sorry to leave this post.

On the other hand, the outlook for any other work seemed bleak. This puzzled Nelly. She was known as a good worker and an exceptionally fine cook. Why was it that she was unable to land another job?

She had haunted the Job Centre. She had asked a dozen or more Thrush Green and Lulling folk if they knew of a job, but always there was some difficulty. One of the reasons, Nelly felt sure, was her past flightiness. Lulling did not approve of wives leaving their husbands, even such unpleasant ones as Albert Piggott, to run off with oil men as glossy and dashing as the one who had persuaded Nelly to throw in her lot with his.

There were other reasons too. Most of the people who were lucky enough to have domestic aid, had employed their helpers for years, as Winnie Bailey had her Jenny, and Dotty Harmer and

Harold Shoosmith their energetic Betty Bell. Others, who might have looked for help in the past, had long ago come to terms with doing everything for themselves and had found the result far more satisfactory, and far less expensive. One way and another, it was plain that there were no jobs waiting for Nelly.

As she returned to her house on Thrush Green, on the last afternoon of her employment, Nelly took stock of her position. Financially, she was a little better off than when she had arrived at Thrush Green. Prudently, she had put aside the money she had earned in her Post Office account. By diligent methods, she had been able to abstract some money from Albert, ostensibly for housekeeping, but a certain amount had been added to her own nest egg.

She owned an ancient gold watch, and a gold locket of hideous Victorian design, and these she knew would bring in a pound or two, if she were really hard pressed. The point was, could she afford to break with Albert?

She had long ceased to feel for him any affection or loyalty, but he did provide a roof over her head and enough to feed them both. But he grew daily more cantankerous, and Nelly knew that, before long, just such another row as that which had sent her into the arms of the oil man would blow up.

Crossing the green, Nelly decided that she would give Albert a week's trial. Who knows? Work might turn up to take her out of the house for a few hours a day. Albert might become a reformed character, though that chance was infinitesimal. She would bide her time for a little longer, and then make her decision.

Albert was emerging from The Two Pheasants as Nelly opened the cottage door. For once, she did not start nagging at him.

Albert was rightly suspicious. What was up, he wondered?

On the appointed Saturday, Miss Watson was collected by her brother and his wife, and departed to the seaside.

Little Miss Fogerty had made her farewells the evening before as she helped Dorothy with her last-minute packing. Watching her assistant's deftness in folding garments and spreading tissue paper, Dorothy thought, once more, how invaluable dear Agnes was, and how dearly she would like to invite her to share the schoolhouse. Perhaps an opportunity would occur during their week together, but, on the other hand, there was always this difficulty of Agnes's unselfishness. If only the suggestion could come from her!

Well, it was no good worrying about it, thought Miss Watson, limping towards the car on that bright morning. Time alone could unravel that problem, and meanwhile she intended to enjoy her much-needed change of air.

Meanwhile, Miss Fogerty set about a number of jobs which she had been unable to tackle during term time.

The position of temporary headmistress, in which Miss Watson's sad accident had placed her, had meant putting aside a great many day-to-day activities which she normally tackled methodically.

Her mending, for instance, which was usually done after ironing, when she studied her sensible underwear and blouses for splitting seams, holes, ladders or missing buttons, had been neglected. The filling of innumerable forms had taken first place, and there had been parents, representatives from educational publishers, and other visitors to the school, who seriously impeded the steady progress of the work which Agnes so much enjoyed.

Now was the time to catch up with her own affairs, and she spent the next day or two replying to letters from friends, doing some shopping, taking shoes to the repairer's, and all the other little chores which she wanted to see finished before embarking on the longed-for week with Dorothy.

But two days before the great day, poor Miss Fogerty received the shock of her life. St Andrew's clock had just chimed four o'clock, and she was about to switch on her kettle and make a cup of tea, when Mrs White called from below to say that she had just made a pot of tea, and would she like to join her?

It was while they were sipping the refreshing beverage in Mrs White's immaculate sitting-room, that the blow fell.

'I've been trying to summon up courage to tell you all the week,' confessed Mrs White. 'Arthur's got promotion, and we're moving to Scotland.'

Her face turned pink with the anxiety of imparting this news.

Poor Miss Fogerty's turned white at hearing it. She put down her cup with a clatter.

'Oh no!' she breathed at last. 'I can't believe it! You mean—?'

'I'm afraid so,' nodded Mrs White, beginning to look tearful. 'I can't tell you how sorry I am about it. You've been a wonderful lodger, and a real good friend too, but Arthur can't afford to turn down this chance. It'll make a deal of difference to his pension, you see.'

'Of course,' said Agnes. She felt numbed with the shock. What a terrible thing to happen! How soon, she wondered, would she need to go?

As if reading her thoughts, Mrs White resumed her tale.

'There's no need for you to worry about leaving just yet. We don't go until the end of August, and Arthur's job starts on the first of September. There's a house that goes with it, and with the extra he'll get we hope to be able to buy our own house, ready for retirement one day.'

Agnes did her best to collect her scattered wits. 'I'm very glad for you both,' she said sincerely. 'The future certainly looks bright. It's just that I'm a little taken aback, you know, and at a loss to know where to find other lodgings. I doubt if I shall ever be so happy elsewhere as I have been with you.'

Mrs White sighed with relief. 'You've taken it wonderfully. I can't tell you how I've dreaded breaking the news.' She turned briskly to her duties as hostess. 'Now let me give you a fresh cup of tea. That must be stone cold by now.'

Like my heart, thought poor Agnes, doing her best to hide her feelings. What on earth would she do now?

Later that evening, she went along the road to Thrush Green and called to see Isobel at Tullivers.

Her old friend was alone, and Agnes poured out all her troubles. Isobel was almost as upset as she was herself.

'If only I had found a place here,' was her first comment, 'you could have taken refuge with me. The awful thing is, Agnes dear, I shall probably be back in Sussex by the time you need another home. Does Mrs White know of other digs?'

'She didn't say anything.'

'Could you stay at the schoolhouse?'

'I'm sure Dorothy would let me stay there temporarily, if need be, but I really must find something permanent.'

'If I were you,' said Isobel, 'I should go and enjoy your holiday, and then come back to face this problem. The best thing to do, I think, would be to put an advertisement in the local paper, as soon as you return.'

'I thought I might tell the rector. He's so kind. He helped with finding a place for you with Miss Bembridge, you remember, and he would know the sort of place I wanted.'

'An excellent idea! I'm positive something will turn up before the end of August. Meanwhile, Agnes, you are going to stay to supper with me, I hope.'

'I can think of nothing nicer,' said little Miss Fogerty, much comforted.

The intense heat ended, as expected, with a crashing thunderstorm which began at seven in the evening and continued for most of the night.

The people of Lulling and Thrush Green waited eagerly for the rain to fall. Water-butts stood empty, flowers wilted, the summer pea pods were shrivelled on their stems, and even the farmers, now that the harvest was largely gathered in, looked forward to a downpour.

For some hours it looked as though nothing would fall. Crash followed crash, angry rumblings echoed round the sky, and sheet lightning lit the scene with eerie flashes, but still the rain held off. It was almost midnight before the welcome sound of pattering drops cheered the waiting inhabitants.

The relief was wonderful. The delicious smell of rain water cooling hot stones and earth was then more appreciated than the most expensive scent. Rain splashed on the parched grass of Thrush Green, and pattered on the great dusty leaves of the chestnut trees. It gurgled down the gutters to Lulling, and formed wide puddles across the road outside St Andrew's church. It sent the local cats, out upon their nightly forays, scampering for home, and encouraged the thirsty wild creatures to venture forth for their first satisfying drink for many a long day.

The air grew blessedly cool and fresh. The wakeful ones sought those blankets which had been unused for weeks, and snuggled into their beds with thankful hearts.

The morning after the storm dawned clear and fresh. The world of Thrush Green sparkled in the sunshine, and everyone relished the slight coolness in the air, and the rejuvenation of all living things.

Even Albert Piggott gave the green a grudging smile as he walked across to St Andrew's. Here he proposed to spend a leisurely hour or two surveying his domain, safe from Nelly's gaze.

Nelly had finished at the Lovelocks, and mightily relieved she was to be able to set to and do her own chores without one eye on the clock. The Misses Lovelock had been sticklers for punctuality, and would not have been above docking Nelly's wages if she had arrived late. Knowing this, Nelly had been very particular in arriving promptly.

She had been paid in full, and wished goodbye by all three ladies. Miss Ada had been gracious enough to say that she would be willing to supply a reference if Nelly required it at any time. Nelly thanked her civilly.

The snag was that there was still no work available, and the thought of being at close quarters with Albert, day in and day out, was a daunting one.

She thought about her future as she dismantled the stove and prepared to scour each part in strong soda water. Albert had been at his grumpiest for the past week. The truth was that he disliked the heat, and that Nelly's cooking was again playing havoc with his digestion. He enjoyed venting his ill-humour upon Nelly, and during the thunderstorm whilst they were hoping for rain, he had been particularly unpleasant about Nelly's chances of employment.

'Can't expect decent folks to take on a trollop like you,' was the phrase that hurt most. It still rankled as Nelly attacked the cooker. The thing was, it was near the truth, and Nelly knew it.

She began to think of Charlie, the oil man. With all his faults, he had never been unkind to her, or insulted her as Albert did. Looking back now, she forgot his meanness, his dishonesty with money, and the long evenings she had spent alone, trying to keep his supper hot without it spoiling. She thought of his attractions, his glossy black hair, the music hall ditties he was so fond of singing, and the good times they had enjoyed together at local pubs. True to her principles, Nelly had stuck to bitter lemon or orange juice while Charlie swigged his whisky, but she had enjoyed meeting his rowdy friends and joining in the songs around the bar piano.

She paused in her scrubbing and gazed out of the steamy window towards Thrush Green. Not much life here, that was for sure! And what would it be like in the winter, when the curtains were drawn at four o'clock, and Albert had left her for The Two Pheasants next door? A living death, decided Nelly, just a living death!

She would have done better to have looked for a place where she was. There was far more scope for her talents in Brighton than ever there would be at Thrush Green. She pondered the matter for a full hour, by which time the cooker had been reassembled, and the frying-pan filled with bacon, liver and sausages for the midday meal.

'Fatty stuff again, I see,' grunted Albert, when his plate was put before him later. 'You knows what Dr Lovell said. You trying to kill me?'

'Chance'd be a fine thing,' retorted Nelly. 'The devil looks after his own, as far as I can see.'

Albert snorted.

'You'd be a far sight fitter,' went on Nelly, 'if you laid off the beer. All that acid fair eats away the lining of your stummick. I was reading about it in my women's paper.'

'You wants to change the record,' snarled Albert, with heavy sarcasm. 'And if you looked for a job instead of wastin' your time with women's papers you'd be a bit better off.'

Nelly rose from the table with as much dignity as a sixteen-stone woman could manage, and went to the dresser drawer. From it she abstracted a cheap packet of stationery and a ballpoint pen, and made her way upstairs.

Sitting on the side of the spare bed she composed a letter to Charlie. It was not an easy letter to write, and how it would be received was anybody's guess. It took Nelly nearly an hour to get her thoughts on paper, and when at last she had sealed the envelope and stuck on the stamp, she descended the stairs.

Albert was fast asleep in the armchair. His mouth was open, and he snored loudly, making a maddening little whining sound as he did so. The dirty dishes still littered the table, and the newly-cleaned stove bore fresh splashes of fat.

Nelly opened the door, and marched straight across the grass to the post-box on the corner of Thrush Green. She was oblivious of the fresh beauty about her, and the bright new world which the rain had created. She dropped the letter in the box, and heard its satisfying plop as it reached the bottom.

Well, she'd done it! She'd burnt her boats, thought Nelly, and now she must face the future!

20. A Proposal

Miss Fogerty travelled by coach from Thrush Green to Bournemouth where she was being met. She determined to take Isobel's advice and postpone all thoughts of finding new accommodation until she returned, but she had called on Charles Henstock, before she left for her week's holiday, and told him of her predicament.

'My dear Miss Fogerty,' said that kind man, his chubby face creased with concern, 'I shall do my very best to find somewhere for you. Try not to let it worry you when you are away. You need a break after all the troubles of last term. Something will turn up, I feel convinced.'

He had told his wife about the encounter, and Dimity at once thought of Ella.

'The only thing is she has said so little about taking a lodger recently, that I'm beginning to wonder if she really wants one.'

'We can only ask,' said Charles. 'Perhaps you could broach the subject?'

Dimity did, that very afternoon, and as she had surmised, Ella did not appear at all keen.

'The point is, Dim, I've been thinking it over, and I've got quite used to being alone here, and I'm not all that hard up. I mean, look at my clothes!'

Dimity looked, and was secretly appalled.

'I've had these trousers five years, and this shirt much the same length of time, and I can't see myself bothering to buy much in that line. And then I don't go out as much as I used to, nor do the same amount of entertaining as we did when you were here. One way and another, I think I'd sooner scratch along on my own.'

'But you thoroughly enjoyed having Isobel,' Dimity pointed out.

'Isobel's one in a thousand and in any case it was only for a week. I just don't want anyone permanently.'

'In a way,' said Dimity, 'I'm relieved to hear it.'

'Not that I'd see little Agnes homeless,' continued Ella. 'If she hasn't found anywhere before term starts, I'm very willing to put her up for a bit while she's looking round. I'm fond of that fanny little soul.'

'We all are,' replied Dimity.

It was soon after this, that Harold walked across to Tullivers to tell Isobel that he had ordered an Alfa Romeo very like her own, and was now bracing himself to part with the ancient Daimler which had played an important part in his life.

The day was cool and cloudy. In fact, the violent thunderstorm had brought the hot summer weather to an end, and there were to be very few sunny days until the autumn.

He found Isobel busy writing letters. She gave him her usual warm smile which affected his heart in such a delightful way, but he thought that she appeared somewhat worried.

'Anything wrong?' he asked, seating himself at the table where her writing things were littered.

Isobel put her hands flat on the table with a gesture of despair.

'A lot, I'm afraid. I was coming to tell you. I shall have to drive home again. There's a muddle about the sale of the house.'

'Can't the estate agent cope with that? Must you go today?'

'Either today, or tomorrow morning. The sale's fallen through again.'

She sighed, and looked so desperately unhappy, that Harold could not bear it. He had never seen her cast down. In all their fruitless searchings for a house she had always managed to maintain a certain buoyancy of spirit which was one of the reasons why he loved her.

He put a hand over one of hers, and spoke urgently.

'Isobel, let me help with this. I can't bear to see you so unhappy, and it's all so unnecessary.'

'Unnecessary?' queried Isobel.

'I've wanted to say something for weeks now, but it has never seemed the right moment. I don't know if this is – but hear me out, Isobel, I beg of you.'

He tightened his grip on her hand, and began his plea. Isobel sat very still, her eyes downcast upon their linked hands, and heard him out as he had asked.

'And will you?' he ended. 'Could you, Isobel?'

She smiled at him, and at last regained her hand. 'Thank you, Harold dear. You must let me think for a day or so. My mind is so confused with all that's happened, I shall need time. But I do thank you, from the bottom of my heart. It is the loveliest thing that has happened to me for a long, long time.'

'You dear girl!' exclaimed Harold. 'And please don't keep me waiting too long! I warn you, I've been in a state of near-dementia for the past months.'

Isobel laughed. 'I promise you an answer before the end of the week, but I must get back and sort out some of this muddle. Oh, the misery of selling and buying houses!'

'You know the way out now,' Harold pointed out.

'You would never know,' replied Isobel, 'if I'd married you or the house.'

'I'll take that risk,' Harold assured her.

As always, the building activity at the Youngs took considerably longer than had at first been imagined, despite Edward's daily exhortations.

To be fair, the builders worked well, but there were interminable delays in getting materials from the suppliers which held up the proceedings. It was plain that the top flat was going to be ready before the stable block conversion, but even so it did not look as though the second bedroom would be ready in time for the Curdles' arrival in September.

Joan wrote to let them know how things were, and was glad to hear that the negotiations for the sale of the fair to Dick Hasler were now almost completed. They would be selling their caravan home when they came to Thrush Green, wrote Molly, and the money would help them to furnish the flat.

But, asked Molly, Ben could not bear to part with his grandmother's wooden gipsy caravan, and could they bring it with them? Would there be somewhere out of the way where it could stand? It might be quite a useful spare-room, and Ben would be very pleased if they would like to use it as such at any time in the future.

Joan felt a surge of happiness when she read this. What could be better? Mrs Curdle's much-loved caravan had always been an important part of Thrush Green's life. May the first had been the highlight of the year, and it was only fitting that the caravan should return to its old haunt for ever, and to stand close to the last resting place of its famous owner.

'There's plenty of room in the orchard,' Edward said, when he heard about the proposal. He was as delighted as Joan to think of having the caravan at Thrush Green.

So were their neighbours and friends. Winnie Bailey, in particular, welcomed the idea, remembering how old Mrs Curdle had visited her regularly every year.

'It's so much part of Thrush Green history,' said the rector, summing up general opinion, 'that it's the *only* place for it. We shall all treasure it.'

Nelly Piggott awaited an answer to her letter with some anxiety. For one thing, she wanted to take it from the postman as soon as it arrived. No one could accuse Albert of undue interest in the meagre correspondence which was slipped under the door, but he might well open a letter which was written by hand thinking it might be from Molly, who was about the only person who did write to him.

Manilla envelopes, with typed addresses, were beneath his notice. They would either contain bills, or some other objectionable enclosures, which would be stowed, often unopened, behind the clock on the kitchen mantel shelf, for later perusal.

Nelly was usually up first, and downstairs by the time Willie Bond delivered the post. If Willie Bond was on duty, he arrived whilst Nelly was on her own in the kitchen.

But if the second postman, Willie Marchant, delivered the mail then he arrived a good half-hour later, and by then Albert was at large in the kitchen with her.

A fortnight had passed and still there was no response from the oil man. Of course, Nelly told herself, he might be away. He might even have moved house, but in that case, surely he would have left an address at the Post Office, and his letters would have been forwarded. It was more likely, Nelly was bound to admit, that he did not consider a reply necessary, and did not intend to waste good money on a stamp for one who had upped and left him comparatively recently.

'Can't blame him, I suppose,' said Nelly to Albert's cat, when Willie Bond had departed after leaving a seed catalogue addressed to Albert, the only item of mail.

But it was worrying. It would be better to know the worst. It would be *far* better, Nelly told herself, to have a rude letter telling her what he thought of her, than this horrible silence.

During this waiting period she had cleaned the house from top to bottom. Any object which could be assaulted with strong soda water, yellow soap and a stiff scrubbing-brush, had been so treated. Anything which could be polished, whether it were of metal, wood or glass, had been attacked mercilessly. Even the cat, once so thin, had been fattened with Nelly's good food, and was given a brisk brushing, and its ears cleaned out with oily cotton wool twisted into a serviceable radish shape.

In between these frenzied spells of cleaning, Nelly took short walks. Sometimes, in order to get away from Albert, she took herself to Lulling and surveyed the shops, or called at the Job Centre, in case she would need to earn again. Sometimes, she strolled towards Lulling Woods, and once went as far as the Drovers' Arms and called on the Allens, secretly hoping that there might be work for her there, if the oil man did not come up to scratch. But there was nothing there, as the Allens made clear, softening the blow by giving her a cup of tea and Garibaldi biscuits, before she made the return journey.

Albert was more melancholy than ever, and Nelly was beginning to wonder how much longer she could stand the suspense of waiting, and the tedium of her husband's nagging.

When, one happy morning, Willie Marchant handed in the letter she had been waiting for, she was able to put it quickly into her overall pocket before Albert realized what was going on.

When he had departed to his duties at St Andrew's, she opened the envelope. The letter was short and to the point:

Dear Nelly,
    Come on back, you old faggot.
Forgiven and forgotten.
        Love,
            Charlie

Nelly could have wept with relief. There was a man for you! Big-hearted, took life as it came, willing to forget and forgive! She wouldn't leave him again in a hurry, that was sure! Why, he'd even put 'Love' at the end! No doubt about it, Charlie was one in a million!

She sat down at the kitchen table and wrote back. Her letter was even more brief than Charlie's:

Darling Charlie,
    Coming Wednesday,
        Best love,
            Your Nelly

She had to walk down the hill to Lulling to buy a stamp, but she was too happy to mind. Normally, she found the return journey, up the steep hill, distinctly daunting, but on this occasion she sailed up it as blithely as a Lakeland fell climber.

Life was about to start again for Nelly Piggott.

*

At Barton-on-Sea, Agnes and Dorothy sat on the verandah of the small hotel, and admired the sea.

It was still difficult for Dorothy to negotiate the steps nearest to the hotel, leading to the beach, and the weather was not as reliable as one could wish for a seaside holiday. The verandah gave them shelter from the wind, and all the sunshine that was available.

'Besides, dear,' Miss Watson pointed out, 'here we are handy for our library books and knitting, or a cup of coffee, if we want it. And sand can be rather *pervasive*. Into everything, isn't it? But don't let me stop you, Agnes, if you want to have a walk along the beach. I'm quite happy here.'

Agnes assured her that she was perfectly contented.

'We'll have a little stroll along the cliff top later,' said Dorothy. 'Grass is so much pleasanter to walk on than sand.'

Miss Fogerty agreed automatically. It was wonderful to be here, taking in the fresh salt-laden air, feeling the warmth of the sun, and the comfort of Dorothy's presence. But her mind still fluttered round her problem, despite her determination to shelve it, as advised by dear Isobel and Charles Henstock. It was easier said than done.

For two days now she had fought against the temptation to confide in her headmistress. Agnes had always found it difficult to keep anything from her. By nature she was not a secretive person, although she could be discreet with other people's confidences.

She gazed out to the sparkling sea, watching the gulls swoop and scream, as they swerved for food being thrown to them by someone hidden from her sight below the cliff. Involuntarily, she sighed.

Miss Watson was quick to notice. 'Agnes dear, are you *sure* you want to sit here? Do say if you feel like doing anything else. I want this little holiday to be *exactly* as you want it. I shall feel *most unhappy* if I am holding you back.'

'Indeed, Dorothy, I am doing just what I want,' cried Agnes.

'But you don't seem quite yourself,' replied Dorothy solicitously. 'Are you quite well? Are you worried about anything? Surely you can tell an old friend any troubles?'

Her kind face, peering so anxiously into that of her companion's, was Agnes Fogerty's undoing.

The floodgates opened, and the whole pitiful story poured forth. Mr White's promotion, his pension, his savings, Mrs White's reluctance to tell her lodger, her tact in doing so, her past kindnesses, all flowed from Agnes in a stream of words, to which Dorothy listened with mingled pity and hope.

'And so,' concluded Agnes, having recourse to one of her best Swiss handkerchiefs, 'I must look for something else. I didn't mean to tell you, you know. It isn't fair to unload my troubles on you when you are still convalescent.'

Miss Watson took a deep breath of good sea air. 'I don't consider myself *convalescent* any longer,' she said robustly. 'And you have taken a great weight off my mind.'

'I have?' quavered Agnes.

'You see, I dearly wanted to ask you if you would consider living permanently at the schoolhouse. There's nothing I should like more, but I feared you might feel I was in need and your unselfishness would prompt you to do something which perhaps you did not really want to do.'

'Not really want to do?' echoed Agnes.

'You must think it over,' went on Dorothy. 'I shall quite understand if you refuse. I know that your independence means a lot to you, and I respect that. I respect it very much.'

Little Miss Fogerty returned her handkerchief to her pocket, and sat up very straight.

'I don't need any time, Dorothy, to think it over. To live at the schoolhouse would please me more than anything in the world, if you're *really sure.*'

'I've been *really sure* for months,' said Dorothy. 'And now I think we might celebrate with that cup of coffee, Agnes dear, if you can reach the bell.'

At Thrush Green, Harold Shoosmith awaited Isobel's answer with anxious impatience. She had been gone for three days now, and he was sure that she would keep her promise and let him know within the week. But what a ghastly length of time that seemed!

Neither Willie Bond nor Willie Marchant had ever seen him so swift to take in the letters. The telephone receiver was snatched from the cradle before it had time to ring twice, and Harold was remarkably short with those who rang up. After all, it might be the very moment that Isobel was trying to get through.

Betty Bell noted his agitation with some sympathy and amusement. 'I bet you miss Mrs Fletcher,' she remarked conversationally, over elevenses.

Harold ignored the remark.

'A real nice lady,' continued Betty, crunching a ginger biscuit. 'Miss Harmer was only saying yesterday as how it would be lovely to have her living here.'

'Here?' interjected Harold. Was it so obvious?

'In Thrush Green,' explained Betty. 'Or nearby. Everyone wants her back.'

Not as much as I do, thought Harold, pushing back his chair. 'Well, I must get on with my hedge-cutting,' he said, making his escape.

It was Betty Bell who answered the telephone half an hour later.

'Hang on,' she shouted cheerfully. 'I'll get him.'

She hung out of the kitchen window. 'Mrs Fletcher on the phone,' she yelled, and admired the speed with which her employer abandoned the shears and sprinted up the path.

She would dearly have loved to listen to the conversation on the bedroom extension, but decided to retreat to the landing where, with any luck, she would be out of sight, and might hear at least one side of the proceedings.

She had to wait some time, for there seemed to be a great deal said at the Sussex end, but at last her vigil was rewarded.

'Oh, Isobel!' cried her employer. 'You darling! Yes, I'll be with you at twelve tomorrow, with a bottle of champagne.'

There was another break, and then: 'I can't say all I want to, but I'll say it tomorrow. Yes, Betty's here, and listening too, I've no doubt. But who cares?'

When a minute later he put down the telephone, Betty sauntered down the stairs with as convincing an air of innocence as she could muster.

'Betty,' said Harold, his face radiant, 'I'm going to get married.'

'Really, sir?'

'To Mrs Fletcher,' said Harold.

'We all said you would,' said Betty, picking up her duster.

Epilogue

* * * *

Epilogue

One golden October morning, Robert and Milly Bassett at last arrived at Thrush Green. The air was crisp and clear, and the sky that pellucid blue which only early autumn brings. The chestnut leaves were turning colour, and some had already fallen, spreading a glowing, crackling carpet beneath the trees.

Over lunch, Joan had plenty to tell her parents. There were still several things to finish at their new home, and Joan insisted that they slept in the old house until she was satisfied that the new plaster had dried out.

Otherwise, the stable block had become a charming one-storey house, sheltered by the Cotswold stone garden wall, and shaded by mature trees. Robert and Milly were delighted with it.

'And how about Ben and Molly?' asked Milly. 'How's the new job going?'

'Splendidly. He's so happy, and Tim Collet told Edward that he'll probably put him into a more responsible job when one of the older men leaves after Christmas.'

'And Molly?'

'As helpful as ever, and relieved to be near her father, of course, especially now that Nelly's left him again.'

'It's little George I want to see,' said Milly.

'He's at school now, with Miss Fogerty. He was promoted to filling in the weather chart this week, so you can see he's happy enough!'

The Hursts were back, Joan told them, and Frank had evidently made a great hit with his lecture tour, and had been invited to go again the following year.

'But our most exciting news,' said Joan, when she poured the coffee, 'is of Harold Shoosmith. He's on his honeymoon at the moment, and you can guess the flutter his marriage made here.'

'Better late than never,' pronounced Robert. 'And he couldn't have chosen more wisely.'

Obedient to the directions of his wife and daughter, Robert went to lie down for an hour and, to his surprise, had a short nap. The journey must have tired him more than he realized.

Much refreshed, he rose and made his way into the garden, and wandered among the falling leaves, admiring the Michaelmas daisies, the golden rod, and the velvet brilliance of the dahlias. It was a lovely time of year to come home, he thought, and sighed with pleasure.

He turned into the orchard and caught his breath with delight. There, beneath a gnarled apple tree, stood dear Mrs Curdle's caravan. Joan had not mentioned this, and he went to investigate.

It was in excellent trim. The paint was fresh, the brass polished, the minute windows sparkling.

The top half of the door was open, and Robert could see that it looked just as he remembered it in Mrs Curdle's day. There was the shining stove, the framed text above it, and the gaudy counterpane smoothed over the bunk bed. It gave Robert enormous joy to see the little home again, and he was smiling as he retraced his steps.

He went of the open front gate and surveyed the scene. On his right was the village school. The younger children were already emerging from the new classroom at the back of the playground, George, no doubt, among them. In the distance, he could see little Agnes Fogerty, and waved to her.

She waved back, and he thought what a splendid thing it was that she and Miss Watson had joined forces. Nothing like a little companionship as you grew older!

Beside the school, Harold's house stood with its windows closed, awaiting the return of its master and new mistress from the Greek islands.

'And if Harold isn't showing his slides at a Women's Institute meeting next season, I'll eat my hat!' thought Robert, knowing his Thrush Green.

His eyes wandered to The Two Pheasants where the hanging

baskets still made a brave splash of colour. Across the expanse of grass, someone was moving among the stones in the graveyard at St Andrew's, where so many of Robert's old friends, including Mrs Curdle, rested for ever.

It looked like the rector, Robert thought, shading his eyes against the sinking sun, and he was about to walk across to greet him, when he heard the front door open behind him, and the sound of voices.

Joan was accompanying Dotty Harmer to the gate, and he turned to greet his old friend, who looked, if anything, even more tattered than usual.

She interrupted her flow of conversation just long enough to say how lovely it was to see him in his own surroundings, and then returned to her discourse.

'Now, I can thoroughly recommend either of the two spaniels. Well, *spaniel-types*, I'd better say. Their tails leave much to be desired, but of course they may fill out as they grow. Both bitches, and a beautiful pale gold.

'I wouldn't suggest the collie. He's going to be enormous, judging by his paws, and I'm trying Percy Hodge for him. I hear he wants another dog, and after all, it was his present collie that was the father. Or *one* of them,' added Dotty, strictly honest.

'That leaves the black and tan terrier-type dog, and the shaggy little bitch. She's going to be *most unusual*, and highly intelligent too. So just think it over, Joan dear. I know whichever you choose will have a marvellous home.'

'Can I bring Paul down to see them when he's home from school? It will really be his puppy. He misses his old dog terribly since she died last winter.'

'Of course, of course.'

She suddenly became conscious of Robert listening with quiet pleasure to the conversation.

'Would you like a puppy, Robert? You'll have all the time in the world now, to train it.'

Robert shook his head.

'I'm too long in the tooth for puppies,' he told her. 'I'll take a share in bringing up Paul's.'

'Very well,' said Dotty, bending to adjust a suspender against her skinny thigh. 'I'll be getting back. Flossie tends to get a little agitated if I'm away for long. Post-natal emotion, of course. Otherwise, she's a wonderful little mother.'

She nodded briskly, and set off across the grass to Lulling Woods, her stockings in imminent danger of collapsing, and one claw-like hand holding on to her disreputable straw hat.

Joan and her father turned back towards their home.

'D'you know,' said Robert, putting an arm round his daughter's shoulders, 'I've thought so often about coming back here. I've thought about the house, and the garden, and the chestnut avenue, and St Andrew's church, and Nathaniel Patten's statue, and all my dear friends here. But the fact is—'

Here he stopped, and drew in his breath.

'The real joy of the place didn't hit me until I saw Mrs Curdle's caravan, and dear old Dotty finding homes, as always, for puppies. Now I *know* that I really have returned to Thrush Green.'